FIERCE DANCER

82ND STREET VANDALS
BOOK NINE

HEATHER LONG

For the found family.
The sister of your heart.
The brother of your soul.
The people who are there for you no matter what.
You matter.

SERIES SO FAR

Savage Vandal
Vicious Rebel
Ruthless Traitor
Dirty Devil
Brutal Fighter
Dangerous Renegade
Merciless Spy
Reckless Thief
Fierce Dancer

FOREWORD

Dear Reader,

Welcome to the ninth and *final* book of the 82nd Street Vandals series. If you have not read the first eight, stop. Do not pass Go. Grab book one: Savage Vandal, and start there.

Seriously.

This is a series that really must be read in order.

Every series has a beginning, middle, and end. Some we can see coming, some ambush us. This one? This one came to life and flourished on its own. Some pieces were incredibly clear, others were a mystery—a genuine mystery—until I found out what happened right alongside the characters.

Did I know every twist and turn the story would take? Yes. And no. Some of it was organic, other pieces were guideposts, set into the bedrock. I knew when we reached them, we would be at turning points in the overall story.

Now… we're here. The last book. So much went into the writing of this book and I'll address some of that at the end. For now, let's do a little previously in the 82nd Street Vandals. Reckless Thief opened with so many of our beloved characters in danger following the cliffhanger in Merciless Spy.

The tattoo parlor where Vaughn worked was burning down with people trapped inside it. Vaughn and Rome rushed in to help, but there were a lot of casualties. Kellan and Milo went to check the alarm at the auto body shop, only to have it blow up in front of them. Kellan took a hell of a knock to the head.

In the meanwhile, the back of Jasper's car exploded and flipped the whole vehicle even as a truck tried to slam into Liam's car with Em inside it. A flurry of activity included Jasper and Liam in a pitched gun battle while Freddie and Em fled through the alleys and backstreets to get to the clubhouse.

Em shot someone to save Freddie and Freddie knifed someone to save her. Jasper came for them while Liam went for his brother and Vaughn. Once he was sure they were safe, he went after his parents. He found his mother Mary, alive but in shock. His father, Jonathon, had died of a heart attack.

Not long after that, he learned that the body left outside of the warehouse belonged to Ms. Stephanie, Doc's sister and the social worker who fought so hard for all of them.

Losing her hurt them. The losses were brutal and they were all suffering. Old friends and new ones converged to help. Em focused on being there for her brother and her Vandals. After everything, she wanted to help them. In the midst of this all, the identity of the king was revealed to be a lot closer to home than anyone could imagine.

It was also war. The guys went after Reginald Sharpe, Em's adoptive father. More revelations ripped open old wounds and allowed some to heal, especially in the case of Freddie who let himself really make a physical connection with Em, albeit one he could control.

In the end, they set a trap, determined to take the fight to

Bradley Sharpe—the man who had triggered all the attacks. They worked out a plan that included getting Em and Milo out of the line of fire but they were betrayed and Reckless Thief ended with Emersyn being buried alive and Milo gravely wounded.

The war is raging and the Vandals have already lost so much. That brings us to Fierce Dancer, our final installment. Please be aware this book contains content with dark themes and intense situations intended for mature audiences only, including but not limited to: sexual assault, flashbacks of grooming, underage/childhood sexual assault, physical violence, emotional and mental abuse, as well as kidnapping, stalking, manipulation, addiction and other potentially triggering topics.

And now, as always, the housekeeping notes:

For those of you who have never read a why choose, or reverse harem before, first let me thank you for picking this up and giving it a shot. Second, the heroine will not make a choice in this book or any other between the guys in her life. It may take her a while to reach that conclusion, but it's the journey that drives it. There are many ways to frame this kind of relationship, currently why choose fits it very well.

Also, this is the final book in a series. While there may be no specific happy endings at the end of each of these books, there will be one to the whole series, that I promise you. Some of these books will have cliffhangers, largely due to the size of the story, but the happy ending has to be earned.

Finally, I wanted to add one last note. Thank you.

Thank you for reading. Thank you for rooting for the Vandals. Thank you for being so invested in their story.

I'll see you on the flip side.

xoxo

Heather

THE VANDALS

82nd Street Boys
   Jasper "Hawk" Horan
   Kellan "Kestrel" Traschel
   Rome "Hummingbird" Cleary
   Vaughn "Falcon" Westbrook
   Liam "Mockingbird" O'Connell
   Freddie "Unknown" Cleary
   Milo "Raptor" Hardigan
   Mickey "Doc" James aka Vandal
   Emersyn "Dove, Sparrow, Starling, Swan, Little Bit, Boo-Boo, Hellspawn, Ivy" Sharpe

Other Characters
   Elaine "Lainey" Benedict
   Adam Reed
   Ezra Graham
   Ms. Stephanie

CHAPTER 1

EMERSYN

"*D*on't take this the wrong way, Ivy," Milo said as we left the warehouse behind. Multiple cars, all identical, pulled out at the same time. I was curled up on the floor of the passenger seat where no one could see me.

"You know," I said, almost idly. "Every time someone says something like that—it's probably something that's gonna piss me off, and that's not the wrong way, even if you're not intending to piss me off."

He chuckled. "You have a point. How about this—I'm really impressed with your choice."

"Better." A real grin pulled at my lips as I peeked up at him. It was funny, he seemed so damned dark and scary when I first met him.

Everything from his rough appearance, to his fierce expressions, to the vicious growl in his voice—he scared and infuriated me. The bossy side of his nature was downright annoying. But he was my brother, and the more I got to know him, the more I understood what he needed from me.

"Anyway," I said. "What did I do that impressed you?" From this angle, all I could see was him as he drove. His gaze was constantly on a swivel, flicking to the rearview mirror, the side mirrors, then back.

The plan was a shell game. Splitting up wasn't ideal. None of us liked it, but we also needed to get out from the under-the-thumbs of our watchers. Understanding what was required didn't make it something I liked, however.

"You let them send you with me," he said. "Rather than insisting on staying there to back them." He raised four fingers from the hand he had on the steering wheel. "Not that I don't think you're tough. You've demonstrated how fierce you are from the beginning, whether I was ready to see it or not."

I didn't laugh.

"Although you have not exactly made it easy to protect you, and Kel has been your staunchest supporter in this." It almost sounded like he was grumbling. "So, not sure how he convinced you..."

Now I laughed. "He asked me," I told him. Which was true, Kellan did ask me. And since they were so devoted to my protection, at least two of them were always with me, which could slow them down or lead to other risks.

That, and they wanted Milo out of there. Sending him with me protected him too. If I didn't go, Milo wouldn't.

"Just like that, huh?"

"Well, I could say he has a talented tongue and persuaded me that way—"

"Nope," Milo said with a laugh, shaking his head. "Don't go there."

"Awww." I grinned, as he wagged a finger at me. "Asking you was enough of an answer."

"Fine," I huffed like it was a real chore, even though it was hard not to laugh. "Why did you decide to come with me?"

He spared me a brief look that said it was a stupid question, but I didn't back off.

"Did he ask you too?"

That earned me a genuine bark of laughter. "Yes, Ivy, he asked—but it wasn't if I would go with you. He asked if I would be comfortable getting you out of town with Doc's people. Doc trusts them. And I've gotten to know them some since they've been here."

"Except you don't know them." I didn't even have to guess how that went.

"No, and I debated sending Freddie with you," he admitted.

"But you didn't."

"Nope. Because I want to be the one who looks after you—and the guys don't need to worry about me flying off the handle. Even if Kel used looking after me to talk you into coming."

"Is that what he did? Huh." I made a show of rubbing my chin. "Sounds sketchy."

He laughed. "You know what...?"

"Are you going to tell me?"

"Actually, I am. I think you're good for them, and while this life wouldn't have been my first choice for you...you do fit really, really well."

Pride fisted in my chest at the declaration.

"It's also not my choice," he said. "And I trust you to know what's good for you."

"We're going to need a hug after this."

He laughed. "Bite me."

I grinned. Even folded up in the well, it wasn't all that uncomfortable. It was almost an hour after we left the warehouse that he pulled into a parking garage on the far side of the city and drove upward. Three levels.

"Stay put," he said before he got out. He circled the vehicle and opened my side, where he pulled out the bags and then let me slip out with him. "Hoodie up."

I'd gotten one of Vaughn's hoodies to wrap up in before we left. It smelled like him, and it did wonders for my nerves. Being with Milo helped, but I missed the guys from the moment I'd said goodbye to them.

I tugged the hood up and made sure it was zipped before Milo jerked his head to the left. "We're going down two flights. Stay on my left."

"Sir, yes, sir," I teased, even if I fell into step right where he wanted me. He just shook his head as we took the stairs down. We didn't pass anyone coming up. On the first level, he headed right for a Mercedes.

It was a lovely dark sedan with dark windows. It reminded me of some of the private cars hired to run me around.

"Front seat or back seat?" Because we had two more car switches to do.

"Backseat," he said, opening the door for me and setting one of the bags on the seat, and sliding a couple of pillows onto the floor. "Next car, you can ride up front."

"It's all good." Once inside, it was a lot more comfortable lying down in here. "I would offer to drive, but I still don't have a license."

Milo glanced over the seat as he started the car and eyed me. "Soon as this is done, we're going to get that."

I grinned. "I'd like it. Kel's been teaching me. I'm not half bad."

"I believe you," he said. "You're also not one to brag about yourself, so if you say you're not half bad, and Kel lets you drive his car, I think it's safe to say you'd pass the test."

A silly grin curved my lips as I settled back against the pillow. I was braced and ready for the movement when he began backing out.

It didn't take any time to drive out of the garage. Traffic was a little snarly, but then we were on the highway.

"You want me to turn on some music?" His question pulled another smile to my lips.

"I'm good," I said. "But I would like to talk, if you're up for it."

There was a beat of silence. "This feels like a trap." He cut a look down at me before looking back at the road. "Definitely sounds like a trap. But what the hell. Hit me, Ivy."

I cracked up. The fact I could see his grin only encouraged my laughter. He didn't tease me more, just waited as I chortled.

Wiping my eyes, I tried to catch my breath. "Right... so... Lainey."

His slow exhale wasn't a promising sign, yet I still pressed onwards. He said to ask him, so I was going to ask him.

"Are you two still seeing each other?" There were just a whole host of ways to ask the question. Lainey hadn't discussed much about Milo, other than to protest some of his caveman tendencies. I didn't press her on those because I didn't want to know as much. At the same time... "I know she's been back east for a while, but...you guys seemed to have a connection."

The silence extended for so long that I thought he might have changed his mind. Blowing out a long sigh, he finally shook his head. "I don't know, Ivy. I don't know what Mayhem and I are right now."

Okay, that was better than saying they were nothing or anything like that. "How did you guys leave it?"

"She hasn't told you?"

"Hmm, no." I considered how I could answer that question. Sometimes the truth was just easier all the way around. "We don't discuss you—other than you're my brother, and I'm getting to know you. Also, she thinks you're stubborn. But—everything else is personal. Not going to lie, if Lainey needed to talk to me, I would absolutely listen. At the same time, I want to know as much about your sex life as you do mine."

That earned me a sharp bark of laughter and he shook his head. "That presupposes there's a sex life to discuss."

"Well—pretty sure her sleepovers with you weren't platonic." Or she wouldn't have had hickeys.

His groan amused me, and I laughed.

"Right, well, it doesn't change my answer. She has her life and her world—this is mine. Not sure where it all fits together."

"That world was my world too—and while Lainey's got a protective grandfather, she's not helpless, you know."

"Doesn't mean I should expect her to give it all up for me, you know?"

Okay, I could work with that. "Do you want her to give it all up and move here?" While I would love to have Lainey closer, she would never leave Andrea. Not while she was still young. Her grandfather was a tough old man, but she wouldn't leave him to wage war with her mother either.

"I just said I can't ask her." He raked a hand through his hair, the grim expression on his face tugging at my heart. I almost hated pushing him.

"That's not what I asked," I said softly. "Do you *want* to ask her?"

"Ivy..."

"You can tell me to shut up and mind my own business," I offered. "Although I don't like to see either of you hurting, and if you're convinced that she's *better* off in her world, I'd remind you that you thought the same thing about me."

A muscle ticked in his cheek. I could almost imagine the gritting of his teeth. "I don't want her world to be like yours was…"

"I know you don't. Just like I know you didn't know. Only that's the thing, making decisions about what is best for someone else without involving them is just a bad idea all around."

"Maybe…I don't want to have to ask," he said slowly. "'Cause I don't know if I'm ready for there to be more."

"That's fair." I folded my hands together over my stomach. "If you'd asked me a year ago if I would be in a relationship like this, I would have laughed. It would seem ridiculous. How could I be with two guys? Now, I'm with seven."

That was a weird thing to say out loud.

"I never thought of myself as relationship material," I continued. "I'm broken—in so many ways. Broken isn't bad, I know that. Rome reminds me—Liam reminds me—all of you remind me. While broken may not be bad, it sure as hell isn't easy either."

"No," he said slowly. "It's not. I wish I could do or say something that would magically fix all this."

I smiled. "I know, I feel the same way. But—I wasn't telling you that to make you feel bad. I wanted to tell you that because relationships are hard. They're even harder when you don't believe in yourself. Maybe Lainey doesn't want a relationship… and maybe she does. However, if you shut her out and don't at least give her a chance to answer that question, you may be cutting yourself off from the relationship the two of you could have too."

Hopefully, I didn't go too far. Milo glanced over his shoulder and down at me.

"I'll think about it."

I grinned. "Thank you."

"I was right, ya know."

"Hmm?"

"It was a trap."

I burst out laughing. Despite his mock eye roll, he was also grinning.

"You know," I said. "You're not half-bad at this brother business. Clearly, you're better at being a sibling than I am…"

He snorted. "You're getting there just fine, Ivy. You have being little sister down to an art."

That pleased me immensely. "Does that mean we can play road trip games?"

His answering groan was downright delightful. "Does that mean twenty questions?"

"Well, it could… or I Spy, or you know… license plate games. Though I don't really know a lot of those."

"How about you tell me about learning to fly?" The question surprised me. "I know part of it was escaping your life there, but that can't be the only reason you learned or how you became so damn good at it."

I nibbled on the edge of a nail. "Do you truly want to know?"

"Yes, Ivy. I want to know—but only if you want to tell me."

That settled the internal debate all at once. "Well, I love to dance. I couldn't even tell you when my first dance lesson was, but I've always danced, and I love it—everything about it. More, I loved how it made me feel…"

CHAPTER 2

EMERSYN

*B*y evening, we'd made it to our third car swap. Smothering a yawn in the passenger seat, I checked the time. We'd gone through a drive-thru for food. Burgers were too heavy, but I'd been too hungry to argue for something lighter.

As it was, Milo killed two of the burgers on his own. He ate with impressive speed. The fact he murdered his French fries at the same rate amused me. When I offered him mine, he frowned.

"You sure?"

"Yep. I'm already full."

"Cool." He took a handful of the French fries and stuffed them in his mouth. I chuckled at the speed to which he ate them and stared out at the dark road. We were on an interstate—somewhere. I'd lost track of the drive.

One of the drawbacks to being driven everywhere was that I rarely paid as close attention to where we were going and how we were getting there as I should—something to work on. We'd turned on the music this time, probably Milo's way to fill the silence.

I kind of liked the station he'd picked. It had a mix of hits from several different decades. I didn't recognize them all, but some had actually been pieces I'd done performances to over the years.

"Do you mind if I ask you a few questions?" He'd finished the fries and shot-gunned some of his soda. At this rate, we would have to stop for another pee break. We'd only used rest stops so far. When he'd stopped for gas, I slouched down in the car.

The hoodie helped to hide my identity and I had my hair pulled into a braid too. Not that I blamed him. I liked the soda for the sugar rush and the caffeine kick too. My bladder, on the other hand, was not a fan.

"Nope," I said. "I don't mind at all. What do you want to know? I don't promise to offer good fashion advice, but I do know what a good tux fit looks like."

"Right," he said, while I couldn't tell if he rolled his eyes—it definitely sounded like he did. "How did you and Mayhem stay friends for so many years?"

"Well," I said, turning that question over in my head. "I would like to say it was me being brave or something, but most of it was Lainey, especially in the beginning. Even when I had to stop being her roommate, we never stopped being friends. We used to eat meals together and we had a lot of classes together."

I swirled the drink around in my cup.

"At one point, she tried to keep up with me in dance classes, but I took so many, and she just didn't love it as I did. Didn't stop her from being supportive in any case, so when I saw that flyer looking for performers of all ages and sizes—she was the first one who told me to go for it."

When I worked on my audition piece, she'd been full of encouraging advice and cheering. Even when she didn't know what to say, she still knew when to say stuff.

"The hardest part was that it didn't occur to me until after I got the spot, that I was going to have to leave the school, leave her—" It had been the one genuine reluctance I had. "But she wouldn't hear of me not going. Said we'd get phones and keep in touch that way…clearly, we could afford them."

Mom had said yes when I asked her for one, and we didn't tell Fuckbucket at first. It had been our secret. Hers. Mine. Lainey's.

"You'd think she'd forget me with me being gone all the time, but she didn't. We messaged constantly, then discovered apps that would delete our messages after they were read. She never asked me why it was safer for me, but she didn't argue when I suggested it. Then again, neither she nor Adam ever liked Fuckbucket, so maybe she understood interfering parents and shitty uncles."

I shrugged.

When Milo reached out a hand, I gripped his.

"I'm all right."

"I know you are," he said. "Doesn't mean it doesn't piss me off that you had to sneak around and jump through hoops to hang onto a friend."

"She jumped through a lot more than I did—including leaving boarding school to take a bus across the country to meet me for my birthday."

"I am still both impressed and appalled that the two of you were set up in that hotel all by yourselves," he said with a shake of his head. "You were way too young to be running around like that."

With a shrug, I squeezed his hand once then went for a drink. "I never felt that young then. But I did feel amazing that Lainey cared enough to spend my birthday with me."

"Yeah, Ivy, I know. Then her friends showed up…"

I snorted. "Did you run into Adam and Ezra?" Had I missed part of the story? Lainey had mentioned something with the guys, but I hadn't even known about Milo then.

"You could say that," he said with a shrug. "They picked up on me following you guys. They were also looking for a fight. Mayhem interrupted…"

In the low glow from the dashboard, I caught the wistful smile on his lips.

"Fierce little thing. All claws and teeth, giving them hell."

"That sounds like Lainey." So much like her. I couldn't even begin to describe how much like her it was. "If I was ever in trouble—" And it had happened. "She was the one I wanted to call. Fearless, tough, and resourceful. She also never made me defend a choice, just asked me what I needed."

"That makes her an amazing friend."

It did.

Absolutely.

Conversation dwindled, and my eyes were getting heavy. Kel had checked in with us only once with a single question mark. We were supposed to limit contact for the moment, so I'd sent him a kiss emoji. We were fine, but the check-in made my heart ache almost as much as it had when I left.

Smothering another yawn, I fought going to sleep. I wanted to keep Milo company. But I must have passed out. When he woke me with a gentle shake, we were at a rest stop.

"Restroom break," he said, scanning the area. "I'm gonna check the ladies and stay out there while you're inside, okay?"

"Yep," I said, smothering another yawn as I climbed out of the car and followed him sleepily across the grass. There were no other vehicles here. Not even trucks. It was like a lonely little rest stop in the middle of nowhere.

Milo checked the interior of the bathroom, then came back out. "You're good to go."

Trusting him at his word, I made use of the facilities. I washed my face and my hands after. The cold water helped to smack a little life into me. When I came out, Milo had me follow him into the men's.

"You know," I said, wrinkling my nose at the smell. "You could have gone into the ladies."

He chuckled. "Stands out more for a guy to be in the ladies than it does for a girl to be in here."

"Not even going to comment on that." Cause, ick. He snorted but left it alone. Fortunately, it didn't bother me to share a facility. Too many times, it happened with the dance company. Nudity didn't even bother me, but yeah, brother and just nope.

He didn't take long. It kind of amused me that he washed up like I did, including splashing his face.

"How much farther do we have to go?" We'd been on the road for more than eighteen hours. "Do you need a break? I can drive for a while."

"I'm good for another couple of hours," he said. Then checked his phone. "Address changed for the meetup, it's an hour closer, so that's something."

Oh, cool. "I was surprised when Mickey said they'd gone so far away, because weren't they supposed to be sticking close to Braxton Harbor?"

"A different job, and they were setting up a safe house," Milo said.

Oh.

"So the plan was always to get me out of Braxton Harbor." I wanted to be annoyed by that. For as much as I'd fought against them hiding me away, the fact they'd gone ahead and made a plan in case they needed to do it was kind of sweet.

"Not sure it was always the plan," Milo said as he opened

my door for me. The breeze was cool, and the air was comfortable and fresh. A big fat moon hung up in the sky and there were more stars than I'd seen in a while. "But it's always good to have a backup, especially after what happened."

That made sense.

It also robbed me of any argument, no matter how much I *wanted* to be annoyed. "You know, as weird as this is," I told him as he climbed into the driver's seat. "I'm kind of enjoying this time."

"Yeah?" He got the engine started and checked the GPS on his phone. His eyebrows dipped as he flipped over to messages. He didn't have any new ones either.

"Yeah. Is something wrong?"

"No," he said, reaching for his soda to take a drink. "Just checking our distance. They wanted a fifteen-minute heads-up so they could double back before they swapped vehicles with us. Then another hour after that."

I made a face. "Are we being too paranoid?" Even as I asked the question, I shook my head. "I don't think so."

"No," Milo told me. "It's only paranoia if they aren't out to get you."

Right now, they were definitely out to get us.

"Try to sleep, Ivy," he said. "It could be an even longer night after we get there."

True. I managed a doze, but it wasn't quite going all the way to sleep. By the time we got to our destination, it was going to be three or four in the morning, at least back in Braxton Harbor. It would probably be later here.

Ten minutes out from our meet-up and five minutes after we sent the message, my stomach started doing little flip-flops. We were literally in the middle of nowhere. It was bizarre. I didn't recognize anything.

We'd gotten off the interstate and followed the instructions toward the final location. It was after sunrise, so the emptiness seemed even *more* empty, if that were possible.

Fields on one side were just thick with brown stalks of something. It kind of looked like something out of a horror movie. Even in daylight.

Maybe especially in daylight.

I was tracking the mile markers as we went further and further from the interstate.

Milo's gaze never stopped moving as he kept scanning the whole area, but his knuckles were white on the steering wheel.

"Why does this feel like a trap?" I asked, echoing his question from the day before. We'd stopped for coffee not that long ago, but I'd downed mine like an addict, and I really wanted more.

"Cause it's too open and exposed," Milo answered with all kinds of gravitas.

I hated the whole idea.

"Maybe because they want to see if anyone is behind us?" I glanced back as if to prove a point and then frowned.

Someone was behind us.

Not super close, but they were gaining.

"I see him," Milo said, his frown deepening. I cut a look at the side mirror then twisted again. "Face front," my brother ordered. "If they impact, I want you secure in that seat."

If they impacted… who the fuck were they?

As we crested a small rise in the flat land, it shifted and changed. Ahead of us was an old church with a rotting roof and damaged brickwork, abandoned by time.

There was also a cemetery.

There were cars ahead of us too.

These were across the road.

"Milo…"

"Hang on, Ivy." He wrenched the wheel to the side and

then we were off the road itself and heading out into the field. The car wasn't meant for off-roading, but Milo didn't take his foot off the pedal as we bounced over the uneven ground.

My teeth clacked together. The noise from the car and the ground was godawful. When the side mirror exploded from a gunshot, I looked at Milo.

"Listen to me, Ivy," he said as he swerved to follow some ruts in the road or whatever it was, he could see that I couldn't. "Gun and knife. Get them both. Phone, too—but it might do us fuck all of good out here. In a minute, we're going to do a spin and generate some dust, and then you are getting out and into that field. You get out there, you get down, and you hide. You *do not* come out. Do you hear me?"

"Milo," I protested.

"No," he said. "You will do this. No arguments. If you can get a call out, call the guys. If you can't, you just stay down. Head down, and you don't come out. I don't care what you hear."

Terror punched me square in the chest *again*. "What about you?"

"I'll take care of me, Ivy." He cut a look at me. "Hang on." Then he began tearing around in a circle over the uneven ground. Dust kicked up everywhere. "When I say go —you go."

All too soon, he said go. Jerking open the passenger door as I clicked off the seatbelt wasn't my most graceful. I hit the ground and rolled, letting the momentum carry me into the taller grass.

Choking on dust, I plunged deeper into the stalks, rushing away from the sounds of engines, tires, gunshots, and *Milo.*

CHAPTER 3

EMERSYN

It didn't matter how close to the ground I was lying, I could still *hear* the vehicles. I could hear the shouts. The crunch of metal on metal when they struck the car with Milo in it, nearly pulled a scream out of me. As it was, I bit down on my lip hard enough to draw blood.

Sticking to the golden brown stalks, I crept through the field. Three times I checked my phone. No bars.

None.

I switched to the settings to see if there was any Wi-Fi or Bluetooth nearby. Nothing. We were well and truly in the middle of *nowhere*. Dammit. Shouts echoed over the field behind me. Everything in me wanted to venture closer to the road. Milo told me to stay out here, to keep moving, to get away.

How far would I have to go to get a phone signal? Dammit, why hadn't we checked before we got out here? Everything had gone the way it was supposed to except…

"Princess…" a very distinctive voice called out to me, and my blood went cold. It didn't matter how far away he sounded. He was *here*. "Princess… I know you're out there. It's time to come home."

Fuck. No.

I crouched closer to the ground. I didn't want to be seen. The dust Milo had stirred up still lingered in the air, but it wasn't a thick cloud anymore. Rustling came from my left and I held my breath as I listened.

"Spread out," a man called. "She can't have gotten far. Start a grid search."

They sounded like they were moving away, but that didn't mean anything. The only way for me to really check was to try and get closer to the road again. Milo was out there. And I didn't hear sounds of fighting. Honestly, not much more than the shouts from the men spreading out and…

"Princess," he called again, his voice carrying like a dark cloud on the wind. "I know you're scared. I don't know what those boys have been putting in your head, but it's time to come home. I'll protect you—just like I always have."

My skin crawled, and bile burned up the back of my throat. Protect me… Swallowing back my insults, I eased through the stalks. They were thick and numerous. If I moved sideways, I could slip past without disturbing them too much. Still, any time there was a rustle, I stopped. The day was growing brighter. Hopefully, Mickey's friends would be looking for us already.

Except… weren't *they* the ones who sent us the change of address? If not them, *how* had Fuckbucket figured out where we were? Hate swelled in my chest. Hate and fear were a potent cocktail. Both could make me reckless. Together, they made me *want* to be reckless. In the middle of that field, I froze.

It wasn't fear holding me captive. It was indecision. Guilt.

Shame. Fuckbucket had Milo. If he didn't, and Milo was also in this field hiding, I wasn't sure how we'd find each other. Except Fuckbucket wasn't calling out to his men to find Milo. The snatches of conversation I'd caught from the guys were also not about my brother.

They were searching for me. The crunch of metal... what if he'd died in the wreck? A fresh wave of fear infused my bones, yet it wasn't alone. Grief threaded around it, sparking a very real sense of fury. Fuckbucket had hurt me all my life. He'd made sure I was always alone. Cutting away anyone who learned the truth. Now, Milo.

He had Milo, or his men had killed him.

Shame left me disconnected from the people around me. Shame kept me small, alone, and vulnerable. Shame had made me *malleable* to him.

Anger spilled into my veins. Yes, I was in this field playing hide and seek with his goddamn men because Milo told me to. But I had a choice—no, I honestly didn't. Leaving Milo wasn't a choice I could make. I'd let the Vandals send us away to *safety* to protect him. I wasn't leaving him now. The moment the decision settled into my soul, the marionette strings drilled into my bones snapped.

All of them.

I checked my phone again. No cell service. Or one bar that kept flickering to life and vanishing again. I tried to call three times. All failed.

Hunkered down in the shadow of the stalks, I weighed my options. I didn't move even when I spotted a rodent snuffling its way through the field. Rats.

That answered one question.

However, it also meant calling them might be compromised.

Testing a theory, I pressed my voicemail button and waited. The call failed. Again. Fail.

Rustling of the stalks froze me in place and I listened, waiting. Voices carried, but they were still pretty far away. The acoustics out here didn't lend themselves to echoes. The wind was blowing, which might play havoc with the sound. Third attempt on the voicemail. Fail.

I crept a dozen feet closer to the road. A single bar. Pressing voicemail, I almost wept when it connected. I chose to record an outgoing message. It was the message anyone calling my phone would receive.

The only people with this number were the eight men and one woman I trusted.

My family.

"Fuckbucket found us. We're on route…" I left the road name, the distance from the highway, and as many details as I could remember about the field: the cemetery and the abandoned church. "He has Milo. I will try to hide, but I can't let him kill him." Please don't be dead. "Please hear this soon." I added what time it was just as the recording reached its limit.

My heart dropped when the call failed. Did the message go through? The bar flickered away and I bit my lip. Twice more, I tried to connect, only it wouldn't go through. I wasn't big on prayer, but I prayed to whoever designed these damn things that the spare amount of connection was enough.

We were an hour early to the rendezvous.

That was thirty minutes earlier.

Thirty minutes from now, Mickey's guys would know we were late. They'd initiate contact with us or him. They'd call…

No doubt existed within me. The Vandals would come. It was only a matter of time.

Just needed to survive that long.

Silencing the phone, I slid it into my pocket then fisted the knife as I set out to work my way through the field back toward the church. Hopefully, my sense of direction wasn't fucked. Hopefully, that message went through.

They would come.

I knew they would.

But I couldn't just wait for them. After I got Milo…

Then we could wait, together.

It took time to creep through the fields. More than once, I had to pause to wipe the sweat off my palms. I'd never been more glad for Vaughn's hoodie. It was like he was right there with me. I got a little turned around as I made my way through the field and came out near the road, farther away from the church and the cemetery.

I found our car.

The hood had accordioned. The front seat was empty.

The cool air seemed so much colder.

"I know you can hear me, Princess," Fuckbucket yelled. I'd almost managed to block his presence as I moved and he was quiet. But there he was—like my past given demon-shape form. "Can you hear him?"

Before I could even quite register what he said, a shout split the silence. Even the rodents weren't moving now. The birds had all vanished.

That was Milo.

I knew pain when I heard it.

"You have one minute, Princess. Then I'll burn him again." He wasn't kidding. They'd been looking for me for a couple of hours now.

A couple of hours and no sign of our guys.

They're coming, I told myself. They're coming.

An agonized sound raked across me as it rippled over the field. It was all coming from the church. Keeping the road in sight, I moved along the edges. Each time I spotted movement ahead, I crouched to go still. The wind had picked up.

That was useful. It rustled the stalks without any help from me.

"How many times do you want me to burn him, Princess? Three? Four? A dozen? I know you're out there—"

I want you to die. The words burned inside of me, even as I didn't give in to the need to yell them out. I want you to die in a blaze of fire, bloody and screaming. I could see it. Never had I craved violence more.

Nearing the church, I could see Milo now. He dangled from ropes that had been looped over an arch formed by columns on an old tomb. That was sick in its dark poetry.

Worse, he dangled shirtless as a man pressed a *brand* to his skin.

"Leave her the fuck alone." The growl in Milo's voice seemed to carry even as low as it was. The wind was coming from that direction. It also smelled of fire, smoke, and something awful—scorched flesh?

Nausea rolled through me.

"She's mine," Fuckbucket declared. "She's always been mine and if I have to gut every single one of you until I cut away your taint, I will."

"She's not coming back to you." The absolute ferocity in Milo's words buoyed me, even as they clawed at my heart.

Then, Fuckbucket moved and there was no mistaking his silhouette or his suit. Nonetheless, he moved slowly and with a *limp*.

If he were saying anything, I couldn't hear it. He circled Milo where he dangled, then Milo slammed a foot into him and knocked him backward. Fuckbucket's guards were on him in a heartbeat.

They were hitting him with fists, canes, and other objects. Milo took it all with grunting exclamations but no shouts of pain. Agony ripped through me at the abuse. More than once, he lashed out at his attackers; at least one went down and didn't get back up.

Good.

Fuckbucket lifted a handkerchief to his face as though to wipe away sweat or blood or whatever. "However I am growing impatient…" he called. "It's been months, Princess. I've missed you." My stomach rolled at the possessiveness in his voice. "And I know you've missed me. I even forgive you for Reginald. Not that I'm going to miss bailing him out."

He coughed.

"With him gone, it will be the two of us—you and me. Where you belong…"

Like my father had been an impediment.

Fuck both of them.

The sky had darkened, black clouds rolling in. I felt that storm in my bones.

"You're hurting my feelings," Fuckbucket said to the darkness.

This close I could see them, the men moving around, and the wind seemed to turn even colder. My mouth was dry, and my sides hurt. My heart hurt. Fuckbucket held up his phone.

I couldn't hear them, they weren't yelling.

"So many good times we've shared, Princess. Do you remember the first time I made you come?"

Ice sliced through me.

"I recorded it for us…"

He *what…?*

"So many firsts for us…" He let out a sigh. "I don't want to lose you, Princess. I never have…" Then he motioned to his men as they lashed at Milo. I tried to get a little closer, and at the same time, everything in me rejected being near him. I wanted to run, but I couldn't leave Milo.

"So tight at first, yet we fixed that," Fuckbucket mused.

"Are you still tight, or have you ruined that by spreading your legs for those criminals?"

You son of a bitch…

A snap among the stalks jerked me out of that obsessive staring and I narrowly avoided the big man lunging at me. Twisting away, I raised the gun, but he knocked it out of my hand with a hard blow that left my wrist screaming.

Yelling as he dragged me to him by my leg, I rolled over and slammed the knife right into the meaty part of his thigh. He backhanded me and I managed to hang onto the knife, slick with blood, as pain lanced through my mind.

He let me go though, and I scrambled to my feet. I didn't make it far before another body crashed into mine. This time, I couldn't get the knife in him as someone else grabbed at my hair and the hoodie. I wiggled, sliding out of it and I was almost free, even if it cost me hair, when someone else hit me right in the stomach.

All the air whooshed out of me and I went down gagging.

Then I was up and staring at the ground as he marched me out of the field and toward the cemetery. Somehow, I held onto the knife, even if everything was bound up in the hoodie. When the guy dumped me, I hit the ground hard enough to bruise my hip. The dirt there dug into my free palm and the last of the hoodie was wrenched away, leaving me with my knife.

Fuckbucket was right in front of me and there were screams and sobs coming from his phone, along with a very familiar slapping rhythm. Bile burned up my throat as he reached for me, his *smile* a grotesque mask of evil promises.

When he reached for me, I slammed my foot against his bad knee. The same one I'd wrenched, and he toppled sideways, so close… I lunged with the knife, except it barely touched him before one of his men had my wrist. He wrenched it hard and yanked my arm behind me.

Pain splintered through me and ripped up my back. My fingers opened on a spasm and the knife fell away.

"You little cunt," the man grunted, but I jacked my free arm back using my elbow. I hit just next to his groin and he yanked my wrist higher, sending renewed agony coursing through me. A second man gripped my free arm, and then I had both wrenched behind me and locked there.

"You break my heart," Fuckbucket said as he made it to his feet and limped toward me,

Then he *touched* me, his hand on my cheek.

I gathered up all the moisture in my mouth and spat. The wad hit his cheek, and his eyes grew incensed as he backhanded me. Fresh blood filled my mouth as my teeth cut into my cheek.

"Burn him again," Fuckbucket ordered. The sound of the brand on his flesh *sizzled*, the noise impossibly loud amidst the harsh panting of my breaths. Milo didn't scream or cry out, but there was a definite muted agony to his groan.

"Stop it," I screamed, and Fuckbucket dug his fingers into my face as he gripped me.

"Do you want me to free him?" He cut a look at Milo briefly. "Do you want him to live?"

I didn't answer. Nothing I said would save Milo. If I begged for his life, Fuckbucket would take it, and if I said I didn't care, he'd keep torturing my brother because Fuckbucket would know I was lying.

"You do...is he one of your lovers too? Has he—"

"You're disgusting," I countered. "He's my brother—my *family.*"

"*I* am your family," Fuckbucket argued. "The only family you will *ever* need."

"I'd rather be dead." It wasn't the first time the thought occurred to me. But no, I'd rather kill myself than go back to him.

Period.

Fuckbucket actually looked *shocked,* then he was furious. The rage in him seemed to hum with its own electric energy and it burned the air around us. "As you wish…"

"Don't you—" Milo's protest cut off as one of the men slammed the handle of their gun into the back of his head.

He dangled there—unmoving—but his chest… he was still breathing.

That relief was short-lived as Fuckbucket jerked my gaze back to him. "Last chance, Princess. You're my everything, but if I don't get to have you—no one does. Choose me, and I might forgive this. I might even let your brother live… provided you behave."

"Go to hell," I told him as his nails threatened to cut into me. Agony radiated through my jaw.

"You disappoint me," he said with genuine sadness. When he leaned in and pressed his lips to mine, the cold sensation spread out. I kept my teeth clenched and my mouth closed no matter how hard he squeezed. "Damn you," he swore and struck me again. This time it left me seeing stars, even though he let go and straightened. Pain registered in his expression, I really fucking hoped he hurt.

Then, the only sounds were my soft sobs on that video as he glanced down at it. "You were so perfect…"

The men holding me had no reaction to his depravity. He must be paying them enough to not care.

Bastards.

"You heard her, she'd rather be dead," Fuckbucket said finally, then he moved.

That was when I saw the coffin.

CHAPTER 4

EMERSYN

"Sir?" one of the men holding me captive asked. The pain from how they wrenched my arms left me in absolute agony, but I kept swallowing back the sound as I stared at the coffin. Was he for real? He was going to put me in that coffin?

"Did I stutter?" Fuckbucket demanded, his voice as cruel as the slash of his mouth and the dark glare in his eyes. "Put her in that coffin and bury her." His gaze dipped to mine. "Unless you've changed your mind?"

"Get in bed with you or get in that coffin?" I choked out the words even as a tear splashed down my face. A laugh escaped me. "I'll take the coffin every time, Fuckbucket. I meant it when I said I'd rather be dead than let you touch me again."

His eyes narrowed as he turned to head back toward me, his limp even more pronounced. I would have lashed out with a foot, but they bent me down to my knees and kept me

27

there. "You used to be so sweet…" He fisted my hair and yanked it until I was forced to stare up at him. "What happened to you?"

"You happened to me, you delusional monster."

When he slapped me this time, my ears were left ringing and more blood filled my mouth.

"Beg me," he ordered.

"Fuck. Off."

The men with him just stood around like they were at some Sunday fucking brunch, where we were discussing whether we preferred jam or cream with our scones than whether I would be in his bed.

"Princess—"

"You know what," I said. "Just bury me. It would be better than listening to you. I've never been more relieved than when I discovered we *weren't* related. That I don't have your blood in my veins and that I *never* did. Course, once a rapist —always a rapist. I hope you're paying these guys a lot. What is the going rate to look the other way? How much does a soul or a conscience cost?"

The disappointment on his face was so apparent. When he trailed his fingers down my face, I debated the distance. If I head-butted him in the crotch, it would hurt.

A lot.

But they weren't letting up on the pressure, and my shoulders were burning almost as much as my arms. The feeling in my hands was gone though. I couldn't even feel my fingers.

"You make me so sad, Princess…" Then he looked past me toward Milo. "Brother…he should have kept to his place and not led you away." With that, he glanced back at the coffin. "I will miss you."

He kept petting my face while holding my hair hostage.

"Yes," he said. "I will miss you." Then he let me go and

limped backwards slowly. "If she begs for me..." His gaze drifted up to the men holding me. "You can dig her out. But only if she begs."

That was never going to happen.

I glared at him as he locked eyes with me once more, then he turned and shuffled away. Vehicles were pulling up on the road and then he climbed into one. When he paused, I got it. He was waiting for me to beg.

It wasn't going to happen.

"You should shout for him," one of the guys said, although I ignored him. "Being buried alive ain't pretty."

"Speaking from experience?" I asked, not that I expected an answer. When they lifted me off the ground, they kept my arms pinned as they walked me toward the coffin. Another guy jogged ahead and flipped it open. I could still see my uncle watching through the open window. I couldn't make out his expression. Truth be told, I didn't care what he looked like.

Whether he put me in this coffin or not. He was going to die. If it was Liam or Jasper or Kellan—someone would find him, and they would end him. Freddie would cut off his balls and make him eat them. Vaughn would break his bones. Mickey would dissect him.

My heart twisted painfully. Rome wouldn't say a word; he'd just torture him until Fuckbucket begged to die. I'd give anything to *see* that. But I wouldn't give myself to him. Not even if I knew the guys would find me. The idea repulsed me on every level.

The guys would come.

They'd find us and if they didn't find me, they would find Milo.

Tears burned as they lifted me up and dumped me in the coffin. The minute their hands were off me, I lunged upward to escape and a fist slammed into my face. Pain exploded through my cheek as I crashed back into the coffin.

"Sorry, sweetheart," the guy said. "Nothing personal. You want out, except there's only one way out and he's about to pull away."

Tears burned in my eyes as I tried to blink past the bloom of pain in my face. The other guy grabbed my wrists and dragged them up. Pins and needles raced up my arm, stabbing me as sensation flared back to life. He looped a rope over and between, tying my hands together.

"We'll be here for a few minutes," the guy said. "Maybe an hour. Not sure how much air you're going to have."

I stared at him as he kept talking. His teeth were yellowed, and he had a zit next to his nose. No idea why I focused on that pimple or the fact it looked ready to burst. It was incongruous with the rest of his appearance. Done with my wrists, he took his time patting me down—which included squeezing my breasts and then gripping my cunt through my jeans.

Not giving him the satisfaction, I just stared at him.

"Like that?" he asked with a half-laugh and the guy with him shoved him over.

"He said bury her, not molest her."

"He wants to fuck her," the groper said. "Apparently, she's a sweet piece of ass."

"Fuck off. We're not getting paid enough for that." The guy actually appeared disgusted. He shot a look down at me before he reached for the lid. "Last chance…"

I ignored him.

Then he shut the lid. The suffocating darkness was immediate. The sound of a latch echoed through the cushion-lined interior like a gunshot. I jerked even without meaning to. Thankfully, no one could see it. Then there was a bump. Their voices were still out there, muffled and unintelligible as they spoke.

I shoved my feet up against the lid, yet it didn't budge. Pushing up with my bound hands, I tested it only to almost cry out from the agony writhing up my arms. They were more than just fiery pins and needles this time. They were pure, bruised agony. I wanted to scream as I banged against the lid.

The muffled voices stopped. Were they waiting? I swallowed the next scream. I needed to conserve my air. How much air was in a coffin? I had no idea. I'd read about people being buried alive, never thought I would experience it.

Worse, I didn't know how long the air would last. So, slower breaths. Shallow ones. I tried to focus on slowing my heart rate down. The ropes on my wrists hurt more on the left than on the right.

The right.

My bracelet. I lifted my hands toward me like I could see them in the pitch black. I rubbed it against my uninjured cheek until I was able to feel the metal along with the roughness of the rope.

Fuck.

Fuck.

I had Liam's bracelet. Curling my fingers into my palm, I focused on that. The message. The fact we missed our rendezvous. The bracelet.

They could find me.

If they were too late for me, they would find Milo.

I managed to lull myself with those words, and then the coffin moved. Adrenaline sparked through me again and sweat slid down my cheek. Or maybe it was a tear. Or blood.

Or all of the above?

I bit my lip, then winced. All of the aches and pains seemed to magnify as the coffin moved. I was in a coffin.

Squeezing my eyes shut could hardly hide it from me. I was already lost in the darkness. I twisted my hands in the ropes. I wanted to touch the bracelet. I wanted to stroke it to remind myself that it was there.

Yes, it had a limited range. But if they were looking for me, they could use it.

Shut up, Emersyn, I told myself. Positive thoughts—*if?* There was no if. They were coming. I just had to hold on long enough for them to get here. I wish I'd thought to leave more of a message for them. The rushed, whispered comments earlier had hardly been more than directions, location, and how many people. Nothing personal.

No word of encouragement for Freddie or comfort for Mickey. No teasing remarks for Jasper or Liam. Rome— Rome would hear everything I didn't say. Vaughn...I pressed my bound hands against my stomach and the tattoo there. Vaughn would too, but he'd blame himself. He was still suffering after the fire. He held himself responsible for the people who died there, even if it hadn't been his fault.

Kellan...

My heart spasmed for Kellan. All of them would hurt. They would rage in their own ways. However, Kellan wouldn't be allowed—at least not by himself. He would spend all his time trying to keep them together. Being a leader was a terrible burden, but Kellan seemed truly gifted. More, he understood all of us. What we needed. What he needed, he always put last.

That was something I needed to change. If, for no one else, he had to come first for me. At least, I needed to show him how to put himself first. They were all going to need him so much. Milo would need him.

More tears slipped out. *I* needed him.

I needed *all* of them. I tried to order the tears to stop, only it proved almost futile. The coffin was being lowered. My stomach dropped at the feeling of hitting the bottom. Eyes open, I stared up through the darkness to the lid. It was right there and seemed a million miles away as the muffled sound of voices filtered down to me.

If they'd seemed far away before, they were in another dimension now. There wasn't even a tone for the words I couldn't hear. Just presence. I kicked at the lid and beat at the sides. Even telling myself to not do it couldn't stymy the panic swirling up through me like a tempest determined to swallow me whole.

Stop.

The more I stressed, the more oxygen I consumed. It was getting hotter inside the coffin.

Coffin.

I was in a coffin.

That made me want to scream all over again.

Eyes closed again, I focused on slowing down my breathing. It was hot in here because I was panting. My breath was hot. At least I'd brushed my teeth the night before when we'd stopped, and there were mints in the car.

A giggle escaped.

Then another.

I might be buried alive, but at least my breath wouldn't stink. It sparked another round of giggles, then something thumped against the top of the coffin and all the humor evaporated.

Straining to listen, I jumped when rain thudded down against the lid. It was like a storm. It must have opened up and started to pour. Licking the split in my lip, I tried to ground myself with the taste of copper from the wound. Another rush of sound, then it stopped.

Even the voices faded.

It wasn't rain.

Terror shivered through me. The heat threatened to

smother me, but I was suddenly brutally cold.

It was dirt.

Not rain.

They'd buried me in my coffin.

The only sounds I could hear were the rapid thunder of my heart in my ears and the sharp gasps I kept taking, even as I tried to slow my breathing down.

How much air did I have?

The absolute lack of spit in my mouth made swallowing almost impossible. The pain in my face was a dull throb, my arms ached, and the cuts in my mouth were sharp. None of it compared to the shattering crack in my soul. Breathe slower, I told myself.

Much slower.

I had to be alive when they got here.

I had to be.

CHAPTER 5

KELLAN

TWO DAYS EARLIER...

The plan had taken some time to hammer out. I wasn't as big a fan of sending them to someone else to guard, but I'd also spoken at length with Doc and his friends. His unit... They knew what they were doing. More, they understood the need to protect and what was at stake. To be fair, they weren't the ones who sold me on the plan.

Their girl had.

I didn't know Grace Black, other than she'd been aboard one of our hijacked trucks. She'd been another nameless victim of traffickers. Well, not nameless; we just hadn't known her. Like most of the others aboard, she'd been a mess. Doc checked them out, called in his friends, and they took in the victims, working to get them home or set up elsewhere. The important part was they were free, and his team handled all the transport and security.

All of that had helped to increase my confidence in them, but Grace—she sealed it. "They're assholes," she mused when I'd been waiting for Doc to finish talking to them.

"Excuse me?" I spared her a look. Beyond an introduction and a few words, I hadn't had much contact with her. The fact that every member of Doc's team gave me a cool appraising look whenever she was around said *everything* I needed to know about their investment in *her*.

"They're assholes," she repeated, a smile curving her lips as she nodded to where Doc and the others stood. Two of them were watching us. "I can't even take a shower without someone standing guard, but they're really good at what they do, and if they tell you they are going to do something—they do it."

"You trust them?" It wasn't a question so much as a confirmation.

Instead of answering immediately, she looked thoughtful. "I trust their word." Then she glanced over at the men, who were *very* aware of the conversation I was having with her. "I don't always like them, but they have proven to be loyal, cunning, and men of their word."

She flashed me a smile. "I don't think I ever thanked all of you for rescuing us from that truck."

"You're welcome," I said easily, still mulling over what she said about Doc's unit. The sincerity in her sober delivery didn't seem marked by affection or attachment. At the same time, she was clearly attracted, and there was a definite touch-her-and-die vibe eddying around those four. Not that they needed to worry. There was only one woman for me. There would only *ever* be one woman for me.

Persuading Sparrow to leave was not something I wanted to do. I never wanted to be away from her. She was the first person I'd ever met that fit all of us. She fit *me*. Time with her was never a chore or work. It was like she filled in this missing piece of me that I hadn't even realized had gone missing. At the same time, I refused to be selfish with her or her time.

Except in this…

We'd all talked. Everyone made their cases, from Doc to Liam to Jasper to Freddie. Vaughn and Rome didn't want her to go—to be fair, *none* of us wanted her to go. Although, they were also willing to go with majority rules. Liam and Jasper, who typically clashed on everything, were in lockstep agreement. They would trust Doc's friends to a point, but they were only willing to let her go if Milo went with her.

Milo or one of us. I couldn't fault that. We wanted one of us there. That said, getting Milo out of the center of this was a good plan. I still couldn't quite wrap my mind around their father being the king. That—that was a live grenade that we needed to not drop. Doc's argument was also sound; we needed Sparrow safe. We needed her out of the line of fire and safe.

That meant a thousand precautions and persuading her to go. The day we had to say goodbye, all of that was in my mind when she wrapped her arms around my neck. I squeezed her close. "You will be safe," I informed her. "You will use that beautiful mind of yours to take care of you and Milo."

When she leaned back, her smile filled all the dark, cracked places in my soul. I never really noticed how many I had before. Protecting her offered a measure of balm that I'd never had previously. But loving her? More, having her love me? Yeah, that sealed up the cracks, knitting them back together.

"You will be safe," she said, her voice fierce as she cupped my face. "I know you guys are going to wage war. I know that's why you want me to slip away with Milo." The trust in her eyes gutted me. "But you all have to be safe too. You have to be here when I come back…"

"…we'll be here. We'll most likely be there, all of us coming to get you."

Her laugh said those were the right words. Then she hugged me again. The ferocious strength she housed had me tightening my arms.

"I love you," she whispered, and I drank those words in.

"Love you, too."

Then it was time to let her go so everyone else could say goodbye. No one wanted to linger. The sooner we got her moving, the sooner we got her back. Still…

Freddie's deep sigh as she climbed into the car and vanished as she ducked down to hide echoed in me too.

The plan was to play a shell game. We would be ranging out behind them, taking turns picking them up until they were out of the city and clear of any tails. Then we'd double back, half of us here and the other half going to hunt. We'd found out where the uncle had two preferred slips. Liam's security people were watching them. He favored one over the other.

The one half back here would deal with Reginald Sharpe. As much as I wanted him to continue to suffer, I also wanted him erased. Leaving anyone at our backs was a bad idea. Three hours after we confirmed Milo and Sparrow were out of the city, I pulled into a garage on the far northern side of the city.

Liam waited with Jasper. Freddie and Rome both elected to head back, with Vaughn backing them. "Where's Doc?" I asked as I climbed out of the car. I'd barely given voice to the question when Doc pulled in. His dark expression didn't bode well when he stepped out. "What?"

I wasn't the only one straightening. The tension crackling

around Liam and Jasper intensified.

"It's not about Little Bit—at least not directly."

Relief swarmed through me, and I wasn't the only one blowing out an aggravated breath. It had only been a few hours, but I was already itching at having her so far away. Milo being with her helped. He'd cheerfully kill anyone and anything that tried to hurt her. That definitely helped, however, I worried about him too.

"Someone hit the clinic last night."

My eyes narrowed as Doc's voice darkened.

"They didn't do much damage, but they were after files…"

"Sparrow's," I said without question.

"Or ours?" Liam asked. Since most of us had seen Doc at one point in time or another… this wasn't a stretch as far as questions went.

"Could be both," Doc answered, his expression a stony mask. "They didn't find anything. I preferred hard copies to digital, and I removed all of them… and never had hers listed by her name even if I did remove them."

Jasper pulled out a cigarette, then lit it with a kind of jerkiness that reflected the wild mixture of relief and anger. "Any other damage?"

"No," Doc said, folding his arms. "Files tossed. Security door pretty much removed right from the hinges. They would have had to hook up a truck and yank it."

I grimaced.

"Police are investigating, but the security camera was shattered too. There was one inside, but they had masks on, so no identifying who they were that way." Not something we could let go, but we'd have to let it lie for the moment. "Gonna add on-site security for a while…"

"I can handle it," Liam offered, but Doc shook his head.

"No, we're using a company and the city is helping since there's a lot of public work the clinic does for pro bono. Off-duty police might be best. It also offers some distance between our problems and the clinic. I'm not there any longer, and there have been enough people 'dropping' by to ask for me to think the uncle is well aware of my absence."

"I want to find that asshole," Jasper said. "Then I want to spend a very long time tearing him apart."

"Thought about it, have you?" Liam asked in a similarly dark tone.

"Have you ever considered how much effort it would take to skin someone alive?" Jasper was utterly serious and Liam looked thoughtful.

"Takes time and a steady hand," Doc informed them both. "I also have very sharp scalpels."

Bloodthirsty smiles, all three of them. It was odd to see it on Doc, except at the same time I got it. These were people who hurt *our* girl. The uncle especially. He'd abused her for years.

Abused.

It was far too fucking gentle a word for what he'd done to her. "Whatever we do to him," I said slowly. "She gets the *coup de grâce* if she wants it."

"*Coup de grâce?*" Liam asked with a grin. "Someone's been doing a little reading."

I rolled my eyes but ignored the teasing. I'd done a lot of things over the years. "The point is, it's hers if she wants it."

"And if she never wants to see him again," Jasper commented. "We can make that happen too."

Yes, we could.

"Right, enough with this. The sooner we find this son of a bitch," Doc said. "The sooner we can bring Little Bit home. My guys will message as soon as she's with them." He checked his watch. "Until then, we're radio silent with her and Milo."

Liam grunted. "Agreed." He passed his phone to me.

"We've got eyes on both slips. I've also got watchers down at the private harbors around here."

"Too many places to put eyes so if he's smart, he won't be in a predictable spot." That was what bothered me about all of this more than anything else. The man had gone decades abusing her, and he'd done it while she lived in a very public spotlight surrounded by others. He'd silenced *any* objections regarding his treatment of her through blackmail, money, and medical incarceration, yet when those didn't work, he had the threats exterminated.

Think what I wanted to about him, and I could think a lot —the man wasn't an idiot. He was as ruthless as he was despicable. The fact Sparrow still had nightmares about us *giving* her to him just added to the complex web he'd built around her. Even in trusting us as she did, there was that doubt and fear he'd embedded in her.

Fear was a choke chain to keep her in line.

I wanted to hang him with it.

"She's going to be alright," Jasper said, gripping my shoulder, reminding me that we were still standing in a parking garage. I glanced at him and the understanding reflecting back at me told me I didn't have to explain.

The pain in Sparrow's eyes, whenever the subject of her uncle came up, shredded me. That she trusted us, believed in us? That helped, but nothing would be enough until that man was dust in the wind blowing across a road we'd left behind. It was going to happen.

"How many hours until the rendezvous?"

Doc checked his watch. "Too many. But that was the point of this exercise, to take them off the radar. Now we need to go make some noise…"

And get the attention on *us*.

I was fine with that.

"Let's do it."

CHAPTER 6

LIAM

Splitting up, we were going to "look" only. But we also wanted to make some noise and get attention. I respected the idea, even though it was frustrating to once again be in the position of 'hurry up and wait'. "I'll take Doc," I said. "You take Jasper."

"Wounded," Jasper muttered. "Here I thought we'd been having a moment."

Shaking my head, I smirked. "We're a work in progress, man. Besides, I can't let you have all the fun."

Kellan rolled his eyes, but Doc laughed. The sound was rusty, and considering the situation we'd all been in, I was glad I could do that for him.

"Let's go," I said, "Anyone hears a word from Hellspawn—"

"We'll alert everyone else," Kellan said. "No one is keeping secrets."

"Not anymore," I agreed, then checked my phone. The

app to track her bracelet was right there. I needed to be a little closer, but she'd worn it when she left. The sight of it on her wrist had settled me. The fact she wore it most of the time since I'd given it to her settled me. I *liked* having eyes on our girl. Bad things happened when I couldn't see her.

"C'mon," Doc said, motioning to my car. "Let's get this done."

I bumped knuckles with Jasper and lifted my chin to Kel before sliding into the driver's seat. I'd be heading to the north harbor while they were taking the on the west side. Before I started the car, I sent a message to my security teams. I wanted a confirmation update on Mom, Moira, and their stakeouts, in that order.

Putting the phone where I could see it, I started the car and then entered the address for the harbor before pulling out. Doc said nothing as I blended into traffic. I wasn't going to offer him platitudes. Ms. Stephanie was gone, just like my dad. Neither of us had time for grief. We'd get that later, *after*.

There would be an after, dammit. I didn't care what we had to do or who we had to kill. We'd lock our city down and deal with any and all comers. But I would be back with my family, my hellspawn, and we'd be building a future.

"She's thinking about doing a tour," I said, more because the silence grated and the direction my thoughts were going would piss me off. I'd indulge my anger *later*. Have the opportunities to vent my grief, my fury, and my outrage. I only needed to temper it so I didn't kill the man *before* he got to suffer.

"I know," Doc said, rubbing his chin. "She mentioned it. But she's also uncertain…"

"We'd make sure she wasn't alone, and if she wants to do her own show without worrying about assholes, I can fund it." Fuck, *she* could fund it once we got her money. "I'm also down with marrying her."

"No shit," Doc said in a dry tone before he shot me a look. "You've made that abundantly clear. However, if all she needs is a ring on her finger to access her money, any of us would do."

"Agreed, *if* that was all she needed." My attorneys were looking into it. It was a challenge to pierce the conditions of the trust, particularly one tied up in stipulations and age restrictions. Moira Sharpe had provided insight into the terms, and marriage was the one surefire way to get her what she needed and free her.

"What exactly do we need to do to get her access to her money?" Doc asked. "Intellectual exercise. Frankly, she doesn't need it, because none of us care about it."

"Yes and no," I countered. "It's security and independence. But it's also power. If she gets her trust accounts, she ultimately takes it away from that asshole completely. Taking power is something that hurts men like that. It also gives her leverage…"

Doc sighed.

"What?"

"Nothing," he said with a shake of his head as he rubbed his shoulder.

"It's something," I countered, keeping my head on a swivel for any tails as we headed north. "Or you wouldn't have sighed."

"She's too young to get married," Doc said, a wry twist in his tone. "She's too damn young for everything that's happened to her—even us."

"Age is just a number." Based on everything we knew about her, she'd never been allowed to be a child, much less a teenager and a budding young woman. No, she'd been forced to grow up way too fast. "Especially where she is concerned. Hellspawn knows who she is and what she wants. Now that she is allowed to explore what she wants, I plan for her to get everything her heart desires."

And then some. Spoiling her was high on my list. The fact she'd let me pick out a dress had been a delight. If she never wanted anyone to buy her clothes, then I'd damn well enjoy the times when she let me dress her up. Not like I couldn't provide her with access to all the outfits she could want, and then she could pick them out for herself.

"That's the problem," Doc said. "She's never been allowed a lot of things, and now…"

"Stop second-guessing this and her," I said. "I get it, you think you're too old for her. She doesn't. You want her—" That much was clear no matter what he said. "She wants you. So, fuck what society thinks or expects. Go with what feels good for both of you."

Silence greeted my comment, and I slanted a look at him. Doc stared at me, his face an unreadable mask.

"What?" I asked.

"Sometimes I forget you guys aren't kids anymore."

I snorted. "Doc, I hate to break this to you. I don't think any of us have ever really been kids. Not you, not us, not her. What we are, though, Vandal—is *Vandals*." Maybe he should remember that. "I know you walked away from this life…"

He waved that off. "I walked away from the criminal shit that killed good people. What you kids are doing? You're not killing anyone who doesn't need it. More, you're cleaning up the place and giving it newfound life. Fuck, Rome is on a beautification tear all on his own."

A laugh slipped out as I shook my head. "Yeah, he is. And yeah, I like to think we're not the lowlifes that stripped our streets and hooked kids like Freddie on drugs…"

"You're not."

"But we have our moments." I couldn't deny that. Not

when I'd done my share of shit work for the king—Julius King.

"Yeah," Doc said, leaning his head back against the seat. "We do. And I'm not pushing her away anymore. I couldn't even if I wanted to, and I absolutely do not want to."

The growl of possession in those last few words made me grin. "She has that effect. Even when you tell yourself a thousand times over, she would be better off without you or that the guys saw her first... that my brother, who has never looked at a woman before, fell in love with her before you even met her and he deserves everything, what business did I have in screwing that up?"

"Let me guess," Doc said. "She decided that you were her business."

I laughed. "Something like that. She's almost impossible to say no to." Not even sure how I managed to for so long, because, looking back? Yeah, we could have truly enjoyed those few months Milo sent her to live with me.

Not that I hadn't enjoyed them...

"Almost impossible," he agreed. "However, sometimes, she needs to have those boundaries, especially concerning her safety."

"You know," I said slowly. "She doesn't take foolish risks. Even with the hell I give her, she listens, learns, adapts...and when we said no to her taking off on her own, she didn't rebel against it."

"No," Doc agreed. "The only thing she's rebelled against has been us sending her away. Against *me* wanting to send her away..." He bumped his fist against the door lightly. "I almost wish we hadn't, even though I know it's better for her and Milo to be miles away from this."

"That tells me we're doing it for her and not for us." Which was what it boiled down to. "We need her to be safe, but more, she needs to *feel* safe." Safety wasn't just about location, it was about trust and communication. We could throw ourselves between her and the world all we wanted, and absolutely would, but if we cut her out of her own protection—well, we risked what we did when we cut any of us out of the planning, one of us going rogue.

She'd done it once to protect us.

Never again. Not if I could help it.

Before Doc could say anything, my phone rang and I flicked a look at the name popping up on the screen. Stiffening, Doc asked, "Is that…?"

"Yep," I said, cutting a look at him. "Can you handle saying nothing?"

He nodded once. "I want to hear that son of a bitch's voice."

A final confirmation, as it were. I respected the sentiment. Hitting answer, I flexed my other hand on the steering wheel. "O'Connell."

"Is your girlfriend with you?" Cutting to the chase.

I glanced at Doc. His jaw was granite and his expression glacial. Well, guess that confirmed things. "No," I said. "Is yours?"

There was a beat of silence. I'd been pushing it with him for months. But after the *dinner* where he basically told her she was working for him, and especially after learning who the king really was? Yeah, he could suck my dick. Even if we needed to keep that particular conflict neutral for now. My brand was belligerent, good for me.

His snort echoed down the line. "She is not answering my calls."

"Good," I said. "You shouldn't be calling her anyway. You can contact her through me or not at all." I scanned the road ahead of us.

"That's *not* how this works, Bishop."

"What was that?" I asked. "You broke up…" I made a

couple of garbled noises then hung up. I didn't want to talk to him anyway.

"I can't believe it really is him," Doc said after a protracted silence.

"You said it was him after you saw Rome's drawing." So had Milo. Their reactions hadn't held any note of hesitance.

"That was a gut check," Doc admitted. "Hearing him, though? I hadn't spoken to him since a week before that fucker walked out on those kids and their mother. Hadn't thought about him in nearly as long—if I could help it."

"What do you remember about him?" This ventured onto new ground for all of us. Our parents, adoptive or blood, weren't usually a subject any of us tackled too closely. Rome and I had no idea who our biological parents were. I could have found out a few times over by now. Mom and Dad even offered to look if I wanted that answer.

Mom and Dad wanted Rome. Whoever gave birth to us hadn't wanted us, or at least hadn't been able to keep us. Either way... not a question I needed answered. Especially not now on the heels of losing Dad. As for the rest of our various parents, only Kellan seemed to have been born to the good kind. At least, that was what we'd thought before he found out about Warrick.

As far as I was concerned, the sperm donor didn't count. He wasn't the parent that helped to shape Kel. Freddie didn't know his. Jasper's dad was in prison. Vaughn's mother died from cancer. Doc and Ms. Stephanie's parents passed away a long time before I'd met either one of them.

That left us with my mom and Hellspawn's. I didn't think much of her mother, though I did have some sympathy for her. My mom... My mom was grieving, and I needed to see her sooner rather than later. The rest of us were our own family, and I liked it that way. We were the family we'd built.

"He could be a real bastard," Doc said. That lined up with

what Milo had said about him over the years. "Sometimes…
he was so smooth you could forget who he was and what he
did. I didn't get it then, but I do now. He was charming and
that was a gift he made work for him."

"Like how Hellspawn can charm you to get what she
wants, or how Milo plays the game when he doesn't let
anyone know what he's thinking?"

Wasn't really sure what answer I was looking for.

"Both," Doc said.

Although that was definitely not it.

CHAPTER 7

FREDDIE

We were back at the warehouse within an hour of the mass exodus. Playing the shell game meant some of us doubled back while others kept going. I'd been riding with Rome. Vaughn was on his own, but we were on the phone the whole time. The guys didn't tend to let me drive that much. I didn't mind. Actually, I wouldn't say I *liked* driving. I enjoyed how happy driving made Boo-Boo.

At the warehouse, JD and a few others of the rats were finishing loading up two of the last shipments we would be sending out before the trucks were scattered to longer-distance pickups. A dozen of them had gone out that morning. These four would be the last go.

For now.

I leaned against the hood of Rome's car as I unwrapped gum and watched the rats moving. They had gotten the box loading down to an art. To be fair, a good chunk of the workers were just locals and not rats. They were pulling down a paycheck, adding some legitimacy to this warehouse as a port hub, and keeping the neighborhood kids out of trouble.

Kellan was a good leader for us and for them. Still…

"Something wrong?" Vaughn asked as he closed his car door and walked up to where I sat against the still-warm hood of Rome's car. Rome hadn't gone far, just moving to stand a couple of feet away.

None of us looked at the office or at the fridge housed beyond. Instead, they seemed to be watching the workers like I was. JD glanced in our direction a couple of times. He'd been around for years. He wasn't my favorite of the rats. He wasn't my most hated.

Frankly, I was kind of indifferent to him most of the time. He wasn't the best or the worst. He wasn't even that particularly memorable most of the time. Other than occasionally pissing off Jasper, JD just didn't stand out. Yet, he was reliable enough, quietly moving up in ranks.

Now, he was more or less a foreman. He spent more time running the rats than we did these days. Saved us a good chunk of time and effort when our schedules were so packed.

"Not sure," I admitted as I chewed the gum slowly. I couldn't put my finger on it, but there was something unsettling about the level of activity over there, the hum of conversation, and the downright—*jovial* air.

"They aren't missing her," Rome said. The quiet observation pulled all my attention toward him, and I exhaled a long breath. "We are."

"Maybe," I said, chewing my gum again. It didn't feel right. What did I care if they missed her or not? Frankly, none of them needed to even look in her direction unless it was to say 'yes, ma'am' and 'get the fuck out of her way'.

"We have stuff to do," Vaughn reminded us both, but Rome didn't seem in any greater hurry to move than I was.

"Yeah." I rolled the gum around in my mouth then chewed again. The gum helped with my appetite. I was a little hungry, but the idea of eating didn't appeal. I didn't like that I didn't know where Boo-Boo would be sleeping tonight. More, I hated that one of us wouldn't be there. She'd be with Milo, and Raptor wouldn't let a damn thing happen to his sister, but that wasn't the same.

Boo-Boo would be out there, away from us.

Away from me.

"Got another piece?" Vaughn asked, and I pulled the pack out of my pocket and handed it to him. When he settled against the hood of the car, I glanced at him. Like us, he scanned the rats who were working with the loaders. Some of their jovial conversations tapered off. Further, they looked over at us more than once.

No, JD looked over at us more and more.

Were we making him nervous?

"You don't like him?" The question in Rome's voice tugged at me and I lifted my shoulders.

"I don't know if I like him or not to be honest. Most of the time I don't think about him. I don't think about any of them..."

"Except you are now," Vaughn's comment didn't need an answer. He scratched at his jaw as he stared across the warehouse.

"Yeah." I couldn't put my finger on it. "Maybe I'm just twitchy about her being gone..."

Neither agreed with me.

"One of us needs to check on Sharpe," Rome said. "I don't want to."

Vaughn chuckled. "Take him a few days to starve."

Rome shrugged. He didn't care.

Couldn't say I felt much stronger on the subject except... "I want to check on him."

That got me a speculative look from Vaughn. "Can you handle it?"

The fact he asked the question was a boost to be honest. Most of the time, they didn't want me in those situations. I slipped a few times with the knife, and they tended to remove me from dealing with any of our "guests" by myself. Sharpe's clock was winding down.

"Yeah," I said as I pushed off the hood and glanced toward the office. "This is gonna be fun." Some of my bad mood drifted away as I began to grin.

"Freddie?" Rome studied me.

I raised my eyebrows. There was a question in his eyes. Not doubt. Not skepticism. Just a question.

"I should be good. I don't want him to die fast."

But I did want him to suffer. I could do this for Boo-Boo.

Neither Rome nor Vaughn said anything for a long moment, but they nodded. "We'll be right here," Vaughn said, pulling out his phone. "You guys want pizza tonight?"

"Don't order," Rome said, and Vaughn sighed. "Once they're gone. We lock up and keep everyone out."

That was the plan. We wanted to be in place on the off chance someone made a run at getting Sharpe free or thinking Boo-Boo was still here. Being down to only a handful could lure them out.

The fact that we'd get to gut more than a few made that proposition more than a little enticing. "Yeah, I think Kel made sure we had leftovers. He said something about instructions on the stuff in the fridge."

Vaughn laughed. "If he put shit in Tupperware, I'm gonna tease him for the next ten years."

I didn't comment. It would be worth it since Kel was a pretty damn good cook. At least whatever he left us to eat wouldn't be likely to give us food poisoning or someone a chance to attack us. Who knew that pizza delivery could be hazardous to your health?

"I won't be long." I set out across the warehouse for the office. With Vaughn and Rome between me and the rats, I didn't have to worry about anyone following or saying anything to me. The office code was something we'd all memorized, and I let myself inside. It was quiet in here, the hush of the air conditioning keeping it cool while also masking any sounds from beyond. The office itself was soundproofed in addition to the fridge.

Frankly, none of us wanted to be bothered by the screams of anyone who earned a stay in this particular accommodation. TA book on the desk, flipped open to the latest schedule. There was also a code we notated for when the guest had been fed, watered, or offered a hose down.

Looked like Sharpe hadn't gotten anything in the last twelve hours.

Good to know.

I grabbed a bottle of water from the fridge, along with a couple of protein bars. They were dry, flavorless, and had the consistency of cardboard. This wasn't a five-star location. He was lucky I was considering giving him this. I checked my pocket for my knife, then stripped off my jacket before pulling on one of the work smocks. There were scrubs for pants if I felt the urge to change completely.

I kept that in mind.

For now.

The smell waiting for me was pretty rank. Yeah, note to self, nose plugs. I managed to block my nose as I flipped on the overhead. Bright light flooded the too-dark room, and Sharpe groaned. He lifted his bruised face to squint in my direction. They'd taken him down from where he'd been hanging by his arms on and off. There was a shackle around his ankle—appropriate—and he was dressed in scrubs for pants and little else.

Huddled against a wall, he had his arms folded tight against his chest like he was cold. A rainbow hue of discoloration showed on his face and down to his shoulders. There would be fist-sized bruises on his back and sides. More than one of them had been by to work him over.

"What do you want?" the man rasped in a painful voice, his eyes tearing despite his attempts to block the light.

I rolled the water bottle across the floor. It was going through a puddle of the man's urine on its way to him. Not my problem. He pissed it out, so it shouldn't bother him to touch it. With the protein bars in my pocket, I walked over to unclip the hose and crank the water.

He'd just picked up the water bottle when I turned the hose on him. The smell was pretty fucking obnoxious. His squeals as the water hit him, the wall, and the floor around him amused me way more than they should. I wasn't the guy who enjoyed it when other people hurt.

Unless they fucked with the people I loved.

Loved.

The water cut off abruptly as I turned that word over in my head.

Love.

Yes. It fit.

I loved Boo-Boo. I admired her, adored her fighting spirit, and her really graceful body. Pretty pussy was not to be forgotten, though even without the sex—she was perfect. The sex was a work in progress. Might always be, but I didn't mind getting horny for Boo-Boo. So yes, I loved her.

And this son of a bitch...

I squeezed the sprayer again and hit him with the full force of the water. It was icy as hell, and he was shaking and half-sobbing by the time I finished. Thankfully, it smelled quite a bit better now. At least I wouldn't be gagging through the stench.

"Why...?" The whole of that one word trembled as he struggled to look up. Time here had not been kind. He'd lost weight. There were deep shadows under his eyes that didn't have anything to do with the bruises on his face. His violent shaking made it hard to open up the water bottle.

I dragged a chair over, letting it scrape and bump over the floor. The noise was like nails on a chalkboard. It earned me a grimace and a wince even as he licked at his lips.

"Why won't you just kill me?" Oh, look at that, he finally got a question out.

I turned the chair to straddle it and rested my forearms on the back. "Do you want to die?"

"No," he said, a hint of defiance in that tone. "I want my wife—and my daughter—"

"Never gonna happen, buddy," I said, pulling out my knife to check the blade. I'd sharpened it a couple of days earlier. Always good to keep it nick free.

"Then what do you want?" He peered at me as he finally got the water bottle up to take a drink.

"From you?" I eyed him, then the blade.

"Yes," he choked a little on the water then coughed. He almost dropped the bottle, splashing a good third of it out before he could right it. I wasn't replacing what he lost.

"Oh, I want you to die," I told him. "Eventually."

"I never—"

I lifted my head and we locked eyes. "What did you never, Reginald?"

"You wouldn't believe me," he said, trying to take another drink. The coughing rattled something in his chest. Oh, that sounded very unpleasant. Maybe we could drown him in his own lungs?

"Probably not," I agreed with him. "But try me. What did

you never? I bet I can guess. You never—protected your wife?" He flinched. "Yeah, we know that. You didn't protect your daughter…"

"I did," he argued, though it was weak and rattly. "I protected them…I tried…you don't know my brother."

"I don't need to know him. I've known men like him." Too many. "Men and women both." Most people thought depravity only applied to the men who dipped their wick into the game. Not the women with them who encouraged it or played along—or got their toys ready. I flipped the knife around, letting the hilt dance over my fingers. "You had a choice. You chose yourself and him, not them."

"You make it sound easy," Sharpe countered. "He—he has a way of getting what he wants. It doesn't matter if she—if Moira chose me. She picked me, and he got mad. So he punished me…"

I snorted. "Excuse me, he brutally raped her for *days* and that was your punishment, right?"

At least the piece of shit had the grace to wince at that.

"Yeah, her pain was about her, dickbag. Not you. Maybe you saw it as punishment, but I guarantee you she saw it as suffering. Then you didn't even bother to avenge her. Instead of getting her far away from him, you stayed close… and when it came to your daughter?"

When it came to Boo-Boo…I fisted the knife as I stood.

"Tell me how you protected her."

"I tried…"

Yeah. Not good enough. I sliced his arm before he'd even noticed I'd moved. A grunt of pain escaped him. It took effort to not cut his throat.

"You tried?" I prompted. "What did you try?"

"I—"

"Come on," I said before I sliced along his chest just below a nipple. "What did you try? I'm listening."

He jerked at the sight of the blood, then looked at his arm before he peered up at me. "What are—"

"Wrong answer." I sliced over the other nipple. He wasn't feeling it. Even watching me cut him, he wasn't feeling it. The knife was that sharp and his skin was that cold. "What did you try, Sharpe? There are a dozen ways I can cut you." Could and would, for that matter. "You won't feel them now..." I dragged the blade down his cheek and he flinched back hard enough to hit his head on the wall. "But you will... and it's going to hurt."

A lot.

The cuts on his feet had closed, so I'd reopen those before I left. It kept him from getting any ideas about running around. His blood drizzled down with the droplets of water to stain the floor scarlet.

"I wanted to protect her," he shouted at me. "I love Emersyn. I always wanted to protect her...but you don't know what my brother can do. Trying to keep them apart only made him more vicious."

"Oh, did he hurt your feelings, Reginald? Did he threaten to cut you off? Did it ever occur to you that if you just..." I sliced him down his chest to his belly button. The cut was shallow but long. "All you had to do was cut him off—his dick, his throat, his head?"

Reginald began to sob and I rolled my eyes as I stood and walked away from him. The man was useless.

"I never wanted him to touch her—at first, I tried to keep Moira away from him. I always took her with me for business. Anytime he sent me away, I took her. Except she wanted kids, and after what happened..."

She couldn't have them. I faced him again.

"You don't care," he said abruptly as he met my stare. "You don't care what I did or didn't do—do you?"

"Not really," I told him. "I know what Boo-Boo suffered. I know her pain. I know what you didn't do…"

Sharpe closed his eyes. "Just get it over with…"

"No," I said, before delivering a pair of cuts to his feet before I cleaned the blood off. The floor around him was wet and the blood stain continued trickling. The wounds would turn sluggish and painful. "You don't get an easy out…" I motioned to the room. "This is a palace compared to the cell Boo-Boo had to live in all those years. You don't understand her suffering… not yet."

He would though.

I dropped the protein bars on the ground and headed for the door. He was shouting something as I turned off the lights. When I let myself out, I wasn't surprised to see Rome or Vaughn waiting for me.

"Still alive," I told them before I secured the door. "For now."

They nodded, but Vaughn gripped my shoulder. "You good?"

I thought about my answer for a moment. "I think so," I said slowly. "I want Boo-Boo more than I want to get high right now. That's a good sign, yeah?"

"Yep," Vaughn said.

"And I want to get a tattoo."

That made both of them look at me. I wasn't as inked as the others. There was a vulnerability to getting ink, one I hadn't always been able to endure. But these guys were my brothers…

"I might need some help," I admitted.

"We'll help," Rome said and Vaughn nodded.

"Food first, then," Vaughn said as he motioned to the door. "Then we'll talk about what ink you want…"

CHAPTER 8

VAUGHN

*R*ome sketched the design Freddie had in mind, and I had to agree with him... it would look good on him. "You know," I said, cracking open a bottle of water. The burns on my shoulders and back had healed—mostly. They were sore, however. The muscle beneath them was sore. I needed to get a workout in to stretch the muscles. "That would look fucking exceptional on Dove."

Pausing, Rome glanced at me, Freddie, and then back at the sketch. "Full color?"

"Hell, yes," Freddie said, leaning so he could study the black-and-white sketch. "I liked it for me, but..."

"But you've never been big on ink." Right now, I needed to get new tools so I could do the inking. I had some of my older stuff here, but the latest equipment had all been at the shop. Didn't mean we couldn't work this out. Still... "Do you want to match her?"

Freddie looked thoughtful as he raked a hand through his

hair. He'd showered after he finished with Sharpe. I'd only asked him if the man was dead, which only made him shrug in response. "Not yet," he said. Fair enough. He would be dying soon enough. In any case, I wanted him to suffer. We all did. How long that suffering took? Well, there weren't enough hours in the world for how long he *should* suffer.

"I like the idea of matching her," Freddie admitted. "But I want mine smaller, I think."

"Cool," I said, then rolled my head from side to side before I glanced at the monitors that held all the camera angles from the warehouse on it. Liam had wired the place up and then some. The interior cameras entertained me. Who knew he was such a peeper—then again, his paranoia paid off when that raid happened. He'd had a bird's eye view of everything going down inside. It gave him time to move when he needed to move.

Right now, I was watching them for any hints of movement. We would take turns being on overwatch while the others rested. If you wanted to exploit our seeming weakness with half the gang gone, now would be the time to do it. *Especially* after we dismissed the locals and the rats.

To all outsiders, it should look like it was just the three of us, and potentially Dove, in residence. We'd increased security, crash doors, and the different types of locks to keep people out of the clubhouse unless invited. The security doors on the clubhouse itself were stronger than anything we'd ever bothered with before—once upon a time, we hadn't worried about locks at all.

Why should we? We were more than capable of handling anything that came for us and very few would try to get us where we slept. There was always someone here.

Then they came for us. Worse—they'd come for *her*.

They'd come for the one person we'd all die to protect—then again, there wasn't a single Vandal I wouldn't die for. I also knew damn good and well they felt the same. Freddie didn't last long before he was snoring on one of the sofas. I settled in, feet up on the table as I watched the cameras. I had a loaded shotgun and handgun ready to go.

Rome continued to work on his sketch, only glancing up when I made coffee or brought him a sandwich. I'd tell him to sleep, but I didn't mind the company and as the day wore on and turned to night, his presence was the soothing calm I needed. It wasn't that I didn't think I could sleep, it was the fact I didn't want to invite the dreams sleep would bring.

"I changed it," Rome said, sliding the sketchpad over after I set a fresh cup of coffee down. He'd done more than change it; he'd switched to a different page entirely.

"What is that?"

"Shrike," Rome said. "Songbird." That fit Freddie, but he wasn't that— "They impale their prey."

I didn't laugh as I caught the hint of a smile on Rome's face. "A songbird with a raptor's habits." That fit Freddie better than any name they'd teased him with over the years.

"Loggerhead shrike," Rome stated. "Black, white, and gray."

"I like it...pair it with the one for Dove, and he can balance them on an arm if he wants or one on each."

Rome flipped the page back to the first drawing. He'd definitely added to it and made it far more elaborate. I approved.

"I need to order more equipment," I warned him. "But if Freddie goes fo—"

Movement on the screens cut me off, and I leaned forward. The exterior cameras hadn't indicated any new arrivals, but the door on the south facing wall was opening. That was one of our favorite entrances. It opened into an alley and afforded us some cover. That was also why I focused on the camera that covered that door from the outside.

"That camera's not working."

Rome set his sketchbook aside and went to wake Freddie. I tracked the movement as the door opened fully. If I hadn't been staring at it, I would have missed the flicker as the camera went back to normal. No movement. The door was closed. I flipped to a different camera that would pick up that area in the distance.

Yep. There he was.

"Who is that?" Freddie sounded far more awake than one would expect.

"Not sure," I said. "But I'm guessing a rat…because they know where the cameras are."

"He's heading for the fridge, isn't he?"

That would be my guess too. He also wasn't alone. Son of a bitch… I picked up the shotgun and the Glock before I headed for the door. Rome was already out there. Freddie was a half-step behind me.

I silenced the door alarms before I opened them. Rome had probably done the same thing. Freddie was a shadow moving with me. I didn't tell him not to move ahead of me, and he didn't try to peel away. A yelp of pure pain followed by a slam had me bringing the shotgun up.

The sound of shoes hitting the concrete registered as our intruder tried to flee Rome. Freddie hit him with the flashlight and it illuminated the gun I had aimed at JD's face.

Sliding to a halt, the rat stared at me before he cut a look at Freddie, then back to me. The big tell was how he had all his weight on his front leg. He was ready to move— his only decision, retreat or charge us? Neither was a good plan.

"Don't," I warned him, hovering one finger over the trigger. I'd rather get some answers, but if he pushed it, I would blow his head off eventually. Right now, I'd start with a kneecap.

JD cut another look at Freddie, but Rome was behind him and the pressure of the gun at the back of his head had him straightening even as he closed his eyes. "I can explain…"

"I just bet you can," Freddie commented. "Can't wait to hear this story."

"I'll explain it to Kestrel or Hawk. Mutes and drug addicts do not get a say—"

Rome struck him hard enough to knock JD to the ground. When he went for his pocket, I kicked him firmly in the chest to flip him onto his back and then planted my foot there with the shotgun aimed directly at his face.

"You're going to explain exactly what I tell you to explain," I said, eyeing him. "You'll answer to Freddie and to Rome. One more crack out of you about either of them and I'll start with your ankle joints and work my way up."

JD glared up at me, but the gun he had holstered in his shoulder rig was on display.

"Freddie…"

"On it…" Freddie leaned down and he used his knife to cut the holster. "Don't mind me, you know, the drug addict—my hand might slip."

The tension in JD communicated itself quite clearly, even with my foot pressing down on his chest. I didn't move the shotgun or my foot as Rome circled round, so he had a gun pointed at JD's head. At this range, he would basically be blood and tissue.

"Start talking," I ordered as Freddie finished removing his weapons, cutting out his pockets and his wallet. Not much was left untouched, and the fact JD was bleeding in a couple of places? Not my problem.

Freddie hadn't slit his throat; he should consider himself lucky—for now.

"Let's start with why you have two phones," Freddie commented while studying both. They were locked—but facial ID unlocked them easily.

Instead of spilling his guts, JD stared up at the ceiling like the answers were up there. "Why are you here, JD?"

"I work here."

"Yeah, not an answer that is gonna work for me." I shifted to put the gun's barrel right at his ankle. "Think before you speak, then try again."

He cut his gaze to me. "You won't like it."

"No shit," I agreed with him. "I don't like it now."

"You really won't like that he has a clone of Kel's phone."

JD closed his eyes, his whole body sagging into the floor. Guilt etched into his face—guilt and anger.

We'd eliminated the problems, but JD had been with us for a long time. He'd bled for us, worked for us, been one of us almost...

"How much?" Rome asked and JD just shook his head.

"You're going to kill me anyway, and I'm not a snitch."

"No, you're a backstabber and a liar. You were going to get Sharpe out, weren't you?"

As plans went...not a bad one.

"It doesn't matter."

Yeah, that wasn't working for me either.

"What's on the phone?"

"It's just got all of Kel's messages—" Freddie frowned then dropped to his knees, knife in hand and a second later, he slammed it into JD's thigh and twisted it. JD screamed, but I kept my weight on him to hold him there. "Who did you tell about where Boo-Boo was going?"

"He wanted Sharpe," Rome said. "Only one person would want the information on Starling *and* Sharpe."

"How long?" I asked, increasing the pressure of my foot. It would make it even harder for JD to breathe as Freddie twisted the knife in his thigh. No way he wasn't tearing through muscle and sinew. "How fucking long have you been working for her uncle?"

All this time...

I had no idea what I wanted his answer to be. We'd known we had a mole. We'd known *someone* was feeding him info. But JD—

"Why the fuck would you work for that man?"

"Because he paid me," JD shrieked up at me, spittle flying. "He paid me a lot of money, more than any of you have ever shown up with...and he gave me *respect*."

"He paid you to be his little bitch," Freddie said.

"Who cares? It was good money, and he just wanted to know what the little cunt you're all chasing was doing..."

Rome's foot connected with JD's face and a tooth went flying.

"Don't call her names," I instructed him.

"In fact," Freddie said, yanking the knife out and then slamming it in again a little higher. "Don't talk about her at all except to answer very specific questions."

"Fuck you," JD said, grimacing as blood trailed down his face and soaked his jeans. "It won't matter after tonight."

"Freddie... go call Kel. Warn him and the others." For a moment, mutiny flashed over Freddie's face then he glared at JD. "Don't worry about him. We're going to take him in to visit with Sharpe..."

I lifted my chin to Rome, who put away his gun and then grabbed JD by the ankles to drag him across the floor on his back. He hit every obstacle between us and the office door. We were going to have a lot of blood to clean up.

I certainly didn't mind that.

"String him up by his legs," I said as I followed. "JD... you're going to want to talk fast..."

"Or what…?" He scowled as he hit the border to the office and Rome banged his head.

"Or you're going to be our object lesson for Sharpe. We need to practice for what we're going to do to him…"

"Kel…" Freddie was saying as the door closed. "You need to lose your phone and get a new one…"

CHAPTER 9

DOC

"**W**hat?" Liam growled the word even as he scanned for an exit. I pointed, and he nodded once.

"Ditch the phones. All of them. JD cloned mine." Kellan's voice was tight, emotion all but drained out of it.

"Kel…"

"I know, ditch the phones. Pick up burners. Call Vaughn for the new number." Then he hung up. I pulled my phone out and stared at it. My backup was in the truck. I checked that all my photos with Steph had gone to the cloud, then I popped open the back and pulled out the sim card. I flung it out the window.

It was late, and we'd been on this search for hours. Liam's whole demeanor darkened as he passed over his phone. "Just the sim card."

"Everything else backed up?"

He nodded once. His sim card went flying as Liam

scanned the exits. We'd been on our way back to Braxton Harbor. No doubt existed in me about where we were headed.

"They were meeting them outside of Lake Valde. They have a safe house there. No, I don't have the exact address. I can get it as soon as we have burners though."

"We'll have them in fifteen minutes."

It only took him ten. I said nothing when he slammed out of the car and stalked into the big box store. He came back with an entire sack of burners, two sodas, and a couple of sandwiches. They weren't the best-looking things I'd ever seen, but I was eating.

Liam stripped open one box and got out a phone, then dialed a number and waited with the phone at his ear.

"Rome, it's me."

That made sense. I gave him a second to talk to his brother while I methodically ate the sandwich that had more in common with cardboard than it did with something edible. It was enough to fill the hole. The soda was cold and helped wash it down. Once finished, I got out one of the burners and called Alphabet.

"Yes?" The singular syllable delivered in that frosty tone did not invite you to stay on the line.

"It's me—our phones were compromised. Your location might have been." I picked up the next phone in the package. "Four, one, five, one. Call me back when you're clean."

Soon as I hung up, I broke down the burner phone to dump it and the packaging in the trash. The second phone was ringing before I finished getting it out. I didn't recognize the number, but I didn't need to.

"How long?" Alphabet asked as Liam motioned to the car. I climbed back in and passed him his sandwich as I put the call on speaker.

"Did you get details from Rome on how long?" I asked.

Liam nodded once, downing a mouthful of soda before putting the car in drive and backing out of the spot. "It could be months. One of the rats had a clone of Kel's phone. Everything goes through Kel…"

Everything. I exhaled a long breath and let go of the absolute irritation. We couldn't change the facts now; just roll with it.

"Then we're going to need to move," Alphabet said. "While we didn't give you guys the actual location, if they were monitoring his calls and messages…"

"They know Little Bit and Milo are heading straight for you. They may have some of the protocols." Not all of them, but enough to be a problem.

"Have you called them yet?"

"Rome tried," Liam said. "Neither of them is answering. They keep getting routed straight to voicemail, so I don't think the calls are even connecting."

Lots of reasons for that.

"That may not be as bad as it sounds," Alphabet said, echoing my thoughts. "But it's definitely not good. Get them on the horn. We need to divert them from the rendezvous."

It was a trap. He didn't have to say it. "Original rendezvous?" I knew the general location.

"I'll text it. Keep trying them, and we'll do the same. Gotta go. We're packing Gracey up and getting her out of here, and then we'll be ready to meet your guys. Watch your six."

Not even ten seconds after the call ended, a message pinged on my screen. GPS coordinates.

I pulled up the GPS on Liam's screen and entered them in.

Hours.

It was easily a full day's drive.

"I can do it in a lot less than that," Liam said as he accelerated.

"They've been on the road for over eighteen hours…"

"Yep. We're doing this differently." He was already flooring it before we were on the highway.

An hour later, we were pulling into a small airport with Kellan and Jasper right behind us. Liam threw the car into park and slammed out of it, striding across the lot toward the tarmac where a helicopter was already warming up and a pilot waited for us.

"You know," Jasper said. "If this weren't so fucking urgent, this would be cool."

I shook my head. "You're not wrong."

Ten minutes after pulling into the airport, we took off. It was late. The dark was going to make it a lot harder to spot them. They still weren't answering their phones. But whether it was because something had already happened to them or because they were out of range, I didn't know.

None of us did.

Bones called us an hour into the flight. "They did not show up at the rendezvous spot."

Of course, they'd gone there.

"It's still early, right?" I checked my watch. It was nearing dawn. Fuck, where had the hours gone? Exhaustion wore on me, but I was in mission mode and didn't have time for it.

"Rendezvous time was fifteen minutes ago," Bones told me. "I've got the area under surveillance. No one is here. No one came here and got ambushed."

Fuck.

"If they intercepted calls, they may have cloned other phones or numbers."

"That's what Alphabet thinks, too. He's trying to hack their phones. We'll find them, Doc. I made you a promise, haven't forgotten it."

"This isn't on you," I told him even as my gut knotted.

"A promise is a promise. Check in soon." Then he was off the phone.

"Angle south," Liam said. He was sitting next to the pilot, and there was a hint of a sunrise in the distance.

Fuck.

"Did she have it on?" Jasper asked, leaning forward. We were all wearing headphones to let us talk. Helicopters were not quiet.

"Yes," Liam said over his shoulder. "I asked her to wear it whenever she was away from us…insurance."

"Wear what?"

"Tracking bracelet," Kellan told me. "She didn't want to be stolen away, so Liam got her a bracelet tracker. We have to be in range, but it will help us pinpoint where she and Milo are if we can get to it."

Focusing out the window, I kept scanning the darkness for any sign of them. Not that I expected to pick the car out even as light ribboned across the eastern sky only to vanish behind dark clouds. We had to land briefly to refuel, and then we were back in the air.

I had no idea what Liam was paying the guy, but he didn't hesitate or argue. Which was good. None of us were in the mood.. Vaughn called with info for Kellan when JD had finally broken. He'd brief us after. Unfortunately, he didn't offer much on how to track the fuckbucket. His final task was to free Sharpe and give him cash and a car. Then he was to wait for his final payment.

Even money indicated JD would have been nursing a bullet to the head for his trouble. Too bad for him, he would find no sympathy among us. Time seemed to stretch into eternity before Liam said, "Got her…"

I wasn't the only one suddenly alert as the helicopter altered course. The storm that had been dancing around us throughout the morning darkened the skies further, but I ignored that as I checked my gun. I wasn't the only one scanning the landscape for any kind of sign.

Come on, I encouraged them mentally. Give us a sign.

"Car," Jasper said, pointing, and I tracked it the moment he did. Son of a bitch. The hood was crumpled, and it was parked—or at least abandoned—at the edge of a cornfield. That was not a good sign.

"Put us down near that church," Liam said, and I leaned over to see where they were pointing, even as Kellan swore. There were bodies scattered around the little cemetery that bordered the church yard.

"Need to take it to the road," the pilot said. "Won't be able to stay there long…"

"That's fine. We may need you to call us in backup." Liam was already pulling off his headset before we were firmly down. I had the backdoor open and we were both ducking the blades as we jogged out. Kellan and Jasper were right behind us.

The first body was obviously dead, his sightless eyes staring up at the sky. I still paused to check before we headed to the next. Bad shit had gone down here. Liam had a device in his hand and he didn't slow as he made a beeline to the disturbed earth where—

"Fuck, Milo," Jasper said as he got to him a half-a-step ahead of us. The minute he flipped him, I saw the problem.

Blood soaked his shirt. Weapon holstered, I swore as I bent down to check on him. His breathing was labored. Blood was flowing from a jagged wound to his abdomen. "I need my gear," I said.

"Is it on the helicopter?" Kellan asked and I nodded. I'd brought my backpack with basic supplies. He took off to get it since, so far, our pilot was holding out with us.

"Thready pulse," I said more to myself than to him as I

looked for other wounds. There was plenty to find—welts on his back and fresh burns. He'd been tortured. Jasper and Liam fanned out and then returned to where we were on the freshly turned earth. Kellan was back with my bag and I was getting the wound cleaned and sealed up. I needed to get him to a hospital.

"She's not here...lots of people have been here... but it says she's here." Liam did a slow circuit of the cemetery.

"She could be hiding," Jasper said. "Swan...Em...baby, you're safe. Come out."

Their yells raised in volume as I worked to get Milo stabilized. "C'mon, kid," I told him. "You're not done. Time to wake up—" He wasn't rousing, at least not easily.

"We can get you both in the helicopter," Kellan said. "Get him to a hospital while the three of us look."

I was worried about his color, the sweat on his face and the depth of the knife wound. Especially with how much blood he may have lost.

Liam and Jasper were back, their expressions fierce and worried. "Does he have her bracelet?"

I patted him down but shook my head when nothing turned up.

"Then how the fuck is she right here?" Liam asked, and there was a beat as I glanced at the disturbed earth we'd found Milo laying on.

Disturbed.

Was she right here, but...

"Fuck." Jasper jerked around. "There has to be a backhoe. Move him." He was already running, and I gripped Milo's shoulders with care as Kellan grabbed his feet. For a split second, Liam just stood there, staring at the earth like it was a viper about to strike.

"Get it together, Mockingbird," I snapped at him. A reminder. He wasn't a fierce raptor, no matter how

75

dangerous he was, but a guy who could be anything and become anyone. "She needs you."

We got Milo clear, and he groaned as we set him down. "Ivy..."

"We're here," I told him. "Do you know where she is?" Was there a chance...

"Buried her," Milo said as he struggled to sit up. "Need to get to her..."

Somewhere on the far side of the church, a motor fired up. However, Liam was already digging with both of his hands into the dirt and Kellan was right next to him.

"Stay here," I told Milo, gripping his shoulder. "Stay with me. We're going to get her..."

There was no other acceptable outcome.

CHAPTER 10

EMERSYN

Fear was an old companion. One I'd grown up around. The feeling had followed me to school, joined my first tour and hung out until my last, and it had even been there when I woke up at the clubhouse for the first time. While some of those memories remained nebulous, half-formed from shadows, fear had always been there.

Until it wasn't.

Opening my eyes took real effort. My eyelids were impossibly heavy. It didn't genuinely matter if I opened them or not. The darkness was everywhere. The cool air had long since vanished, leaving warm, humid, and far too thin air. My breathing had grown shallower and shallower.

I had stopped trying to control my breathing, relaxing, bit by bit. Had I fallen asleep? The silence above was almost suffocating, and at the same time, it was kind of peaceful. Being in this coffin should terrify me.

Should.

But it didn't.

This coffin was far preferable to my uncle. Did he think this would break me? That I would beg to be let out? Was he up there, even now, waiting desperately for the sound of my screams?

Fuck. Him.

I wouldn't give him the satisfaction.

The melancholy, unlike the fear, did not want to go away. It was—painful. Loneliness for the guys. They would look after each other, I hoped. Jasper and Liam would look after Freddie and Rome. They would protect Milo too—oh, Milo. They had to find him. Fear surfaced briefly at the idea that Milo might be in another coffin.

No, Fuckbucket didn't want Milo in a coffin immediately. He wanted to punish him for taking me away. That might buy him some time. Then images of his torture danced through my head like some sick old-timey cartoon, right down to the out-of-tune piano music.

Uncertainty pushed aside the fear to climb out of me like some ghoul in the dark. The Vandals would look after their own. They would kill Fuckbucket. Chances were they'd already killed Reginald.

Good.

Mom was safe. They didn't have to like or even want to see her, but they'd already gotten her out for me.

Tired entwined over me and I fought the yawn stretching my jaw. I really was ready to go back to sleep. The tightness around my chest grew even more restrictive. The pressure aborted the yawn, and I stopped fighting the sleepiness pulling me down. I wanted to see them... just...

One...

More...

Shouting came from the distance. Muffled as it was, there was a raucous sound of an engine as something banged against the coffin. That should probably bother me more than it did, but the sounds stopped as soon as it hit. I drifted—

Something yanked against the coffin and then the lid peeled back with the most agonizing sound that ripped right through me. Cold air flooded in to brush against my face, and I took a deep breath.

"Fuck my life, Hellspawn," Liam swore, and it was the most beautiful sound I'd ever heard. Even as I tried to get my eyes open, he pulled me upward. Pain shot through the fuzziness and dragged me back to wakefulness. Moaning, I tried to lean into him as he kept an arm tight around me. "Goddammit, I'm going to kill them…"

"Yeah," Jasper said and I wanted to cry as he was right there and caught me. "C'mon, Swan, reach up—there she goes, good girl." My shoulders were screaming and the throbbing pulse seemed to beat in every limb.

"Give her to me." Mickey—oh, Mickey was here. My eyes finally obeyed me and opened. There was light everywhere—headlights. I squinted away from the too-bright lightness and turned to Mickey. His chest was right beneath my cheek. I could smell him—the dirt—and the smell of grass and…

"Milo." My lips were almost unbearably dry and cracked. I started coughing.

"He's fine," Kel was there. "Can she have water?"

"Yes," Mickey said as he settled me down. The minute I was flat, I turned my head. Milo was right there. His eyes were half-open, and when he reached over with his hand, I clasped his tight in mine.

Time grew a little more fluid. Kellan gave me a sip of water. Then we were being lifted and loaded into vehicles—no, not a vehicle—it was a helicopter. Where did we get a helicopter?

Other voices came and went, but I was curled up in

Kellan's lap. "I've got you, Sparrow," he murmured, rubbing my back. "Sleep."

They'd come for me. They'd come for Milo.

I could sleep now.

The next time I woke up, Rome was sitting in the chair next to the bed with his sketchbook in hand. The déjà vu flooded me as I stared over at him. Unlike the last time, I knew exactly who he was, and there was a fist of warmth in my chest at the sight of him.

"Rome," I said, his name as much a gift to me as something sweet to taste. My voice came out rough and broken. His head came up and his gaze fastened onto mine. "Your name definitely makes me feel better—" I coughed, ruining the effect. Although the flash of his smile didn't seem to agree with that sentiment.

Instead, he set aside the sketchpad to slide onto the bed next to me. When he stretched across me, I followed the motion to see the cup with a straw sitting on the nightstand.

"We're at the clubhouse."

They'd brought me home.

"Yes," Rome said, carrying the cup over to let me get a sip. The first brush of water on my tongue was heavenly. I paused for a moment, then took a longer, deeper drink. The water was perfectly soothing on my throat. "Slowly," Rome cautioned. "Doc said it could make you sick if you drink too fast."

"Okay," I said, resting my head against the pillow. How long had I been out? Long enough to get back to Braxton Harbor. I didn't do anything to be this tired. My arm cramped when I tried to lift my hand and Rome set the water aside to catch my wrist gently.

The careful massage of his fingers against my forearms had me damn near sobbing at the relief. It hurt so bad, and at the same time...

"Milo." The image of my brother flicked through my head and I tried to sit up. Rome kept me in place, his fingers careful as he worked his thumbs up and down the inside of my forearm. The scars didn't usually hurt and right now, I was pretty sure it was just my arms themselves and not the scars.

"He's asleep in his room," Rome told me. "Doc is with him. Lainey is coming…"

Lainey… "It's dangerous."

"Yes, that's why Liam and Jasper went to bring her, along with Ezra."

Oh.

I smiled. "They're being careful with her."

"Yes." Rome lifted a hand to brush the hair away from my forehead. "We're going to be careful with you, too."

"You guys are always careful with me." A yawn stretched my jaw that turned into a groan when he found a particularly sore spot and dug his thumb in.

"Not as careful as we should be."

"This wasn't your fault… Somehow, they sent us a message from—"

"We know," Rome said. "JD is dead."

JD? "The rat?"

One nod. His eyes had gone flat, almost blank, as he focused on me. It was the most profound, unfriendliest look I'd ever seen on his face. "He betrayed us. Betrayed you. He's dead."

Relief unfolded within me. "He worked for Fuckbucket."

Another nod.

"Then I'm glad he's dead." I covered his hand with one of mine, and he laced our fingers together. "Rome…?"

He gazed at me.

"I need to pee and I want to shower." I licked my lips. "And more water? Please?"

Warmth infused his expression, chasing the emptiness away. Rome lifted the water back over so I could take a couple of sips. "Can you walk?" He saved the question for after he put the cup back on the nightstand. There was a dull ache behind my eyes. It paired well with my sore throat and cramping arms.

"I think so," I said, letting Rome help me sit up. I was dressed in only a t-shirt, and that was fine. It was clean. He stood but kept my hand. "Catch me?"

"You won't fall," he promised.

There was so much more to that oath than just the simplicity of the words themselves. I tightened my grip on his hand as I swung my legs down. It wasn't pretty when I stood. My calves threatened to revolt, but Rome was rock steady as I got my legs under me. Then step by step, he moved with me at my speed to the bathroom.

"I feel like crap," I admitted. Even with the water, my voice was still rough. "Kind of hungover."

"Dehydration and hypoxia." Rome guided me into the bathroom and, thankfully, I didn't have to deal with panties. He turned on the shower while I peed. When I was done, I flushed and then stripped off my shirt. "Do you want help in the shower?"

"Yes, please." I truly did want the help. Everything was shaky, and what wasn't shaky was sore and stiff. "I feel beaten..."

Rome zeroed in on me. With light fingers, he carefully traced a path down my arm to my hip, turning me. There was a technicolor bruise all along my side.

"That's where I jumped out of the car," I told him.

There were fingermarks on my forearms, bruises. He touched each one, carefully tracing his fingers over them. Then he lifted my hands to kiss each palm.

"Those were from the guys who caught me and pinned my arms so I couldn't hurt Fuckbucket."

The measured look in Rome's eyes kept me captive.

"He didn't touch me."

Then he brushed his hand against my cheek and nudged my chin to look at the mirror. There were fingerprints on my face.

"Oh, I forgot about that." To be fair, I'd rather he punched me... "He dug his fingers into my face, then backhanded me."

Rome's expression tightened. When he traced his fingers against the larger bruise on my upper cheek, I sighed.

It all kind of hurt in different ways, but to be fair, the bruising on my face barely seemed noticeable.

"The guy who put me in the coffin punched me."

Rome nodded once, then nudged me toward the counter. "Stay here."

He disappeared back into my room then came back with a phone. Closing the door behind him, he held the phone up to scroll through some photos.

Three dead men.

There was no mistaking the fact that all three of them were dead.

"Him," I said when he got to the last one. "He was the one who punched me."

"Good," Rome clicked off the phone. "He's already dead."

I touched his cheek, the strain of lifting my arm added to the burn in my shoulders, but I didn't care. Rome ducked his head down, and when I would have pushed up on my toes, he gripped my hips and picked me up so I could kiss him.

It was infinitely light and gentle. The brush of his lips was warm against mine. Warm and welcoming. When I wrapped my arms around his neck, he turned to carry us both into the shower. The hot water was a kind of blissful torture. Rome didn't put me down as I leaned my head back to let the water spill over my face.

Oh, that stung on my cheek and my eye. Hands on Rome's shoulders, I balanced myself as he reached up to stroke his hands through my hair. When he nudged me to turn out from under the spray, I almost sighed. I needed to wash my hair but almost didn't want to move.

He did everything, from the shampoo into his palm, to beginning to massage it into my scalp. I drifted as he rinsed my hair and then again when he used the conditioner. After, he helped me soap down and clean up. With care, Rome inspected every single one of my bruises. The feathering of his fingers down my sides, to my hips, then over my legs. At one point, he turned me to check my back and when he tugged me back against his chest, I sighed as I faced the water and he rinsed the soap from my breasts and then my belly.

Every single caress of his fingers soothed as much as it explored. Then he pressed his lips to my shoulder as he cupped my cunt.

"No," I promised him. "He didn't touch me like that this time."

Not again.

"He wanted me to pick him," I said, swallowing around the sudden lump forming in my throat. "Wanted me to go back to him, and I told him I'd rather be dead. Then he had them put me in the coffin…"

When Rome nudged my chin up, I found his steady gaze fixed on me.

"But I'm glad you guys found me," I whispered. "I knew you would."

I just hadn't been one hundred percent certain it would be in time.

"I love you," I told him, and he smiled as he hugged me close. The feel of his lips against my throat as he stroked his hands down my sides had me sighing. Yes, I hurt. Yes, I was sore. But this… I pulled back and Rome met my gaze. "Touch me?"

I barely said the word and he slid a hand back into my hair as his mouth brushed mine. Rome's movements were as direct as his language. I asked him to touch me and he did. When I traced my fingers over his shoulders and down his arms, I was shaking yet also a little desperate.

Inside the coffin, all I'd wanted was the chance to see them again. To touch them. To hold them. When I reached his cock and slid my hand along the already thickened length, he sighed into my mouth. I hitched my thighs to his as I teased his cock against my cunt.

"Not enough…" Rome worried, and I kissed the corners of his mouth, teasing the seam of his lips with my tongue until he opened to me again.

"You're always enough." More than enough. He balanced me even as I began to sink down on him. The slow stretch and the soft burn were perfect. Rome was perfect.

There was something about shower sex I had come to truly adore. When Rome shifted so my back was to the wall, I groaned softly. The first thrust was everything, and I sucked against his tongue as he mirrored the rocking motion of his cock as he filled me.

Every brush of my nipples against his chest, the stroke of his fingers on my skin, and the taste of heat in his kiss left me drunk on the feel of him. But he moved so slow, so careful, and I needed—wanted more.

"Rome," I pleaded against his mouth in between kisses. "Please…"

"No hurt for you." I adored him for the promise, but he wasn't hurting me.

"I need you." That declaration had him lifting his head. His slow nod was everything as he increased the pressure and friction, so when the next time he thrust into me, I lit up.

This—this was what I needed. I clung to him as we surged together. No more words, no more sound. My orgasm ambushed me and I was still spiraling when he came, even as I forced my eyes to stay open. There was always this moment of surprise in his expression that I savored, and the last push of him filling me before his release sent erotic ripples through my system.

Then we were just clinging to each other, panting.

We needed to get out of the shower. Only I didn't want to go anywhere, not yet.

Soon though.

Very soon.

CHAPTER 11

EMERSYN

*W*e lingered in the shower until my fingers were wrinkled like prunes. Rome didn't urge me to go faster or complain. He even knelt to let me wash his hair. It was soothing on a lot of levels. When we finally climbed out, I had to sit down. He dropped a towel over the toilet seat so I could sit on the closed lid and helped dry me off.

The muscles in my arms were jumping and twitching as they spasmed. My shoulders ached all the way down to my lower back. I'd bruised, pulled, and otherwise strained just about every single part of my body. At the same time, as bad as I felt, elation filled me. I was home. My body hummed from the sex and his smile buoyed my soul.

Rome helped me get dressed and pulled socks on my feet. After I combed my hair, he scooped me up to carry me back to the bed. Instead of setting me down, he paused. "Do you want to go out to the sitting room?"

"Are the guys up here?" Because it had just been the two

of us. He said Jasper and Liam were gone to get Lainey, but not where the others were.

"Yes."

"Then yes, please."

Rome pressed a kiss to my forehead and then carried me to the door. I hadn't meant for him to carry me around, but I was worn out from the shower. I could probably go right back to sleep.

The conversation from the sitting room spilled over us as he opened the door and then cut off.

Vaughn was just right there. The heat in his topaz eyes offered me every bit of the hug his arms did as he lifted me right away from Rome. I wrapped my arms around his neck and hugged him tight. Then Freddie was there, he gave me a long studying look before he hugged me, and I sighed as he pressed a kiss to just below my ear. When he turned and handed me to Kellan, I nearly laughed.

We'd barely even made it three steps from the bedroom, and I was being passed from one to the next. I fucking loved it. Kellan's gaze was dark and fierce as he carried me over to the sofa and settled with me in his lap.

"Hi." My voice was still more than a little rough. His expression seemed to tighten as he stroked soft fingers along my throat. Like Rome before him, he cataloged the bruises on my face. He couldn't see the others, but maybe he already had. The care he took with where his hand rested on my hip suggested he had.

"Sparrow," he said gently. "Are you hungry?"

"Um…" I had to actually think about that for a moment. "I have a headache." I was pretty sore everywhere else too, but not cripplingly so. "Maybe?"

"I'll bring coffee and donuts," Rome said.

"Don't go out alone," Kellan ordered, and the warmth in the room fled for the chill of reality.

"I got him," Vaughn said as he stood from where he'd dropped to sit next to me and Kel.

"Me too," Freddie agreed, already bouncing from foot to foot. "Want anything special? Maybe Kolaches, too? What about breakfast burritos?"

"It all sounds good," I confessed. "Especially the coffee."

Rome nodded, then closed on where I was sitting with Kel. Vaughn shifted to the side. With care, Rome cupped my bruised cheek then brushed his lips to mine. "I love you too."

The soft words made me smile. Even when the pain made my cheek jump and twitch, I reveled in the soothing words.

"I forgot to tell you in there," he murmured, then kissed me again. "We'll be back soon."

Vaughn and Freddie were both grinning widely as Rome straightened. I had a feeling that my smile was as wide as theirs. "We'll be back, Boo-Boo," Freddie said with a wink, and Vaughn blew me a kiss before the three of them vanished out the door, leaving me with Kellan. Sighing, I shifted a little in his lap to find him staring at me with the most unreadable expression.

"You okay?"

He let out a little huff. "I should be asking you that."

"But I'm asking you," I countered, and he lifted a hand to smooth the hair away from my face. It was still damp, but I hadn't wanted to take the time to blow it dry. "You—look sad."

Sad wasn't the right word. Not even close. He looked *troubled* and distressed. Both were things I wanted to fix, maybe even erase for him if I could.

"I signed off on a plan to send you and Milo into hiding, where you were both supposed to be safe. Instead, someone we trusted cloned my phone and had it cloned for fuck knows how long. Probably all of our phones..." He shook his head, the darkness in his voice growing more ragged. "Then they set you up…"

"Kel…"

He touched his fingers to my lips, silencing me as he stared into my eyes. There was no looking away from the raw intensity in his gaze. "Sparrow, protecting our own is the one driving goal we all share. You—you mean everything to us, and Milo has been my brother for most of my life. I didn't *know* that we'd been compromised, and that lack of knowledge landed you in a coffin…"

A shiver raced up my spine. "I'm okay…"

"That's not the point, Sparrow." He tightened his arms around me and I relaxed into him. I didn't want to be anywhere else right now, not when he needed me. "You were supposed to be safe, and instead—you both drove right into his trap."

"Fuckbucket's fault—not yours," I told him as I shifted to straddle his lap. My legs protested the movement. I wasn't totally sure why everything was quite so sore, but I was sure it had something to do with jumping out of the car, the fight, and then being forced to lie still for so long. "Kellan—I *knew* you guys would come. I knew it. I knew you would find me. You would find Milo."

"If we'd been even a half hour later…" He slid his hand around my throat but only cupped it gently. "Sparrow—"

"I'm here," I promised him. Then pressed a hand over his heart even as I took his free hand and pressed it over mine. "Feel me, Kel. I'm right here. Still breathing. I wasn't afraid… that whole time in there—I wasn't."

He frowned.

"I know it sounds insane, and maybe it is. I was scared when I realized *he* was there, but not for me. I was scared for Milo—he tortured him." That hurt me on a level I didn't even know I could be hurt on. "He—played a horrible video for him."

That admission cut deep.

"Video?" Kellan's eyes narrowed.

"He made videos." I shuddered and then shook my head. "Videos of us." I grimaced. "It was disgusting, and he watched it like it was some kind of fond memory."

His expression turned to stone. "I don't know if there's enough pain on the planet for that man, but I intend to find out."

"I know," I said, and surprise crept through his expression. "I want him to suffer for everything he did to Milo and to Mom…"

"And to you," Kellan said. "Milo would take a bullet for you, and trust me, we will exact vengeance for him. But what that bastard did to you? I want him to feel every single fucking minute of it."

"I don't know if that's possible—but you want to know what I *know* is possible?"

For a moment, I wasn't sure if my light quip would work. His expression was so ferocious. Then he exhaled a long breath and shifted me closer until I lay against his chest, and he settled for running his hands up and down my back. The contact was infinitely gentle, yet I felt hugged all the way down to my soul.

"What do you know is possible?"

"Surviving him." He tensed as if his surprise surrendered to shock for a moment. "Yes, I know what I'm saying—and if you'd asked me even six months ago if I thought that was a possibility, I don't think I could have said it was. Before, I told Freddie—" I shook my head. "Before I chose to come back here after the first time I ran, and before I gave myself up to protect all of you, I didn't think escaping him was possible, much less surviving him."

He pressed his thumbs gently against my lower back, right at the base of my spine. Apparently, my bruises just weren't there because the massage actually felt pretty good. Pushing up, I gazed at him. I wanted to memorize every detail of their faces, every nuance of their expressions. Everything.

"But I survived him. He hurt Milo, and I will stab him for that..." It came out fierce and Kellan's expression gentled. "Still when they put me in that coffin, I was fine with that, because he wasn't in there. The only thing—the *only* thing I wasn't fine with was the idea I might not see you guys again."

Lifting my hand to touch his face, I lightly traced his features.

"I'm not a victim anymore." I hadn't been for a long time; I just hadn't seen it.

"Sparrow, you were never a victim. You've always been a survivor." He sighed softly. "You've had to survive so damn much— you've been fighting since you were old enough to walk."

I laughed a little, even as hot tears burned in my eyes. "And now I'm here—with you and with—"

He kissed the words right off my lips. The firm pressure of his mouth against mine had me sighing at the contact. His tongue swept tenderly along the seam of my lips until they parted. I drank in the touch, the taste of him, and when dampness hit my cheeks. His tears or mine, I wasn't sure, but I leaned into the kiss. The soft, gentle licks and nips turned me inside out.

When I lifted my head, he used a thumb to gently swipe away my tears, even as I carefully removed the evidence of his. "Thank you, Sparrow," he whispered. "Thank you for surviving everything. Thank you for just surviving..."

"Thank you for coming for me," I answered in a similar hush. "Though, I think in the future..."

"Yeah, where you go, we go, period." His voice was gruff, but there was laughter again and some of the shadows in his eyes retreated. We stayed in that position, trading little kisses and soft pets, but it was more for comfort and cuddling than anything passionate. If he wanted more, I'd do my damnedest to give it to him, but as it was, I was so damn tired.

The sound of the locks on the door tumbling roused me from my half-doze and I blinked as I glanced at the door. Awareness of Kellan lifting a gun from behind the cushions registered, but he set it back in its holster when Mickey came in. He looked like hell.

Like Kel, his eyes were raw with all the terrible things he'd seen. Kellan lifted me onto my feet even as I began to shift, and I made it two steps to Mickey before he scooped me up into his arms. He crushed me to him in an embrace that had me sighing even as I tried not to groan when I raised my arms.

Raising his head, Mickey swept his gaze over me from head to foot. "You should still be in bed."

"I wanted to cuddle with Kel," I told him. "And I needed to check on everyone." My voice was still rough. Like everyone else, Mickey just carried me as he moved back to sit on the sofa. Kellan was already handing me the water to drink. "Thank you," I murmured before I took a sip. My throat was really sore.

"Milo is sleeping," Mickey told me. "I'll head back there in a bit. I had to do some stitching. I also hit him with some pretty heavy antibiotics and painkillers. He was not staying down."

I frowned. "But he's going to be okay?"

"Yes, Little Bit," Mickey said as he settled on the sofa with only half a cushion between him and Kellan. Mickey shifted me so I was sitting in his lap and my legs were over Kellan's.

"He's going to be fine. I'll keep his stubborn ass sedated for as long as I have to so he doesn't tear his stitches again."

I made a face. "Wait—that's why they went to get Lainey?"

They being Jasper and Liam. Kellan smiled and Mickey laughed. "Yes," Kellan told me. "That, and we knew you might need to talk to her. Doc didn't find anything..."

I glanced at him, and Mickey's scowl deepened. "You were pretty out of it..."

I rubbed my hand against his chest. "It's okay. He didn't touch me—I mean, yes, he gripped my face and backhanded me." I motioned to my bruises. They were hardly the worst I'd ever had. Honestly, beyond the light throbbing, I barely felt them. "But he didn't touch me otherwise."

Mickey cupped my head before he pressed a kiss to my temple. Relief seemed to shiver between them and I curled up, tucking my unwounded cheek against his shoulder. I needed to feel them as much as they seemed to need to hold me.

The silence blanketing us was still fraught with all the things we weren't discussing, although that also began to gradually relax. "How long does it take to get coffee and donuts?"

"They're probably bringing you half the bakery," Kellan said with a laugh. "And Rome knows where you like your coffee from."

Yeah, but I liked them more, and there was a coffeemaker downstairs.

"Let them fuss, Little Bit," Mickey told me, even as he traced a circle with his thumb against my bruised hip. "This was not a good few hours for anyone..."

No, I suppose it hadn't been. "How did you find me?"

Kellan blew a breath before lifting my hand and stroking my bracelet. "This helped."

Good.

"However, we already knew you were in trouble before we went looking, because JD snuck back in here to release your father…"

I made a face but didn't interrupt as they filled me in. Reginald was still alive—so far. It didn't sound like that would last for much longer. JD was very dead and wouldn't be around to bother us again.

I was more than fine with that.

Kellan tried to beat himself up again about the phone, but I gripped his hand. My uncle was a devious, dangerously narcissistic, and controlling man. I listened to them tell me everything and all the things they didn't say when they described tracking us to that cemetery.

They'd come for me in a helicopter. I kind of wished I could have seen that.

My eyes grew heavier, and Mickey kept massaging the back of my neck. I was mostly asleep when the door opened to let the guys back in, wreathed in the scents of coffee and sugar.

Both roused me immediately, but the truth was as much as I was hungry and thirsty for food and coffee, I wanted *them* more.

Almost never getting to see them again was going to take me time to get past. I didn't want to waste a single moment, not ever again.

CHAPTER 12

JASPER

"We could have just taken my family's jet," Ezra said, his tone bored and irritated. I didn't know why Liam liked this jackass, and if Emersyn weren't fond, I'd have suggested throwing his ass out on the tarmac before we boarded the flight Liam had chartered.

"Because they're being watched," Lainey said without looking up from her phone. "As Liam explained to you three times, with far more patience than you deserve."

He scowled at her, but she didn't so much as flinch, much less glance up from her phone. "If they're being watched, you shouldn't be going."

"We're not having that conversation again," she told him as she unbuckled her seatbelt and rose. "I'm going to use the restroom, do try not to kill each other in my absence. In the event that doesn't work, try not to get blood on anything."

I almost laughed. Freddie called her Ball-Cracker for a reason, and that name *definitely* fit. As soon as the door closed to the private bathroom, which was way bigger than anything I'd ever seen on a plane in the movies, Ezra swung his chair to glare at Liam.

"A heads up would have been nice."

"You shutting the fuck up would be nicer," I commented when Liam said nothing. He'd been looking at his own phone. If I were a gambler, I'd bet he was dialed into the security cameras at the clubhouse and was checking on Swan. I wouldn't mind doing that. The last text from Freddie said she woke up and was smiling.

That—that settled a lot of tension for me. The sooner we got back, the happier I would be.

"No one asked you, dickhead," Ezra snarled at me, and I smirked.

"No one cares what you have to say, either. You're only here because you were present when we came for Lainey. I have no problems dumping your ass somewhere." Not only that, I would *enjoy* it.

Ezra started out of his seat. One nice thing about a chartered jet, is I couldn't get arrested for beating the shit out of this—

"Sit down," Liam said, glancing up from his phone to fix Ezra with a glare. "Stop baiting him, Jas. He's useful, even when he's an asshole."

I snorted.

"Making me regret saving his ass," Ezra grumbled.

"You didn't save me—that was Liam and Emersyn." If he wanted to keep score, I could do that.

Liam sighed and shot me a look. The faint smirk on his face amused me. I lifted my shoulders and leaned back in the chair. "Fine."

"Thank you." Then he focused on Ezra. "You know we would protect her—you didn't have to come."

"If you think I'm letting her—"

"You're not *letting* me do anything," Lainey informed him as she opened the door to join us again. Her expression was calm, collected, and at the same time, *ferocious*. "I'm going to see my best friend who was hurt *again*. I'm going to see Pretty Boy, who was also hurt."

The pretty boy comment earned a real scowl as Ezra shoved out of his chair this time. "You don't need to be around that—"

"That?" She arched her brows, daring him to continue.

"That man, you don't need to be around. He went to fucking prison." The man's arrogance dipped into dark territory. "For rape. You want to date a fucking rapist—"

"Ezra," Liam said in a far steadier voice than I could have managed. "Don't."

"Or what?" He turned to face Liam and narrowly caught the first fist Liam threw. Yet he didn't catch the second strike because that one-two from Liam had always been a vicious assault strategy. He went down, and only Liam's slight head shake kept me in my chair.

"Oh, please," Lainey said with so much disdain it was almost amusing. She stepped right over Ezra and slid into the seat Liam had abandoned, which put her on my side of the plane. She snapped her seatbelt into place and crossed one leg over the other. "If you want to just go by background checks, do one on yourself. I know what things it doesn't say and what it does...ask yourself if what sent him to prison was reality or not. Or don't—I don't actually care."

He growled as he shoved to his feet, but Liam planted himself between the two of them. I steepled my fingers together, ready to move if needed. Despite her nonchalance, Lainey paid as close attention to the throw-down between the two men as I did.

"How—how can you defend him?" Ezra demanded as he got to his feet. Blood flowed from both of his nostrils. I was impressed that Liam hadn't broken the damn thing. Though I'd give the fop some credit, he took that punch and got up again.

"Because I took the time to get to know him," she said, lifting her gaze to meet Ezra's. "I will always protect my friends, even when they're being idiots."

"Never thought you'd let your cunt make decisions for you…"

"Ezra," Liam said. "Don't make me knock your ass out. You are here as a courtesy and because we're friends. Talk to her like that again, and nothing I do will save you when Hellspawn gets her hands on you."

The warning landed almost perfectly, Ezra swung his head around to stare at Liam, and then he shook his head as something resembling a laugh escaped. "She's too damn tiny to do any damage."

I snorted. "If she comes for you," I said. "*All* of us will be."

"Agreed," Lainey said with a hint of a smirk. "Pretty Boy is her brother and she's very protective. And I'm extremely protective of her."

"No shit," Ezra muttered, slinging himself back in his chair.

"Good. You've remembered how to think," Liam said. "It would be nice if you learned to do it before you spoke."

"You're asking for miracles," Lainey commented, absolutely ignoring the heated glare Ezra threw in her direction. I couldn't pinpoint what it was between them. Was he interested in her? Absolutely. But how much of it was genuine interest and affection, and how much was possession?

Honestly, I didn't give a fuck what he wanted. If she indulged him, her call. Her loyalty to Swan was indisputable, although the fact she called Milo *Pretty Boy* was fucking delightful. I would save that. Liam said something else but pitched his voice lower as he moved to take the seat Lainey had abandoned. The conversation was clearly between him and his friend, so I pulled out my own phone.

"Is he all right?" Lainey's question came out soft and almost inaudible. If she hadn't been sitting just a couple of feet away, I doubt I would have heard it. As it was, she didn't glance up from her phone more than to stare at the other two before returning to it again. "Really?"

"He will be," I said, keeping my tone at the same level. This subtle shit was not my favorite. I'd rather stand my ground and throw a fist or a verbal jab. Fuck knew I had the temper for it. But if that asshole called Milo a rapist again, I might rip his head off. So—soft it was. "We got to them in time."

If I lived to be a hundred, I don't think I'd ever get over seeing Swan in that coffin. When Liam ripped it open, I thought my heart had failed on the spot. It didn't beat, move, or even twitch until her eyelids fluttered.

Then and only then, did I allow myself a breath. Doc being there also helped. He knew exactly what to do for both of them and put us to work. That motherfucker buried her, for real.

We only got lucky in as much as he didn't kill her first. I'd gotten a look at Milo though; they'd burned and battered him. Sick bastard. The stabbing had been bad. Doc said it was infected and could have been poison, but he hoped like fuck it wasn't. The last check-in said he was improving, so maybe not.

Fuck, we needed a break.

"What did he do to her?" The question pulled me back to the present, and I glanced at her without lifting my head. Like me, she kept her face angled toward her phone but her gaze was on me.

"He failed to break her," I said. "Again."

She sighed. "I hate him."

"Yeah, same."

To be fair, I hadn't had much in the way of conversations with Lainey when she'd been at the clubhouse before. Her absolute loyalty and the deepness of her friendship with Emersyn—were qualities I admired. It also made her one of ours *before* Milo developed his genuine interest in her. The jackass traveling with her better get his shit together, cause if he spoke to her like that when Milo was there—

Well, he wasn't long for this world.

I wasn't sure whether I was pleased or disappointed that Ezra kept his shit together for the rest of the flight. He limited his conversation to Liam. When we landed, Liam's security people were there and that was fucking weird.

Still, I appreciated the paranoia. An hour later, we pulled into the warehouse and I was out of the car and halfway to the door by the time Swan stepped out of the clubhouse. She seemed perfectly fragile. I picked up my speed, aware of Kel and Vaughn being just steps behind her and that Rome was already out here with Freddie.

Then she was in my arms and I picked her up to cradle her close. When we left, she'd still been out. While she'd roused a couple of times on the return journey, exhaustion and trauma had well and truly knocked her flat. Doc insisted it was normal, particularly when coupled with the reduced oxygen.

Holding her was a visceral reminder that she was alive. She *survived*. She *endured*. She was my goddamn hero, and she was right here. I lifted my head and searched her eyes, but then she was cupping my face as her lips pressed against mine. I drank in her kiss like a dying man in the desert.

Love and lust blew threw me and I wanted to devour her. The strength in her grip buoyed me. The taste of her was exactly what I needed to soak up. That and the way she felt in my arms.

"Share when you have a moment," Liam commented. "I'm patient. I can wait." The undeniable dry tone made me laugh for the first time since we realized fucking JD had sold them out. I twisted, still holding her and she kept one arm around me even as she reached for Liam. I held her until he had an arm around her and then passed her over to him easily. She melted into him with the same fierce grip she'd had on me.

My own relief echoed in his expression. When they kissed, I grinned and caught Kellan looking similarly relieved. I raised my brows and he shook his head once. No changes since we last messaged. That was good. When his gaze flicked past us, I gave it a beat, but Freddie interrupted everyone with his, "Ball-Cracker!"

Swan lifted her head and her smile was damn near transformative. Liam grunted, but he set her on her feet and she brushed his arm on her way to Lainey. The girls crashed into each other, even as I shifted and so did Vaughn. We weren't the only ones. Freddie had ranged out further. We were keeping our girl in a safety circle. Now that Lainey was here, she would be in it too.

Ezra had evidently developed some discretion following Liam's punch, because he filled in a gap in the circle. He didn't close in on them or scowl. He also kept that mouth of his under control where Swan was concerned. When the girls pulled apart, there were tears on their faces. An unreasonable amount of rage spilled into my veins.

She was crying—again. She was crying because of something that bastard of an uncle did to her. To her and to Raptor.

A hand gripped my shoulder and I dragged my attention off the girls to lock eyes with Doc. "Get it together," he said in a low voice. "Little Bit is putting on a face for all of us, but this hit her harder than she wants to say."

That didn't surprise me. From the tense look on Kellan's

face, which probably matched my own, it had hit all of us harder. I nodded once. "Milo awake yet?"

"No, whenever I lighten up the meds, he gets downright violent, and I don't blame him. But I don't want those stitches to be torn out. Really hoping she can help."

He nodded to Lainey, and I blew out a breath. "Let's get Swan in there with her. He's gonna need to know she's okay."

Fuck, he'd collapsed right where she was buried. That—that would leave a mark too. Doc patted my shoulder. "Ladies…" He moved to intercept them. "Would you like to see Milo?"

"Yes," Emersyn's whole demeanor shifted. For a split second, the mask dropped and the raw worry was right there. Yeah, I got it. Doc was right, she was fighting to take care of us, and I was more than willing to let her do what she needed. But I—we—needed to look after her too.

"Please," Lainey said, locking arms with Emersyn. The pair headed for the clubhouse door that Vaughn opened, with Doc escorting them. Ezra didn't make a move to follow.

Smart guy.

While I'd rather follow, I shifted to focus on Kellan. "What's next?"

CHAPTER 13

EMERSYN

*L*ainey's hand was firm in my grip as we climbed the stairs. Mickey followed us up, then took the lead as we headed down the hall to Milo's rooms. I'd only poked my head in there briefly earlier. He was asleep, and I didn't want to disturb him. At the same time, I *needed* to see he was alive. The last time I'd seen him previously had been before they thrust me into that coffin—ice spilled into my veins.

When Lainey flexed her fingers where our hands clasped, I squeezed in response. She glanced at me. Her eyes held a tangible combination of worry and sadness. "How bad?" she asked, and I shook my head.

"Bad, but he's tough."

"He's stubborn, too," Mickey advised. "He's had worse, but you two are the best medicine he could ask for."

I hated the idea that he'd "had worse." Hated that he'd been caught up in the tumultuous storm of my past. Opening the door to Milo's room, Mickey ushered us inside. There were two low lights on in the corner. The dimness offered something soothing to ease the jagged nerves.

Music filtered in from somewhere, accompanying sounds of water trickling and were those birds? It was almost endearing that he enjoyed spa-like sounds. Lainey passed Mickey with me in tow as we headed straight for him. There was no mistaking the genuine concern on her face as we got to his bedside. There was a swath of bandaging visible on his bare chest that came up and over one shoulder.

"The wounds were significant," Mickey said. "He was definitely tortured." Lainey's nails dug into my hands. "The worst was where the knife penetrated through his lower abdomen. I worried about internal organ strikes, but it seems to have gone out of its way to miss hitting anything vital."

When Lainey sat carefully on the edge of the bed, I steadied her as she reached out with her free hand to cover one of Milo's. His knuckles were bruised and scabbed over. The signs of his fight were visible.

"What about the burns?" I couldn't miss those. I'd heard the low, stressed tones of his screams that he'd fought to keep behind clenched teeth. It would have been impossible to miss —those or the cane strikes.

"Not infected, which is good." Mickey slid a hand around my nape; the comforting squeeze eased some of the tension locking up my muscles. "They aren't pretty, and I've treated them. We're going to have to be careful. There are a couple of cracked ribs and I set his dislocated shoulder back into place."

Lainey lifted her tormented gaze to glance at Mickey. "He hasn't woken up since you found him?"

"He's tried," Mickey told her in the calmest of tones. It was like a soothing balm against the more jagged portions of my soul. "He's woken up and spoken. I've kept him sedated because he wasn't totally rational and Little Bit was also asleep."

"But I'm awake now," I said as much to remind myself as well as to assure Lainey.

"Exactly," Mickey murmured, a smile easing the lines around his mouth before he pressed a kiss to my temple. "So, we'll let him wake up now that you're both here. He will probably be a little disoriented, but take it easy and let him focus. Do you two want some privacy with him? I don't want to go far, but…"

"Lainey?" I was fine with Mickey being there, but it was up to her.

"A few minutes," she said. "Please. You can leave the door open…"

"I can do that." Mickey focused on me again. "I'm getting you a chair, or you move around and sit on the other side." His tone allowed for no arguments, and I let out a little sigh. "I need you to rest, Little Bit. So, indulge me?"

"As much as I can," I told him, and he tilted my head to give me a very firm kiss. The possession in that press of his lips to mine had me curling my toes against the carpet even as I leaned into him.

"Thank you," he whispered, before letting me go. I squeezed Lainey's hand once before letting go to circle around to the other side of the bed. It was large enough that there was room for me to climb up and sit next to him while Lainey kept the space she'd claimed right next to him. "I'll be close."

I glanced over at him and he held my gaze for a long moment. There was no mistaking the worry or the tiredness in his eyes. I mouthed, "Love you." His smile deepened, and I could almost hear the sigh he didn't release as he blew me a kiss before he touched his fist to his heart and pointed at me.

When he slipped out silently, I returned my attention to

Milo and Lainey. She was holding his hand and her focus was intent as she stared at him. When I settled my hand over theirs, she glanced at me. "How bad?"

"Pretty bad," I told her. A part of me wanted to lie, to sweep it away in the corners and the shadowy places. But each time I did that, I allowed myself to be complicit. "He set us up—bribed one of the rats to clone a phone, then used our own plans against us. We were going to Mickey's friends, where they'd set up a safe house. The idea was to get me out of the line of fire—to get both of us out."

I looked at my brother again. It was weird. I'd never seen him asleep. Not really. There was something just—peaceful about his expression right now. Most of that was probably the meds keeping him out, but at the same time...

"By the time we realized what was happening, it was too late. He did circles in a field, kicked up dust for cover and I jumped out of a moving car." At Lainey's grimace, I squeezed her hand gently and grinned. "It was fun—not that I advise doing it."

Her indelicate snort made my smile grow. "I'm not sure I approve of your ideas of fun," Lainey scolded, but there was as much affection as there was worry in her voice.

"Different strokes..." I teased, but even that sobered. "Still, they cornered him—crashed into the car. There were so many of them and just one of him. I was hiding in the field. They were looking for me and tortured him to get me to come out—" Then I locked eyes with Lainey. "Fuckbucket tortured him."

"You stayed hidden." It wasn't a question.

"I didn't plan to abandon him, yet at the same time—if I gave myself up, would he just kill him?" I couldn't let that happen. I didn't dare. "I wasn't sure what I was going to do, but his men were sweeping and even as Fuckbucket yelled for me, they found me—" Letting go of her hand, I reached up to brush the hair from his face. There was a shadow of stubble on his cheeks and chin. He was definitely in need of a shave.

"He didn't—"

I shook my head. "He has videos, Lainey."

I didn't have to look at her to feel the plunge in the ambient temperature.

"He played a couple of them. Milo heard…" I didn't know if he'd shown him. Maybe? The whole idea made me want to vomit.

"I'm going to cut his micro penis off with a spoon," Lainey declared and I smiled, even if it didn't have much strength. "That son of a bitch."

"Maybe just throw acid or something. I don't advise touching him." That just sent a shudder through me.

She caught my fingers. "You don't have to keep talking."

"I know," I assured, returning my attention to her. "But he gave me a choice…come back to him or die. Weird, right?"

Her brow tightened. It was weird to me. All my life, he'd treated me like his personal possession, his pet. I was *his* property, and he actually gave me a choice.

"I picked death," I said with a shrug. "The very last thing I wanted was to ever go back to him."

"Em…" She squeezed my fingers.

"I know, Lainey—I really do. He had them put me in a coffin and told me if I begged…if I *begged*, he'd let me out."

"Fuck. Him." Milo growled, and we both glanced down at him. Through the tears in my eyes, his face wavered as he was blinking slowly. "You aren't begging him for anything."

"No," Lainey said with equal ferociousness. "She's not. We're just going to make him hurt—a lot."

"Mayhem?" The tangle of confusion and hope in his voice had us both gripping his hand.

"Hey, Pretty Boy," she murmured almost softly as she

lifted his hand. His eyes opened further, and he curled his fingers when she pressed his hand to her face. "A little bird said you were going to extraordinary measures to get my attention."

"You shouldn't be here," he warned in a low voice.

"There's a lot of that going around," she teased almost gently. Her worry and fear for him had to be at an epic level for her not to be scolding him.

His eyes drifted closed again. "Ivy…"

"I'm right here," I promised, and he turned his head to look at me, but there was no mistaking the way he curled his fingers against Lainey's face. Maybe he thought it was bad for us to be here, but he *wanted* us here. He wanted *her* here. "Safe and sound—"

"They buried you." The agony in his voice tore at me. I captured his free hand and pressed it between both of mine. "The boys came—they got me out. Mickey, Liam, Kel, and Jas. They were there…got me out, saved you, and we're okay. Both of us."

For a moment, I thought he'd gone back to sleep then he squeezed my hand. "Where are we?"

"You need water," Lainey told him firmly. She let his hand go, but he snagged her before she could move away. "I'm not going far," she said, this time her voice was a scold. "Talk to Em."

"Mayhem—"

She pressed a finger to his lips. "You have to get better to give me orders. Until then, Mister, you're mine to boss around. Got it?"

The corner of his mouth kicked up. "Yes, ma'am."

"Better." Then she kissed his cheek once before feathering one against the corner of his mouth. "I'll be right back."

He let her go this time, but his eyes opened to track her

movement. I had to swallow my own smile at the way he stared after her. "She shouldn't be here," he whispered.

"Hush," I said. "She's where she wants to be—for both of us."

That pulled his attention to me. Then he seemed to be registering the room around us. "The clubhouse."

"Surprise," I murmured. "They brought us home, and we're not going anywhere. This time when we move, we move together…"

"How?" He frowned.

"JD," I told him. While I didn't have all the details, I didn't think I'd have to explain what that meant. His expression darkened. "Don't worry about him. It's been dealt with." The hint of a smile touched his lips.

"Bloodthirsty."

"When they hurt my brother? Or any of the Vandals?" I raised my brows. "I just wish I'd gutted him myself."

"Agreed," Lainey said as she returned to the bed with a cup and a straw. She eased onto the bed next to him again. Milo's whole being seemed to focus on her, and I had to hide another smile. "Next time someone needs to be gutted, make sure I'm there. I'm starting to feel left out."

He huffed, but it sounded more like laughter than a scoff. When she pressed the straw to his lips, he took a long drink. Then another. He grimaced when she smoothed a hand over his face.

"Sleep," she whispered. "I'm not going anywhere."

"Not safe," Milo protested, but I gently touched his chest.

"It's safe enough. You rest and let us look after you. Mickey's in the hall if you need him…" I was worried about his pain as Milo grimaced.

"He's gonna knock me out."

"Good," Lainey said. "Then I'll have some quiet to enjoy your pretty face."

I didn't laugh. It took real effort, but I didn't. I really didn't want to laugh at him. I wanted him to rest. I also wanted to give them a moment. I pressed a kiss to his cheek and then touched her hand before I slid off the bed to go in search of Mickey. A glance back from the door showed me Lainey leaning down with her forehead to his. My heart did a little twist. That was another good thing to come out of all this darkness, and I'd hold onto that spark of light with everything I had.

CHAPTER 14

LIAM

Ezra paced circles around the pool table to the point I was ready to stab him myself. As it was, I managed to keep my focus on lining up the cue ball. Silence lay like a shroud over the whole of the downstairs while we played pool. Jasper settled in to lean against the wall, waiting to play the winner. Freddie flung darts at the board almost idly, like he wasn't paying attention to what he was doing.

Everyone else settled around the room, drinking coffee or working on their phones. The thing was, no one except for Rome seemed to actually be focused on what they were doing. Unlike the rest of us, my mirror stood near the base of the stairs, focused on where Hellspawn had vanished with Lainey. Doc hadn't descended again, so chances were he was keeping an eye on Milo and the girls.

I supported his attention being where it was. Milo's injuries hadn't been light. If anything, they rivaled some of the worst we'd seen. The burns branded to his lower back were going to scar. Nothing we could do about that except take the brand and ram it up Fuckbucket Sharpe's ass.

My phone chimed and I straightened to check it rather than finish the next shot. Ezra gave me an impatient look, but I turned the phone to show him Adam's text.

He was on his way.

For a moment, all the irritation in Ezra's manner bled away. He braced the pool cue against the floor and bowed his head. If I didn't know better, I'd think he was praying. Not something either of us did that often, if at all. Still...

I sent an acknowledgement, then glanced at Kellan. "Thirty minutes."

He nodded once, then rose as Rome straightened a split second before Hellspawn appeared at the bottom of the steps. She walked right into his arms and leaned into him.

"Where is Lainey?" Ezra demanded.

"She's sitting with Milo so he'll sleep," she answered in a perfectly reasonable tone. Despite how cool and even she sounded, a ragged note pulled at the rough ends of her voice. Eyes closed, she leaned into Rome and he cradled her before glancing over at Ezra. I didn't turn my head, trusting Rome to alert me if Ezra was about to do something stupid.

"How is he?" Ezra asked after a prolonged moment in the gruffest tone. That absolutely cost him to even ask.

She tilted her head, then glanced toward us. Her smile when she met my gaze steadied me then her expression sobered as she looked at Ezra. "He's going to be okay. He needs rest and antibiotics."

Blowing out a breath, Ezra nodded. "Can I do anything?"

"Coming with Lainey was a lot, and keeping her safe is everything. So, thank you."

I didn't grin as Hellspawn completely neutered the bastard's grumpy mood. "Tell me if you need something else."

"We got our girl," Jasper said. "You don't need to suck up."

Ezra glared at him and it was my turn to laugh as I focused on the table again. "Don't bait him," I said, lining up the next shot. Hearing that Milo would be okay was one thing, but seeing the relief in Hellspawn's face and hearing it in her voice offered far more comfort.

"Who?" Ezra asked. "Me or him?"

"Both," Hellspawn answered, drifting closer to the table with Rome following her. She paused to wait for me to finish the shot. When I straightened, lifting my arm, she glided to me and slid up to my side. Wrapping that arm around her, I took a deep inhale of her hair and pressed my cheek to hers.

The tension knotting my spine released and I had to lock my legs to keep from leaning on her. Turning around and leaving five minutes after we got them to safety at the club-house burned. But she and Milo both needed Lainey Benedict. Ezra was being a raging dick about bringing her here, so I wasn't going to fight that battle on the phone. I showed up and Jasper went with me, then we brought them back.

It protected them and shut Ezra up. The reward was right here, cuddling against me. The relief was profound. "I'm alright," she whispered against my chest. I felt more than heard the words. I soaked in the content as I rubbed her arm and pressed my lips to the top of her head again.

"Need you," I told her, and she pressed a hand to my chest before she tilted her head back. I didn't need another invitation to kiss her. She parted her lips at the first brush and I sank into the kiss, half wishing I was fucking into her, but this was enough. The delicate, kittenish licks were enough to make me insane on a good day.

Today? They were the cure for everything ailing me. She sucked on my tongue then nipped my lip like I was taking away her favorite treat. When I deepened the kiss again, she let out the most delightful little groan.

Someone coughed.

Then a second person.

When a third person cleared their throat with almost obnoxious loudness, I growled. It was hard to be irritated when she let out a wild giggle that succeeded in breaking our kiss and I lifted my head to marvel at the light dancing in her eyes as she grinned. "Hi."

"Hi," I murmured. "Don't mind me when I steal you away and lock these assholes out."

"Awww," she elongated the complaint with a laugh even as Freddie echoed it. Then the little pair of comedians glanced at each other with equally wild grins. I rolled my eyes. "Don't be mad," she teased. "I'm perfectly fine with being stolen by one of you. You just have to bring me back."

"Fine," I huffed with all the mock impatience I could muster. When she flicked my nose then kissed me again, I adored her with my eyes. "Look at that, you've kissed me right into submission."

"Bullshit," Jasper sneezed and Ezra, the prick, burst out laughing. An alarm went off on my phone—and everyone else's. I slid Hellspawn right back to Rome and pulled the phone out to check.

"Friendly," I said, before I headed to the door. Adam had arrived and it was good. I didn't leave the clubhouse alone. Vaughn and Freddie trailed me, and there was no mistaking the sawed-off shotgun Vaughn carried. Yeah. We weren't soft balling this.

I messaged Adam to pull inside and hit the remote to open one of the exterior rolling doors. He didn't answer, just drove his black Mercedes-Benz SLS AMG inside without hesitation. As soon as he cleared the threshold, Adam shoved the door open and stalked out.

"Is she safe?"

"They both are," I told him, betting he was asking about Lainey every bit as much as he was Emersyn. Relief trickled through his expression, easing some of the icy emptiness he often adopted. He cut a look at Vaughn and then Freddie before staring at me. "Ezra's inside, hopefully not picking a fight, but I already belted him once."

Rolling his eyes, Adam just shook his head. "Typical."

I shrugged. "C'mon. I'll get you a drink, then we all need to talk."

Freddie raised his phone, while flicking his eyes to the side door. I made a face then shook my head.

"Fine, fuck it—Vaughn, can you take Adam in and get him a drink?" I locked my gaze on him. Preferably, he would keep him from starting a fight too, or sit on him if he did. Vaughn lifted his chin once in acknowledgement before jerking his head toward the door.

"C'mon in. People are a little on edge, so I recommend minimizing any and all assholish tendencies if you don't mind."

"If I do?" Adam asked.

"Well, then when someone hands you your ass, you'll know why..." Vaughn deadpanned that delivery perfectly, and I had to swallow my own chuckle as Freddie rolled his eyes.

Once Vaughn and Adam were inside, I focused on Freddie. "When is he due?"

"Soon," Freddie said. "I texted him. I know you're not a fan, but Bodhi came through for us."

Yeah, I was aware of Freddie's trust in the guy. "Fine," I said. "But you let us control how much Cavendish knows."

"Why don't you like him?" Freddie asked, and I sighed.

"Long story. It begins and ends with money, privilege, and the ability to buy your way out of just about anything."

"And?" The dry question served to deliver a point. Frankly, he wasn't wrong. I had that kind of money. So did Ezra and Adam.

"Cavendish is a loose cannon," I told him. "The family wealth covers up a lot of crimes and crazy."

"I like him."

"I know you do," I said, then clasped Freddie's shoulder lightly. "I trust your judgment." The surprise flickering through Freddie's eyes at that declaration was humbling. "I need you to trust mine here too. If he can help, I welcome it. Just like Doc's guys. But..."

"Bodhi isn't one of us," Freddie said, and the understanding there helped. "Yeah, I get it. Though if he can help..."

"As I said, we'll take it. We're already bleeding, Freddie, and this last battle—" It had come too fucking close for Milo and Hellspawn.

He nodded. "I got it. I'll follow your lead."

Fortunately, we didn't have to wait that long before Bodhi arrived. Just like Cavendish always did, he blew in when he was ready. The man ran on his own timetable and acted like the whole world was just here for him.

Dick.

Thankfully, Doc's guys arrived hot on his heels. While he didn't say much after greeting Freddie, Bodhi seemed to be studying Doc's guys the same way they were studying him—too many unknowns. Once we had them inside, the clubhouse felt too crowded. Hellspawn was sitting with Kellan, curled up in his lap, half asleep. Probably because he was rubbing her back and she was exhausted.

Jasper and Vaughn formed a barrier between the rest of the room and Kellan. Yeah, even if Doc trusted his friends and we were trusting him—adding Ezra and Adam to this volatile mix wasn't helping. As it was, Adam and Bodhi were glaring daggers at each other. Then Lainey descended the stairs and her arrival seemed to toss a match right into the kerosene.

"Elaine Benedict," Bodhi said with a wide grin as he crossed the room. Her expression would have been entertaining if Ezra wasn't already storming across the room.

She raised her brows at him. "Cavendish," she said slowly. "When did you get here?"

He dipped his head and pressed a kiss to each of her cheeks like they were French, and she gave him a light shove before she headed toward Hellspawn. Vaughn shifted to let her slide onto the sofa next to Kellan.

"Right," I said, watching the girls confer for a moment. "I think it's time we all put our cards on the table…" Kellan and I had discussed some of this but not all of it. "Before anyone starts throwing their dick around about who is the bigger badass, listen. We all have pieces of this puzzle."

I tracked my gaze to Hellspawn as she slipped off Kellan's lap to let him stand. The guys moved and then we formed a loose circle around the girls while facing Ezra, Adam, Doc's guys—Lunchbox, Bones, and I forgot what the last guy was called. Alphabet wasn't here, so I'd guess he was with their girl wherever.

Doc had come down to join us and seemed to read the room as easily as I had. This was a seriously volatile combination of people.

"We're going to start with what we know," Kellan said. "You guys have all helped us in different ways since this began, but I'm making it clear right now—there's going to be more blood spilled before this is over. None of you are committed, yet. If you want out, now is the time to go."

No one moved. Not that I expected them to make that choice. If anything, Adam turned his brooding, studious gaze on Kellan and seemed to be assessing him. "Read us in…if we can help—if *I* can help, I will."

Ezra sighed. "Fine, fuck it. You guys are always good for a fight."

"We're here for Doc," Bones said like that answered everything, and granted it probably did.

"Is there going to be pizza?" Bodhi asked and I rolled my eyes. "Cause I'm hungry and think better with food."

Fucker.

Hellspawn laughed and I almost forgave the son of a bitch for being a son of a bitch.

Almost.

"Right," Kellan said. "Pizza later. Everyone take a seat, this is going to be a minute."

CHAPTER 15

EMERSYN

*W*hile Liam got us started, it was Kellan who took the lead. Lainey clasped my hand after she settled on the sofa with me. Bodhi's response to her had been *interesting*. Even more, was her response to him.

"You know each other?" I'd murmured in her ear, and she gave me the barest of nods.

"Tell you later," she promised and I squeezed her hand. I was nosy enough to want to know, still she didn't have to give me any details she didn't want to share. Ezra staring bullet holes through Bodhi was hard to miss. Equally as difficult was Adam's regard resting on me, although I didn't think it was *me* he studied. But I also didn't think he wanted to make a show of needing to know Lainey was all right.

I wish there wasn't so much going on right now so we could tackle these more interpersonal issues. I wanted Lainey happy, but the guys needed to know that I was firmly on *her* and *Milo's* sides. Period. That said, I wasn't immune to the way they watched Lainey. What irked me was how they treated her. Dislodging their heads from their overprotective asses might go a long way toward getting what they all wanted.

Covering our joined hands with my free one, I kept an eye on Kel.

Exhaustion circled him like an angry storm front blowing in. It worried me. What happened to us *haunted* him. He seemed to be taking total responsibility for all of it. Nothing I'd said so far had penetrated. I didn't blame him. No one blamed him. Everything that happened was due to Fuck-bucket's actions and *JD's* actions, not his. It didn't seem to matter though, since Kel blamed himself.

I needed to find a way to help him with that.

"We've been debating how to tackle this issue," Kel said, his voice gathering strength and direction as he continued. "We've all got our strengths, as well as weaknesses. To ignore one in favor of the other? Bad idea. We've learned that lesson and never let it be said we don't take these lessons to heart."

Mickey folded his arms, a frown tightening his forehead. He wasn't alone in that dark expression. Jasper had one eye on Kel, but it was Freddie that I nudged with my hip. He'd claimed the free spot next to me when Kel stood up. When he settled a hand on my thigh with a raised eyebrow, I twisted to press a kiss to his shoulder. The corners of his mouth tipped a little higher, and some of the tension eased out of him.

"That said," Kellan stated. "This fight has already gotten bloody, and it's only going to get bloodier." He wasn't looking at us but at Ezra, Adam, Mickey's guys, and Bodhi. "If you want out, now is the time to go. There are no guarantees any of us are making it out of this one unscathed. For most of us—we've already gotten chunks taken out of us."

He pivoted to look at me, and I raised my brows. I wasn't

going anywhere. I'd agreed to the former plan and still thought it was good.

"We've learned who we can trust," Kellan continued as I held his gaze. "Those people are present in this room."

"Fuck yeah," Bodhi said with a laugh. "I made the cut."

"Mostly," Kellan continued, his tone dryer than the Sahara at Bodhi's interruption. Freddie snickered and the corners of Lainey's lips started twitching.

"Damn, dude," Bodhi groused. "Gonna be like that?"

"Keep it up," Kellan told him. "You'll find out."

Jasper laughed aloud at that one, as did a couple of Mickey's guys. Lunchbox just shook his head as he flicked a look at me and then at Mickey.

"Shut the fuck up, Cavendish," Adam said in a droll tone. "He's too polite to say it, but I have zero compunctions."

"Bite me, Reed," Bodhi told him as he motioned to Lainey and me. "PPG and Lainey B need me, which means you try to remove me and I'm going to gut you like a succulent pig at a roast."

"Gentlemen," I said, even as Ezra took a step forward. Adam straightened as Bodhi looked positively gleeful, and Liam sighed.

"Just don't," Mickey growled in a tone that cracked through the room. Bones smirked, but I didn't miss how he and Voodoo shifted their positions. The whole room seemed to bubble with increasing tension.

Bodhi sighed and slanted a look at me. "Really, PPG?"

"Really," I stressed the word. "Thank you for wanting to help, but baiting people *isn't* helping."

"It could," he muttered. "It's definitely fun."

Lainey rolled her eyes. "Phillip."

"Fine," he said, elongating the syllable. "Only because the two of *you* asked."

"I hate him," Ezra said with a scowl.

"I heard that," Bodhi told him, his glee seeming back in full force. "But I'll let it go because PPG and Lainey B asked. *You*, however, are an asshole to keep interrupting."

Kellan blew out a breath. Everyone was staring at Bodhi, and he smirked as he raised his hands. When Lainey patted the sofa next to her, his grin grew and he dropped onto the couch hard enough to bounce me and Lainey both. Freddie cocked his head to look at Bodhi.

"You good?" Freddie's question had me biting back a laugh because there was just so much doubt in his voice.

"Not even on my best days." But Bodhi slung an arm around Lainey's shoulders then gave my ponytail a little tug. "But I will behave." Though I could have sworn he added, "For the moment," under his breath.

"Kellan," I said, focusing on him and pulling his gaze to me. "Go ahead. We'll gag him if he starts talking again."

The tension around Kellan's eyes softened. "Thank you, Sparrow."

"My pleasure," I promised.

Lainey jabbed her elbow into Bodhi before he could say another word and Kellan held my gaze for the most prolonged moment before pivoting to face our gathered allies.

"We have two enemies at the moment," he said. "One we want to remove from the board immediately—the other... the other is open to some debate. If we can skip the interruptions, I'll bring you up to speed."

Fortunately, Bodhi kept silent and no one else commented, letting Kellan brief them on everything he knew about Fuckbucket without diving deep into the specifics about me. That said, he still had to address it—particularly in light of his most recent escalation...

"So basically, she chooses him, or he keeps coming to kill her and everyone else in the way?" Adam clarified, his expression thoughtful and focused on me, then Lainey, before he regarded Kellan again.

"In a nutshell," Liam answered. "Hellspawn is always with us. We'd initially planned to move her and Milo into the safehouse while we took care of drawing Sharpe out."

"Not a good idea now," Bones said without adding more to the explanation. "Full frontal assault—but she has to be the distraction."

Mickey glared at him, but it was Vaughn who actually leaned forward. "Excuse me?"

"No matter where we try to point him towards," Kellan said, facing us, "it won't matter. He wants Sparrow. So, we're going to use that against him."

"You want me to put on a show." My insides did a very uncomfortable flip-flop at the idea yet at the same time... "You want me to play bait to lure him out."

"No, I don't want that," Kellan told me. "However as plans go, it has the greatest chance of success. It also comes with an incredible amount of risk. Maybe too much."

I wasn't sure whether it was the gravitas in Kellan's voice or the fact we had company, or that I was present. Perhaps it was some combination of the above. The arguments against it didn't explode instantly.

"That's—going to take some work," Lunchbox said with a measured expression. "Because to make him take the bait, especially after she evaded the last trap, will require she appear vulnerable..."

"Or," Liam said, locking his gaze on me. "We make our own power move that forces his hand."

"If you're proposing to my sister," Milo said from the doorway, his voice ragged and his face gray. "Get on one fucking knee and at least give it a measure of romance, jackass."

"Pretty Boy," Lainey scolded even as she rose to her feet.

Bodhi shifted to let her go, and I was a half-step behind her, but Mickey got there first.

"I'm fine," he said, leaning on Mickey as we approached. "If we're talking strategy, I should be in on it."

When Lainey got to him, he curled an arm around her, and the temperature in the room plummeted. The shifting feet behind me warned of the changing climate. While I half-expected it, I didn't want to plead for peace at the moment.

"Dude, take another step in their direction, and this isn't going to go well for anyone," Freddie's warning resonated. "Give him a minute to sit down."

"What happened?" Adam asked.

And I glanced behind me to see he and Liam both had a hand on Ezra while Freddie stood right in front of him, knife dancing on his fingers. "Fuckbucket's men stabbed him when he tried to get me out of the coffin they'd buried me in."

Ezra's expression transformed as he ripped his gaze from my brother to me. "He put you in a *coffin*?"

"Yes."

Adam's eyes flattened and when Ezra cut a look at him, relief swarmed me. Maybe it shouldn't have, but even Lainey seemed to lose some tension. I recognized those overprotective looks. Whatever else went down, they were on board for dealing with Fuckbucket.

"Milo," I said, turning to him. "Can you sit down? I know Mickey doesn't want you popping stitches."

"No, he doesn't," Mickey agreed. "Listen to Little Bit if you're going to be a stubborn asshole and drag yourself down here."

Milo was so gray and sweat dotted his face. "I'll sit, but I'm staying for this discussion."

"Then sit down," Kellan ordered him, and Milo scowled as Lainey and I got him moving. Bodhi abandoned his spot so that Milo could sit. Once Lainey sat on one side of Milo, I dropped to sit on his other. We were both careful to not jostle him too much. His pallor didn't improve as he sat, but Rome joined us and brought water for Milo and a blanket.

"Thank you," I told him as I helped to tuck Milo in.

Kellan gave us a beat to get him settled then he picked up the conversation again. "So, we have some threads we're going to pull to get his attention—those threads will be discussed separately among us. For now, what we need is increased security. Sparrow and Milo need backup at all times—"

"We'll take care of that," Adam said, arms folded. "I have some ideas on the other subject that I'll save."

"The second problem is Julius King and the Bay Ridge Royals."

"I knew you had to have invited them for a reason," Bodhi commented, the barest hint of a smirk in his voice.

"Actually," I said, as much to Bodhi as to Ezra and Adam, "We invited them because they are our friends. So, hush." I mimed zipping it, and Bodhi grinned at me, then pressed both hands to his heart.

"PPG, I'd do anything for you." He made a great show of zipping his lips, locking them up, then handing the key to Lainey.

It was hilarious but earned him a side eye from Milo and a snort from Liam. "And you guys wondered why I wanted him gone..."

"Nope," Jasper said. "Not something I'm wondering anymore."

Rome whistled and it shut everyone up.

"Thank you," Kellan said. "This is worse than when you assholes *were* in elementary school." Despite a handful of snickers and a mildly amused head shake from Mickey, they kept their commentary to a minimum. Which was good.

So far.

"We know who Julius King is and why he targeted Milo—or at least we suspect why. We also believe we get why he has developed an interest in Sparrow and why he wanted you killed." The last went to Adam.

Lainey jerked her head to look at me, and I reached over Milo to hold out my hand to her. Milo's hand came down to rest on both of ours.

"I think I'm going to hate this answer," Adam said. "Who is he?"

"Well, when I knew him," Mickey said as he straightened. "His name was Jeff Hardigan, and he abandoned those kids when he walked out on their mother."

"Oh my god," Lainey muttered and focused on me before she looked at Milo.

"Yeah," I said softly. "We still don't know everything—just that he didn't want Adam to marry me and he caught a hint of his plan when he proposed—" I shot Adam an apologetic look. "It's why he wanted you killed."

"Don't worry about me," he said, lifting his chin. "That offer still stands for all the reasons I made it before." It was almost sweet how easily he offered that, but Lainey dug her fingers into my hand. "The big question, though—is *what* do you intend to do about him?"

I glanced at Milo and I wasn't the only one. I didn't really know what to think about King. I had no memories of him, only Milo did. Milo had been abandoned and then punished by this man. What he decided to do about him? I would follow.

"We're going to use the son of a bitch," Milo said. "For once, he's going to help us."

CHAPTER 16

EMERSYN

*I*t was late by the time the guys ran out of questions for the plans. Locating Fuckbucket had moved from a first-round priority to secondary because of the trap they wanted to set for him. A trap that *I* would be setting for him. That earned me more than one steely-eyed stare.

A trap I had to be in in order to spring, but one I wouldn't be waiting inside of alone. I was fine with it as long as none of them were hurt. Considering how many people we'd involved in this plan, I didn't care what happened to me. I wanted Fuckbucket gone. Once Mickey's guys left, Lainey and I helped Mickey bully Milo back up to his room and to bed.

I left Lainey to get him settled and when I came back out in the hall, Vaughn and Jasper stood like a pair of sentinels keeping Adam and Ezra out of Milo's room. Oh, this had all the potential in the world of going badly.

"Milo all set?" Vaughn asked as I came out. I pushed up the sleeves of the sweatshirt I was wearing.

"Mickey is checking his stitches since he came downstairs, and Lainey is basically sitting on him to make him behave." I lifted my shoulders. "So, I'm going to go with yes." I glanced from Ezra's tense expression to Adam's too-calm but unreadable one. "Everything okay out here?"

"We're fine," Adam answered before they could. "I want to speak to Lainey." He glanced at Jasper and Vaughn. "Although it can wait until your brother is settled."

"Thank you," I said, then folded my arms. "I'm going downstairs for coffee—if you'd like to have some."

It was late and I was tired, but I didn't think sleep would happen anytime soon.

"You don't have to entertain them," Jasper said, sliding an arm around me. I curled into him. It had been a while since I'd had a hug from him. The need to be around them seemed to have magnified since my time in the coffin. Just the thought sent a freezing cold chill through my blood. I wasn't sure if I shuddered or if the tension communicated it somehow because Jasper tightened his arms.

"Tell you what," he said. "You two head downstairs, and if she's up for it, she'll come down in a minute."

"Right," Vaughn said. "I'll show you the way…"

"Wait," Adam said, raising a hand, and I stole a glance at him. "We're not going far. You take the time you need. However, I need to talk to Lainey and you."

I nodded against Jasper. "I'll be down in a minute." Because right now, I needed this minute. I needed all of them. "Thank you, Vaughn."

"You got it, Dove," he murmured, brushing his knuckles down my cheek and then herding the other two toward the stairs, where the twins had just appeared. Liam said something, his tone biting, but I couldn't distinguish the words.

Jasper rubbed a slow circle against my back as we waited for them to go. Only Rome lingered at the top of the stairs, and he looked toward us.

"I'm okay," I mouthed to him, and he gave me a slow nod then pointed to the stairs before miming a cup of coffee. "Please," I said, and he glanced at Jasper.

"What she's having times two," Jasper said. "Thanks, Rome."

He waved and then disappeared down the steps. Closing my eyes, I burrowed into Jasper's warmth.

"What's wrong?" he asked. "Beyond the obvious."

I laughed a little, then tilted my head up to look at him. "I don't know...I'm fine, and then I'm not. I'm worried about Milo, and I'm angry. I want to rip Fuckbucket's spleen out with a rusty spoon."

"That's my girl," Jasper said, cupping my face. "It might take time to get there, I plan on removing every joint in his body as brutally as possible."

That—made me smile. "He's walking with some kind of cane..."

"Good."

It was good.

"So, tell me, what else is bothering you right now?"

"I don't want anyone else hurt because of all this." I wouldn't say because of me, even if that was how I felt. They'd all made their feelings intensely clear on the subject. Since I'd take a bullet for them, I could hardly fault them for what they wanted to do for me.

That said...

"We're going to do everything we can," he promised, stroking the tendrils of hair back from my face. "Everything, sweet girl. You aren't in this alone anymore and we're all going to get you a few pounds of flesh before this is over."

I licked my lips. "What happens then?"

"Whatever we want," he said, then pressed a kiss to the tip of my nose. "One step at a time…"

Pressing my forehead to his chest, I closed my eyes again. "I'm worried about Kel."

"Me too," he confessed in a hushed whisper. "But we got him. Just like we have you. Need me to help wrangle him somewhere you can sit on him to make him rest?"

"Maybe," I said, twining my arms around his neck. Jasper picked me up and cradled me closer. The hug was undeniably everything. "I just—I feel weird."

"Weird, how?"

"I want to run away and take all the danger away from you guys," I admitted, turning the words over in my head even as I said them. "At the same time, I don't want to let any of you out of my sight." I rubbed my nose to his before I pressed a kiss to his lips. He held the kiss there, sweet and gentle but still possessive. "I want him dead, but I am not willing to sacrifice any one of you to do it."

"Let me tell you a secret," he said in a soft voice. "The only people we're sacrificing is the dickless wonder who married your mother—cause fuck him for what he did to her and to you. Then there's the fuckbucket himself, who should be taken apart piece by piece for what he's done to you. Trust me when I say, we can burn everything down—every goddamn thing. We'll rebuild if we have to when it's over, but no more losses, Swan. And we're going to avenge every single drop of blood they spilled."

Another shiver danced through me.

"Believe me?"

I swallowed. "I want to."

"Okay, that's enough," he told me as he set me on my feet. "Now, go downstairs and stick close to the guys. I'm staying up here to guard Milo's door while he's down. Doc will probably head down to find you when he's done too."

"You don't trust Adam and Ezra."

"Not even a little bit. They seem pretty loyal to you and Liam. But they have their eye on your friend and don't like Milo being with her."

I couldn't really comment on that. Did I think they'd go after Milo when he was down? Maybe. I didn't want to think that though.

"When Mickey comes out, will you tell Lainey Adam wanted to see her?" I wasn't sure I wanted to interrupt, especially if it would set Milo off.

"I'll let her know." He stroked my cheek. "Stop worrying. Go see the guys. Find out what's up, and then I'll help you drag Kel off to rest."

"Love you," I whispered and pushed up to give him another kiss.

"Best part of my day," Jasper said with a wink. "Go on. I'll be right here."

I squeezed his fingers before I headed for the steps. Rome was waiting for me at the bottom with a cup of coffee in hand. He offered it to me even as I curled into him. The need to be close to them held me fast and hard.

"Tired?"

I nodded against him. "A little. How about you?" When I glanced up, he pressed the coffee into my hands.

"Some," he said. "They're waiting with Liam."

They, were Ezra and Adam. "Okay. I think Kellan needs to get some sleep."

Rome tilted his head thoughtfully for a moment, then nodded. "We'll take care of him." I pushed up onto my tiptoes and kissed him lightly.

"Thank you."

He grinned. "You're welcome."

I stood there with him, soaking up the closeness while I

sipped the coffee. Both his presence and the coffee chased away the chill.

"Hellspawn," Liam said, and I lifted my gaze to find him watching us, a frown tightening his brow. "You look beat. Maybe you go up and go back to bed."

"Adam and Ezra..."

"Can wait," he continued with a slow shake of his head. "You've been through a lot the last seventy-two hours. Tonight wasn't easy, and tomorrow doesn't promise to be much better. You need to rest when you can."

"I don't know that I want to marry you," I told him absently and he narrowed his eyes. "You're already bossy."

Rome chuckled as Liam stared at me with his own lips twitching.

"I'll marry you," Rome offered.

"Hey," Liam countered, even as his grin was growing. "You can be bossy."

"Can and are..." Rome shrugged. "Two different things."

A giggle escaped, followed by another. When I reached out an arm to Liam, he curled one around me and then Rome folded up against my back. Sandwiched between the two was safety, security, and solace.

"Sorry," I whispered to Liam.

"Nothing to be sorry about, Hellspawn. Just challenging me to work harder to get you to say yes." Then he winked. "Worth it."

Another kiss, and then I blew out a breath. "Okay, let's talk to Adam and Ezra."

"They can wait," he reminded me, and I touched his cheek before leaning back against Rome.

"They can, but I don't know that I can." I wanted to focus on the guys, but we also needed to focus on our allies. Especially with Julius King out there and the fact we needed to play him.

The twins moved with me as I headed through the living room. Kellan was in the kitchen with Adam. That was fortunate. I didn't see Ezra, but since we'd been blocking the stairs, I was less concerned.

Kellan looped an arm around my waist when I got to him. I could almost feel the weight of his measuring gaze as he studied me. "I'm okay," I whispered as I pressed a kiss to his cheek. "But I want to sleep with you tonight." It wasn't subtle or even fair, but I didn't think Kel would sleep if I didn't.

Right now, I wasn't sure I wanted to sleep, so maybe we could just sit up together.

He gave me a squeeze then glanced at Adam. "Adam has some questions for you—none of which you have to answer."

Liam and Rome were right there, and Rome slid a chair over for me to sit in. He then took the one on the other side of me. I didn't even know when they replaced all the kitchen chairs. I'd ask later. "Where's Ezra?"

"Outside getting his ass kicked by Cavendish," Adam said with a shrug. "Don't worry about him. He needs to blow off some steam."

Alarmed, I glanced up at Liam, who groaned. "Fine. But that's two you owe me, Hellspawn."

"I adore you," I said and his smile grew.

"Good." He dropped a kiss on my lips, then eyed Adam. "Keep it respectful."

"As if I'd treat her any other way, dick," Adam said, and Liam scowled but still headed out. I had to wonder if Freddie was out there. Vaughn must be, 'cause he wasn't here either. "Emersyn…"

I took a sip of my coffee and met his gaze. "Adam."

The corner of his mouth kicked a little higher. "I'm sorry."

"For—what?" I wasn't entirely sure what I expected him to say, but that wasn't it.

"I've never liked your uncle. He's—well, I'm sure there are

135

a lot of names for him. However, I've never liked him and never wanted Lainey around him. To be fair—I didn't think anyone should be around him, but instead of listening to Lainey and just helping you—I tried to keep her away from you."

Real regret shone in his eyes.

"You weren't very good at keeping her away from me."

"Yeah, well, she's as stubborn as you are, apparently." The rueful comment just made me smile wider. "But I am sorry. I should have done more. I thought—if you needed help, you'd ask. Sometimes, it's hard to remember that families with dark secrets don't encourage faith in others."

Then because I understood, maybe not as well as I could, I reached over to touch his hand. His father and Lainey's mother made for a complicated situation. "Thank you."

"I didn't do enough—"

"But you did do something. Maybe it wasn't what you think you could have done now, but at the end of the day, you hated my family and were willing to help me because of Lainey. So that's something."

He sighed. "That makes asking my question kind of more challenging."

"Well, you're a tough guy." I settled back in my seat with my coffee and met his gaze. "You can do it."

"I have a job to do," Adam told me. "Part of that job is killing Julius King."

Oh.

"I didn't think it would be a problem until I found out who he is to you and your brother."

Nope, we still weren't following a script. I bit my lip. "It's not about who he is…" I said slowly.

"No," Adam agreed, glancing at Kellan, then Rome, and finally me. "It's what you need from him."

"We."

"Well, *I* need him dead so I can get my life back…"

And we needed him alive, at least for right now, so we could use him against Fuckbucket.

Dammit.

Why couldn't this be easier?

CHAPTER 17

KELLAN

*A*dam Reed puzzled me. The man was a contradiction. Arrogant, wealthy, and privileged. It set the stage for him to be one type of man. Yet, he didn't seem defined by any of them. I didn't have to wonder if he was dangerous. He appeared as comfortable in our world as he was in his own. He'd been playing dead for months, avoiding his family, friends, and life while maintaining a low profile. He'd traded himself for Sparrow, essentially turning himself over to someone who may or may not be a friend.

Just being the enemy of my enemy didn't make a person trustworthy. These were the people who had taken Rome and Sparrow, believing Rome was Liam. They'd forced Rome to take a beating by threatening her. Yeah, anyone who used her as leverage was not a friend—I didn't care who their enemies were.

"Tell me about the job," I said, settling my hand on Sparrow's nape. She'd drifted from one of us to another all day, and I was fine with that. If she needed nearness and contact, I was more than happy to provide it. If I lived to be a hundred, I would never get over the fact that the son of a bitch put her in a goddamn coffin and then buried her.

Buried her because he wanted to own her, and if he couldn't—well, then she had to die. I'd killed people in my life. Killed more than a few. I'd wrecked a few more. To protect my brothers, there was very little I wouldn't do.

To protect Sparrow? I'd burn it all down. To give her the vengeance and the justice she deserved? Fuck the world and everyone else who wasn't us. If that meant utilizing their biological relationship to the king to get what we needed done? Fine. We'd beg, borrow, and steal to do what was needed.

"The job is pretty straightforward," Adam said. "My current employer wants the king eliminated in order to create a power vacuum. Then, they will use that vacuum to force other players into the light. Nature abhors a vacuum and fuck knows the wealthy do..." He actually sounded weary. "Currently, he has a wide array of controls in place— not the least of which is, no one knows what he looks like or who he is."

"What I don't get...is how he managed to amass that kind of power with no one knowing it was him," Sparrow said, her voice low and thoughtful as she leaned more into me while I kept up the massage.

"Manipulation," I suggested. "He sent Adam and Ezra to recruit Liam when they were all sixteen."

Adam raised his brows. Maybe Milo and Liam had kept their plan under wraps for years, playing everything too damn close to the vest. They didn't anymore. They'd read us all in. No. More. Fucking. Secrets.

"When did he recruit you?" Sparrow focused on Adam in an almost sleepy-eyed, relaxed way. If I wasn't perfectly content and confident in her devotion to us, it might bother me. As it was, the look seemed to make him uncomfortable.

Or maybe it was the question.

Could be both.

"Fourteen," Adam admitted. "Though I had inklings he was out there before then."

"Fourteen," I said as I eyed him. "That didn't strike you as odd?"

The other man shrugged. "You don't get what you deserve at that level. You get what you negotiate and what you earn. I had my reasons for looking to secure a power base." He blew out a breath, then knocked back the last of the beer I'd gotten him. He turned the bottle in his hand, studying it for a moment then glancing at us. "It started out simply enough—information for information. Not everyone made the cut. Not everyone had the fortitude."

"But you did," I said, rolling my thumb up and down along the side of Sparrow's neck until some of the tension there began to drain. The bruises on her aggravated me on a different level, so I had to concentrate on *not* focusing on them.

"I had my reasons." He set the bottle down. "The point is —getting in wasn't nearly as hard as it appeared. Getting out has proved a task."

"Lainey was his leverage over you," Sparrow said softly. When Adam said nothing, she sighed. "You *have* to tell her."

"No," he said. "I don't. I'd prefer if you would mind your own business on this one, Emersyn. I appreciate how much you care about her. I appreciate and respect all you have done to protect her when she would have been firmly on your side. There are too many risks for both of you already, especially with how involved the two of you are..." Leaning forward, he set his hands on the table and focused on her. "I know you don't like secrets. I respect that desire to open up all of these old wounds…"

"But you want to protect Lainey."

I wanted to protect Sparrow, so I got where he was coming from. The damned thing was, she clearly got it too.

"Yes." And I'd give Reed credit, for as important as this was to him—the tension in his hands and his jaw were a tell for all that affected calmer air—he kept his tone measured and his manner quiet for Emersyn. "I do."

"I won't lie to her," she told him, leaning into my hand. I glanced down to find her studying me. "I don't want to lie to anyone—but if she doesn't ask…"

Did she want my permission? The look was hard for me to interpret. "Trust your instincts," I told her. "We'll back your plays." That message was as much for her as it was for Adam.

A hint of a smile flickered over her lips. "Then no, I won't lie to her. However, if she doesn't ask me specifically, I won't tell her—for now." Then she locked her gaze on Adam. The way he straightened his spine at her regard amused me. "Find a way to read her in, she deserves to know, and you can't fight what you don't know is out there threatening you."

She raised her hand as if to stifle his arguments before pushing up from her chair. Not wanting to lose the contact, I rose and slid an arm around her waist to pull her back against me.

"Before you tell me you don't want her fighting, think about all the fights she takes on without you knowing… because she doesn't want to have to fight you too." That information set Adam back. "And remember, she's a lot tougher than she looks. You're not doing her favors cutting her out and treating her like a child." That was definitely a warning. "Thank you for protecting her."

The corner of Adam's mouth lifted. "Of course..." He glanced at me. "We're staying. Ezra will get his head out of his ass sooner or later, but we're here. I take it you want me to help guard Hardigan as well as Emersyn?"

"Something like that..." It was my turn to study him. "You understand that she's with him right now." It wasn't a question. "Is that going to compromise you?" Cause if he was willing to eliminate his competition—we would have a problem.

"I give you my word, nothing will happen to them on my watch." He rose so we could lock gazes and I read the frankness in his stare. "If anyone kills Hardigan, it will be me."

Sparrow glared at him. "Not funny."

"Not joking," Adam told her. "It's not a threat. My issues with your brother can be tabled for the immediate future."

"If that changes?" I challenged.

"I'll remove myself before I endanger Emersyn or Lainey. Harming Hardigan would do that—so for now, trust my feelings toward them."

And he'd made those feelings abundantly clear over the last few months, as well as proved his loyalty.

"Adam..."

The other man glanced at her, then sighed. "I've given you my word. It's going to have to do."

I believed him. It might be easy to just let the competition get killed, but he had to recognize the issues that would cause.

"Fine, I'll work on you more later," she informed him, and he gave a half-laugh.

"You have enough men in your orbit," he said with a hint of affection. "Go torture them."

"That's a good plan," she said then peered up at me. "Can I steal you away now?"

I smiled at her, then stroked her cheek. "Give us a minute?"

"Only one," she teased, kissing my jaw before leaving the kitchen. When I glanced at Adam, he shoved his hands in his pockets.

"Need more than my word?"

"Oddly," I said, pushing the chair in before picking up my coffee cup I'd emptied earlier. "No. I believe you want to protect both of the girls. I believe you don't want to hurt them."

Surprise flickered across his expression, followed by something undefinable.

"Don't take that as carte blanche, though. As much as I believe you don't want to hurt them, I also think you'd be willing to do it if it protected them."

His expression tightened and his mouth flattened.

"I understand," I said, because I did. "But let's be clear—if any action you take hurts Sparrow, I won't care about your reasons." There was no reason to pull out a gun or a fist. Retribution would be swift, and it didn't necessarily have to come from me. "Hurting her brother will hurt her. Hurting her best friend will hurt her."

Adam blew out a breath. "Subtle."

I ignored the little dig. "Not trying to be subtle. Keep in mind, you getting yourself killed would hurt her too. If you think I'm opposed to digging up a body to set it on fire, think again."

That actually earned me a laugh.

"I don't think you're a bad guy," I told him. "But I recognize the determination, I've shared it. Stay on this side of the line and we'll be fine."

"If I don't?" He almost seemed curious.

"You won't see us coming."

He gave a slow nod. "Understood."

"I hope so," I told him. "Vaughn will sort you two into a room. You will stay out of Milo's unless directly invited. We'll go over the full scope of security tomorrow. In the event of a raid—covering Milo and Lainey is your primary task."

"Got it. I take it you will all have Emersyn?"

"She goes nowhere without one of us." Ever again.

"Good plan." Adam extended a hand. "I like you, Traschel."

I clasped the hand and smirked. "Jury's still out on you."

He laughed, then shook his head as I left him in the kitchen. The door opened to let in a staggering Ezra, who sported a rapidly reddening eye, a bloody nose, and a split lip. He was also limping. Liam followed behind him, along with Freddie. Both were shaking their heads as Bodhi strolled in—sporting his own share of bruises.

Sparrow stared at them with raised eyebrows.

"It's all good, Boo-Boo," Freddie assured her. "They just needed to work a few things out."

"Uh-huh," she said, accepting Liam's hug then curling around Freddie when he all but fell into her. I liked the way they looked together. I liked that Freddie let himself reach out more and more. "If you're sure."

"Don't worry, Dove," Vaughn assured her as he detoured into the kitchen, only to return with Adam and a couple of ice packs. He delivered both with a distinct lack of gentleness. "They'll be fine."

I didn't laugh as Adam gave Ezra a baleful look. Not my circus or my monkeys for the night. When I held out my hand, Sparrow glided right to me. "Bedtime," I told her. The fatigue was reflected in the bruises around her eyes.

"Only if you're going to bed too."

"He's absolutely going to bed with you, Hellspawn," Liam

said. "Want me to haul his ass up there and dump him in the bed for you?"

I would have rolled my eyes, but Sparrow actually looked thoughtful. "Unnecessary," I told him. "Keep these guys out of trouble."

"Damn," Liam said, hand over his heart. "I miss a few minutes and get stuck with scut work."

"Sounds good," I told him and clapped him on the shoulder. "I'm gonna take three hours."

"Six," Sparrow informed me. "Although I'll settle for five."

Freddie grinned. "Boo-Boo has spoken, Daddy-K, you are banished for at least five hours. I bet she can persuade you to take more."

I would have argued, but I didn't want to... so I caught Sparrow's hand. "Good night, gentlemen. Behave."

"Do I have to?" Freddie called, and I chuckled as Sparrow tucked herself up against my side.

"Just clean up the mess," I said and Freddie laughed.

"That means I don't have to behave..."

"He didn't say that," Sparrow teased, and more laughter rippled. It helped.

All of them helped.

CHAPTER 18

EMERSYN

*U*pstairs, I glanced to where Jasper kicked back in a chair with his feet up and his phone out. Mickey hadn't left the room yet. Kellan didn't hesitate to walk me toward the door when I frowned.

"It's all good, Swan," Jas said as he stood up. "Doc is giving Milo the lecture, and he's really into it at the moment, so we're gonna let him have it."

"The lecture?" I was a little mystified. Kellan chuckled as Jasper reached for me. Kel let me go, so I slid into Jasper's arms and sighed as he wrapped himself around me. Then Kel pressed against my back and all the tension seemed to bleed right out of me. These hugs—the memory of them had sustained me in that coffin; the feeling of suffocating pressure was erased with the steady thump of their hearts.

"Doc periodically likes to remind us that we are mortal, especially the more thick-headed among us." Kellan's explanation spilled laughter into my veins, particularly when Jasper grunted.

"For once, it's not me." The salt on those words had me pressing my face into Jasper's chest as I tried to contain my laughter. It didn't work, particularly when they were both chuckling. I stole a look up to see the amused look Jasper shot Kellan, one that carried elements of concern. "You need sleep man, you haven't gotten any."

"I could say the same to you," Kellan said in a firm tone.

"Not true. I slept on the fancy-ass plane Liam stuck us on to get the bestie." Then Jasper peered down at me. "Need help hog-tying him to the bed?"

Soft laughter escaped. "Probably not. I think he would prefer to hog-tie me to it."

Mouth closing with a soft little click, Jasper pursed his lips. "Okay, soon as I get someone up here to cover the door, I'll come help."

That made Kellan laugh as he slid an arm around me then gave Jasper an indelicate shove even as Kel pulled me back. "Nope, no help required. I promised Sparrow five hours. She gets five hours. You get guard duty."

"You suck..." Jasper said without an ounce of malice. Then he winked at me. "Have fun, Swan. Go take each other's minds off of this." Not that I needed the advice. I had every intention of trying to get Kellan to relax and rest. The darkness writhing around him and the blame he cast on himself were both things I wanted to ease.

"I will," I promised, stretching up to give him a kiss. "Look after Milo and Lainey."

"Promise." He winked. "Go on. I'll see you in the morning."

"I don't even know what time it is," I admitted, and he grinned.

"Time for bed, Sparrow," Kellan said as he tugged me with

him. I blew Jasper another kiss. The sitting room was quiet, but then again almost everyone was downstairs or otherwise preoccupied. It was just me and Kellan.

On our way toward his bedroom, he scooped me up like a bride and carried me through the door. Once inside, he shut the door and locked it. For a moment, he just stood there unmoving as he gazed at me. Tilting my head, I raised my brows.

"See something you like?"

"Oh, very much so," he said before walking me over to the bed. With care, he set me down, and when I would have reached for him, he shook his head. "No touching."

I scowled. The indulgent look on his face shifted and he wrapped a hand around my throat. The necklace he made with his fingers almost immediately settled the buzzing hum under my skin.

"You're going to be a good girl for me," he said. "I need this."

Three words changed everything. I wanted to touch him. I loved touching him. But I wanted to give him what he needed more. Relaxing into his grip, I tilted my head to bare my throat to him. The intensity in his eyes warned me of him studying every mark on my face. The bruises on my cheeks were dark and pronounced now. They'd gotten worse, which was just a sign they were healing.

With his hand firm on my throat, he used his thumb to stroke my pulse. The way he gazed at me was a caress all of its own. He studied me, the penetrating focus in his eyes seeming to dig deep and look at all the layers beneath— Superman with his X-ray vision. Amusement rippled through me. Kellan tilted his head.

"What are you thinking about?" He continued to stroke my pulse. His nearness, along with everything else at the same time, left me wanting more.

"You remind me of Superman," I admitted, and Kellan's eyebrows shot up. Startled mirth reflected in his blue eyes.

"I'm going to regret this," he half-muttered. "Why?"

The hints of exasperation in his voice just made me laugh. "Because—the way you look at me. It feels like you can see everything down to my bones—maybe deeper."

The hints of a smile on his lips seemed to grow, and he let out a rough chuckle. "Sparrow...how do you do that?"

"Do what?" I wasn't trying to be coy. Honestly, I wasn't going to pretend to be anything other than who I was. I didn't have to with these men. They loved me for me. They accepted me for *me*.

"Just—say what I need to hear."

Pleasure flushed through me at the affection and relief tangling together in his voice. "Well, if all you need to hear is that you're my personal superhero, then I will tell you every single day. I would touch you and tell you, except someone said no touching." I raised my hands like I was surrendering and wiggled my fingers.

His expression gentled as his smile deepened. "I'll take that under advisement." His smile faltered then as he frowned. "I can't believe I let you go—that I—" The harshness of his exhale had me reaching forward. His hand flexed on my throat, but he didn't scold me when I pressed a hand over his heart.

"Don't," I ordered, and the command seemed to register with him. "I mean it. I'll go back to behaving in a moment. But please don't blame yourself. You didn't make the decision alone. You made it in consultation with *everyone*, including me. You *talked* to me about why you wanted me to go, and I didn't like it—but I *agreed* to it. We didn't know about JD. We didn't know he'd been working for Fuckbucket all along."

"But I should have known," Kel said, the shadows

writing in his eyes. "I should have known. We knew they had a mole..."

"And we thought we identified them." Though that begged the question, were the ones we'd identified set up by JD? Would we ever know? "Kellan—you did everything right. You put my safety first. You put Milo's safety first. When you knew something was wrong—you came for us. If nothing else convinces you—I'm here, and I'm alive, breathing. I wouldn't be without you."

He loosened his grip, stroking my throat with his fingers. "They hurt you—"

"He hurt me a long time ago—all he did this time was bruise me." That was the truth. "The funny thing is—I wasn't afraid of him. I didn't like what he did...I hated that he has videos and played one for Milo." Maybe he played more than one. The thought made my skin crawl. "But what I felt wasn't fear. It was fury. It was frustration. Then when they put me in that coffin—I freaked out a little—then I made myself calm down."

"How?" Surprise flickered over his expression.

"I knew you were coming," I told him. "I knew you were all coming. That you wouldn't stop until you found me...and even if it was too late for me, you'd find Milo. My only real worry was that—I didn't want to leave you guys and I didn't want you to hurt—"

His lips fusing to mine silenced the next words. Despite what he'd said about not touching, he wrapped his arms around me and dragged me onto his lap. Then there were just no words. I could barely breathe without tasting him and didn't care enough about oxygen to break the contact.

When he pulled back, I was gasping, and then his hands were at the hem of my shirt, whipping it up and over. His sudden stillness resonated with me as he feathered his hands over my ribs and the mottling of bruises.

"I'm going to rip him apart," Kellan said slowly as he nudged me back so he could examine the marks.

"I don't want him here," I said, wrapping my legs around his torso to keep him from bending down further. "Not with us. Not with you *or* with me. This—*this* is about us, and when you touch me, I don't want him anywhere near us."

"It's going to be like that?" Reluctance seemed to mark his words, but he didn't look away from me. Not once.

"Yes," I informed him. "It is. We have rules."

The corner of his mouth kicked up. "Planning to spank me if I disobey?"

"No," I told him. "But if you want me to…"

That earned me a genuine laugh, and then he carefully cradled my face in his hands. "Sparrow…I adore you."

"Well, the feeling is mutual," I promised. "Can you be here with me? Just me? Nothing else? Or do I need to find another way to distract you?"

His lips pursed. "I can do anything for you." The raw, elemental truth in those words unlocked the tightness in my chest. Some part of me had been holding my breath this whole time. Holding my breath and fisting the torrent of emotion that lashed at me to escape. "Anything."

"I love you, Kellan," I told him. "I love all of you so much, but never forget that I love you and can and *will* do anything for you too."

For all of them.

"You're my home."

They were—all of them. From the renovated spaces they —no, *we*—carved here in the clubhouse to the areas they'd created next to them.

"I love you too," he murmured. "But that doesn't mean I still don't dream of tying you up and eating you out until you can't see or feel anything that isn't me."

My cunt clenched at the declaration.

"Or testing your limits with toys—you like having me in your ass now, don't you?" The bluntness of that question sent another shiver of anticipation through me.

"I like having you everywhere," I promised. "In my mouth —" His pupils dilated. "In my cunt." He pressed forward against the cradle of my hips, grinding himself gently. Our clothing reduced the friction, but couldn't hide the weight of his erection or how it felt when he moved against me. "My ass—yes, I love feeling you there. I love the care you take with me." The care they were all taking. It wasn't something I'd done with everyone, but I trusted them. I understood it could feel good if done right, and more, I'd taken it back. "I love touching you and having you touch me."

He pulled up, then hooked his hands into the sides of my leggings. One gentle tug, and then he was peeling the clothes down. When I was naked, he stood next to the bed, studying me, and I'd never felt more on display, or experienced such a dizzying high from it.

"Legs spread," he murmured, tracing a finger around one nipple and then over to my Vandals tat before tracing his hand down to my abdomen. When he reached my cunt, he moved his hand to my thigh. Everywhere he touched, fire lit me up. "Freddie might be a goddamn poet," he said and then dared a teasing look up at me. "You really do have the prettiest pussy."

A laugh escaped me on a cough, and then he was stripping off his own clothes. When I would have sat forward, he shook his head sharply.

"Hands on your ankles, Sparrow. Give me a good stretch." When his cock thumped against his stomach, thick, red, and damp with pre-cum, I licked my lips. He gave himself a couple of strokes while I did what he asked, only I pulled my feet back to tuck them behind my head. "Goddamn…"

I grinned, then pushed the stretch by arching my hips.

"My cunt is very empty…"

"You just want to push me."

Yes, yes I did. "I want to *feel* you."

I didn't have to say another word, because he surged forward and rubbed his cock along my slit. The motion teased us both, but I didn't complain. The way he looked at me right now, devouring me with his gaze, kept me right on the precipice. "I'm going to be gentle," he informed me, "and you're going to be feeling me for hours, Sparrow."

Oh, that temptation had me smiling and then letting out a low shout as he thrust inside. The stretch was perfect, the burn was there but also the clench of my cunt wrapping around him and he braced his hands onto the bed on either side of me as he dipped his head to nip my lower lip.

"Ankles on my shoulders." The order wove through me, and I shifted so that they were on his shoulders.

"Be a good girl for me, and now play with your nipples… pinch them tight enough that they sting, then tease them again." He gave a little roll of his hips, the action easing him out before he thrusted back in.

I covered my breasts with my hands and began to toy with my nipples. I pinched the right one tight enough that the sting had me clamping down on him.

"Perfect," he said with a smile. "Keep it up and hold on, Sparrow… neither of us will be walking easily tomorrow."

Oh, that was a—and then he thrusted again. His fierce and frenetic pace scattered my thoughts, but I kept toying with my nipples under his approving gaze, and when the first orgasm swamped me, he followed me over. Only he didn't soften. So maybe he didn't, he just lay there with me for a few, and then he began to move again.

At some point, he flipped me onto my stomach and there was a toy attached to my clit as he filled my ass, and the only thought I had was his name over and over again.

CHAPTER 19

ROME

After Doc finished with Milo, he descended the stairs to find the rest of us and get coffee. He took one look at Ezra's busted lip and bruised face. "Do you need stitches?" It was a concession on his part; one Graham just shrugged off.

"Might need to patch up my hand," Bodhi volunteered. "He seemed determined to bust my knuckles with his face. Dude needs to learn how to fight."

"Fuck you," Ezra said over his shoulder, and Bodhi flashed him a grin.

"You're not my type," Bodhi said. "I like my partners a little curvier, a little smarter, and a hell of a lot prettier."

That declaration fell like pebbles in a pond rippling out, earning him a more baleful look from Graham. But the guy refrained from reacting—at least physically to the taunt. Instead, he just glared. Only Adam chuckled, as did Liam.

Freddie burst out laughing for real and I let myself smile as Doc rolled his eyes.

He scanned the room, not paying them any attention.

"Starling went up to sleep. Kellan needed her." We all needed her. It was written on every face and etched into every expression. Well—I glanced at Bodhi, Adam, and Ezra —not every face. That was fine. They cared… it was enough.

"Good, he should rest. Milo is resting, and his girlfriend is staying with him." The last comment from Doc earned more than one dark look from Ezra and Adam, though Adam's expression went almost neutral as soon as it darkened. Doc's smirk was not like him; he tended to be kinder.

Maybe this was kindness.

"Huh, little Lainey B got a boyfriend." Bodhi leaned back in his seat and hooked his bruised hands behind his head. "Good for her."

"Fuck. Off." Ezra spit out each word but didn't lunge out of the chair. Huh. Maybe Liam should have beaten him up harder.

Definitely, something to save for the future.

"He's just jealous," Bodhi continued like he didn't have a care in the world.

"And he's also armed," Doc told him. "So maybe a little healthy survival instinct wouldn't be amiss."

"If he could kill me, Doc," Bodhi said, "he'd have already done it. Right now, he's just sore 'cause some other guy is dipping his dick in a girl he thinks belongs to him."

"Asshole," Ezra said as he stood, but it was Adam who stopped him this time.

"Let it go…"

"You're okay with him talking about Lainey like that?" Ezra's temper flared with every single word.

"The words aren't for her," Adam advised. That made sense. Bodhi was quite happy with baiting both of them. He seemed to like baiting Liam, too—the rest of us, though? He left us alone.

Food for thought.

Ezra and Adam were now glaring at each other, and Liam rolled his eyes. "I'm going to separate all three of you. We do not need this shit."

"I think we should make popcorn," Freddie said with a grin. "It's kind of like our own personal sideshow."

"Except," Vaughn said in a measuring voice, "none of us need this kind of distraction right now."

That sentence seemed to pierce the bubble around those three, and Bodhi let out a long sigh. "Fine, I'll stop baiting the thin-skinned dickless wonder."

"If you want to choke on my dick," Ezra said. "That can be arranged."

"Enough," Liam said, anger flash-firing through the word. "I'm about to gag all of you. And I swear to god, Ezra, if you even think about opening your mouth one more time, I'll break your fucking jaw. You can be useful with it wired shut."

Instead of responding, Ezra turned and flung his bottle at the far wall, where it shattered, splattering the paint with dregs of beer.

"Feel better?" Adam asked him. Ezra just flipped him off and stalked away to head up the stairs.

Liam turned his gaze to the ceiling. "Follow him, or I will."

Adam sighed and rose from his seat. "Fine. I'll settle him down. Keep the lunatic away from us."

"I'll think about it," Liam retorted.

"I feel like I should be insulted," Bodhi said. "Fortunately, I don't really give a fuck what they have to say."

"Freddie," Doc commented. "Give those two a minute to get to their room, then set your friend up somewhere *else*."

"Yep," Freddie said, giving Doc a thumbs-up. "Who has Milo guard duty next?"

"I do," Vaughn said. "I'll relieve Jasper in a bit, then Liam. We will rotate until these fuckers figure out if they're here to help or not."

"Works for me."

"Me too," Bodhi volunteered though no one else seemed to be waiting for his response. I smiled. Everything Bodhi did was to drive others away from him—except the ones he liked.

Freddie.

Starling.

Lainey.

He liked them.

He didn't give a damn about the rest of us.

Fine. As long as he protected Starling, I didn't care who he liked or didn't. I didn't like Ezra, either. Adam—I gave a mental shrug. He had given a lot, but he also had his own agenda.

"Whatever, I'm getting coffee." Doc disappeared into the kitchen. Liam tracked him with his gaze then glanced at me. Something was up with Doc. We all knew that.

Liam said nothing and didn't move until after Freddie got Bodhi moving. Vaughn just shook his head once they vanished up the stairs.

"Letting all three of them stay is a bad idea," Vaughn commented. "Bodhi has a death wish."

"If only he did..." Liam scrubbed his hands over his face. Tired seemed to bleed into every action.

"We should call your mom tomorrow," I said, and he pivoted to face me, confusion clouding his expression, and then...

"Fuck. She wanted to go out to dinner with us..."

"I know. We can't right now. It's not safe for her." Our

birthday only came once a year. "So we call her, and we talk to her. Then we go out to dinner with her when it's safe."

Liam rubbed the back of his neck and gave me a weak, almost sad smile. "You don't have to talk to her. I know—you're not always comfortable with it."

"More family isn't a bad thing." I liked the O'Connells. I didn't love them the way Liam did, nor did I need them. But she might need us, and I was okay with that too.

"Now you say that."

I shrugged. "She didn't need me before."

His mouth curved upwards, but the smile didn't touch his eyes. "I think she'd like it if you called her."

"We…"

"Yeah," he said, then exhaled another long sigh. "She'll like it more if we call. If Hellspawn is up to it…"

"She will be." Starling loved her family. We were her family. Mary O'Connell was Liam's family. That made her Starling's family too.

"Glad you're sure of it." But there was no heat scorching the words. "I need more coffee."

"You need sleep." He hadn't been. I'd tracked it.

"Not yet," he said with a shake of his head. "I don't trust my dreams right now."

Nightmares. Not dreams.

"I want to see Sharpe."

My other half pivoted to stare at me. "What?"

"Sharpe is still alive." I shrugged. "Or he was when Vaughn checked on him."

Doc appeared from the kitchen, his coffee in hand. A lot had been going on since we discovered what JD had done, and they had gone to get Starling and Milo. More still since they'd brought them home. Liam snapped his gaze to Vaughn.

"He was. Smells terrible. Looks worse. But he's still alive.

Pretty sure he's nursing an infection in some of his cuts." Not that Vaughn cared.

"Infection could still take a while to kill him," Doc said.

"Yep," Liam agreed. "I'm torn on that. I don't know if an infection is painful enough."

"No," I said. "Or quick enough."

"Tired of having him around?" Doc asked, but he was looking at me and not Liam.

"Don't want him there to come after her again." That was one reason.

"And one of JD's tasks was to free him," Vaughn said.

"So, the fuckbucket wanted his brother back," Doc said slowly. The change in the timbre of his voice attracted Liam and Vaughn's attention. "Then I say we give him back—we can start by gift-wrapping him."

"We still don't know where to send him," Vaughn pointed out.

"Maybe," I said. "We have JD's phones in the safe." After verifying one was a clone of Kellan's and the other was JD's own, we'd powered both off and stored them for the moment.

"True," Vaughn said. "But can we crack them?"

"Alphabet can," Doc stated. "Why didn't we give him the phones earlier?" He stared at me, the bite in his tone audible, but Doc's anger wasn't directed at me.

"Been a little busy," Vaughn answered. "Getting Dove back with Milo was way more important."

"No shit," Doc almost snarled as he stalked toward me. "Of course, we were getting them back, but the guys were here. We could have—" He cut himself off even as I put a hand on Liam's chest to keep him from cutting between me and Doc. Doc wasn't going to hurt me.

He was hurting.

Liam was hurting.

Starling was hurting.

Everyone was hurting.

"We can do it now," I told Doc. "Do you want to call them before I go talk to Sharpe?"

'Cause I wanted to end this with him. He didn't get to cause Starling another ounce of harm. No one did. The tension vibrating through Liam communicated through the stiffness of his frame.

"Yeah," Liam said, his voice low and aggressive. "We can fucking do it now, and you can take a damn step back —*Vandal*. Rome had a good idea. He doesn't need you acting like an asshole."

"But clearly, he needs it from you," Doc said with a bland look.

"Yes," I admitted. "Liam is always an asshole."

My mirror jerked his gaze to me, and so did Doc. Vaughn began to laugh behind us. The sound cracked through the room and Doc's lips twitched, as did Liam's. It wasn't long before they were all laughing.

That was fine. It was better than fighting. Starling didn't need us fighting—unless we were fighting everyone else. She would be okay with that.

"Right," Doc said as he caught his breath, then picked up his coffee. As he turned away, he scrubbed a hand over his face. "I'll call Alphabet. Someone grab the phones. Then I want to get another phone so we can make that son of a bitch a video of our own."

"I have a phone," Liam said in a very unfriendly tone. "We can get more. How many cameras would you like?"

"Oh boy," Vaughn said behind me. "I recognize those tones. Should we wait for Kel?"

"No," I answered before anyone else. "Kel needs Starling. We need to deal with Sharpe ourselves."

"And Kel, Jas, and I took care of the dance partner." That

wasn't really a factor for me. We all protected Starling. I didn't need to keep score. Vaughn, however, needed to share. "Fair enough. I'll get the phones. We need to run security and ensure Freddie knows what's happening."

I nodded. "I'll tell him." When I looked at Liam, I studied him. Could he handle this?

He gave me a little shrug. Nothing would bring back Jonathon O'Connell, or even remove the history that Starling had suffered. But we could inflict harm on the fuckbucket through the brother.

Sharpe needed to be punished anyway.

I agreed.

"So we're decided?" Doc asked after the silence dragged. I didn't look away from Liam. The anger orbiting him had its own turbulence. He needed Starling soon too. But he needed violence more right now.

"We're agreed," Liam said before flicking a look at me. "You want first dibs, don't you?"

"I just want to know he's dead." What I needed was for Starling to be free from the shackles of her past. To be able to spread her wings and not worry that someone was coming to break them again. I wanted to erase the Sharpes. Moira could have a different last name. "Starling needs a new name."

"Cleary?" Liam challenged and I shrugged.

"I don't care—just not Sharpe." She might want to keep it, and that could be her decision. If she wanted it, we would eliminate everyone else with the name and make it hers.

"She has another last name if she wants it," Doc reminded us. "Hardigan."

"Yeah," Liam said slowly. "And we need to deal with that other son of a bitch."

"We will," I said, before heading toward the stairs. Vaughn was already descending with the phones in hand. I would inform Freddie and Jasper. Milo and Kellan both needed to rest.

We could take care of this part.

CHAPTER 20

FREDDIE

"Can I ask you a question?" I'd just gotten Bodhi settled into my previous room. It was cleaner in here than I remembered it ever being, and someone had repainted after we moved me into the new suite.

Huh. It was more than enough for Bodhi. Since Jasper's old room was bigger and closer to Milo's, we'd set that aside for Adam and Ezra. If the pair opposed sharing a room, they could bitch to someone else.

"I could say you just did," Bodhi stated as he stood in the bathroom doorway, blotting his face with a hand towel. He'd washed up and shaved while I grabbed fresh sheets and blankets. Dude could make his own bed. But we had a whole storage closet and someone had doubled up on everything.

I really needed to pay closer attention to the shopping. The clubhouse had always been a sanctuary, though now it was turning into a home.

"But I'll reserve my asshole for the jackasses who deserve it."

A snort of laughter escaped me. "You like antagonizing them."

"That's not a question," Bodhi said before tossing his towel back into the bathroom before he looked at me. "Spit it out, Freddie. Not planning on killing you today."

"Damn," I said. "Still waiting for the epic way you'd do it."

He didn't bother to respond to the rather bad joke. Instead, he just folded his arms and gave me a long stare.

"Right. What's your deal with them? Liam, Ball-Cracker, and the two assholes." Liam didn't like him—or maybe, better put, he didn't trust him. Interestingly, it was Ball-Cracker who seemed more familiar and relaxed with him. Small world where Boo-Boo's bestie and our new friend were tight.

Or maybe…

"Or was that why you were at Pinetree?" That idea rocked me a little. Was that possible? Ball-Cracker came to get us. Had she called Bodhi too?

He shrugged. "Lainey's a hottie and kind. Never seen her be a bitch to anyone who didn't deserve it. No, she didn't ask me to go to Pinetree. Haven't seen her in a couple of years." It was as direct an answer as I supposed I could have asked for. "I like Ball-Cracker for her. It fits. Reed and Graham—those two are always running an angle. They live for control. It gives me hives."

Huh. "And Liam?"

"He doesn't like me. Fortunately, I don't give two shits about his opinion." He walked over to the duffel bag he'd brought with him and unzipped it. "Dumb luck was why we met, Freddie. Don't dig at it too much more than that."

Arms folded, I studied him. "I'd like to not second guess everything…"

"But betrayal leaves a bad aftertaste." Bodhi pivoted to face me. "What do you need to feel comfortable again?"

I almost laughed. Chances were, I'd never feel comfortable as long as some people were alive. Sadly, I didn't know all of their names. If I did?

Yeah, I could go on a road trip and collect ears or something until I was done. Not the life for Boo-Boo or for me, so I'd lump my demons in with hers and kill them. That was a good start.

An image of her writhing against me as I rubbed my dick against her ass until I came, and the feeling of her dripping down my fingers as I teased an orgasm out of her, had my dick hard in a flat-second.

Right. No thinking about Boo-Boo like that right now. All that wood was for her and her alone.

"Not sure you can," I admitted, aware Bodhi waited for an answer. "I like you. Think you're not a bad guy."

"I am a gift to all who know me."

I didn't laugh, but it was amusing. "Not everyone trusts you."

"I am perfectly fine living with that disappointment."

I snorted. "Boo-Boo does."

"Ah…PPG has nothing to fear from me, Freddie. Neither of you do. Look, trust me. Don't trust me. It's all the same to me. I like you. I like PPG. I like Lainey B. Trust that when I like people, not much I won't do."

That, I had gotten.

"And the people you don't like?"

He made a face. "Which of them am I not allowed to kill?"

"Liam, for certain," I said. "He's my brother."

A grunt was his only response.

"As for Adam and Ezra? Boo-Boo likes Adam, and he's tried to help her a few times."

"So, Ezra is fair game?" The sudden flash of his smile shouldn't amuse me so damn much, even though it did.

"I'd say within reason. Didn't hear anyone complaining about the fight earlier."

Cocking his thumb and forefinger like a gun, Bodhi pointed at me. "Understood. Now, I like sleeping naked, and you're not my type. So—we done?"

"Yeah. Sleep well. Try not to wander too much. Everyone's a little jumpy, and if I didn't say it before…" I went to the door and gripped the handle before I glanced back at him. "Thanks. I owe you."

"Nope," Bodhi said. "You don't owe me shit. I'm where I want to be. Or I will be when you get out and I can crash."

"Night, Bodhi."

"Night," he said, then added, "Hey, Freddie…"

"Yeah?"

"If you can work out a really good and bloody fight for me, that'd be sweet."

I chuckled. "I can think of a few people who need to get scratched off, and it sounds like the fuckbucket has a lot of security."

Bodhi clapped his hands together. "It'll be like Christmas."

Closing the door, I chuckled and turned to find Jasper kicked back in the chair outside Milo's room, his feet stretched out in front of him. "You good?"

"Not a day in my life," Jasper retorted. "Go get some sleep. You look like hell."

I snorted. "I look better than you."

Pressing a hand to his chest, Jasper gasped. "Goddamn, kid. That wounds."

The earlier amusement spilled back in. "You need anything?"

"Nope. Vaughn's gonna spell me in a couple of hours.

Then I'll be sleeping. Liam, Rome, and Doc are dealing with the trash. Then they're gonna get some sleep too."

The trash.

They were gonna kill Sharpe.

I debated going to join them... No, there was no satisfaction in killing that shitstain. For as awful a human being as he was, his neglect and selfishness kept him from helping Boo-Boo.

The fuckbucket was the one I wanted to dismember. Well, him and the dicks who helped hurt Milo and Boo-Boo.

"Jas?"

"Yeah?"

"Why did you pick me?" The question surfaced from the same deep, dark place all thoughts seemed to emerge when it was late and we were all exhausted. Most of the time, I tried to drown out those thoughts, especially the ones that threatened to choke me out. But tonight... "When I was such a shit. I tried to knife you once."

"I know."

"And the drugs...I know you wanted me to get clean, and you kept helping, but I always went back to them." I turned that over in my head. "And I didn't listen for shit about picking fights or reacting to others."

Jasper didn't say anything as I pulled out and examined each piece of that.

"I just—what did you see in me?" That was the part I didn't get. Before the rest of the Vandals, it had been Jasper who saw me. Jasper, who dragged me out of fights, ended others, and more than once beat the shit out of the guys determined to beat me up for shit that I probably deserved to have my ass handed to me over.

"Me," Jasper answered when I finally locked eyes on him. "You reminded me of me. Always an eye on the exits. Always looking for who you could provoke, because when people react, they aren't thinking. They just lash out. You covered up your pain with shitty jokes and sometimes shittier behavior. And the drugs? You were never chasing the high, Freddie. You were just trying to escape."

"You don't do drugs." I was still trying to process the rest of his explanation. Fuck, they were all so uncomfortably close.

"Nope, but I had an alcoholic father who hated himself and everyone around him. A guy who lashed out with his fists as easily as you smart off with that mouth of yours. I come by my temper pretty fucking honestly." The raw openness was even more uncomfortable.

"You're not your father," I told him. "You've never struck me in anger. You wouldn't do it to Boo-Boo."

A wry smile turned up his lips. "Pretty sure I've popped Vaughn, Kel, and Milo though. Liam more than a few times." Dry as hell, Jasper dared me to deny it with a raise of his eyebrows.

"Well, you got me there," I said, spreading my hands. "But you're still not your father."

"Thank you. I never want to be him." The naked emotion in his eyes was even more uncomfortable. "So yeah, kid. I saw a lot of me in you. Especially with how much you didn't trust others at your back, how you reacted to the violence around you...and the fact you were kind of scrawny."

"You're a dick," I commented.

"Yep," Jasper said. "Sad but true."

Chuckling, I shook my head. "Thanks."

"For being a dick?" Yeah, he was teasing me, except I didn't mind it so much.

"Sure," I said, flipping him off. "I think I'm gonna crash for a few hours. Bodhi's got my old room. The assholes have yours."

"Good. Get some rest." Jasper popped his neck. "And Freddie?"

I paused to glance back at him. "Yeah?"

"You reminded me of me," Jasper said. "Only you're better than I am. You never tried to hurt other people."

"Doesn't mean I haven't wanted to hurt some of them." I wasn't a hero.

"No, you're misunderstanding me. You run from your past the same way I do—only you lash out at yourself and not others."

Oh.

"And in my book, that makes you better than me, at least in the coping department."

"I don't know about that."

"Well," Jas said with a shrug as he leaned back in his chair. "I do...and Swan has taught you to smile again and brought real light back into your eyes."

"I love her." It was as simple as that, and three words I never thought I'd say just...wow.

"First time you admitted it?" Jasper asked with an almost indulgent smile.

"Yeah," I said. "I mean she's always been special..."

"Yep, and you don't need to explain it to me. Loving her is the second-best thing I've done in my life."

"The first one was stealing her, wasn't it?"

Jasper grinned wide. "Damn straight. Now—go to bed, kid. Get some rest. We have a lot more shit to deal with before this is over. Then we're going to take some time and just celebrate our girl."

Our girl.

I liked that.

"Night, Jas."

"Night, Freddie."

All the way back to my room, I turned those words over and over in my head. I loved her.

I love Boo-Boo.

Whew. I blew out a breath as I stood in the sitting room. Evidence of our shared living space was everywhere. A couple of books Jasper was reading. Art books for Vaughn and Rome. Sketchpads. A couple of the latest mechanic magazines. There was even a dancing one.

On a stand, in a place of prominence, was her stapler. Glancing around the quiet sitting room, I checked the doors. The only one closed all the way was the one to Kel's room. So she wasn't in her bed, that was good. Doc tended to crash in her room when he slept over.

Still, I went to the stapler and ran my hand over it. Just cold metal. A practical tool, but it meant everything to her.

Because she'd fought and freed herself with that damn stapler. It had grounded her in a place where they tried to rip her away from herself and some other fuckbucket tried to help himself to her.

How many times had he done that to her before...The uncle deserved to have staples driven through his nuts.

Oh.

I paused, one hand on the stapler. That was an idea. I'd mention it to Boo-Boo. She might never want to see that part of him. No problem, the rest of us could make sure it happened.

The image of that carnage warmed me up. Yeah, let the others deal with Daddy Sharpe.

I wanted a piece of the uncle.

One last pat to the stapler, then I headed for my room. There was a sticky note on the door that I didn't even see until I got there.

You and me, donuts at dawn or—you know, when you get up. Or when I get up. So, early but maybe not dawn. Your Boo-Boo

"My Boo-Boo," I whispered, then kissed her note. "Damn right, you're mine." She was all of ours, and fuck knew we were hers. The warmth the carnage ignited turned positively incandescent at the note.

Blood and Boo-Boo. I truly was a simple guy.

I texted Jasper and Vaughn before I collapsed on the bed. We needed donuts at dawn. Jasper sent back a laughing face. He'd take care of it.

Perfect.

When I fell on the bed, all the tension melted from my body, and I closed my eyes. The only thing I could see was Boo-Boo and all that soft skin.

Definitely perfect.

CHAPTER 21

DOC

ll the way to the fridge, I debated—internally anyway—what the hell I was going to do with Reginald Sharpe. Rome wanted him gone. Erase him from the board, remove him as any kind of a threat where Little Bit was concerned.

I agreed. Wholeheartedly, I agreed.

Years had peeled away from my life when I found Milo unconscious and bleeding on that freshly churned grave. More fell away upon discovering the horror of Little Bit being *buried* in that grave. Thank fuck the guys were with me, because I had to stabilize Milo while they *dug* her up.

Fucking *dug* her out of that grave. A shudder crept along my spine. We used to joke about the chills coming from someone walking over our graves. This time, we were walking on hers. The agitation transformed into pure incandescent anger. Little Bit already had trauma. Her trauma had trauma. What had I told her? Never be ashamed of the scars. The scars showed we survived.

Even as that thought took purchase, Liam secured the office door before he coded us into the fridge. The fact they'd hidden the fridge behind another panel added more security. The soundproofing was perfect. I appreciated it.

The smell that rolled out was eye-watering.

"Rise and shine," Liam called as he flicked on the lights and strolled across the room. I tracked the figure huddled on the floor who flinched away from the lights. How long had we had him in here? His eyes were sunken, and his face had a gaunt look. Sweat dotted his face while he was shaking.

"Is Emersyn here?" the man asked in a raspy voice.

"No," Rome said as he walked over to the hose. He pulled it off the rack then turned to crank the water on. Sharpe shrank in on himself as the hose came on, and Rome sprayed him.

The stench of urine, feces, blood, and the unmistakable smell of puss wasn't so easily washed away. Sharpe released yelping cries as he tried to twist away from the water hitting him. Rome washed away the evidence from the ground around him, rinsing it all down the drain. By the time he finished, Sharpe was huddled in a pathetic little mess of humanity.

Liam stared down at him, his expression seemingly carved from stone.

"What do you want?" Sharpe asked in a weeping tone. "I can't give you Bradley...if I could, I would. But I can't." He sobbed against his hands as if barely able to lift his head. "I can't undo the past..."

"If you could undo the past," Liam said, his tone as disinterested as if he was discussing a bus schedule. "What would you do?"

I hadn't moved from the doorway, where I watched

Sharpe as he lifted his trembling head. He gave Liam a bewildered look. "What?"

"You said you can't undo the past," he stated in a leveled, emotionless voice. "If you could, though—what would you do?"

"I—" Sharpe hesitated, glancing from Liam to Rome. He blinked, tracking back to Liam as if just realizing they were twins before he looked at me. Or maybe he was just checking out the three blobs in the room. I didn't know if the guy even needed glasses.

Honestly, I couldn't be fucked to know either.

"I—don't know..."

"You don't know?" Liam scoffed, then shook his head.

The man shook, his eyes feverish. Yeah, he had an infection of some kind. The part of me that went to medical school—the doctor who had been trying to repair all of his mistakes—that part wanted to react. The rest of me? Vandal, Steph's brother, Little Bit's lover, and Milo's brother?

We were just fine with letting him suffer. At the rate he was declining, he'd die on his own in a few days. It would be a miserable few days too.

"I don't know," Sharpe said, his lower lip wobbling as the words vibrated out of him. "What does it matter? You're just going to kill me...my wife...my wife doesn't want anything to do with me." The broken note in his voice and the sag to his shoulders were that of a man with little left to live for.

"You gave up the fight a long time ago," I said before Liam could launch into him. The need for violence shimmered over him like some kind of heat wave rising up from the pavement in the midst of summertime.

The man swung his head to look at me. "What?"

"You gave up fighting a long time ago," I said as I pushed away from the door. I crossed the distance, separating us slowly. "You don't care what happens to you."

"How do you know what I would do?" Sharpe demanded, staring up at me. The man couldn't even push himself upward to stand. He just sat there, waiting to die. He'd given up. I'd seen men like him before. Fight or flight could keep a man alive, but that primal response had to be sustained, and it could be broken. It could be defeated. You could wear a person down until they just stopped fighting. They stopped running.

They stopped.

They would lay down and die.

"Because you're not offering to negotiate. You aren't begging or pleading. You're not even being belligerent." I rubbed my jaw. "You don't think you have a chance in hell of surviving. You're right, by the way. You signed your death warrant the day you let your brother put his filthy fucking hands on a *child*."

Reginald Sharpe flinched. "I didn't know." He shifted his gaze away.

"Liar," was all Rome commented, and the man jerked his gaze up at him. The look held shock and resentment.

"I *didn't*."

"I can't tell if you're delusional or you genuinely believe the bullshit coming out of your mouth." Liam's upper lip curled.

"I didn't know," Reginald screamed. "Do you think I would have allowed him to spend time with her—"

"You let him rape your wife," I said, keeping it conversational. "Apparently, for days. Then merrily just picked up as if nothing happened. Why don't you lie to us some more about what you did or didn't know…"

"I love my wife," Sharpe said, a real sob breaking out. "I love her—she may never forgive me, and I deserve that. I failed her."

"Well, on that, we can agree," Liam stated as he walked

over to one of the tables and picked up a hacksaw. "You are a complete fucking failure."

I glanced at the hacksaw then back at the man who tracked Liam with his gaze. Sharpe blanched, his defeat taking on a new dimension as Liam looked over the weapons.

"Your brother is never coming for you," I told him, wanting to steer the wretched thing's attention back to me. "You have to know that. He doesn't give a damn about you... only what you can do for him."

"Which, currently," Liam said, picking up the thread, "is absolutely nothing."

Head back against the wall, Reginald Sharpe stared at us. He seemed to be searching for an element of an ally, although he wouldn't find it in any of us. His shoulders sagged and his chin dipped. "Can I see Emersyn once more—before you kill me?"

"No," Rome answered. "She doesn't need to see you."

I cut a look at him. Were we really making that decision for her?

"She said all she had to say," Liam stated, ice slicking over every word.

"You could ask her..." Sharpe suggested, sweeping all of them with a look.

"She knows you're here," Rome said. "She doesn't care anymore. You made sure of that." He wasn't wrong about that. He abandoned her. Abandoned her and her mother. They didn't owe him anything.

"Moira—"

"Left," I told him before he could get his hopes up. "You don't deserve their love, affection, or time."

Sharpe sagged further. "So—now you what? Torture me to death?"

"Was thinking about it," Liam said. "I thought we'd carve out that pound of flesh you owe Hellspawn."

"Then the one you owe her mother." I motioned to the hacksaw. "I think we're going to make sure that those ladies are paid in full for your neglect."

"I never wanted them hurt," he said, the plea as empty as his soul. "Never. You don't know Brad—you don't know what he'd do to me."

"You're right, and I don't care what he'd do to you," I told him. "What I care about is what he *did* do to your daughter."

"What he *did* to your wife," Liam caught the thread as I started forward and he moved too. We should probably put on scrubs and masks. It was going to get fucking messy in here. For once, I was looking forward to it.

"I tried to protect them…" But even his plea faltered. He couldn't conjure a convincing tone in the slightest. "I wanted to… so much."

"Except?" Rome asked, and that stopped Liam and me both in our tracks. We loomed over the man. The broken piece of refuse didn't deserve an ounce of pity. One part of me just wanted to put a bullet in his head and be done with it.

Doc still had mercy.

Vandal did not.

"It doesn't matter…" Sharpe muttered. "None of it matters. My gambling…I was always right on the edge of a big win. Then I could push him out, take over, and he wouldn't be able to touch them and never…"

Gambling addiction.

Personality disorder.

Weak-willed.

"And what does it matter if they were hurt as long as someone kept bailing you out?" Because it all made sense. "You sold off your wife and your child…for what?"

"It—" Sharpe lifted his miserable gaze to Liam and me. Mistake.

Liam struck him so hard with his right cross that Sharpe went down. Blood exploded from his mouth and he spit out a tooth. A gasping sound escaped him. The pitiful wail he released aggravated me, and I kicked the son of a bitch in the stomach hard enough to make him gag.

He rolled onto his side and tried to cover his more vulnerable organs. It didn't matter. Nothing we did to him would change what happened to Little Bit or her mother. It wouldn't take away their pain. They had survived his brother. Survived him.

Reginald Sharpe, on the other hand, was not going to survive us.

"Who wants to go first?"

We wouldn't be doing rock, paper, scissors for this one. No—

Rome walked forward and eyed the man for a moment, then put his foot down on Sharpe's wrist. His right one.

"What are you doing?" Sharpe asked as Rome knelt, all of his weight on that wrist. The man began to struggle. Survival instincts always kicked in. But he didn't lay a finger on Rome. Liam blocked him and braced his legs.

"Knife," Rome said, flicking a glance at me.

I retrieved one from the table—a scalpel for Rome and one for me.

It took some effort, but Rome removed four fingers and left him a thumb. Sharpe passed out by the second finger. The blood spray wasn't as impressive as it could have been. Dehydration on our side. Blood painted Rome as he stood.

Liam retrieved the smelling salts.

Sharpe barely woke up before he was screaming again. There was pleading this time. Begging. Swearing. Sobbing. Then Liam removed his feet. The hacksaw took a lot of effort, and Liam was sweating before he was done. Sharpe lost his battle with consciousness.

I used the torch to heat up one instrument to cauterize the wounds. It woke Sharpe. Some distant part of my mind cataloged his screams when it was my turn. I took his whole left hand.

He hadn't lifted a finger for the women in his life, so Rome took those. He couldn't even go to them when they needed them, so Liam took his feet. The only thing this man knew to do was have his hand out to his brother—so he had no hands.

"Elbow or knee?" Liam asked, and I nodded to his knees. Dislocating them woke Sharpe again. Maintaining a grip with how much blood sprayed from his wounds was hard.

By the time I cut off his dick, he was dead.

There was no satisfaction in his torture or his death.

Only a quiet sense of justice. I eyed the body parts. Dismembering was a lot of work, and we still needed to remove his arms, the rest of his legs, and his head.

"Box up his dick," I said.

Rome glanced at me but retrieved the shriveled organ, dropped it into a medical container, and then sealed it shut. Liam eyed the dead man then me. "I'm going to like what you're going to do with that, aren't I?"

"Probably," I said. Because Bradley Sharpe started all of this. He began with Moira, then Little Bit, then he came for us.

We were already going to tear him apart for his crimes.

Now?

Now, we were going to make sure he suffered.

"I have an idea…" He probably wouldn't enjoy receiving his brother's dick in a box. But it would put him on notice.

CHAPTER 22

EMERSYN

*A*rms folded, I studied Milo where he slept. Lainey needed a shower and food. So I'd sent her to shower while I sat with my brother. Mickey assured me that, like Jasper before him, Milo would be fine. But I couldn't get over the...

"Ivy," he said on a groan, and I frowned. "Come here."

"Sorry," I murmured. "I didn't mean to wake you."

"Shh." He made a face as he braced a fist against the bed, and I was moving.

"You're not supposed to get up," I scolded, but I helped steady him as he fought to get to a sitting position.

"Not laying on my back more than I have to." Weariness scraped along each word as though it took effort to voice them. The gruff notes in his voice tore at me, as did the way he exhaled sharply once he was upright and leaning against the pillows. "Bad enough Doc and Mayhem are giving me shit and bossing me around."

"I just want you to get better," I said, pulling the blankets up. Mickey and Jasper had changed them the day before, while Kel and Vaughn helped Milo into the bathroom. Lainey had been the one to help him wash up. Based on all the expletives, it hadn't been the highlight of Milo's day.

"And I will," he promised, then patted the bed. "Now, come here."

I'd barely sat down before the tears burned in my eyes and he seemed to waver in front of me.

"Ivy," he said in a rough voice that turned soft and gentle. When he opened his arms, I scooted forward to hug him.

"I'm so sorry," I whispered. He'd been hurt because of me...

"Shh," he murmured, stroking my hair. "I mean it. You have nothing to be sorry for. I'm glad I got a good look at that son of a bitch. I just wish I'd managed to gut him like a fish."

A little laugh escaped that sounded more like a sob. "But he tortured you..."

"Pfft," Milo said, leaning back to meet my gaze. Then he brushed a calloused thumb against my cheek to swipe away the tears. "Jasper hits harder. Fuck knows, Liam does."

"Milo..." They'd burned him and hit him with the cane, and at some point, they'd stabbed him.

"Yes, Milo. That's me. I know what I can survive. I know what I did to survive. None of that was your fault, do you understand me?"

I bit my lip.

"You did everything the way I asked you to. You tried to get away...you didn't come out easily. You hit back. Sweet moves, by the way..."

Heat scalded my face at the pride in his voice.

"And you survived," he finished with a firm look. "You

stood up to the guy who terrifies you and has terrorized you for most of your life. You didn't give him an inch…"

I licked my lips then swiped at my own tears. "I just wish he hadn't hurt you."

"He couldn't hurt me," Milo said, and when I made a face, he shrugged. That shrug hurt however, because despite the tightness of his expression, he grimaced. It would be hard to miss this close.

"But he had…" I didn't want to bring up what he had. I still couldn't believe he had recordings. Then again…it almost made a sick, perverted kind of sense that he would have them.

"I know," Milo said, and a muscle ticked in his jaw. "We're going to make him regret those too…and I don't care what it costs, we'll make sure they're all erased and destroyed."

I swallowed at that declaration. "I don't—I want to say I don't care. Not when…it's hard to even think about those, much less talk about them. And yes, I know I'm the one who brought it up."

In the few days we'd been back, I'd been very focused on the guys, especially after Lainey arrived to look after Milo. There had been no disguising her worry. She hadn't even tried to, and while Ezra and Adam had become permanent fixtures, they'd left her alone in here.

A damn miracle by my book. Then again, she'd made a point of speaking to them each day and checking on me too. I knew she didn't believe me when I said I was going to be okay.

"You don't have to lie to me," Milo said as he leaned back against the wall. A sheen of sweat showed on his brow. "You don't have to try and make me feel better either. What he did —*he* did. What we do to him, *we* will do to him." He cut a look toward the bathroom door that was closed. The water was still running in there. "When is Liam setting up the meeting with King?"

"He's avoiding it," I admitted. "He's angry and doesn't want to risk it."

"We need to risk it," Milo said, that muscle ticking in his jaw again. "How do you feel about going around him?"

"Around Liam?" I raised my brows. Curling my leg up, I shook my head. "No, I won't sneak around behind their backs."

"Ivy, they are always going to put your safety first, and after this...the chances of any of them taking their eyes off you are slim and none. And as much as I want to bury that asshole for playing this game..." The anger turned practically molten in his gaze. "We could use him."

"But I'm still not going around Liam. I can convince him, but it will take time. I don't want to risk any of you, either." Considering what Fuckbucket did to Milo and he only *thought* Milo was a lover and not my brother. I almost hated to think what he would have done to him if he'd known sooner. Maybe Milo didn't remember that Fuckbucket wanted to take him with him, but I had. "He's a cruel man— Fuckbucket, I mean. He always has been."

"I don't give a shit about his forgiveness. In fact, I want him to choke on his pride and his perverted sickness...then I want to stuff it down his throat until he drowns in the shit he's poured over you all these years." The hostility in his voice amped up. "We are going to kill him...*and* we're going to make him suffer."

I glanced down at his hands. The livid bruises on them were still an ugly shade of greenish-black. He was healing, but not as fast as I would like.

"Hey..." He raised his hand to my face but hesitated until I lifted my gaze to meet his. I leaned forward, and he cupped my face. "Do you want to kill him?"

I frowned. "I just want him to leave us alone... I want him to never hurt anyone again. Do I want to be the one who kills him?" Cold shuddered through me, and I rested my cheek in his hand.

"Ivy, you don't have to do a damn thing," he said. "We can, and will, deal with him. But if you want the final say—it's yours."

"Don't you have to talk to Kel about that?" I was trying to lighten the mood, but I didn't think it had worked and the shower cut off.

"I have," Milo said, his gaze steady in all its fury. "Not that I needed to. There's not a man out there who won't kill to keep you safe. Who won't extract every ounce of vengeance you are owed. But the only one who can tell us if this is the justice you need—is you."

"I hurt him."

"I know you did," he said, wiping away a tear, and his smile turned almost indulgent in its pride. "You also wouldn't bow to him, so you cut his ego as effectively as you bruised his pride and his knee."

I swallowed. The limp...Fuckbucket was still limping. I'd done that to him. Messed his knee up... It didn't seem like that much payment to extract considering everything he'd done to me, to Ms. Stephanie, to the people at Vaughn's work, including Lauren, to Kellan, to—all of us.

"I want to get him," I said slowly. "I just don't want any of you to get hurt anymore."

The door to the bathroom opened, and we both glanced at Lainey as she stepped out with her damp hair, looking like a million bucks. She was dressed in comfortable clothes, more like me than her. Then again—she didn't need anything fancier here.

When I glanced back at Milo, I raised my brows and he

nodded. I didn't have to stress that Lainey was one of the people we had to protect. He already wanted her safe.

"You two have the worst poker faces," Lainey commented as she moved to her bag and stowed a small cosmetic bag.

"No, I don't," I said at nearly the same time as Milo said, "No, we don't."

I shot another look at him, and we both laughed. He gripped his side a little as Lainey walked over to us, but he was still chuckling.

"And you are supposed to be lying down," she informed him, even as she wrapped an arm around my shoulders for a hug. "And you're supposed to badger him into taking care of himself."

I peered up at her and smiled. "He just wanted to sit up, he's still in bed."

"Hmm," she hummed in the back of her throat. "I'm going to go make coffee." She fixed Milo with a stare. "Going to behave for me, Pretty Boy?"

"Going to bring me coffee, Mayhem?"

"Maybe."

"Then I'll consider it."

She chuckled, then gave me a squeeze. "What about you?"

"I'm not going to behave." At that admission, Milo laughed for real and Lainey's expression eased.

"So, no coffee for you, then." She winked and I smiled.

"I'm okay for now. Go ahead. Or I can go make it for the two of you..."

"No," Lainey said with a shake of her head. "I promised Adam I would talk to him this morning. This is a good time to do that, and it has a time limit since I don't want to bring back cold coffee."

Milo's face went expressionless at the mention of Adam, but he didn't say anything.

"Call me if you need me," I said to her, and she caught my hand in a quick clasp before she strolled toward the door. I didn't miss the way Milo tracked her every movement as the door closed behind her, then he looked at me.

"Don't start."

"I don't have to, you already did."

He groaned and leaned his head back. "Not going to threaten me?"

"Pretty sure I already did...kind of like how you threatened all the guys."

He chuckled. "Fair enough..." His humor vanished as he held out his hand to me and I set my hand in his. "Think about what you're willing to do and how far you want to go. I won't take this away from you for anything in the world, Ivy. But that man has to be erased. He needs to pay for what he's done. To you. To Moira. To everyone. I want you to have your justice...only I don't want you to have any regrets in any direction."

I chewed my lower lip as I mulled over the words in my head. "I will...and thank you."

"For what?" He frowned.

"For not pushing. For not demanding I make a choice..."

"Sweetheart," he said with a heavy sigh. "I know when we first met again—I was bastard about a lot of things. I'm still a bastard about them. Although you're right, you are one of us. You get a say. Especially when it's about you."

"You know...you're not half-bad at this brother business."

"Thank fuck," he said, even as the corners of his mouth quirked upward. "I've waited a long time and been practicing."

I was so glad he was okay, that he was going to be okay. I was so happy we were here, together. "Do you think we have a future? All of us?"

The question slipped out from the dark corners where it had been lurking.

"I know we do," he said. "You, especially. Besides…haven't you noticed? When Vandals want something done…we get it done."

"You honestly believe that?"

"I do," he promised. "Maybe…maybe because I have lost everything. Because I gave it up to protect the people I cared about. I know what it is to have nothing and what it is to have nothing but the people I choose as my family. You have a future, Ivy."

"Then you better have one, too," I told him, and his expression softened. "Because I need you…"

More, I wanted him in my life.

"I like having a big brother…even when he can be an asshole."

"Sometimes, you need me to be an asshole." He half-closed his eyes. "Just like I need you to be a brat sometimes, too."

Well, he wasn't wrong. We did need that. "That sounds like permission to me."

"Sure," he said. "Why not?"

A genuine smile tugged at my lips. "I'll talk to Liam. We'll go see King and…I don't know what to do with the idea that he's our father."

"He's not—he's an asshole who we're going to use to get what we want, and then we'll deal with him like we do anyone else that uses, abuses, and leaves us."

"You said we."

"Yes, I did, little sister. You and me? We're a package deal."

I liked that. "Can I give you a hug?"

He opened his arms, making the decision easy for me, and when I crawled into his embrace, I was careful, but Milo's hug completely encompassed me.

A package deal.

We were going to do this, and then we were going to have our future. Dammit.

CHAPTER 23

LIAM

"Are you sure I can't talk you out of this?" I leaned back against the counter, studying Hellspawn as she added the barest hint of cosmetics to her eyes. She'd already covered the bruises on her face with a combination of concealer and foundation. The skill it took to blend away those dark marks had been acquired over time, and it just pissed me off all over again.

"You probably can," she admitted, peering up at me. The openness in her eyes was a kick to the abs. "I would prefer it if you didn't, though."

The urge to sweep her off to bed was right there, but the lightness in her tone did not match the sobriety in her expression. "Tell me again what you hope to accomplish?"

"Freedom," she said slowly, pausing mid-lash stroke with the mascara. The thoughtful look on her face held me riveted. "I don't know Jeff Hardigan. Arguably, I don't know Julius King either...or why he changed his name. I can guess and speculate. But one of the king's goals was to eliminate Milo—he had to know Milo was his son."

Yeah, that part had registered with me as well.

"So, I don't know what *he* wants from this. From trying to get me to work for him like you do, unless it's more leverage over Milo."

"He doesn't have any leverage on Milo…"

"Except, we all think he's the reason Milo went to prison." Her gaze went distant as she blew out a breath. "So, leverage or not…he wants something from Milo. I want to know *what*." She finished the light touch of mascara before flicking her gaze up at me. "I want to know what he wants from me… am I just a means to an end? The Sharpe fortune is something he wants to acquire?"

Dislike kissed that last sentence. Dislike and determination. The worst part of all of this…Kel agreed with her, even though he didn't want to send her in any more than I did.

Finished with her cosmetics, Hellspawn turned to face me. The dress I'd picked out was a simple wrap-around, but it also let me put a lighter vest on her, where then the jacket covered both. "How do I look?"

She'd partially braided her hair, pulling it all over one shoulder and leaving the rest to spill in a cascade. Dressed in the dark chocolate dress and matching boots with a cashmere jacket in a paler color provided the contrast to hide the vest under her clothes.

"You'd be gorgeous in a paper bag," I said, then chuckled. "Or out of it. It isn't the clothes, Hellspawn."

Dropping a hand to her hip, she smoothed her palm over the dress and definitely pulled my attention to the suggestion of curves. She'd lost weight again. I wouldn't harp on it, but she had. It was the stress. All at once—all I could see was her pale and frail inside that coffin when we ripped it open.

"Hey…" Soft hands framed my face and drew me back to

the present. The woman in front of me wasn't pale or frail—she was infinitely precious. "Don't go away..."

Looping my arms around her, I hauled her to me and she all but melted against me. The press of her ear over my chest and the tightness of her arms were another form of a visceral reminder that she wasn't in that coffin.

She wasn't buried alive.

She hadn't *died*.

Lips pressed to the top of her head, I inhaled the sweetness of her. It was a combination of citrus, vanilla, and something I couldn't quite put my finger on. Maybe it was just Hellspawn herself. Fuck knew I loved the way she smelled, looked, spoke, and even pushed back against me.

"I want so badly to just take you away and hide you—" Fuck did I ever. "And, no, I know we just tried that and it didn't work out. However, Ezra has an island..." Squeezing her, I whispered, "What would you say about... you know... taking Lainey and hiding on the island? I could send most of the guys with you."

It was futile.

Fucking hell, I knew it was futile.

At the same time...

"And leave you out here on your own?" Her fingers dug into my back, her grip on me every bit as fierce as mine on her.

"Yeah, I didn't think you'd go for it."

"Liam," she murmured, the taste of the sweet emotion my name on her lips provoked going straight to my cock. When she made the barest noise of resistance and began to pull back, I loosened my grip so I could meet her gaze. "I love you."

Whatever I had expected her to say, those three words detonated against my psyche like a bomb.

"I love you all so much," she said, focusing on me. I

refused to move a muscle. Nothing was allowed to interrupt this moment. "And if I thought for an instant that it would be better for me to stay gone—I would go."

"But it wouldn't be better," I confessed. "Goddammit, I want to lie to you, to myself, to the world…"

"No, you don't," she said, the sexy shape of her mouth curving upward. "You haven't lied to me since you met me."

I frowned.

"You haven't. You just didn't answer my questions or told me you wouldn't when I wanted to know…"

That really felt like splitting hairs. "I didn't tell you I wasn't Rome."

A laugh peeled out of her. "You didn't tell me you were him, either."

Yeah. I supposed. "You're getting me off topic."

"Not intentionally." She spread her fingers against my chest. "I love you. I'm one of you. I'm right here and ready to fight. We've already decided separating is not the way to go."

"Don't come at me with your logic," I grumbled, and she laughed again. I couldn't hold onto my grimace or sour mood. If anything, she just made me want to smile more. "Losing you—not an option, Hellspawn."

"That goes ditto for you." She toyed with one of the buttons on my shirt. "Now—if you really don't want to meet with King, then we need a new plan."

"It's not that I don't want to meet with him…"

"It's that you don't want *me* to meet with him." Smart and beautiful.

"Exactly—that said, he has taken an interest in you *and* we might be able to negotiate that to our advantage. I just don't want you making him any promises."

"I don't plan to make him any promises," she said, lips pursing. "You see, I have something he wants. If he wants it, he needs to earn it."

"We don't know exactly what *it* is."

Her half-shrug had me shaking my head. "It doesn't matter—whatever he asks for, we might say no. And I'm okay with that. Or it might be something I don't care about, and it doesn't hurt to say yes. Either way, he won't get an answer until he's scratched my back first."

Lightning in a bottle. That was what she was. "Hellspawn certainly does fit you."

"Thank you," she said with a kind of happy glow. "I kind of love it." Because she loved me. While she didn't repeat the earlier sentiment, it was in her every gesture and expression.

"You're armed?"

She pulled back to open her jacket to show the small shoulder holster in place. While I'd watched her put it on, I still wanted to check. The pistol was a smaller caliber. But it would get the job done.

"Knife?"

"In my purse," she said, motioning to the bag. "Along with the taser and the pepper spray."

"Are you giving me shit, Hellspawn?"

Head canted to the right just slightly, she grinned. "Would I do that?"

Looping my arm around her waist, I bent my head toward her and the fact that she didn't hesitate to push up to meet my kiss just made me smile. I whispered against her lips, "Absolutely, you would do that, and I love that you do."

I kissed the laughter right out of her mouth. From the moment the subject of Julius King resurfaced, I knew we were doing this—*again*. Even considering how I could possibly talk her out of attending the meeting wasn't a solution. She opened to the first sweep of my tongue, and I sighed as she teased and toyed with me. The dueling kiss wasn't so much a struggle for power or dominance as it was playful, filled with affection, and a promise in its own right.

Breaking the kiss was the last thing I wanted to do, yet I did it anyway. Forehead to hers, I said, "Follow my lead, and I'll back your play. If I call it—we walk away."

The faintly puzzled look on her face gave way to amusement.

"Plan to share with the class?" I challenged.

"I just didn't know you were a poet..." Mirth danced in her eyes and I groaned. Smoothing my hand over her ass, I gave into the temptation and landed a resounding smack there. She gave a little groan as she exhaled. I was careful to massage the heat around. "If calling you a poet gets me that..."

"Don't," I ordered. "Hellspawn...you start that now and the only place we're going is that bed."

"You make that sound like it's a punishment," she teased, and it was my turn to groan, especially when she grabbed her purse and sashayed that sweet ass of hers out ahead of me.

Freddie and Vaughn were out in the sitting room. "Um..." Freddie said. "Boo-Boo looks edible. I don't think she should go out looking that fantastic."

"I'm armed," I retorted.

"So am I," Hellspawn promised as she ducked her head to drop a kiss on Freddie's lips. It was a very careful contact, light and ephemeral. She understood what he could take and what he couldn't. When he caught her hand, she smiled.

"You might need backup," Vaughn said.

"I have it, but I won't say no to a follow car." I wouldn't say no to anything. Vaughn rose at the suggestion.

Instead of commenting, Hellspawn perched on the edge of the coffee table, focusing on Freddie.

"Everything good?" I asked Vaughn, turning my head enough to keep the movement of my lips from being seen.

"Yeah," Vaughn said. "Freddie's getting a tattoo... he might be telling Dove."

He was getting a tat? I glanced back to where Freddie played with her fingers and traced his other hand over the bracelet on her wrist. That bracelet steadied me. I'd put it on her initially to help assuage her fears of being taken. Never had I imagined it would be how we saved her.

Thank fuck for her liking it.

"Cool."

"I thought so."

"It's a date," Hellspawn said as she rose and Freddie grinned.

"Do you think I can talk you into another dress like this?" Freddie shot us a quick look but kept his attention on her.

"Only if you intend to talk me out of it later." The tease pulled a real laugh from Freddie, and some of the tension bled out of him. I liked who Freddie was around her, who Freddie let himself be. He was still him but with fewer jagged edges. She did that for all of us.

"Deal," Freddie said, then looked at me. "Boo-Boo back in one, unblemished piece, please."

"That is my plan," I told him, and he saluted before falling back on the sofa. "Get some rest."

"That's my plan," he told me with a grin. "At least until Bodhi is up. Then I gotta help Doc with some stuff."

Hellspawn blew him a kiss before she gave Vaughn a proper one. "See you later?" she asked him.

"I'll be here, or there…depending on who gets bodyguard duty."

"Well, my body will definitely be looked after." She was killing me with the flirting, even though I didn't mind it —'cause what a fucking way to go.

Downstairs, Ezra was waiting for us along with Rome. Both of them were in suits. I did a double-take at Rome's. He just shot me a bland look. Right. No way he was staying behind, and I'd bet money he had on a vest.

Good plan.

I cut a look at Ezra.

"Don't start with me," he said. "Now that we know a little more about this son of a bitch, you couldn't keep me away. Besides, Lainey wants Em safe, so—that's where I'll be. Adam gets to deal with the brother."

"Milo has a name," Hellspawn reminded him and Ezra just gave her a cocky grin.

"I know—still don't care."

She chuckled and shook her head. It was good that the guys understood how important Milo was to us, or this could be going another way entirely.

"Enough play," Kellan said as he arrived with Jasper and Doc. Adam was absent, but then so were Milo and Lainey. Yeah, not a conversation I wanted to hear, so I focused on Kellan. "Let's talk about the plan for tonight before you four go…"

The plan.

It was pretty basic, but we were all feeling the loss we'd *nearly* suffered hot on the heels of the losses we did suffer.

I had no problem with going over the plan a hundred times. We weren't fucking this up again.

Period.

CHAPTER 24

EMERSYN

*T*he drive to our dinner meeting was almost too silent. Ezra rode up in front with Liam while Rome sat in the back with me. Awareness of the guys watching us leave weighed on me. They hadn't been alone out there. While Lainey stayed with Milo, Adam came out. He'd actually spoken to Ezra and Liam briefly; the measure in his eyes, when he glanced at me, struck me just a little odd until I recognized the concern under the blankness.

He was going for neutrality. Like everyone else, he didn't want me to go. I could hardly blame him. It was my fault King ordered Liam to kill Adam. I didn't ask for his proposal, but he'd offered it nonetheless. So, his being on edge made a certain amount of sense. My guys, on the other hand, were unsettled. Particularly those staying behind, because the last time they'd seen me off...I'd ended up in a coffin. A cold hand wrapped around my spine and dug its fingers in. Tonight wouldn't end similarly... I hoped.

Rome linked his fingers with mine, pulling my attention off the guys we were leaving behind and to him. I wasn't alone. This wasn't me leaving them all. We were together. Him. Me. Liam. Even Ezra. The steadiness in his eyes held me riveted and chased away the chill of the grave. They hadn't left me alone, not once. One or, more often, a few of them were always with me.

A couple of months ago, I might have suffocated under the way they surrounded me, buffering the world before it could even attempt to reach me. Hell, I'd chafed when they'd taken me and kept me all but prisoner. Looking back? Yeah, I was a prisoner, but their reasoning made so much more sense to me. I adored them for taking the initiative. Loved them even more for letting me lash out at them while refusing to back down.

Now?

Now, I loved them, period. They weren't caging me. If they were? Well, they were all stuffed inside the cage with me. This was a team effort. I wasn't just the one being protected; I got to protect them too. It was why this evening was such a challenge for them. Squeezing Rome's hand, I leaned my head against his shoulder. The lightest brush of his lips touching my hair rippled through me as I caught Liam's gaze in the rearview mirror.

The sharp gleam in his eyes promised me he missed very little. Right now? He wanted to be as far from this particular battlefield as possible. Instead, he was leading the charge right into it, because that was what we needed him to do. We, meaning me, the Vandals, Rome, Ezra, and even Adam.

I mouthed the words "love you," His eyes softened before they flicked back to the road, all business.

The drive took forever and almost no time at all. The tension in the car was thick when we pulled into the parking garage of a building downtown. So—we weren't going to some special club. Good. The last one had been... unsettling. Right now, I needed distance. Security waited for us just inside. Liam held up a hand before they even closed on us.

"You can tell Mr. King, if he wants us to stay, we walk through as we are. One of you even considers laying a finger on anyone here and I'll break the arm off and beat you all to death with it."

"I was just gonna shoot them," Ezra said. "Your way sounds way more fun."

Where Ezra was flippant, Liam was most assuredly not. The security detail was seven men. Rome said absolutely nothing. He didn't have to. Whatever Liam did, Rome would back him and so would I. As it was, wariness reflected in the gazes of every single man staring at us. The guys formed a triangle, with Liam at the point and Ezra and Rome just behind him. I was the other end of the diamond. It put me closer to the door and all three of them in the way of someone coming at me.

They hadn't even discussed it. I adored them so much, but I would shoot the security guards myself before letting them touch my guys. Even Ezra. He was a good friend, even when he was being an asshole.

Liam didn't respond to Ezra's comment. His stare locked onto the first guard who'd stepped forward. Probably the guy who was in charge. While I couldn't see Liam's face, I didn't need to. Whatever the guard saw on his face, he believed. He fell back a step and touched his finger to the device in his ear.

"Yes, sir," he said in a formal tone. "I believe Mr. O'Connell is not kidding."

Huh. The fact he took the threat at face value and even confirmed it without breaking a sweat was kind of impressive.

And more than a little terrifying. The guard's gaze moved over Liam, Ezra, and Rome before finally latching onto me.

"Yes, sir, she is here."

Liam's whole body seemed to stiffen. Whatever was on his face now backed two of the guards off even further. One guy actually seemed to pale. I fought against the smile on my face, but it was hard to contain. They were afraid of Liam.

They were *very* afraid of him.

All I could think was, good.

They should be terrified of all three of them. They would learn—if they pushed it, well, they only had themselves to blame. The chill on my spine became a bit of a thrill. Maybe it was adrenaline and dopamine hitting my system at once, but part of me was almost eager for the fight.

Too eager.

"Yes, sir," the guard said for a third time. "I will send them up."

Just like that, the guy lifted his hands and backed off. The other guards followed suit.

"The king will see you now," was all he said.

Liam didn't comment, nor did Ezra. Rome held a hand out to me and I glided forward. Ezra folded to one side as Liam kept point, and Rome was on my other. They framed me as we headed for the elevator. The guys had this, so I simply focused on one foot in front of the other. Clearly, we were being observed, and King had verified that I was present—dick.

Anger flash-fired through me. This man hurt Milo. Sure, yes, he was my biological father. I couldn't care less about that part, *except* he hurt Milo. He abandoned us—abandoned *him*. Based on what Liam and Milo had both shared about the Royals, he'd also been targeting Milo for years. Started targeting him when Milo was still a teenager.

What the fuck was wrong with him?

"Relax," Liam said, holding the elevator door for her to slide in. The guys coordinated it like they practiced. You know, maybe Liam and Ezra had. Ezra had definitely backed us before. Liam and Rome needed no practice. There were times when I was convinced they were absolutely extensions of each other.

Once in the elevator, I pivoted to face the guards behind us. Not that I got to see much of them. The guys all nudged me back out of sight and into the corner.

"It's a good thing I like you," I teased. He reached a hand behind him and I clasped his in my free one. Rome had one hand, Liam the other. They were the perfect balance. The contact calmed me in a way I couldn't express. This wasn't stage fright or even nerves before a particularly tough performance.

This was anger, grief, frustration, and on a profound level. Fury for my brother. We'd been split apart for years. The adoption had taken me away from Milo and cut me off from the Vandals. While they had been out there, keeping a distant eye on me—I'd been utterly unaware of them. That part I hated more than anything.

Now, this man we were about to see *again*, had known all of us. *All* of the players. The more I thought about his questions at our previous encounters, the decisions he'd made, and even the actions he'd taken, as relayed by Liam—the more the fury grew.

Julius King or Jeff Hardigan, or whatever he wanted to call himself, left us, left *Milo* and rather than try to help or support? He'd gone after Milo to punish him. For what? For standing up to him when he was seven or eight years old?

What a dick.

The doors opened with a ding, and instead of some functionary or assistant waiting for us—it was the man himself.

Julius King stood in the reception area of the office. Like

the guys, he was dressed in a suit. His tie was neatly knotted, and the tailoring of his clothes suggested expensive handling and fine materials. He had his hands clasped behind his back and his focus direct. While he'd been clean-shaven the first time we met him, stubble decorated his jaw and his eyes were narrowed as he glanced over us.

However, when he reached me, his gaze fixed as he gave me a studying look that I couldn't quite decipher. It was like someone struck a match and lit the fuse on my temper. The very last thing I wanted to deal with was this man, his manipulations, lies, and games. Yet, here we were because Milo was right...

We needed the son of a bitch.

"Gentlemen," King said as he nodded to Liam and Ezra. They took point, stepping out together. It forced King to withdraw a step or two even as he shook their hands. "Mr. Cleary," he continued, regarding me and Rome. "Emersyn."

"I think we're going back to Ms. Sharpe," I corrected him. No, this wasn't the plan, yet the hot coals of anger were burning inside me. Close enough to touch the man who'd abandoned us and left us to our fate—worse, then consigned Milo to another fate? I wasn't in the mood to pretend.

"Really?" Intrigue filtered through his expression as he held out a hand to me. "I thought we'd come to an under-standing."

I glanced down at his hand, then up at the man as I made no move to take it. I could *feel* Liam and Rome weighing and measuring every single word and maneuver. Ezra probably was as well, and I would likely need him to be a smart-ass here soon.

"We came to *something*," I said, but this was not a game I wanted to play with him or anyone else. "I've been in a coffin since then, and I'm a little sick of betrayals."

The moment the last six words left my lips, I shifted my

approach and strode around King to head toward the office. I assumed that was where he intended this little meeting to occur. Rome moved right with me, and I didn't have to glance back to check where Ezra and Liam were. They flanked King and the power dynamic around us began to change.

It wasn't something I could define so much as sense. King hoarded control by limiting knowledge, by creating the illusion that his reach was far and his awareness limitless. Except—it wasn't. It hadn't been.

Or why would Adam and Liam have been able to run the scam on him? Or Liam having played him for so long?

King could suspect, yet he couldn't prove what he knew. Or if he could, he couldn't do anything about it. The neutering of his influence hadn't been more apparent than Liam's open declaration of rebellion in the lobby and King acquiescing to it. The fact he'd allowed us up without a search or removal of weapons divulged something, and until we were standing right in front of him, it hadn't registered.

I let myself into the office, grasping both hands and turning them to push them inward. A part of me half-expected an ambush. If I admitted that to the guys later, I had a feeling Liam would make good on his offer of a spanking. Plus, it probably wouldn't be half as fun as the last one.

The interior of the office, however, was empty. It reminded me of our first meeting. Although this was a different building. How many did he own? Did he move constantly to keep from being tracked? The security he kept around him was at ridiculous levels. Who was he hiding from?

I had so many questions.

A fire burned in the fireplace and Rome paced me as I strode ahead to the sitting area framing the fireplace. It didn't surprise me to find King following us, his expression guarded but also—puzzled.

"You said a coffin?" Well, at least I knew the man paid attention when I spoke. That was something. I glanced from him to Liam. His gaze was on King, but it was as if Liam knew the moment I focused on him. Confidence and anger were tightly wound in his gaze. There was no mistaking it for anything else.

He lifted his brows. Was I really about to do this? While I know we hadn't discussed it, I nodded. Then I gave him a beat. If he didn't want to go with this plan—well, we'd figure something else out.

Saying nothing, Liam held my gaze for what seemed a long moment. Then he flicked a look at Rome. One of those wordless pulses passed between them before Liam nodded. If I wanted to do this, then he would back my play.

"Yes," I said, loving Liam so much at the moment. Loving all of them. Then I transferred my attention back to King. "It would seem that my uncle is opposed to my choices in life, particularly those that don't involve him. So, he had me buried alive."

As flip as I made it sound, including adding a shrug, apprehension curdled in my stomach.

King's eyes narrowed and his expression grew stonier. "Are you playing with me, Emersyn?"

"Oh, please," I scoffed, making Ezra's posture shift. Both he and Liam were ready to go for their guns. "You're one to talk about games, Mr. King." I almost called him Hardigan, but that was Milo's name and I wasn't going to give it to this bastard. "You've been playing games for years—what is this little meeting about, if not another game?"

Challenge offered.

King's nostrils flared, and his stare bored into mine like

he could see right down to the depths of my bone marrow. Honestly—I'd stared into Fuckbucket's eyes.

This man *didn't* scare me.

Not anymore.

"You have a point," he said, finally. "And as I told Liam before, your enemies—are my enemies. Therefore, your uncle is now my enemy."

Challenge accepted.

CHAPTER 25

EMERSYN

$\mathcal{I}$ snorted.

The sound echoed in the room and King's expression darkened. Only it was Liam's smirk that kept my chin up.

"You don't believe me," King stated. It wasn't a question.

"No," I confirmed for him. "I don't." And I wouldn't. I cut my gaze from him to survey the room again. He had drinks and appetizers out. "Also, what is it with you and party food?"

"Excuse me?" King said as I pivoted on my heel to walk over to the spread that had been set up. Rome was my shadow. His fingers trailed over my spine before he settled his hand at the base of my spine.

"I asked what was with the food and the setup?" I gestured to the room. "You bark orders. You set up goons to search us. You change locations more often than I change shoes. You provide meals and appetizers and..." I lifted the bottle of wine that had been opened to breathe. "Expensive, if gross, French wine." It was one of Fuckbucket's favorites. I put it back on the table like it might scald me. "No one pairs caviar with this. One is too sweet, and the other too damn salty."

I caught King's reaction from the corner of my eye. He gave a little jerk as he turned his attention to the table. Folding my arms, I walked the length of it then away. The last thing I wanted was food; after seeing the wine, I'd rather flush all of it.

Honestly, I'd kill for a cheeseburger.

Finally, I was near the fire and the heat barely touched the ice enveloping me as I pivoted to face them again. Ezra's expression was priceless. He wore the most manic fucking grin. It would be disturbing on a stranger, though I also couldn't say it wasn't a bit off-putting on his face. As it was though, I just went with it. Liam's face was a little more calculating, his attention solely focused on King.

As for King? If he were aware of his bishops, it didn't show. If anything, I had all of his notice and I planned to keep it. His agitation was a living thing, shrouding the room in stinging static. It was like being on stage, setting up for the next stunt. I knew the moves, for the dance was as much a part of me as the music. All I had to do was hit the beats.

Rome, though, was an island of calm in the middle of the storm. He didn't care about the dance. At least not this one. He was right there, his support a buffer against the crackling tension in the air.

"You are angry with me," King said after a significant pause, as if puzzled by my irritation. He glanced at the spread again, unbuttoning his jacket. "If you don't like the wine or the food, I can have something else sent up."

"I don't care about you one way or the other." Oddly, until I opened my mouth, I hadn't realized what I was going to say.

Obviously, *he* hadn't expected those words either. "We're here because you demanded to see all of us for some reason, and you have some unhealthy fascination with me."

"Unhealthy?" Insult discolored the word.

"Yes," I confirmed. "Unhealthy. So, let's cut through all the social bullshit and the dance of words that often accompany the knives in order to distract your opponent while you plant a blade in their back or order their companions and friends to kill them, and just talk honestly."

His mouth closed with a little click of his teeth coming together. The silence ballooned like hot air rushing in to fill the vacuum, only to explode with Ezra's laughter.

King jerked his eyes from me to where Ezra had moved to lean against one of the sofas. He looked like he didn't have a care in the world. More, his laughter carried a natural element of humor, even if he was deliberately provoking the bull. A smile pulled at my lips, for Ezra had to know what he was doing. The thing was—he clearly didn't care. King ordered Liam to kill Ezra's best friend. The only reason Ezra hadn't retaliated was because we had so many questions that needed answers.

Questions we may never actually get answered.

As long as we got rid of King and he couldn't hurt anyone again, I could live without the answers. Too many shadows in our past had suffocated me for too long. I didn't want to keep looking back.

I had too much to look forward to...

"I seem to have truly offended you," King said finally, reminding me that he was in the room with us. Leaving Ezra and Liam at his back, he crossed the room to where I stood. Rome shifted minutely. When he lifted his arm, I accepted the invitation to lean into him. The comfort of having them there, coupled with the awareness that all of them were waiting for us, and if we didn't come back from here?

They'd come and fucking get us.

"What makes you say that?" Infusing those words with polite curiosity was as easy as breathing. Mom taught me there were rules to every social interaction. Controlling those conversations took practice. I'd never mastered it. Mostly because I rarely went to those types of events of my own volition. I might be flying blind here, but I wasn't flying on my own.

"You just accused me of playing games."

I shrugged. "Do you deny it?"

Liam suppressed a smile, then cut a look at me. Warning gleamed in his eyes. I couldn't help shrugging. Not when King continued to stare at me. "No," he said slowly. "Though I wouldn't call this a game."

"Great," I said, taking comfort from Rome's strength. He wasn't holding me up, but he was keeping me steady. "Then what do you call it? Or—you know what, I don't care what you call it. What I want to know—is what do you want? What do you want from them? What do you want from me?" And since I could *not* let this go. "What do you want from my brother?"

Now, King's eyebrows rose. "Your brother?"

"Don't play dumb." Liam picked up the baton on this one and yanked all of King's attention away from me. "You sent Reed and Graham to recruit me because of my ties to the Vandals. It helped that my family had money—and I came with connections. Connections in the business world, in the world of the elite... and the Vandals."

I loved Liam so much as he took the tone I'd set and made it his own. Rather than stay where he was, he moved to stand next to me. It was like filling in the missing piece. When I ran a hand down his arm, he stared at King. I didn't try to take his hand. He needed those free, but I needed the contact.

Maybe he did too.

"I know for a fact you targeted Milo Hardigan." The verbal jab landed. It slammed into the king even though he didn't respond—at least not immediately. "You wanted me to help you set him up. You wanted him *removed* from the board. Ostensibly, because you perceived the Vandals as an obstacle to your plans for Braxton Harbor."

Rome snorted. He didn't buy that story any more than I did, or Liam, for that matter.

"You put me to work, asked me for information. Attempted a run at Rome—" Liam's voice dropped precipitously into a frigid territory. "Tested me every chance you got. You wanted me to deliver Milo to you on a silver platter, only I didn't play ball."

"So, you involved us," Ezra joined in, and that actually did what Liam's interruption hadn't—it *startled* King. Oh, did he not see the rebellion coming? Too bad. Ezra didn't shift from where he leaned with all the casual ease of a royal. If anything, he seemed kind of bored. "You wanted me and Adam to break Liam, to get him to cooperate enough with information to go after the guy. Didn't know him, didn't care about him. Still don't."

I didn't call Ezra on the lie of that last bit. He was digging the hole deeper for King. Unfurling the trap.

"When Liam cooperated though, you didn't get much. Frankly, you didn't get much from us either." Ezra shrugged. "There wasn't much there—and then he was arrested."

"Smelled suspicious," Liam said.

"It was suspicious," Ezra continued. "Even more when you realize that Adam was directed to remove the one witness who could have put Hardigan somewhere else."

Oh, they were both leaning into the Hardigan name. I wanted to smile, but I fought that need while I kept an eye on King. His demeanor had gone frostier and frostier. Someone was very unhappy with us.

He also wasn't confirming or denying.

"Witnesses are troublesome anyway," Ezra said. "You can't always trust memory. Especially traumatic memory. The threat worked, along with the money, to get the woman to agree to bring the charges."

"Are you insinuating that I set him up?" The warning in King's voice echoed loud and clear.

"Nope," Ezra said.

"We're saying it straight out," Liam added. "You did set him up. I've known Milo for most of my life. He didn't do what he was accused of. The measures taken to make sure he pled guilty were pretty extreme. They also involved blackmail."

"On more than one front," Ezra picked up the thread, batting it back and forth with Liam like a pro. "It wasn't *just* the witnesses, but law enforcement, from the cops to the D.A.'s office. You need money to pull that off."

"And influence…" Liam spread his hands. "You have both. Once he was off the board, you wanted the remaining Vandals scattered. You were willing to let *them* go…"

"Because your brother was still one," King reminded Liam like he needed it.

"And without Milo, you didn't give a damn about them anymore." Liam stared at King. "You didn't care until he was out of jail, and then suddenly, it was all you could talk about." Liam cut a look toward Ezra. "Sound about right?"

"Mostly—at least until Em there came along." Ezra winked at me. "Then it wasn't just this Hardigan boy you wanted to know more about, but her…"

"That didn't truly occur until after she was kidnapped," Liam countered. "With Rome."

"Eh," Ezra said. "She hadn't been kidnapped when he wanted you to kill Adam."

"You have a point."

"I often do."

"Are you two quite finished?" Oh, they'd made him mad, for the cultured tone vanished under a faint growl.

"They might be," I said. "I'm not."

It was like jumping into the middle of a game where you thought you knew how it was played but didn't know all the rules. In fact... I didn't know any of the rules.

"Of course, you aren't," King said, his expression darkening. The weird thing was, no matter how much I studied him. I couldn't see Milo or me. "Though your objections feel a little more performative, as does Graham's. Neither of you knew Hardigan before last year."

"Doesn't make him any less my brother or any less protective of me." Perhaps he needed to remember trying to force a little boy to choose. Or maybe he didn't care. "However Ezra's right, you had Adam killed because he asked me to marry him. You didn't wait to find out what I decided or why—you just swept him off the board like he didn't matter. You sent Milo to jail. You killed Adam. You tried to go after Rome—testing Liam's resolve or not. What next? You kill Ezra? You kill Liam?"

A muscle ticked in his jaw. He truly didn't like where this conversation was going.

"Maybe you want to kill me now. Honestly, I'm getting kind of used to it." Rome squeezed me gently, a reminder he was right there. "Trust isn't something that can just be given. It has to be earned. It has to be maintained. It has to be *valued*. Nothing I've seen or heard about you indicates either. You've manipulated, blackmailed, and abused your control over a group of *boys* for years."

"They aren't boys," King argued.

"Not now. Maybe they really weren't then, either. Only how old was Liam? Fifteen? Sixteen? You had Adam and Ezra before then. How old were they?"

"Your point?"

"Why were you recruiting children to do a job? Why did you go after another teenager—"

"He wasn't a teenager." In four words, he confessed what he hadn't actually admitted to from the beginning. King blew out a breath. "None of this has anything to do with why you were in a coffin." Someone wanted to take control again.

The memory of the lid closing and the dirt raining down on it spilled through me like a torrent.

The sounds of the video Fuckbucket played for Milo.

The pressure of his fingers on my face.

All of it, like a surgical incision, rolled through me. It was razor sharp—the pain, the loneliness, the fear...

...and the hope.

"It has everything to do with you, you son of a bitch," I said. "If you hadn't walked out on Milo and me when we were children, I would never have been adopted by the Sharpes."

Yeah.

I was done playing.

CHAPTER 26

ROME

Starling walked into this meeting quiet, reserved, and while not *withdrawn*, she wasn't *quite* in the same space as the rest of us. From the moment we stepped out of the vehicle, she let us make the calls. She moved with us when we closed in, and she held position. When the guards challenged us, she was ready. When we stepped into the elevator, she didn't complain about being nudged into the corner.

Arriving on this floor though, everything changed from the moment we stepped out of the elevator. I'd seen my mirror walk into a room and own it by the force of his glare alone. I'd seen him dominate in the ring, his determination rolling over the other guy before they even realized what was happening. Jasper had that effect on people, especially when he was looking for a fight. Milo could take over a room with a simple look.

Kel and Vaughn were quieter, yet it was a mistake to

think they didn't know every inch of the space they were in. Know it and own it. Doc flew lower, but he was always there and ready. Starling, though, was like Freddie. She took and took until she was done—then she struck. The beauty and grace, though, were all her.

Watching her square off against King was a marvelous thing. The man, a threat in his own right, had been caught utterly off guard, and she wasn't backing down an inch. Liam wasn't a fan, but he wasn't going to squash her, either. Even Ezra, the asshole, seemed to be all in.

Good.

"Walked out on you and your brother?" King repeated slowly.

"Problem with the truth?" She straightened from where she'd been resting against me. Riveted as I was by the sudden spread of her wings and the way she lifted her chin, I didn't miss Liam shifting his weight onto the balls of his feet. If King made one wrong move in her direction, we were going to end the game right here and right now.

Instead, King's gaze turned thoughtful and measured, as he smoothed a hand down his tie. "What gave me away?"

"I didn't come here to answer your questions," she countered. "I came to ask them."

"And to tell me someone put you in a coffin." No, the man hadn't forgotten that part. I was glad I hadn't been there to see that. Liam had described it to me, the jagged pain inside him slicing deep into me. The image would forever haunt my mirror and me.

Haunt all of us.

She shrugged. "Do you honestly care?"

"What I said earlier stands. Your enemies are my enemies."

"That's a problem when *you* might be one of *my* enemies." It was like watching Freddie work with his blade. The slices and cuts were vicious, delivered with a kind of deliberate grace that was almost artistic. Starling was not a timid bird. She had never been, but she'd never been the fierce predator she was right now.

I liked it.

"Why would I be your enemy, Emersyn?" King kept his focus wholly on her. It might be foolish to think he wasn't aware of them, but he directed his responses to her.

"You didn't want me—*then*." Her voice's absolute lack of emotion was a cut of a different type. One that pushed me closer to her. I just wanted to wrap around her and take her away from this place and this fight. It was her call to make, but King had hurt her before she even knew who he was. His disregard continued to hurt her.

"Did your brother tell you that?"

"Don't," she said with one slice of her hand, and King's gaze went flat. "Don't pretend you didn't know. You asked me why I didn't ask for protection for him. And don't begin to try and drive a wedge between me and Milo. You seem to excel at pitting people against each other. Makes sense. Men in power hold onto power by denying others the support structure to challenge them." Confidence flooded every single word she said. If I could capture the moment our broken bird became a blazing fiery bird, this would be it. "Isolate. Insulate. Triangulate. Whatever it takes to make each person wholly dependent on you and untrusting of others."

Spreading his hands, King offered no apologies. "You look like your mother. However, you are a lot tougher than she was."

Starling didn't respond to that compliment, if it was one. "Fine. I didn't know her."

Milo had though, she didn't add that piece.

"Are you going to answer the questions, or are you going

to keep playing this game?" So fierce and determined. For a brief moment, King looked thoughtful as he glanced at me, then Liam and Ezra, before gazing back at her.

"Let's sit down," he said. "I understand your feelings are strong and you have some issues. I have questions, and you have questions. You answer one. I'll answer one. We'll work our way through them that way."

Liam spared Starling a look. Did she want to do that?

"I don't really want to sit."

That answered that question.

"Nevertheless, you want answers," King countered.

"And you won't offer them any other way?"

"Everything is a negotiation, Emersyn. The sooner you accept that you cannot control everything, the simpler this will be."

I focused on him now. "That was a threat."

Surprise appeared in King's eyes. Yes, I could speak. I just didn't usually choose to speak to him.

"Not exactly," he countered. "My—" The hesitation echoed in the silence around us. "Emersyn," he corrected, catching himself redirecting his attention back to her. "Please, sit."

It was the please that signaled his capitulation. At least for this round. I wasn't the only one who heard it. Some of the tension leaked out of Ezra and Liam, but not all. None of us trusted him.

None of us would.

Least of all Starling.

"I don't need to sit. In fact," she continued. "I don't want to."

"Then what do you want?" King asked, his brows tightening as his jaw tensed.

A dozen unspoken answers lingered in the room all around us.

Rather than dismiss his question out of hand, Starling looked thoughtful. "Liam?"

He glanced over his shoulder to where we stood, staring at her. Did she want him to answer the question? I didn't think so. Based on the assessment in his eyes, he didn't think so either.

"It's your play, Hellspawn." The concession was huge for my mirror. Then again, what wouldn't we do for her?

Then, as if remembering King was still present, we all looked at him again.

"I want Bradley Sharpe," she said, distaste in every single word, then held up a hand when King opened his mouth. "His location. His hiding spots. His security."

"If you want him dead..." King began.

"Did I stutter?" She kept her head up and her shoulders back. King appeared more amused than irritated.

"No," he said slowly. "I suppose you didn't." Amusement seemed to gloss over the darker parts of his expression. "Very well, you want information. What do I get?"

"What do you want?" There was a warning in her tone, a warning King would be wise to heed, because Starling had enough pieces carved away from her.

She didn't owe him anything.

He *wouldn't* be taking anything, either.

"To be determined," King said and it was Liam who sliced a hand through the air.

"That doesn't work for me," he said. I was glad my mirror interrupted. It didn't work for me either. "No open-ended favors. She wants information. You can ask for something of equal or lesser value, or you can just do this as a show of good faith in the hope that she might actually deign to speak to you again."

Liam's tone stated that the chances of her actually speaking to him again were located somewhere between never and not a chance in hell. This man walked away from her. Walked away from Milo.

On the one hand, we wouldn't know them if he hadn't. On the other…

They had *suffered* because of him.

We wouldn't allow him to hurt them again.

Ever.

Taking a step back, King rubbed his jaw and then moved over to the bar, where he took some time to drop ice cubes into a tumbler before splashing it with an amber liquid. He downed the whole measure before he added another splash of alcohol.

The silence in the room grew taut as he kept his back to us. The reflective surface above his bar gave him an excellent angle of the room. It would be a mistake to think he couldn't see us coming.

Killing him, while an option, wasn't the goal today. I didn't think. His reactions to Starling were hard to read. Even more difficult now that he seemed to be guarding them after he'd been called on his identity.

He confirmed, but he didn't explain. I glanced at Starling, who tracked King's every move with a kind of lethal focus. She'd become more and more of who she truly was over the last year, but the past week had changed something in her irrevocably.

I wasn't sure if everyone saw it or if it was just me. But Starling wasn't a broken bird anymore. She didn't have damaged wings. Her pin feathers were no longer absent.

She'd been remade in fire and smoke. The ash of her destruction was torn away in a flash, leaving the truest form of herself. My hands itched for paint. I wanted to capture all of this.

For now, I settled for memorizing it all for later.

Finally, King turned. "I will find Sharpe. I will get you

everything you want. I am assuming you also want access to your funds..."

She gave the most careless of shrugs. "If I want my trusts now, all I have to do is marry."

King cut a look to Liam, who met his gaze steadily.

"That didn't answer my question," he informed her.

"Good. Find where Sharpe is. Get me that information—then I'll think about talking to you again."

"Your brother?"

She shook her head once. "You don't get to ask me about him. I won't tell you anything."

King swirled the drink in his glass as if the answers he wanted were in there. Somehow, I doubted it...

"Very well. Does this mean you will not be staying for the meal?"

"It does mean that," Liam said in a flat voice. "She already said she wasn't a fan of the food options."

Eyes narrowed, King quirked his lips. "Very well. Next time—and there will be a next time—I will request a list of acceptable dishes and wines."

Starling surprised us all when she laughed. "You sound very confident that *there will be a next time.*"

"Because I am. Those two still work for me," he said with a nod toward Ezra and Liam, "at least for the moment. Though, I suppose if I directed you to protect her, Bishops, this wouldn't be a problem."

Ezra snorted and didn't bother to answer. Liam just stared at him.

"Times change," she said. "Call Liam when you know where Sharpe is."

Not call me.

Not message me.

Liam.

I approved.

So did my mirror.

"As you wish," King said. "Nevertheless, understand I am doing you this favor. I will not ask for repayment, but I will require another meeting."

"Require what you want," Starling told him as she reached for my arm. Liam and Ezra were already moving to block King from us. "Right now, I'm going home. I would suggest, however, if you want to invite us to dinner—you issue the invitation and let us RSVP at our convenience."

King actually seemed puzzled, but Starling no longer paid any attention to him. She focused on me.

"I'm tired."

That was all I needed to know. Liam motioned me toward the elevator, and I took point with Starling tucked next to me. Behind us, Ezra and Liam said several pointed things, but I didn't care about King anymore.

The ride down in the elevator was silent. Still, Ezra smirked when the doors opened as security cleared the way for us to leave via the garage exit. It wasn't until we were at the car and Ezra held the door open for her, that he said anything.

"Remind me never to piss you off," he said. "That was very entertaining but also very dangerous."

For her part, Starling shrugged. "I don't care about his opinion, and he wasn't touching me when you guys were there."

No one was touching her without her permission again.

"Hellspawn," Liam said on a sigh once we were back in the car.

"Scold me later?" Tired filtered through her voice, and I pulled the seatbelt over to lock her in before wrapping an arm around her again.

He studied her for a moment then locked gazes with me.

Worry reflected back at me from my mirror—a worry I shared.

I nodded once. We would take care of her. "Let's go home," I said, and it was Liam's turn to nod.

Starling wanted to go home.

We were going home.

CHAPTER 27

EMERSYN

I was shaking by the time we settled into the back of the car. I wasn't even aware of it until Rome tucked me closer and rested his head against mine as he covered my hands in my lap.

The temperature in the parking garage, and then in the car, was almost too brisk. But I couldn't make up my mind if I was cold or hot. Either way, when Rome wrapped me up, I curled into him. The seatbelt kept me from just crawling into his lap, but I tried to steady myself with the even cadence of his heartbeat.

The ride back to the clubhouse carried a wealth of tension in the silence. It wasn't oppressive, but awareness of Liam's gaze tracking to mine in the rearview mirror accompanied Rome's slow stroke against my back. Even with Liam driving, I was wrapped up in the cocoon of both of them.

Back at the warehouse, Rome didn't exit the car until Liam and Ezra were out, and Kellan was already crossing to us from the clubhouse door to greet us. Rome slid out first, then reached a hand in to me. As soon as I was out, Liam crushed me to him and I returned his fierce grip even as I met Kellan's worried gaze.

Some of the tension in Kellan seemed to ease as he gave me a once-over. "I'm in one piece," I promised.

"Even if someone wanted to wave the flag at the bull and challenge him on every level." Liam's growl sent a shiver through me as he flattened a hand against my back and kept me in place. Since I was drinking in his nearness, I just settled there. The thump of his heart was as steadying as Rome's had been.

"Look," I said, trying to get a grip on my own fluttering emotions. It was so much easier to hold it together when I'd been standing in that office than now. My reactions had been arrested, and now I was shaking everywhere. "You were the one who called me Hellspawn."

Kellan scrubbed a hand over his face, but exasperation joined his relief as Liam chuckled. "Too late to take it back, huh?"

"Yep," I said, and when I eased backward, I lifted my gaze to Liam's worried one. The last thing I wanted to do was scare them. But I was done hiding. "Nothing was happening to me. You guys wouldn't have allowed it. And I had your backs."

"You know," Ezra mused. "I *almost* miss the timid Emersyn."

"I don't," I told him, perhaps a bit too vehemently, because Liam scowled at Ezra, who immediately raised his hands.

"Right, shutting up. Going to get a beer and check on— well, check on the dead and the not-so-dead…"

Silence blanketed us until he vanished inside the clubhouse doors, and then Kellan stared at me for a beat before lifting his gaze to Liam. "How did it go?"

"Starling verified that King knows who she and Milo are." Rome shrugged, the ease in his statement put another smile on my face. "She also challenged him to find Bradley Sharpe—"

Kellan frowned.

"Information only," I admitted. "If he kills him—well, I won't be that disappointed."

"I will," Liam grumbled. "I want to skin that son of a bitch."

Head tilted back, I smiled up at him. "I don't want King targeting any of you. Especially after his vague and not-so-vague threats."

"I don't want you taking him on either," Liam retaliated, but his eyes softened as he stared at me. "Hellspawn, we just dug you out of a grave. I need you to not dare someone else to toss you back into one."

Intensity blazed in his eyes. "Did I really scare you?" Because if I had—

"No," Liam complained even as Rome said, "Yes."

Liam scowled at Rome, and his twin just stared back at him, unperturbed. Kellan, however, chuckled and the rough amusement pulled at all of us. "In other words, you did scare him, but he enjoyed your feistiness."

"Fuck both of you," Liam muttered, but some of the rumblings eased when I curled into him again. "The guy has an agenda. One we've always known he had, just not the details."

"His agenda didn't include Sparrow before," Kellan admitted, and I had to turn that over in my head. I didn't think it had either. At least until...

"I don't know if he knew about the Sharpes *immediately.* Maybe he did—and that's why Adam's move annoyed him. However, Milo said I looked just like our mother."

Kellan glanced at me where I had my ear pressed to

Liam's chest. For the most part, I wanted to hug all of them, but it was Liam who had a faint tremble going on. Anger, adrenaline, or fear? Maybe some combination of the above. It seemed to vibe in time with my own. I wasn't afraid of King. Not when we were in his office. Not now.

"He wants something from me," I continued. "I don't know what he wants, specifically, but he wants something. From the moment he *met* me, he's acted like I was one of the Royals. And if that were all it was, I wouldn't care…" Liam was one of them, too, even if he was only one because he'd allowed himself to be recruited to protect Milo.

Adam had been one until King ordered him killed. Ezra? Ezra was in the middle of all this, and I didn't think we knew half of what he was involved in. His guard remained up. Then again, did any of us know what he'd been dealing with in Adam's absence? Maybe I should talk to Lainey.

Arms folded, Kellan dipped his chin. "So, while he may not be an enemy we need to worry about right now, he's not a friend."

"No," I said with a slow shake of my head. "I don't trust him. Not at all."

"Agreed," Liam said, finally loosening his grip on me. He squeezed my arms gently before he rubbed them up and down. Even if he was relaxing, he wasn't letting me go.

"He wants Starling's approval," Rome said, and we all stared at him. If Rome were as worried as the others, it didn't show.

"How so?" Liam asked, his attention shifting to his twin.

"The food," Rome said with a shrug. "She criticized it. He didn't like that."

Had I? Oh, I guess I had. "I *hate* that wine," I admitted. "It's one of Fuckbucket's favorites."

Kellan's expression darkened.

Rome shrugged. "He wants to impress you."

"Why?" That was the part I didn't get. "He didn't want me before."

"You were a baby before," Rome said.

"You are definitely not now," Kellan said. "You're also an heiress."

I didn't care about that part.

"And your family has power," Liam reminded me. "So maybe he wants access to that wealth."

I made a face.

"I know you don't want to think of them as yours, Sparrow," Kellan said slowly, and I shook my head.

"It's not that—it's just that all of it comes with so much baggage. Even if we kill him—then what? I inherit everything?" I made a face. Was I really just talking about killing Fuckbucket as we would talk about the weather? "We could use the money and at the same time…"

"You don't want anything he touched," Rome said, and I twisted to look at him. Liam looped an arm around my waist and kept me tucked to him with my back to his chest.

"No," I said. "I don't want that…"

"It's your money," Liam said softly. "I know you hate him, and you have every right in the world to hate him. But the Sharpes adopted you. They made you their family. That means that inheritance is *yours*."

Head to his shoulder, I lifted my gaze to the ceiling. The catwalks up there were easy to forget.

Somewhere up there were cameras, nested amongst the metal walks and braces. We had them everywhere.

Inside and out.

I still needed to get a look at Liam's private collection. If he recorded us, I wanted—

All at once, my stomach pitted. He wasn't the only one who had recordings. The difference was all in the two men, my age, and who I chose to be with.

"We don't need to decide anything right now," Kellan said. The three of them kept me steady. They chased away the shadows. They all did. I wanted to be able to forget. What if I never could?

Could I just replace those bad memories with better ones? Or what...?

Sadness crept out of the shadows to curl through me. Milo had wanted me to talk to someone other than them, someone to help me cope, and that person had been Ms. Stephanie. I'd never told her...but that hadn't protected her from Fuckbucket's wrath. The sadness turned to anger all over again.

"I'm tired," I admitted.

As if propelled by my confession, the guys shepherded me inside where the others were waiting. Milo was sleeping. But he was doing fine, according to Mickey, with some marked improvement, and Lainey had gotten him to eat. The infection also seemed to be getting better.

The news unlocked so much relief that I might have fallen if Liam hadn't been holding onto me still. When it came time to crash though, there was a debate on who would sleep where.

"Why don't we all just crash out here?" I suggested. When we were renovating, we added this massive sofa and set up the sitting room so there was plenty of room for everyone. "If we squash the ottomans in—"

"Blankets," Jasper said as he peeled off to one room.

"I'll get pillows," Freddie said, disappearing into his room.

"Go get changed, Little Bit." Mickey pressed a kiss to the side of my head. "I'll get us some popcorn and..."

All of us were out here to sleep, which meant we'd probably turn on movies too. "Hot cocoa?" I asked. Mickey grinned, and Vaughn gave me a thumb's-up behind him.

"Hot cocoa it is."

Liam prowled right into the bedroom with me. Instead of following me around my room as I changed, he leaned against the door. His expression didn't invite conversation, but I kept an eye on him as I stripped out of the jacket, then my gun harness. With each layer I peeled off, I checked on him. I hated this—weight of him, the tight lost feeling expanding and contracting around him.

Still, he said nothing until I came out from washing my face in the bathroom and stood there holding one of Vaughn's t-shirts. I had a whole drawer of their t-shirts. I'd pilfered one from each of them, but it hadn't escaped my notice that more had also been creeping into my drawers.

"What can I do?" I asked as I faced him.

"I took my eyes off you the first time, and you got up on a stage and danced in a damn topless bar." Focusing on me, Liam exhaled a long breath. "I took my eyes off you—and you got on a plane to go back to your uncle to save us."

My stomach bottomed out.

"I took my eyes off you, and you ended up in a facility with wounds, drugs, and who the fuck knows what else..."

I closed the gap and put my hands on his chest.

Covering my hands with his, he kept his gaze fixed on mine. "I took my eyes off you, and you disappeared with Rome because some asshole took you thinking it was me."

His throat bobbed as he swallowed.

"Then I took my eyes off you, and when we found you—you were in a grave."

If I could do nothing else, I just wanted to soothe the raw pain in his voice and eyes.

"My dad died, Hellspawn. They killed him. Tried to kill all of us. Killed Ms. Stephanie. But we made it...and then I found you in a grave." His voice broke on that last. "I don't dare take my eyes off you again—and tonight? Tonight, you walked in there and waved a red flag at a bull, then tasered him until you ensured he would charge at you."

The words "I'm sorry" were glued to the roof of my mouth. I couldn't apologize for that. King needed to know where I stood, but at the same time...

"I have never loved another person the way I love you," Liam confessed. "You fill this space inside me that I didn't know was missing. You complete all of us. You paper over the cracks and fill them with gold."

Tears burned in my eyes.

"I *love* you, Hellspawn. I will do everything in my power to avenge you, to help you get vengeance. And I will kill anyone who puts a hand on you that isn't one of us..."

There was no boasting in that statement. No bravado. His calm, almost cool tone never wavered. This wasn't blistering fury, it was ice-cold confidence.

"But?" It seemed like there was one there, hanging unspoken. Except Liam just shook his head.

"But nothing—if you want King dead, I'll make it happen. If you never want to see him again, I'll make that happen too." He let go of my hands to cradle my face. "If you want to declare war on every single one of those families involved in the Bay Ridge Royals, I will be the general in that army. The only thing you have to do—is *stay* alive. Do you understand me? No more crazy fucking risks or stunts. You don't do anything without us."

"To be fair," I said slowly. "I didn't do this without you. I know I lashed out when that wasn't the plan, but from the moment I saw him—all I could see was him hurting Milo."

A smile pulled at the corners of Liam's mouth. "You wanted to protect your brother."

"You know a little something about that," I teased, and he leaned in to press his lips to my forehead.

"I know everything about that. But I need you alive,

Hellspawn. I need you alive, in my life, in my arms, in my bed…and not necessarily in that order."

A laugh escaped me. "I need you too…"

"Good." When he closed his arms around me, I pressed my forehead to his chest.

"I am so sorry about your father."

"Me too," he whispered, and my heart ripped for the loss there. He really hadn't had time to grieve. None of them had. "Promise me, Hellspawn, no matter what…"

"I promise."

"You don't even know what I was going to ask."

"I don't need to—you want me alive and where you can see me. I'm not going anywhere. I promise."

"Good." He blew out another breath.

"Can I ask for one thing?"

He pulled back to give me an almost indulgent smile. "Just one thing?"

"Just one thing right now."

"Better," he said with a genuine smile, more of the tension easing from his face. "What can I promise you?"

"Will you fly with me again? You and Rome?"

"Yes." Not even a moment of hesitation and it buoyed me higher. "Whenever and wherever—I'll make it safe for you."

I had an idea for that—but later. "Thank you." Then, because he was still wound taut, I stripped off the rest of my clothes. Liam's gaze fastened to me as I stepped out of my shoes, and then my dress was next.

When I finally pulled the Velcro on my vest, his eyes heated, and then there was just me in a bra and panties. Head tilted, I spread my arms and did a slow turn.

"Where do you want me?"

He straightened and then crooked his finger to me. I narrowed that gap and when I would have reached up to him, he caught my hands and put them on the door. "Hands stay here, Hellspawn." His lips barely moved as he whispered into my ear, punctuating the sentence as he nipped my earlobe. "Not a sound," he continued. "I want you to stand here and take it for me."

Anticipation shivered through me as he palmed my ass.

"I think you earned four tonight..."

"Four?" I let out a breathless whisper, and Liam's low chuckle had my cunt clenching.

"That's five," he said in a voice so satisfied that I shuddered. Then he landed the first slap on my right ass cheek. It burned before he massaged the warmth and spread it out. "Yes, definitely five—now that was one. Are you going to be a good girl for me?"

I licked my lips. Did I want to be a good girl? Not particularly at the moment. But Liam needed me to be a good girl, so I nodded—just once, and he kissed my shoulder before unhooking my bra and sliding it off. I didn't lower my arms, though. He hadn't said for me to take my hands off the wall.

"So good for me, Hellspawn. Lose the bra." I dropped my arms so it could slide off. "Hands back on the door."

Control threaded every word, and they looped over me like his own personal caresses. When he peeled my panties down, I waited for the word to lift my feet. Another low chuckle escaped him, dark and delicious.

"Good girl, lift your feet one at a time." Once my panties were off, he bit down against the curve of my ass where it met my leg. A whimper wanted to escape, but I sucked on my lip to keep it in place. Then he nuzzled kisses to where my legs met and teased his tongue along the slit of my cunt. When he tapped the inside of my thighs to spread them, it took all of my control to stay quiet.

Every lap of his tongue made me shiver, and when he slid his finger along to tease my clit, the whimper escaped. This time, his chuckle was positively devilish. "That's another two."

Before I could protest, he circled my clit with more pressure as he thrust his tongue in and my knees went weak, my whimper turning into a mewling sound. I was right there and he backed off. I couldn't even slap my hand against the door. All at once, Liam rose.

"Hold on, Hellspawn," he murmured, and then his hand landed six slaps, three to each cheek. Then, he massaged the heat to spread out the fire on my ass. I didn't have time to catch my breath before he thrust into me. The angle, coupled with his thickness, pushed all the air out of my lungs, and I fought to stay quiet as he drilled into me.

Every thrust lit me up. I put pressure on my hands to stay coherent and then he cupped my breasts and pinched my nipples as he bit down on my earlobe.

"Fuck I love you," he whispered in my ear, and I think I came from those words alone. The orgasm tore me apart and pulled me back together again as he pumped a few more times. Each time his hips ground against my burning ass, the pleasure seemed to unravel within me. When he came, I would have collapsed if he didn't hold me up.

A knock sounded on the door. "Let Boo-Boo out, Liam. We're having a slumber party."

Laughter escaped me, and Liam pulled me from the door to rest against him. He cupped my face, then stroked his thumb along my cheek. "You and me," he whispered.

"Forever," I panted. That was a promise I intended to keep.

After brushing a whisper of a kiss to my lips, he said, "Don't ever leave me again, Hellspawn. I can take pretty much anything, but not that."

I didn't want to leave him. I didn't want to leave any of them.

"You're stuck with me," I told him, and he tightened his grip on me as someone else knocked on the door."

"Let's go," Jasper said. "Get your asses out here."

"Fuck off," Liam grumbled, and I laughed. He pulled out of me and I shuddered at the sudden absence, even though he was already turning me around. After a long, thorough kiss, he carried me into the bathroom. The cool tile felt fantastic against my ass and he was gentle while he cleaned me up. He waited until I wore a t-shirt and panties before walking me to the door.

"Go on," he urged, giving me one gentle swat. "I'm gonna change, and I'll be out." He leaned out of the door to eye the room. "And whoever thinks they're next to her, don't get comfortable. At least one of those spots is mine."

"Hey…" Freddie protested with a grin, but Liam just shut the door. I laughed as Freddie slung an arm over my shoulders. "Possession is nine-tenths of the law."

"True," Vaughn said, scooping me up and carrying me to the sofa. "And now I have her—" He barely set me down before Jasper plowed into him. In turn, they dragged Kel into the shoving match that Rome avoided as he eased over the side of the sofa to land next to me.

"Oh, for the love of…" Mickey scowled as he tried to separate the guys, and that just got Freddie involved. Fifteen minutes later, and one dumped bowl of popcorn, we were all settled across the sofas. I was tucked between Liam and Mickey, with Freddie beside my feet. The others sprawled out on the couch as the movie started.

I had no idea what we watched, but it was amazing.

Or maybe that was just them.

CHAPTER 28

DOC

*T*he vibration of my watch woke me. Sleeping light was something you did in the field. It was also something I would be doing whenever Little Bit was near me when we were sleeping: discipline and focus. I wouldn't risk her again. It was dark in the sitting room; the soft sound of multiple snores at varying levels reminded me of where I was and who was there.

Scrubbing a hand over my face, I checked my watch when it vibrated again. The messages were from Alphabet. Right, I needed to answer him. I checked on Little Bit, and she was curled up on top of Liam, sound asleep. It was kind of funny. While she'd been between us during the movie and drifted off there, somewhere in the night, she'd rolled over.

Liam had an arm around her and one hand splayed against her back. Her whole body blanketed his, but she was too slight to make an effective blanket. A sweet one? Yes, effective? Probably not. Easing forward, I draped my blanket over the pair of them. At least the illumination from the television let me see to step over where Jasper was sprawled. The huge sofa was at least comfortable.

I stretched, popping some of the vertebrae as I picked my way off the sofa and over the guys. Vaughn lifted his head, gave me a look, scanned for Little Bit, and then grunted before rolling over. Made sense since I had needed to know where she was too. Tugging on a pair of jeans, I zipped them up before I grabbed my phone off the charger and let myself out of the suite. The clubhouse was quiet as I eyed the hallway. Milo and Lainey were in the room at the far end, and Adam Reed sat in a chair just outside the room, head back as if he were sleeping.

He wasn't, because he sat forward briefly to stare at me before resuming his napping position. There was no sign of Bodhi or Ezra. That was fine. My watch vibrated with another message and I headed for the stairs. I rolled my head as I walked into the kitchen. It was cooler down here, with only the hum of the fridge to provide background noise.

I scanned the messages from Alphabet, then called him while I got a pot of coffee going. The fancy coffee maker was great for Little Bit, but I was fine with real coffee.

"Morning, Doc. Thought I was gonna end up calling you, but since I didn't know if you had your girl, I kept it to texts." Alphabet sounded a little jittery. "I've been tearing through firewalls and found the little bastard."

Swallowing my criticism for his caffeine intake, I said, "Sharpe?"

"Let me correct this, I found his money. I'm still playing whack-a-mole with his hiding places, and he's hired a damn good team to relocate him. Not the best team, for that would be us, and we don't work for pricks like him." The words spilled out of Alphabet in a rush. "But I found his money. The thing with big corporations, they have to keep legitimate books and cash on hand. Sure, they can borrow against profits and interest, but eventually, it must be paid back. Now, if you borrow from yourself and raise the interest, then get a loan to consolidate, you can actually double your profits while cutting your bottom line in half."

The coffee hissed and spit. "Alphabet—we getting to a point in this financial lecture?" 'Cause I wanted Sharpe. I wanted to filet him until he was a skinless husk, dead and buried. No—not buried. That conjured images of Little Bit in that goddamn coffin. I wanted to burn the motherfucker alive, make sure it *really* hurt.

"Yeah, definitely a point. See, here's the thing about hiring a solid team, you gotta pay 'em. They aren't the kind that will take an IOU or wait around for you to move some money through numbered accounts, launder it carefully, then transfer it to Bitcoin to be paid out somewhere else totally untraceable. No, they want cash, and they want it upfront. If you were stuck guarding a piece of shit, you wouldn't want to give them a chance to weasel out of it."

That made sense. "They aren't going to accept anything not tangible."

"Exactly," Alphabet almost hissed the word, triumph punching it up. "So, to keep himself solvent while on the move, while hiding his assets, he did two things—one is really fucking smart. Almost too smart to have come from this piece of shit—" Real anger discolored that description. "The other is so common, I damn near overlooked it. And I feel like a fucking idiot."

"You didn't overlook it." Bones was with him, and his voice came in loud and clear.

"I didn't, but I almost did and while I want praise, I deserve a punch to the face."

"I'll sign an IOU to be paid on delivery if you get to the fucking point." I didn't mean to growl, but the coffee was hissing and spitting, my eyes were gritty, and any conversation that involved Bradley Sharpe just pissed me off. We should have killed him a long time before.

A.

Long.

Time.

Before.

"' If only's' will make you insane if you live your life that way," Steph said as she glanced at me over the rim of her coffee cup. I'd just told her why I was taking the deal for the army, and I couldn't believe... "I'm not letting you off the hook for the actions you took or the responsibilities you have. But you will go mad if you try to live your life based on 'if only's'. The past is immutable. We can't change it. We can only learn and do our best to build a better future."

"I wish it was that easy." I rubbed my face, but her expression only gentled.

"Mickey, are you going to make the same mistakes?"

"I fucking hope not," I said, then grimaced. "I won't be cavalier."

"Then that's all you can do." She reached across the table and gripped my hand. "You're a good man, Mickey. You may not have always made good decisions, but if you learn from the ones you have made—good and bad alike—I think you'll be just fine."

Fuck, I missed her.

Alphabet laughed, then groaned. "Sorry, Doc. I'm a little hyped up at the moment because they've really made me work to find them. If I didn't think he was such a waste of fucking space, I'd be impressed. As it is, I'm annoyed."

"Alphabet," Bones said, his voice steady and commanding. It was enough to hook Alphabet back around to the point.

"Right, money. Much of the family capital has been rolled into three major trust accounts."

Little Bit.

"Corporate accounts are untouchable, but they are

floating on solvency right now. They have just enough to meet all obligations and very little extra because profits are bled off into four separate accounts—but only three are trusts."

"The fourth account?" I asked because Alphabet had been busting ass on this, and I appreciated his efforts.

"That's the one I found most interesting. It's a shell within a shell within another shell, where the money goes in and doesn't come back out to another account, but once you drill down, the cash isn't there either. It's been removed, steady withdrawals, all standard amounts, just enough to fly under Federal radars, but done daily until each new infusion is bled out."

Cash.

"He's literally working with straight cash."

"Yep," Alphabet said, the smug note in his voice giving away to irritation. "You can't track cash as easily unless you've marked the bills, but that still requires a lot of intervention..."

"You can't move that much cash easily either."

"You complete me," Alphabet said with a laugh. "See, Doc, this is why you're my favorite. Because no, you can't. Particularly when we're talking *millions*, quite possibly *billions*."

"Trucks."

"Then step on my moment," Alphabet grumbled. "Yeah—trucks. Makes sense. I feel stupid that I didn't think about it. Been digging into a lot of these different companies for other reasons—so I don't know why I didn't make the connection. Trucking companies have the inside track on the best routes. They have eyes everywhere, and you know what weigh stations are open and which ones aren't. So, you bypass the ones you don't want to have a look at what you're doing. That said, moving cash is heavy work, but you can *hide* it easier than you can drugs or contraband because no one trains *cash* sniffing dogs or devices."

I lifted the carafe from the machine and poured a large cup of coffee.

"Do you have a line on the trucking companies they're using?"

There was a beat of silence.

"He does," Bones answered for him. "This is where it gets tricky."

"They're in the Network." The Network was useful; they provided many opportunities over the years, but you had to be willing to get your hands dirty most of the time. That had begun to shift in recent months, but I was still much more invested in the wait-and-see than trusting these rather brutal changes to the structure. There were pieces of the Network that had been excised like a cancer, but they hadn't been eradicated.

Yet.

"Not precisely," Alphabet said. "They're not all the way out of the Network. Reportedly, they still do business inside it enough to keep them protected—"

"But not enough so that they are wholly insulated or controlled by the new rules."

"Yep," Bones said. "So—we take a risk going after them."

"It'd be a risk going after anyone. If they have all his cash, I want it—burn it if we have to—but cut him off from his funds."

"You want to burn *billions*?" Alphabet sounded like he would cry. There was a light thwap sound. "Ow, I didn't say we wouldn't do it. Just—man, that's a lot of money."

"Blood money. Not saying we couldn't do something else with it, but I want it completely out of his hands." And at the same time... "I need to get Kel up. Brief him. Now that we know what company is doing the hauling? What do we know about *them*?"

"I'm—ow, shit, Bones. I said I'd sleep, but I had to call him and he needs more info."

"I'll work on it. You go to bed." Bones wasn't asking. "He's pretty hopped up on caffeine and junk food. The sugar high is only going to last so long. Brief your people. I'll get you everything I have—then recommend that we talk to the Network directly."

"I'll keep it in mind, and Bones is right, Alphabet. Knock it off and sleep. Doctor's orders. You're no good to anyone if you collapse."

"Goddamn, you wanna give me a kiss before you slap me on the ass like that?" His grumbling made me smile.

"Sorry, A, I'm taken."

"Yeah, yeah, yeah," he muttered, before he sobered. "Sorry, I didn't make the connection sooner. We have the scent now, though, Doc. We'll get the bastard."

"You did good." Then there were shuffling, muffled comments.

"It's just us now," Bones said. "Lunchbox and Gracie are gonna sit on Alphabet until he sleeps."

"Good." I downed a long drink of the almost too-hot coffee. The scald against my throat hurt, but I kind of wanted the pain right now. It brought clarity and helped to dull the pain in my heart which was still a gaping wound.

"Talk to me about the end game here," Bones said. "We take the money, burn it. Cut him off from his security, then what? We just erasing the problem or…"

"No," I said slowly. "I just need you guys to box the target. Elimination will come from our side."

"Understood."

Silence held us on the phone, and I stared at the fridge as I took another drink of coffee.

"Bones?"

"Yep?"

"Thanks."

"Anytime."

Then the call was over and I drained my coffee. One more cup, and I'd roust Kellan. We had plans to make.

CHAPTER 29

JASPER

*L*arge gatherings were something I was getting used to again. With all the people crammed into the clubhouse, it was hard to believe how commonplace this used to be—though, to be fair, we had seven more bodies here than normal.

Technically, nine, but Swan had always been with us, even when she hadn't been here physically. Scratching at my beard, I turned that concept over in my head. It was more than fifty-fifty, I guessed. She had been here, but the spirit of her that we held onto could not hold a candle to the light her presence created.

Then there was Milo's girl...and I couldn't really say she had always been with us, she *fit*. Not like Swan did—Swan was in our blood and bones. But her BFF fit. I wouldn't have pinned her for it when she first showed up—then again, I didn't give a damn about "Ball-Cracker," as Freddie called her, except she earned our gratitude and protection for her absolute loyalty to Swan.

I tracked my gaze to where our girl perched on the arm of Vaughn's chair, with one foot against the side of Freddie's. We'd had to drag all the spare furniture in for this.

Bodhi, Adam, Ezra, and Doc's guys were ranged around the room, threading in and around us, but Ezra and Adam were firmly planted near Milo and Lainey. Milo shouldn't even be at this meeting, but he'd been every inch Raptor when he refused another day in bed. So much, he'd walked himself down here despite the objections from Doc and Lainey.

Surprisingly, or maybe I should have seen it coming, it was Swan who backed her brother and supported his damn stubborn notion. Took one to know one, I supposed. Kellan nudged me, and I glanced at him.

"You good?" He offered the question in such a low voice that I doubted it carried.

"Worried." The moment the word left me, I tasted its absolute truth. "We have a lot to lose."

"Yeah," Kellan said. "I feel that." We weren't just looking at Emersyn but the room filled with friends, lovers, brothers, and allies. There were definitely wild cards in this room— Bodhi Cavendish was one of them—but every single one of these people had come through for us.

"Not sure how I feel about relying on so many outsiders." That was the other part. Loyalty and friendship weren't always so tightly intertwined. I trusted a relatively small group of people. Now we had to expand that circle.

"Something has to give," Kellan reminded me. "This is the journey. We have only one way to go."

Through.

The only way out of the darkness was to plunge through

it and just go. Trust those who had our backs and fight our way to the other side.

"Any idea what that's gonna look like when we get there?" 'Cause it seemed a lot like hope, which was also really hard to trust.

"Nope," Kellan said before he flashed a real smile. "I think that's the surprise at the bottom of the box—for all of us."

I snorted, even if I liked the sound of it. To be fair, nothing in our lives had been fair. The bright spots were even brighter now, though, because they truly illuminated our journeys.

"Focus up, people," Kellan said as he took command and the varying conversations fell away as everyone turned to look at him. Another net positive to come from my choices—while it hadn't been my intention, Kellan stepping up to take the lead from Milo after he returned was one of our better decisions.

He had the level-headed focus to see the choices in front of us without letting his own bias control the narrative. I was so much better as "the bash their heads in guy." If we needed a door kicked in or asses handed to people, that was my specialty.

And I *liked* doing it. Right now, I really wanted to kick in whatever doors we had to in order to get our hands on Bradley Sharpe.

Erase him from the board, then Julius Fucking King, if Milo and Swan wanted it. Whatever it took. Erase them, get on with our lives, and give Swan the freedom she'd craved all these years.

It would be Christmas come—well, not early. But Christmas, nonetheless.

"We have a lot of data to go over and a lot of decisions to make." Kellan clasped his hands behind his back. He was almost standing at parade rest. There'd been a brief moment where he'd flirted with going into the military. Looking at him now?

I believed it. I was just glad he'd stuck around. I flicked a look to Doc, glad that he had come home. While I might always resent those years he was gone—there was a rational and reasonable explanation for it, didn't change my feelings on the subject—but I was ready to let it go as much as I could.

"We've got a lead on the money," Kellan said. "Both the money in the trusts and the cash Sharpe is using to pay his mercenaries. The transport company could be a problem, but I've reached out to our contact in the Network to try and smooth over those cracks."

He spent exactly five minutes making sure everyone had the same info. Doc's team had given it to him, and Alphabet filled in any gaps. Milo's frown deepened as we got the complete picture.

"It's going to require us to split up," he said, and the distaste for that idea was one we all shared.

"To a point," Kellan said. "But we're not sending anyone off alone or in ones and twos. We'll be assigning groups and moving as teams, coordinating all efforts centrally."

"With Alphabet?" I confirmed and nodded to the man in question. The guy gave a thumbs up.

"The most effective strike is the one they don't see coming."

Yeah, we'd already experienced that ourselves.

"To that end, if we coordinate our strike on the money transport, the merc team, the trusts, *and* the corporate boards, we don't give him time to set up a defense anywhere else." Bones folded his arms. "This is not a fishing expedition. Every single strike needs to be surgical in its precision. We need to have the timing down, and we need to know each domino will fall on schedule."

"That means we all need to be in position *before* the first domino hits the ground," Adam Reed rubbed his jaw. "How does this affect our more vulnerable participants?"

While he didn't look at Milo or Lainey, I didn't doubt he was referring to them. Then again, he could also mean Swan. But we had her buttoned up and planned to keep it that way. Where she went, at least four of us were going.

Period.

The plans had worked until they hadn't. I almost wished JD was still alive so I could be the one to kill him.

Prick.

"We'll discuss that," Kellan said. "While we'd all like those we want to protect out of the line of fire, I'm not denying anyone their pound of flesh. If they want to be there, they will be there."

That ended any argument anyone wanted to make for keeping Swan out of it. Did I want her safe? Abso-fucking-lutely. Safe right next to us. Where she went, we would follow.

That meant where we went, she got to do the same. Milo wanted Sharpe. So did I.

Fuck it, we *all* did.

No one was being left out of that justice.

"Right now, we need to discuss what each of us is going to be doing—and as Bones said, we're going to plan this down to the minute. There will be no cowboying or going off script unless there's a pressing, life or death reason, and then you *have* to notify Alphabet—*he* will coordinate all of us."

"In other words," Alphabet said. "If you don't tell me, don't fucking do it. If you have an assignment, we're trusting you to get it done. You don't check-in, I'm going to assume there's a problem. Don't make me assume shit, period. I can be an ass on my own. I don't need your help."

I rolled my eyes, but I appreciated the sentiment.

"Do we get to volunteer for jobs?" Bodhi asked, his expression bored, but it really didn't match his eyes. The guy was a hard read, but I got why Freddie trusted him. Freddie trusted so few and so little, it was an endorsement we couldn't ignore.

"No," Kellan said, then raised his hand. "Save your questions. Let's take this from the top…"

The next two hours were grueling in a way that I hadn't experienced since we'd been in high school, and Kellan wanted to get the best SAT score he could. We'd drilled down in a similar fashion, repeatedly going over the data until we could recite it in our sleep.

No part of the plan was left out, and every step was carefully outlined, from the timing down to what had to happen before and after each particular step. Timing was *everything*. We wanted everyone in position. Alphabet would keep us in touch; he would be the central location to help avoid distractions.

Contingencies were also outlined, save for— "We aren't going to go over *every* contingency. I don't want anyone mistaking a contingency for the plan. So be ready to be flexible if a contingency is called in."

Then another round of going over the plan until each group could recite their part perfectly. As detailed as the plan was, it didn't leave a lot of room for error. The coordinated hits were definitely dominoes, it would start with the first slash at the accounts and the trusts and end with Sharpe in our hands and the threat neutralized.

Then avenged.

There were many steps in between. But we had this. The big brains had all put their minds to it. That said, no plan was without its flaws. The flaws in this one seemed limited to human error. But the best part of the plan? The whole plan didn't revolve around her being the bait. Even if she was still *part* of the bait.

That already made it a thousand percent better than the plan we'd been debating.

I was still turning that over when the weight of a gaze feathered over me and I caught the quiet question in Swan's eyes.

Was I all right?

Yes, I was.

Did I need her?

Always.

Now?

I grinned as she raised her eyebrows and curled my fingers at her. She put a hand on Vaughn's shoulder, then murmured in his ear before she rose. It registered with me that the meeting was ending, which meant we could get out of here.

Well, at least go upstairs and away from everyone else. We were going to take a blowtorch to the bars Sharpe had erected around us in his effort to recapture Swan. Particularly since his default to not having her was killing her.

Fucker.

When her hand slid into mine, I clasped it and tugged her closer. Pressing my face to her hair, I took a deep breath before murmuring, "We're done down here. Think I can kidnap you away for a little while?"

"Is it kidnapping if I go willingly?" The tease made me smile.

"I like kidnapping you," I reminded her. "It's kind of our thing."

Laughter bubbled out of her, pulling more than one gaze toward her, but I tucked her under my arm. Mine. At least for a couple of hours. I lifted my chin to Kellan and he nodded.

Conversations were breaking out all over the room as the guys intercepted anyone who might delay me getting our girl out of there. She brushed her knuckles against Doc's spine and gave Liam a pat on the ass.

His look was fucking priceless and I snickered. That earned me a pinch, and I just grinned at her. She could slap my ass any damn time she wanted. All the way upstairs, she just leaned into me as we walked. A certainty and a calm washed over me as we entered the suite.

Her gaze shifted to where the stapler sat on its little pedestal and a smile curved her lips.

"You're hot when you're bloodthirsty," I told her, and she pivoted to look up at me. But since I had a destination in mind, I just scooped her up, bracing an arm under her ass as she wrapped her legs around my waist.

"Am I now? I thought it was you torturing people that turned me on?"

Goddamn, there was a reason I loved this woman so fucking much.

"These things," I informed her as I let us into my room and kicked the door closed, "are not mutually exclusive."

"Good to know," she whispered against my lips before she kissed me and I threw the lock on the door before walking us over to the bed.

Those things were not mutually exclusive at all.

CHAPTER 30

EMERSYN

The stroke of Jasper's tongue against mine, the warmth of his hands on my face, and the softness of his beard under my palms delighted me. His kiss held a bite conveyed in the scrapes of his teeth against my tongue, my lip, and then back again. It was like he was intent on devouring me. All the plans we'd made downstairs seemed to melt away under the blazing intensity of his kiss.

Every kiss with Jasper was both battle and caress. It almost felt like forever since the last time our lips connected when in reality, it was the day before. I couldn't soak in his nearness enough. Desperation edged every place we connected, from our lips to our hands to the pressure of his weight against the cradle of my thighs. I *needed* him like a flash fire in my veins, threatening to burn me alive, and I couldn't wait to be consumed.

With hot hands, I tugged at his clothes, and he pulled away from me long enough to strip off his shirt and toss it away, and then he was back devouring my mouth. I stroked my hands over his skin. Tightening my legs around his hips, I flipped him so that he was on his back and I was straddling him.

He broke the kiss with laughter, and I took a moment to straighten up and strip off my own shirt. With helpful hands, he cupped my breasts before he found the hook in the front and then it was open and I was shrugging it off while he teased my nipples.

When he sat forward and caught one nipple in his mouth, I arched my back. Rocking against his erection where it strained against his jeans was a whole new sense of personal torture that I delighted in. The suck of his mouth, the nip of his teeth, and the heat he laved with his tongue over my nipple had my cunt clenching as liquid pleasure unspooled inside of me.

"Jasper," I gasped out his name even as I fisted his hair. He didn't relent, though, the intensity increasing when he bit down gently. The splash of pain amidst the hedonistic assault added another layer to it, and I wanted us naked. I wanted to drown out the rest of the world with the feeling of him. "Jasper…"

"I'm busy here, Swan," he whispered, his breath teasing the dampness on my nipple and causing it to pebble tighter. I tugged his hair lightly and he cut his gaze up to me. The storm in those gray eyes promised me a furious ride, and I was so ready for it.

"I want you inside me," I informed him, and the huskiness of my voice was a little shocking to my ears. "You can suck my nipples in a minute. I need your cock."

Wanton desire twined with need, amping up the demand within me. He studied me for a beat; the only sound between us was the sharp sound of our breaths escaping in pants.

Whatever he searched for, he must have found it because he gripped my hips.

"Up…" He lifted even as he spoke and plucked me off his lap. When he set me down, he hooked his fingers into the waist of my leggings and peeled them straight down. His eyes seemed to catch the light from the fairy lights he'd strung around his new room, as he had in his old.

It was never dark in Jasper's space. Never cold. Never isolated.

I always felt at home here, warm, filled with passion, and as much a visual and environmental embrace. Kind of like the man himself. "Someone isn't wearing panties," Jasper said on a half growl as he ran a hand up my leg. There was the barest hint of stubble beginning to return. I needed another laser appt—

Later.

"I didn't have time to find any," I admitted, enjoying how his pupils widened and his nostrils flared. When he tapped my thighs, I spread them so he could see. "Rome was in a mood this morning…"

He chuckled at the black ink circling my thigh where Rome had been drawing birds. There was one for each of them and smaller ones fluttering, a flock that circled the whole thigh. "I see that." Tracing his fingers over each one left me shivering from the light contact and what those birds meant. "He added a sparrow, a dove, a starling…" His grin grew a little smug. "A swan right here on the inside of your thigh. I approve."

Grinning, I butterfly spread more so he could see the rest of it. The fact he pressed a kiss to my cunt, then teased my clit with the barest of brushes from his tongue, sent another shudder through me. "Do you really like it?"

"I do," he said, glancing up to meet my gaze. "Going to get Vaughn to ink that permanently?"

Biting my lower lip, I nodded slowly. "I think so…I wanted—" Hesitation raked through me. Not three minutes ago, I'd been focused on his cock and where I wanted it and now…

Rubbing my thighs gently, Jasper focused on me. "Talk to me, Swan. What do you want?"

"You," I whispered.

"You have me. But that's not what you were going to say." The affectionate tease in his scold sent heat to my face. "Talk to me, Swan…"

"I wanted to ask Vaughn for another tattoo anyway…and I love these birds. But it's not the only one I want."

"Okay." Simple. Easy. No hesitation.

"Okay?"

"Swan, if you wanted Vaughn to paint you up as colorfully as he has himself, I'd say okay. Your body. You do with it what you want. I will love you with all the art or none of it."

Your body.

Your body.

You do what you want with it.

He went all wavery as tears filled my eyes, and I couldn't get the words out past the lump in my throat.

When he pulled me to him, I wrapped my arms around him and held on. "Shh," he whispered. "It's all right."

It was more than all right, but the lump in my throat kept all the words trapped. I dug my fingers into his shoulders and held on. The press of his chest to mine, combined with the steady thrum of his heart and the soft, almost soothing hum helped, but the tears still escaped and splashed down.

"I love you," I whispered, pushing the words out.

"I love you too," he whispered. "More than I could ever begin to describe." Pulling back, he cradled my face in his palms and stared at me with so much emotion. The tears pooled and escaped, sliding down my cheeks to his hands. "Swan—I know that I'm not the guy with the pretty words or the easy temperament. I'm a hell of a lot more comfortable with anger and violence than I will ever be with flowers or poetry."

I sniffled because he so was, but I didn't want to interrupt him to tell him that.

"But this—beautiful body of yours with all of its power and talent—it's *yours*. You let us play with you and make love to you, and when you demand it, we give you all the cock you can handle and more."

Laughter actually escaped this time, with more tears. Because that was both sweet, erotic, and hilarious in equal measure.

"But *never* mistake that this body isn't yours. We won't let anyone else make that mistake, either. It's your choice, or it doesn't happen. Period." The last came out a warning growl that had all the hairs on my body standing up. "Do you believe me?"

I swallowed that lump and nodded slowly. "It's just—it's hard to remember that sometimes. I mean—I know it now." I tapped two fingers to my head. "Here, in my mind. I know it. I see it every day, how you guys take care of me and let me take care of you. That you trust me, and you let me learn to trust you…"

"But in this survivor's heart," he murmured, gliding a hand down to rest over my breast where my heart seemed to beat faster in eagerness to get to him. "It's a little harder to remember."

Licking my lips, I nodded slowly. "I know you guys will never hurt me and my heart knows it too…" Just like I'd known they would come for me. They would always come for me, and I would damn well do the same for them.

"You still want my cock, Swan? Or do you want to cuddle

up here and just be?" The offer wrapped me up in an entirely different kind of embrace.

"I want everything," I whispered. It was so hard to want and, at the same time… "I want you. I always want you."

"Then open my pants and get my cock out," he told me, and another shudder went through me as I swallowed around that lump again before I dropped my hands to his jeans. Even though my fingers were shaking, I freed the button and lowered the zipper. The hot weight of his cock was right there and I chuckled.

"I'm not the only one who's going commando."

"Nope," he said, a smile quirking his lips. Then he pulled away long enough to take his pants off. I enjoyed watching the way the shadows played over him. I tracked my gaze to the scar on his abdomen. It had mended so beautifully, but it was there, the ridge of skin still pink from being so recently healed.

So close.

Too close.

"Eyes up here, Swan," Jasper said, and I glanced up to find him watching me. "I'm fine."

"Yes," I said slowly, grinning. "You most definitely are."

It was his turn to laugh, and he moved to sit on the bed again. When he laid down, his cock was angled upward, jutting up as he wrapped his hand around it and gave it a couple of strokes. "This the cock you want?"

That was a dare and an invitation. Answering both, I shifted to straddle him and then covered his hand with mine as we both angled him toward my cunt. When I sank down, he thrust up and then moved his hands to my breasts. The thrust pushed him balls deep and shoved all the air out of my lungs.

This was what I wanted, to feel him. To be connected. To

be held, and when I glanced down at him, there was a look in his eyes. That connection was what he wanted too.

"Ride me," he murmured. "Take all the cock you want."

I clenched around him on the last couple of words and he grimaced before he slid a hand upward and I dipped down at his coaxing. When he gripped my nape, my mouth was already open to his and my hips rolled. I could control the flexion of muscle, and it didn't hurt in the slightest, even as I flattened my chest over him.

Each time I rose up, he pulled back his tongue, then thrust it again as I sank down. Tears splashed from my face to his, except his cheeks were damp already. The salt lingered in our kiss and then I was gripping his hands, or maybe he was gripping mine as I sat up. I wanted to go faster, and I wanted to add a little twist...

"Fuck me," Jasper exhaled as I increased the pace, and, this time when I laughed, there was no lump in my throat to dislodge.

"I'm working on it," I promised him.

The friction was perfect, and so was the angle. Every thrust bumped my clit against his pelvis as his cock kept hitting that spot. With our fingers threaded together, he offered me the balance to control the pace and his gaze held me riveted as we rocked together. The pleasure came in a rush, splintering over us almost like a surprise. The orgasm stole my breath, and then he groaned as I fluttered around him. Another couple of thrusts, and he came in a hot rush.

When he tugged me to him, I met his groaning kiss with my own. This one was longer, sweeter, and far more relaxed than the earlier biting kiss. It held all the emotions we'd shared and more.

Our skin was tacky where we touched, but I craved that nearness like I did his kiss and his cock and his laughter—

"I like your growls," I whispered against his lips.

"Yeah?"

"Hmm," I hummed, then nipped his bottom lip. "Want to kidnap me again?"

He was softening but slowly.

"Give me ten minutes, Swan, and I'm going to kidnap you so hard, you'll feel me for the rest of the week."

Oh. I liked the sound of that.

"Yes, please?"

He grinned and then held me to him as he chuckled. "Coming right up."

I couldn't wait.

CHAPTER 31

VAUGHN

*L*eaning against the wall while Dove danced was the second-best way to start my day. The first would always be sliding into the slick heat of her glorious cunt while she cried out in pleasure, but I got to do that often enough that I enjoyed a little variation. They could start with the dancing today and get right to the second when she was up for it.

The way she moved to the music was effortless in its grace, and utterly captivating. She danced like she truly did have wings and that gravity didn't affect her in the slightest. Ethereal in the poetry of how she moved and, in the same breath, earthy as hell because she wasn't an angel or other-worldly being—she was our girl. I couldn't sometimes breathe for how fucking magical she was when she moved.

Awareness of the plan in motion had me on edge—all of us, really. The door opened to let Liam and Freddie in. It had all of us on edge. Rome and Jasper would be along soon. I checked my watch. Yeah, Kel and Doc were back. Except Doc was checking on Milo, and Kel probably went with him to sit on Milo if he needed it.

Since they hadn't grabbed me, I got to enjoy this part of the morning. Liam wordlessly passed me a cup of coffee, and I lifted my chin to him. Freddie leaned against the wall next to me, and Liam took a sip of his while he watched. She knew we were here. Every day she danced, one or more of us drifted in here to watch. It was like we needed the movement every bit as much as she did.

Every second ticking by brought us closer to the moment we would move. I couldn't wait for the time to get there, and at the same time, I dreaded it. The skin on my back itched, and I shifted to rub against one of the seams in the wall to scratch it. The burns had healed, but the irritation was there.

Liam nudged me and I glanced over to see the question in his eyes. Was I alright? No, I wasn't, but I didn't want to discuss it now. So I just shrugged and lifted my chin to where Dove was spinning. Any minute she was going to go for those silks. The fact Liam and Rome coaxed her back into them settled something in my chest that had been tight since she vanished to go home and ended up in Pinetree.

She'd always been exquisite—but there was such raw power to her now. Power. Focus. Intensity.

The fire had damn near consumed our broken bird, but she'd emerged so much more—*her*. Maybe that was the best way to describe it. My dove brought so much peace into our lives, and she deserved so much more than she'd ever been given. The door opened to let Jasper and Rome slide in, with Kellan and Doc right behind them.

They made it just in time for her to leap and take the first silk, stealing my breath as she moved. Fuck, she was gorgeous. Dressed in only a leotard and dance shorts, every muscle ripple was on display. Most performances took place in a darkened theater or venue with only the lights tracking her motion. Usually, her costumes had sparkles or glitter, all of it designed to pick up the light and reflect it back

There was something magical about those performances, magical and effortless. What the audience couldn't see or enjoy was the control and the discipline reflected in the way her muscles moved and shifted. The earthier part of her. Yes, she could fly, but it was *her*, not the silks or the costumes, just her. Her talent. Her strength. Her skill.

"Fuck my life," Doc muttered.

"Right?" Jasper said, his grin growing.

"Shh," Freddie said with a scowl, barely tearing his eyes off from where she was moving on the silks. Not that I blamed him. Honestly, I barely listened to them or the music. Distraction wasn't possible as she twisted and twined her way up. The sudden dead drops were heart-pounding.

It didn't matter that I trusted her skill, admired it, or that I'd been the one to secure the harnesses and the silks. I'd reinforced every hook, bolt, and D-ring. Nothing was allowed to harm Dove, certainly not carelessness. At the same time, the speed at which she would spin down and then extend her arms without hesitation was so downright defiant and fearless.

Head up, wings out. I'd inked that onto her skin, and she was the living personification of it. Rome let out a slow sigh that I echoed, and Kellan shook his head. My dick twitched when she twirled, twisted, and then bent back to hang suspended above us. When her gaze locked on mine, she grinned and then let go again.

The downward spiral stopped abruptly, with her body in perfect form. Yep. I was hard as a stone and desperate for her to do more, even if I was ready for her to slip out of those silks and right into my bed. The next thirty minutes passed like an exercise in sensual torture. When she finally slid free of the silks to land lightly on her feet, she dripped with sweat. Her cheeks gleamed, and a smile graced her lips. What held me in place though, was the radiant joy in her eyes.

Freddie began clapping, and every single one of us joined in. "Boo-Boo, you're a goddess."

Laughing, she dipped into the most graceful curtsey. "I'm still a little rough in places."

"No," Jasper said firmly, a syllable all of us echoed in varying forms from Liam's "bullshit," to Doc's "you were magnificent," and Kel's simple, "magical, Sparrow, absolutely magical."

Freddie chose a different response. He took three steps forward, raised his hands, and she tracked his every movement. His expression in the mirror held a question, and she nodded once. When he cupped her face and then kissed her, I was torn between laughing, applauding, and just fucking whistling. 'Cause, goddamn, it was about time. They'd been getting closer but nurturing the trust between them was as much about leaving them alone as it was encouraging them.

I wasn't the only one grinning, especially when Freddie dipped her. Jasper put his fingers to his lips and whistled as Liam whooped at them. For her part, Dove let out a breathless laugh as Freddie straightened them. He smirked and hooked an arm around her. "I'm all sweaty and stinky," she protested.

"My kind of woman," Freddie declared, pressing another kiss to the side of her head to prove his point. The smile she gave him relaxed the fist of tension crushing my heart since we realized JD had betrayed us, which led to her being buried in a coffin.

"Good morning to you, too," she teased, and he winked before looking at us. Dove glanced at all of us as well, her soft smile dimming as she tilted her head. "What's wrong?"

"Nothing is wrong," Kellan answered soberly. "However,

we are here for a reason—well, a reason besides enjoying how beautiful and talented you are."

A hint of red bloomed on her face, adding more of a glow to her already flushed cheeks. "Okay," she said slowly, and worry flickered in her eyes for a moment as she studied each of us. The searching look and the worry tugged at me.

"It's nothing bad, Starling," Rome assured her.

Freddie had welded himself to her side. "It's not, but I think you stunned all of us, Boo-Boo. I mean, all the blood runs south and the brain turns off."

Head tilted back, she took a deep breath then exhaled a long sigh. "Should you guys sit down, then?"

I groaned, but it was Doc who laughed. "I think we can handle it, Little Bit. Although it's not sitting down that we need to do…"

He was the first one who took a knee. Goddammit, I hit mine a second behind him. The other guys dropped one right after another, even Freddie. But it was Liam who took three steps forward to take a knee right in front of her. Her breath caught and she shivered, goosebumps rippling over her damp skin.

"You're safe," I told her. "I promise, Dove. You are safe." We were scaring her and that wasn't okay.

"You can handle us," Liam said as he held out his hand to her. "Can't you, Hellspawn?"

Our fierce girl may not be fearless, but she didn't let fear dictate her. This wasn't genuine fear; she was just unsettled. All of us on one knee in front of her? I was with Liam. She could absolutely handle us. "Yes," she whispered. "I can."

Liam didn't nudge her or do anything more than keep his hand out, and when she finally settled her palm against his, I wasn't the only one who let out a breath.

"Good girl," Doc murmured, and she stole a look at him

with a tremulous smile before Liam steered her attention back to him.

"We rock-paper-scissored for this," he said. "And I won."

She blinked, shock and surprise startling away the fear. "Really?"

I didn't slap my forehead, but it was damn hard not to laugh.

"Not really," Liam teased. "Nonetheless, you're not afraid anymore."

That was the point.

"We did discuss it, though," Kellan said. "All of us."

"And we argued," Jasper stated.

"A lot," I added. The fact we'd managed to argue without yelling? That was a miracle, though it didn't make the fight any less fierce.

"But we all agreed," Freddie said. "It just took some of us longer than others."

Dove licked her lips as she swept her gaze over us.

"Some of us are stubborn," Doc admitted.

"Some of us are really stubborn," Jasper agreed.

"Fuck that, we're all stubborn," Liam declared and Rome snorted. "Fine, we're all stubborn, and Rome just does what he wants anyway."

That earned a laugh from her and I couldn't help my own grin.

"The point," I said, pulling us back, "is we're all on the same page with this…"

"Maybe we're not all in the same place," Freddie caught the thread, and I wasn't the only one who braced. "Our relationships—they're all different. What you have with Vaughn or Jasper is not what you have with Liam or Rome…"

"Or me," Doc agreed. "It's okay."

"It's *more* than okay," Kellan emphasized. "I love what you and I have."

"So do I," we chorused it like we'd planned it that way.

"I adore what I have with you," I added.

"So do I," Jasper said. "You make me a better person."

"Make us better people," Doc agreed.

"I can't get much more perfect," Freddie admitted, and we were all laughing again, but the tears sliding down her face threatened to gut me. "Though, you do make me shine, Boo-Boo. You make me want to take more risks."

"You make me want to be more careful," Jasper said.

"You make me want to come home," Liam confessed.

"You make me remember what it is to have a home," Kellan whispered.

"You give me hope, Little Bit," Doc told her.

"You give me peace," I said. "The kind of peace I haven't had in so long, I'd forgotten what it was like."

"I love you," Rome said.

"We all do," Liam agreed. "While this may not be the romantic proposal you deserve and will get—we want you to marry us. Legally, yeah, you can only marry one of us—and, yes, this is for the plan—but Hellspawn, I want you to be my wife. I don't give a rat's ass about the money or the trusts or the plan. That's all just a benefit."

"We want you to be our wife," Jasper said firmly. "You might get his name, but you're *our* girl."

"Ours," Doc agreed.

"All you have to do is say yes," Kellan said.

The moment elongated, stretching as the silence ballooned between us all, and throughout it, Dove stood there with tears on her face, gripping Liam's hand so hard her knuckles were white. When she glanced at Rome, he smiled.

"That's a yes. She just needs a minute…"

CHAPTER 32

EMERSYN

 couldn't take my eyes off any of them, and I couldn't look at all of them at once, even if they were all on one knee. Liam gave my hand the gentlest of squeezes, despite the fact I was digging my nails into his hand. Freddie held fast to my right hand, grounding me.

"I'm nineteen." It wasn't the best answer in the world.

"Almost twenty," Freddie reminded me. "But we can buy the booze, don't worry."

The random comment cracked through the glass cage that had slammed down over me at the sudden swell of emotion coming from all of them.

"We can buy you anything you want," Liam said, pulling me back to him. "This isn't a cage, Hellspawn." It was like he read my mind. "If it was, you'd be the only one with a key."

"Never make the mistake of thinking this body isn't yours."

"You think we can really get out of here?"

"I know we can. Liam and Rome are that far away. If they

don't hear from me soon, Liam's gonna raise hell. Boo-Boo, we're going to get out of here. You. Me. We're going home."

"Broken isn't bad, Starling."

"Welcome home, Dove."

"Waited too damn long for this..."

"Make me work for it, Little Bit..."

It was what they'd been telling me all along. No more cages. No more chains. No more *ownership* except...

I licked my lips, and despite my hesitation, none of them moved. None of them got angry or hurried me along. If anything, they just waited me out. When I dropped my gaze back to Liam with Rome a half step behind him... They wanted *me*. Not my money or my name—fuck, they didn't want me to have that name. They wanted me safe; however I wanted my life so they would make it happen.

It was what they'd been telling me every goddamn day since they'd taken me. Even if we hadn't had the exact words then. Hell, even if I hadn't known who I was then.

Who I was to them.

Who I was to me.

Who we were together.

"Trust us?" Liam asked. Two words. Two simple words, while at the same time, they were everything.

"All of us?" I said slowly.

"Yes." One answer. Seven voices.

"Emersyn O'Connell?" It sounded odd and kind of beautiful.

"Or Cleary, or Hardigan or James or Horan..." Liam said. "Hellspawn, I don't give a damn about the last name you pick. You can just go by Emersyn or Ivy. I just care about you."

Tears spilled down my cheeks again and I let out a little laugh. The trust was there, shining in every single one of their eyes. "Maybe my last name should just be Vandal."

That earned more than one snort or chuckle.

I took a deep breath, and Freddie squeezed my hand. Rome lifted his chin even as Jasper dipped his a fraction. Kellan's gaze remained steadfast, as did Vaughn's. Mickey gave me a little nod. Confidence swirled around them, yet it was more than that. They were united. It had been growing for so long and I'd loved seeing them get closer—forgiving each other for real or imagined mistakes and tightening those bonds.

"I always wanted to be worthy of the kind of loyalty you guys showed Milo," I admitted. "I wanted—I wanted to be a part of all of you, too." I'd said this before, but the hollow inside me was gone; the places inside my soul scraped raw to eliminate any other connections. The only one I'd managed to hang onto over the years was Lainey, and only because I'd hidden it.

Sniffling, I licked the tears off my lips again.

"You guys are my family. You're my people. This is my place—where you are." It didn't matter if it was the club-house, Liam's apartment, Doc's place, the clinic, or the mechanic's shop—we needed to rebuild Kel's shop and Vaughn's parlor... we needed to do so many things.

I was shaking. Even my voice trembled, but there was nothing but steadiness, patience, and confidence in their eyes.

"Yes." One simple word. Yet, it meant so much more than just an affirmation. It was acceptance and binding, and it threw open the cage; they were my lifelines. My home. "Yes, I'll marry you..."

Liam shocked the hell out of me then by producing a ring that he slid onto my finger. It was a gorgeous yellow gold that seemed to shine under the light with a heat all of its own. But it wasn't just any ring, it was a bird—

"It's a phoenix," Freddie said. "A firebird. When they die,

they are reborn in their own flames, remade, stronger and more perfect than they already were."

"Just like you," Vaughn added. "A firebrand who brought all that heat and color into our lives."

"You were born Ivy Hardigan, then became Emersyn Sharpe—but who you are is *our* girl, our Phoenix," Liam caught the thread. "My Hellspawn."

"Swan."

"Sparrow."

"Starling."

"Dove."

"Little Bit." Laughter edged those syllables, and there were tears in Mickey's eyes.

"Boo-Boo," Freddie completed the nicknames as they were all laughing and so was I.

"But you're our phoenix, too," Liam said soberly. "You have been through the fire, Hellspawn. It tried to consume you and I think there were times that it did, but that fire is a part of you, and now—*you're* the one who burns with it."

He pushed the ring along the ring finger on my left hand. There were perfect pink stones in the eye as I studied it.

"That's a rose quartz," Liam continued. "The debate over the stone was long and hard..."

"I won," Rome said without a trace of self-consciousness or arrogance. Amusement surged around the guys as they laughed.

"It's the stone of unconditional love," Kellan told me.

"There's a story," Jasper said, and I wanted to wipe away my tears, but that would mean letting go of Liam or Freddie. Which I definitely didn't want to. "Aphrodite battled Ares to protect her wounded lover Adonis. When she was wounded and fell next to Adonis, their blood combined, turning the white quartz around them pink. The fusion is what made

Rose Quartz—love and war. Battle and blood. Unconditional and perfect—just like you."

Vaughn let out a low whistle. "Exactly."

"I love it," I whispered then let out a real breath. "And I love all of you."

Liam surged up and caught me, then his mouth fused to mine and the guys surrounded us. I was hot, sticky, covered in sweat and tears, and I'd never been happier or safer than I was surrounded by all of them. Liam gave way to Rome, who kissed me with such fierce possession that my toes curled.

Then I was caught up against Kellan and he nuzzled a promise to my lips before surrendering me to Jasper. His kiss was as much teeth as it was lips, and his grin was so damn beautiful. Vaughn was next, picking me all the way up and cradling me to him as he kissed me. Then I turned to Mickey. His kiss was no less sweet as he teased my lips apart.

It was Freddie who waited for the last kiss with a shy grin. I opened my arms to him and let him come to me. His choice. He could touch me, I wouldn't touch him unless he asked for it. However when he pressed just a chaste kiss against my lips, I accepted it. Freddie had already kissed the hell out of me. But he didn't let me go. Instead, he pressed his forehead to mine.

"I'm getting a tattoo," he told me, and that was such a big deal, I held my breath. "A phoenix...for you."

And for him.

"I want one too," I said almost immediately and his eyes shone. Freddie was every bit the phoenix I was. We'd both been consumed by those flames.

"Yeah?"

"Yeah."

We both looked at Vaughn and he grinned. "Done."

Then Freddie brushed one finger over the pen-drawn birds on my legs. "These?"

"Yes." No hesitation. I loved what Rome had drawn on me and wanted to make it permanent.

I wanted to make them all permanent. One glance at my ring, and I felt a permanence resonating through me. Tears kept slipping out. I swiped at them as I turned to find them all watching me with varying degrees of affection and adoration. I hope my eyes were shining as much for them.

Before I could say anything though, my stomach grumbled. The sound punched through the room. Laughter exploded and even I was giggling.

"Right," Kellan said. "Breakfast. Sparrow, go shower."

Vaughn held out a hand to me. "C'mon, Dove." I stole a look at each of them. Liam winked. Rome looked peaceful and happy. Jasper appeared fierce and proud. Mickey was smiling, and Freddie seemed delighted.

"Liam, you're on coffee. Jas and Freddie, potatoes. I'll get the omelets going. Doc, go get Milo and company for food, and we can make our announcements and plans."

The orders flowed around us as Vaughn and I headed up the stairs. I was riding on air. I caught sight of Ezra down the hall as we got to the top. He lifted his chin but didn't get up. It was weird to see Ezra and Adam splitting guard duty with the guys while Milo continued to heal.

More, it gave me hope for Lainey.

All the way to my room, Vaughn stayed with me. While I stripped off the leotard, Vaughn got the shower going, and I caught him watching me as I stared at my ring.

"You like it?" The tender question made me smile.

"I love it."

"Good." Then he held out his hand to me. "Mind if I shower with you?"

His cock was already jutting out, thick and heavy. The piercing was right there, shimmering almost. Or maybe that was just the pre-cum on the heavy tip. "The first time we had sex was after a shower."

"I know," Vaughn said, his smile licking fire right through me. "The next time we have sex is going to be right now if you're up for it."

Was that even a question?

I made the two steps to him as I took his hand, and then he lifted me up and walked us into the shower, even as I wrapped a hand around his cock. The hot water sprayed over me as I hit the tile wall and then I was sinking down on that gorgeous dick. The thickness stretched me out. There was no patience in me as our mouths fused together. But I was also more than ready to take Vaughn in.

Once he sank to the hilt, he lifted his head. "We're gonna wife you up so damn hard, Dove…"

Oh.

Yeah.

"I want you, Vaughn," I whispered, feathering my fingers against his face. "And I want my tattoos as soon as possible."

"Before?" We didn't usually discuss plans during sex. Not battle ones, anyway.

"Hell. Yes." That was all I had to say on that subject. His smile grew as he spread his hands over my ass and lifted me a little higher.

"Then you will have exactly what you want. Lean into the wall, Dove. And relax…you're not leaving this shower without at least two orgasms."

He made it four. The first came as he rocked his hips into mine, the piston force dragging that piercing against my g-spot until my vision whited out. He slowed only while I was gasping then eased back in to do it all over again while teasing my nipples. I was loose-limbed and floating when he pulled out of me to turn me around.

This time, I pressed my hands on the wall at the end of

the shower, and he thrust into me from behind. It was so much deeper this way that my cries turned ragged as he filled me over and over. The third orgasm tumbled into a fourth, although I ended up shuddering all over when he pressed his thumb right against the rim of my anus.

"Fuck," he groaned as he came with me this time and I would have fallen if he hadn't been holding onto me. He twisted to lean back against the wall, keeping me with him. He didn't soften that fast, and I loved the feeling of being impaled on him. The door opened while we were leaning there.

"She needs to eat more than your cock," Jasper informed us.

A giggle escaped me, then another and another. They kept spilling out of me until I swore my side would stitch from the laughter. Jasper waited patiently, watching me even as Vaughn dipped his head to kiss my shoulder.

"I have six more cocks to swallow," I finally said to startled silence. "Lots of cock for me to consume. I could live on a diet of cock."

The silence ballooned, and then their masculine laughter flooded the bathroom and I grinned.

I was engaged.

I was home.

I was *happy*.

CHAPTER 33

KELLAN

*C*haos reigned as Milo and Lainey descended to join us. Conversation was loud and bombastic. Ezra followed Lainey, but it was Milo he had his gaze on. Despite his protests, Milo leaned on Lainey as she kept an arm around him. He was doing better. His color had improved, and Doc said the infection had finally begun to clear. Bloodwork was good and his lingering fever had broken. Blood loss had cost him some time, but in the past week since rescuing them, he'd rallied.

His gaze locked onto mine as they made it into the living room. "Party?" One word question.

"Yep." One word answer.

Adam appeared behind them, still buttoning his shirt and his hair damp. Bodhi wasn't far behind him. He swung around that little cluster without a second glance and looked at Freddie.

"So? What did PPG say?"

That snared Milo's attention for a split second before he swung that dark gaze back to me. His expression could have been carved out of granite. I was ready for this fight—*if* it became a fight. But almost as soon as it registered, the tension around his eyes eased. "Yeah?"

I grinned. "Oh yeah." The proposal had been a surprise. We'd already discussed the fact that marriage was another tool in our arsenal to take down Sharpe. But marrying her—that was never going to be about that piece of shit.

Ever.

That proposal was about us. Just like the ring—the debate we'd had over what ring to give her and what shape it should take we could revisit another day, if at all. The ring we picked was the one we had all agreed on and if we wanted to give her others? Well, we could do that too.

Letting go of Lainey, Milo held out a hand to me, and I clasped it. "Congratulations—you ever hurt my baby sister…"

"And I will deal with it," Sparrow announced from behind him, much to Milo's consternation. Lainey burst out laughing as she twisted to look at Sparrow, who drifted more than walked across the room and right into the hug Lainey had for her.

Milo's low humming growl actually made both Adam and Ezra smirk, but they were watching Lainey look at her ring. "That's different," Lainey said.

"I know…" Sparrow said with a breathless little sigh. Jasper and Vaughn were right behind her, both smiling indulgently at her. I could feel the same smile on my lips. "It's perfect."

She hadn't been so certain at first, but that was another hurdle to cross when she was ready for it. Though—maybe she already had. Milo patted my shoulder as he turned to face his sister.

Sparrow met his gaze, even as Lainey wrapped an arm around her shoulders, and the pair of them faced him with the exact same expression. They were ready for this fight. Good thing that Milo wasn't going to give it to them. If anything, his chuckle disappointed Adam and Ezra both.

I almost wanted to apologize to them, but Sparrow didn't need the grief. Ever.

"Just tell me you're happy and that you're not just doing this for the plan." That was what it boiled down to, and I couldn't say I blamed him. None of us wanted this just for the fucking plan. If that was the case, fine, we'd have done it like a legal contract and given her all the outs.

"I am happy," Sparrow told him without hesitation. "And it's not just for the plan. It's too scary to be about the plan."

I frowned but it was Lainey who asked the question. "Are you scared?"

"Yes," Sparrow told her. "And no…don't ask me to explain it. No one is making me do this and I really can't wait, but… it's a lot." Then she looked past all of them to me and the fingers digging into my chest relaxed their grip. "You guys are a lot. But I can handle you."

"Oh yes, you can," I murmured. "Not a doubt in my mind." Thank fucking God.

Milo opened his arms and Sparrow all but flew from Lainey to him. While she didn't throw herself at him, she did hug him as carefully as she could. Unsurprisingly, Milo picked her right up off the ground, and the tears were in her eyes again as she held him but met my gaze.

"Proud of you, Ivy," Milo said, then added something in a low voice, probably a threat, that made her laugh, and she slapped his shoulder.

"You will not," she ordered, and he shrugged. Yeah, that was a threat. "I mean it, Milo. I will fight you, and I don't want to fight you."

He gave the most long and aggrieved sigh. "I'm supposed to threaten them."

"And you can threaten them all you like, because they can handle it." I grinned at the absolute certainty in her voice. "But they are still mine."

For his part, Milo was biting back a smile as he pivoted to face me again. "Not a word."

"Wouldn't dream of it," I commented.

"I would," Freddie called from the kitchen. "C'mon, Boo-Boo. Food is ready."

I chuckled as she slid her hand into mine and pushed up to give me a kiss. I met it easily, then studied her for a beat. The comment about being scared. That brief moment in the studio—"You good?"

I just wanted to know.

"Nope," she declared. "According to Liam, I'm a hellspawn."

"Yes, she is," Liam said from the doorway. "And stop with all the chattering out here. In the kitchen, we're feeding her then making plans."

"One sec," I murmured to her as I tugged her to me and let the others file into the kitchen. Jasper shot me a look, but I shook my head. Only when we were alone did I glance down at her. "Tell me the truth, Sparrow. You okay?"

"I am," she whispered, spreading her hand out against my chest. The precious weight of her would keep me right where I was, because I'd rather tear off my own skin than move her hand. "I promise. I know I got a little wobbly—and it was—a lot. I mean we'd talked about it because it was the plan, and I don't have a problem with the plan but…"

The hand on my chest was the left one with the ring right there on her ring finger. "You don't have to wear it. You've told us about being dressed up—" She pressed the fingers of her right hand to my lips.

"I want to wear it. I love it…" There was a marvel in her voice. "It's beautiful and it's different and it's—it's not a chain."

"Never," I promised, even as I kissed her fingers. "We would *never*."

"I know you wouldn't. But when you guys all came in and everyone went to one knee—it just—we're doing this, right? We're okay? All of us? There's seven of you and one of me and…"

"There's eight of us, nine if we count your brother, ten if we count his girlfriend. The point is, yes, we're an us. I want to do this. They want to do this. But Sparrow, you don't have to do anything you don't want to do."

She smiled, then tipped her head back and closed her eyes. "I don't ever want to bring Fuckbucket here with us—he's the past. While he might not be gone yet…"

"Oh, he *will* be." There would be absolutely no mistake. When we were done, we would freeze what was left of him then feed it to a woodchipper and burn the results before we sowed it with salt.

Overkill?

No such thing.

When her eyes opened again, they were shining. "I love you," she whispered. "I love all of you so much. The scary part is—not being enough. I never pictured this… never pictured a real life and now, I have so much to lose. I can't stand the idea of losing any of you. *Ever.*"

"We're going to protect you and each other," I swore to her. "If that's something you need me to repeat over and over again, I will. Getting married? That's just a step. There's gonna be another after that and then another… There's always going to be more steps."

A tremulous smile touched her lips. "Like a dance?"

"Absolutely like a dance." Then I covered her hand on my

chest and traced my fingers over the ring. "Ask Liam about the ring when you get a chance."

She tilted her head.

"Just ask him—but when he tells you, remember, we all agreed. We decided together, we proposed together, we're going to be there for whatever the ceremony looks like, and every single day after that. This is just a step in our dance, Sparrow." I was already reaching for her when she pushed up to hug me, and I cradled her. "I promise," I whispered against her ear. "We have you."

"And I have you," she whispered back, and the last of the tension released. "Thank you."

When I set her down, it was my turn to tilt my head. "For?"

"Being you." She swallowed. "For loving me. For saving me. For pushing me. For... for dancing with me. Thank you for letting me be me."

"I don't want anyone else." The good. The bad. The terrifying. "My worst day with you is a thousand percent better than any day without you." And we'd had some bad days.

Her stomach growled.

"Now we're going to feed you before Liam launches out of that doorway to thump me for keeping you away from the food."

Her eyes widened a fraction, and she leaned to the side to look around me. "How did you know he was there?"

"Cause he's pushy," I said with a laugh, then wrapped an arm around her as I turned to face the man in question. Liam just gave me a droll look, but he flicked his eyes to her once then raised his brows to me in question.

Was she all right?

I nodded.

"Yeah, I'm pushy. Now get in here and eat." Liam crooked a finger. "Please."

"He said please," I commented, and she laughed.

"He's actually gotten really good at it," was all she said, then she pressed another kiss to my jaw before she skipped ahead and leapt up to meet Liam's hug. He crushed her to him with care. The concern in his eyes was the same one I shared. We all did.

But like I told Sparrow. This was just another step.

The noise in the kitchen seemed so much louder when we stepped in there, as if they'd all been trying to keep it down but now there was no such need. We needed a bigger dining area, especially if we were going to do more family meals like this. Liam parked Sparrow in a seat, and then Vaughn eased her into his lap so I could sit down.

Lainey was seated on the other side of Vaughn and sandwiched next to Milo. Sparrow grinned at her as she took a bite of bacon. There were pancakes, orange juice, fried potatoes, eggs, and more. Doc was at the stove, and when I would have gone to help, he waved me to the table.

"The sooner we all eat, the sooner we plan. Freddie and Rome have clean up after."

"Hey," Freddie protested. "Who volunteered me for that job?"

"I did," Rome told him. "Eat."

"Oh." Freddie studied Rome for a minute. "Okay, big brother, but understand, I expect an allowance if I get chores."

Jasper flicked food off his plate and nailed Freddie right in the cheek.

"Don't," I said before Freddie could retaliate. "No food fights."

"Awww," Freddie and Sparrow said in the exact same tone. There was a downbeat then an upbeat before laughter rippled around the table.

"I'll help with the dishes," Bodhi volunteered. "Call it a wedding present."

"Dishes are not a wedding present," Sparrow informed him.

"I'll work on that, PPG."

She just grinned, and when she caught my eye, her smile grew. She was all right. Good.

I dug into my own pancakes as Liam fired up the coffeemaker. "Barista in the house. After Hellspawn and Lainey get theirs, I'll take orders…"

"I see who the favorite is," Jasper teased, and Liam just flipped him off.

Chewing my bite thoughtfully, I turned over what Sparrow had confessed out there. We all had a lot more to lose. Then…

We had a hell of a lot to gain too.

CHAPTER 34

EMERSYN

hree days after the proposal, Liam and I were on our way to the county clerk's office with a full escort, including Mickey's guys in a forward car. Adam and Ezra were with Lainey and Milo in another car. It was quite the entourage for a civil service, or so Lainey teased when she gave me the dress this morning.

I smoothed my hand down the pale cream dress with the deep blue jacket. The lace overlay was so delicate, creating an illusion neckline, and the skirt that went to my knees. The ballet flats weren't as classy as heels, I supposed, but I preferred them. The jacket was Lainey's concession to me going armed.

"I never thought I would have to find a gun holster that went with a nice dress," she'd said while perched on my bed. "But I have to admit, I did enjoy the challenge."

Laughter swirled through me. "Thank you for doing this…" There had even been a garter, in deep blue to match the jacket. I was wearing a pair of her earrings for something borrowed. The dress would work for new. The jacket and garter for blue. Then Milo had given me a necklace that belonged to our mother. It wasn't anything fancy, but he'd managed to hold onto it over the years. It was a hammered penny from an amusement park.

"I made it for her when I was like three," he'd admitted with just the barest hint of embarrassment. "It was one of her favorites. I don't even know why I kept it after, but I want you to wear it today." The story made it even more special because it was Milo and he was the one giving it to me.

"We can call this off right now," Liam said, glancing over at me. I blinked back to the present and looked at him. I'd been running my finger over the phoenix ring over and over. "I mean it, Hellspawn. We can find another way. Fuck it, we can fake the papers if we need to do it…"

"No," I said, shaking my head. "I haven't changed my mind."

"Okay. You want to talk to me about what's going on inside that head of yours?"

We were at a traffic light, and Freddie was in the car right next to us. As soon as they pulled up he made a face that had me giggling. As soon as Liam glanced toward Freddie though, he sobered like nothing happened. I bit my lip when Liam shot me an amused look, then he sobered again.

"Talk to me, Hellspawn. I can't fix it if I don't know what it is."

"You sure? You seem pretty good about fixing a lot of things, even when I didn't know what the problem was."

He smiled. "I try. But you're too important for guessing. Is it the ring?"

I glanced down at it where I was stroking it. "No, I love the ring. It's—it's different, perfect."

"Okay, so it's not the ring. Is it going to the clerk's office?

This is just the paperwork. We can see a Justice of the Peace and get it all squared away. But if you want a real ceremony..."

I laughed. "Actually, no—I don't want a 'real' ceremony, whatever that would look like. This is going to be real, right? We're going to get married, and legally, I'll be your wife and you'll be my husband—but I'm marrying everyone."

"Exactly. I get the legal leg up but—I don't even care about that if you're unhappy." The worry decorating his voice tugged at me, and I reached for his hand. He caught mine easily even as the light changed, and we started forward again.

"Liam, I'm not unhappy—not that way." This was so hard to explain. "I'm not even sure I understand it myself. My life has not been normal. Or at least—my normal is not everyone else's normal. I can't imagine anyone who had this kind of 'normal' except..."

"Freddie?"

"I don't want to talk about his secrets."

"You don't have to," Liam said, squeezing my hand. "We know it was bad even when he doesn't want to talk about it, and if he's talking to you? Then I'm *glad* he is."

"Me too." I blew out a breath. "But that's the thing. I never imagined a big brother or one lover, much less seven, or getting married, or getting rid of Fuckbucket, or finding my biological father—it feels like so much, and when good things happen, bad things follow."

"You're scared for us," Liam said, and his whole demeanor shifted. "Emersyn..." The use of my name rocked me. "Hellspawn, that's what being a real family is. We take hits for each other, we dish out the pain to those who hurt us, and we take care of each other. I know a lot of bad shit has gone down for you. Fuck, do I know it has..."

I swallowed.

"Finding you in that coffin? That's never going away. But I refuse to not pursue every drop of happiness we can have and the life we can build, together. You, me, the guys—fuck even Ezra and Adam, pair of asshats that they are."

I laughed. "Bodhi?"

He growled. "Fine. But he's riding in someone else's car."

"I know," I said, squeezing his hand. "I do know that. In my head, but my heart? It's hard to hope. It's even harder to not be afraid of something happening to any of you. It would kill me…"

"Then we keep protecting each other. We make sure we take care of each other. Yes, even if it means protecting fucking Cavendish, well, maybe I sacrifice him first, but otherwise, we'll do our best."

He wasn't altogether teasing about that last part. So I just squeezed his hand. "Thank you."

"You never have to thank me," he said. "I mean that. What I have is yours. What I can do, I will do. If you never look afraid again it will be too soon."

"I didn't mean to worry all of you. The proposal was beautiful…"

"And terrifying."

"But not because of you," I promised. "I know I'm stubborn, and I know what I said about Fuckbucket and clothes and the jewelry and…" It wasn't all that many years ago that he'd leashed me during a gala. "But I hate giving him that kind of power, and this ring…this ring is from you and the guys. I don't know why you picked out this one exactly but…"

We pulled into the lot, and he parked before he looked over at me, catching my hand between both of his. "When we argued about the wedding—and yes, it was an argument, but no blood was spilled, I promise."

I had to bite back a smile at that.

"We all talked about the ring. We wanted to give you something that meant something to us but also to you. I know you don't like all the jewels and the fancy clothes, but this..." he lifted my hand to show me the ring where it wrapped around my finger. The phoenix was beautiful, and the rose quartz just made it even more ethereal, even as it added to the heat. "This is you. Fierce. Beautiful. Fiery. A survivor. A firebird who gave birth to herself and saved herself, and no matter how much darkness that son of a bitch coated you in—that fire was right there. It's unique, like you. It's something we could all give you, and it meant something from all of us—but even more? It's new, and it's a new start."

"A new start," I repeated slowly. "For all of us?"

"Hell yes, for all of us," he promised. When Rome knocked on the driver's side door window, Liam held up a hand, then cracked the window. "Give us a sec. We'll be out." Then he closed it before he focused on me again. "Before you came along, Hellspawn? We were pulling apart, treading water in places—drowning in others. The guys didn't trust me anymore because of all the secrets I was keeping. Rome was torn between them and me. Milo was in jail. Doc—Doc was focused on the clinic, and Jasper kept everyone at arm's length. And Freddie..."

"Freddie was dying," I said softly, and Liam gave me a small smile.

"Yeah, he was. We were—weren't who we'd been, and we were nothing like we are now. When Jasper kidnapped you, he did more than just save you, Hellspawn. He saved all of us. Just some of us were too fucking stubborn to understand it at the time."

"I mean," I said slowly. "That could apply to me too."

He grinned. "I know it does."

"You like me stubborn."

"Damn straight." He touched a finger to my jaw. "But this

is a new start for all of us. We're going to bury the past. Every damn bit of it that we don't want. We'll burn it down if we have to, then we're going to all get the life *we* want, because we'll damn well build it. If that means you want to do shows or open a school or just sit around and eat bon-bons all day, then that's what we'll do."

I giggled. "Bon-bons?"

"Sure, they're sweet."

"I love you, Liam. I really do."

"I love you too, Hellspawn." The brush of his lips to mine was almost painfully sweet. "But you need to get back into fight training again."

"I promise." When I lifted my hand to his cheek, I said, "And going forward? I think I want us to just be us, which means you get to get me presents if you want…"

"We'll take baby steps there," he said, taking my hand and kissing the ring before he focused on me. "But right now, will you give me the privilege of taking me inside and making me your husband?"

"Emersyn O'Connell." I tested it out. "That's gonna be weird. But a good weird."

"We approve of good weirds." That was such a bizarre way to phrase it that I laughed all over again. "You ready?"

Nodding slowly, I said, "I am, and Liam?"

"Hmm?"

"Thank you. I needed to talk that out." While the nerves were still there, it was more anticipation than dread. He winked.

"Anytime, Hellspawn. Now get that gorgeous ass in gear. We've got places to be and people to kill."

I was still laughing when Mickey opened my door for me and offered me a hand to get out. The guys were all there. More than one had their heads on a swivel, but Lainey slid up to hook her arm through mine.

"I know this is just civil, but I'm maid of honor," she informed me as she held up a tiny bouquet. "But I refuse to catch this."

I burst out laughing. "Done," I said and gave her a hug. Milo watched us with an indulgent smile, but it wasn't long before we were all heading for the doors. Once inside, we'd fill out the paperwork.

Liam was right about one thing, money definitely smoothed the wheels. It was midday. The clerk's office was open. We'd just made it to the top of the stairs when the door to the building opened and all the laughter drained out of me.

Julius King stepped outside to meet us, and I forgot how to breathe.

"You son of a bitch," Milo said. "What the fuck are you doing here?"

CHAPTER 35

EMERSYN

*T*he tension in Liam turned his arm to stone. Vaughn and Mickey just moved right in front of me. Mickey's back was rigid, and the others closed in, forming a box that cut King off from me *and* Milo. Lainey's fingers tightened on my arm.

"It's good to see you too, son," King said in a slow, even tone that he had no right adopting when it came to either of us, but particularly not Milo. "Mickey."

"Jeff." Mickey's voice was dead flat.

"I'm sorry about your sister…"

"Fuck right the hell off with that," Mickey retaliated. "I don't want your sympathies or anything else. In fact, I don't want you anywhere near Little Bit or Milo."

"Right, because you have a leg to stand on with my daughter who is nearly half your age…" If King was worried about the reaction from everyone on the steps, he didn't show it. "In fact, why don't you go away and let me talk to my kids."

"Your kids," Mickey said with a scoff. "They haven't been *your* anything since you walked out on them and their mother."

"Not your call," King informed him, his tone going colder and his gaze stonier.

"It *is* mine," Milo said, pulling King's attention back to him. "And Ivy's. Mickey's been here. You haven't. So in this we agree, you can fuck right the hell off."

A chill wrapped around my spine when King locked eyes with Milo. I squeezed Lainey's hand then stepped forward, aware that Liam moved with me, and when I was standing with Milo, King flicked a look to me then to Liam and back.

"What do you want?" I was proud of the fact my voice didn't tremble.

Sliding his hands into his pockets, King created a hell of a stir because Mickey's guys were already surrounding him, and there was a grunt as his security guys were intercepted. No weapons were out, but this whole situation was a powder keg and a flash of Freddie's knife danced in my periphery.

"I believe you're here getting married."

"And?" I wasn't going to confirm or deny it.

"I came to give the bride away."

My snort echoed and I wasn't the only one, but it was Liam who said, "She isn't anyone's to give away. Hellspawn belongs to herself, and she gives herself to who she wants. If that's what you came for, I suggest you go away."

"Actually, Bishop," King said, sparing him a look. "The fact she wants to marry you is the only reason you're still breathing. Particularly because I can see that Adam Reed is *not* dead."

"Sorry to disappoint," Adam replied in a sardonic voice that didn't carry even a trace of apology.

"She's not marrying you, not disappointed in the slightest on that front." King's possessive tone irked me, and I rolled my eyes.

"You didn't want Ivy when she was a baby, a fact you made brutally clear," Milo all but snarled. "Don't pretend you want her now. What you want is her money and the companies she's going to inherit. You want the power she represents and the influence. It has *nothing* to do with her."

"It's almost sad that you think so little of me," King said. "And a debate for another day. As it is—Emersyn asked me for something. I'm here to deliver."

Shock rippled through me. He didn't have Fuckbucket here right now? Did he? The ice on my spine thickened, and the chill invaded every part of my body.

"It's up to you," King said, his focus on me like he wasn't surrounded by a number of hostile Vandals. "Do you want the answer or not?"

Tension threaded through Milo, and I lifted a hand to rest on his arm. That pulled his attention to me. "You don't have to say a damn word to him, Ivy."

"I know, but I did ask him for something." The fact he'd actually... "How did you know we would be here?"

Amusement touched the man's cool gaze. "I make it a point of being informed."

"He's following us," Liam said flatly.

King didn't respond to that. He focused on me. "It's up to you, Emersyn. If you want the information, I have it for you..."

"And if you don't give it to me now, I don't get it at all?" Was that the deal?

"We can find the son of a bitch on our own," Milo said. "We don't need or want anything from you."

I didn't *want* to want anything from him *or* need it.

"I didn't say that," King said, ignoring Milo.

"What do you want for the information?"

"Five minutes of your time, and to watch the ceremony."

"There isn't going to be a ceremony," I told him. "Not the way you're thinking, and you have already taken up five minutes of our time." No way I was walking off with him for some private conversation.

When he pulled his hand out of his pocket, Mickey cut in front of me again, and King merely sighed. "It's paper, Mickey." He held up the slip, and when Mickey held out his hand, King closed his fingers over it. "It's for Emersyn. Not you. Not Milo. Not Liam. Emersyn."

Kellan let out a slow sigh. "Sparrow?" Did I want to do this? Did I want the information? What did I want them to do?

"You give that to me and then what?" was how I chose to answer all of them. I kept trying to relax my white-knuckled grip on Liam. It didn't work, and he didn't flinch from the way my hand dug into his arm.

The violence wreathing the air could be choking, I supposed, but it offered me a kind of comfort I didn't want to examine too closely right now. The words I'd said to Kel echoed in the back of my mind. I had so much to lose. No doubt existed within me that they would protect me. But I wasn't willing to trade their lives for mine, period.

"I stay long enough to see this through, then I leave. You call me when you're ready to talk," King said.

"I don't get it," I admitted, and he canted his head even as Milo flicked a look to me. "Why do you care so much now?" Before the Vandals took me, I hadn't even known I was adopted. This man was literally *no one* to me, except that he'd caused *Milo* pain, and ordered *Adam* to be killed, and was a threat to *Liam* and *Ezra*. To be honest, he was a threat to all of us, but it didn't offer an explanation.

"A conversation for another day," King answered. "For

now, I'll accept your word that you will call me when you're ready to talk."

I had no idea what answer to give him. But if he knew where Fuckbucket was... "And that's his location?"

"It's where he will be in six days."

Six days.

"You know where he is going to be in six days, but you don't know where he is right now?" Mickey asked, skepticism rifling every word. I didn't blame him for that or for the anger he and Milo held toward this man.

Rome pressed a hand against my lower back, and I almost sagged into him. I glanced up at him and met the steadiness in his gaze. For a moment, just a few seconds, the world faded away and so did the noise. Rome wanted to know what *I* wanted.

Trusting everyone else at my back, I glanced over to meet Lainey's gaze. She lifted her shoulders in the barest of shrugs. She didn't have the answers either. Kellan wasn't watching me, but he did have his gaze on King. So did Jasper and Vaughn. They were all watching him and waiting.

Waiting for me to answer.

"Adam?" Because he'd already paid one price for me, I looked at him.

"Do what you need to do," he advised, and I didn't miss the way his gaze flicked to Lainey. I blew out a breath and glanced down before Milo shifted next to me. There was a slight movement as the guys rearranged themselves until Milo and I were shielded once more. The only one who didn't move was Liam. He did cut his gaze to us as Milo glanced down at me.

"What do you want to do?" was what Milo asked me, and I loved him so damn much for not ordering me around.

"I want to *not* need that information," I admitted, and his small smile promised he understood.

"I know," he said. "I've got you, and if you have to see him again, you won't be doing it alone."

"No," Liam agreed. "She absolutely won't be doing it alone."

I never had to be alone again, and I was more than all right with that.

"You don't want him here for this," I said, splitting a look between them. The guys closest to us could hear every word.

Liam shrugged. "We can make up for it later." There was just the barest sliver of tease in his voice. When Milo rolled his eyes, I couldn't hold back my smile. "Look, Raptor, just because you got a dirty mind, doesn't mean that was where I was going with that."

Milo snorted. "Doesn't mean it wasn't either."

"True."

Exhaling, I nodded. The teasing helped. The contact helped. It all helped. I squeezed Liam's arm once more before I peeled my fingers off and gave Milo's hand a squeeze. Touching light fingers to Mickey's back, I circled around him, and no one tried to haul me back or jerk me out of the way. Milo moved with me though, his steps matching mine until we were face to face with King.

"I don't want you here for this," I told him flatly, and if it pissed him off—whatever. "Today isn't about you. But I do want the information, and I did ask for it." King held my gaze. "So, if you will take my offer to call you when—and *only* when—I am ready to talk, then yes, I would like to know where Fuckbucket is going to be."

King withdrew the paper from his pocket and held it out to me wordlessly. I took it carefully. "If you need or want anything else, you have my number." Then he glanced past me to Liam. "You marry her, you will take care of her—"

"He already takes care of me, and if you threaten him or anyone else, it will be me you're dealing with."

With a light chuckle, King inclined his head. "You really do look like your mother." Milo stiffened. "But you are far more like me. That's good." He flicked a look at Milo. "Very good."

Turning, he walked away, and I frowned. "You're leaving?"

"You didn't want me here," King said, glancing back at me. "I'm respecting that. Like I said, you know where I am when you need me. I'll be looking forward to the call."

Then he just—left.

I stared after him, almost bewildered, and when I looked at Milo, I read the same confusion there.

What the hell had just happened?

CHAPTER 36

EMERSYN

"Well, I guess you don't have to play dead anymore," I offered to Adam. That seemed a small recompense for the ambush. I glanced down at the paper in my hand. When Kellan covered the folded piece with his hand I turned to him.

"Save this for later, Sparrow. Let's do this and get you two secure again." Lines of worry and tension tightened at the corners of his eyes and mouth. Mickey had moved to track where King had gone. I could almost make out the anger vibrating off of him. King shouldn't have brought up Ms. Stephanie.

"Kel's right," Liam said, his voice eerily calm. He wasn't remotely that relaxed about any of this. They were all scanning the area, and we were just standing out here on the steps. How was it possible to be so cold with the sun shining down on us? Liam held out a hand to me as I surrendered the note to Kellan. With care, Kel tucked it into the inside pocket of his jacket.

None of us wanted to open it right now.

That was for *after*.

"You still up for this, Hellspawn?"

Worry coated his words, and I slid my hand into his. "Hell, yes." What nerves I might still have evaporated with King's presence. I had no idea what game he was playing, but we'd just shown our hand with Adam and more. "You're not going back to him," I said to Liam, and he lifted his brows. "Not after today. He doesn't get to have you anymore. You're ours. Period."

"Agreed," Rome said. "Marry Starling and come home."

Liam chuckled. "One step at a time."

That wasn't a no.

"Let's go," Kellan said. We'd lingered too long, and we'd definitely drawn attention. Lainey passed me the bouquet back. I was glad she'd held onto it. I'd forgotten all about it thanks to the interruption. Mickey's men swept ahead of us and held the doors as Liam and I went inside.

Ten minutes later, we were crammed into the registrar's office, and the woman working the desk with her steel gray hair and dark eyes gave us a measuring look before she focused on Liam. "What can I do for you?"

"We're here to apply for a marriage license." Liam pulled out a small portfolio of papers from his pocket, including the application all filled out. "We didn't sign it yet…"

"Oh good," she told us with a smile. "And congratulations, when is the happy day?"

"Right after we get the license. According to the calendar, the Justice of the Peace is available today?" Liam said as he pulled out his ID and mine to hand over with everything.

"Oh, that's so sweet," the woman said as she went through

the paperwork. "Give me a couple minutes, and I'll call down the hall to make sure they book you right in."

It didn't even take her that long to go through everything and make the call. Then she asked us to swear we were not currently married nor had we been married and then divorced. She passed the license through to have us sign it. Liam passed it to me first, and my fingers were trembling a little.

This was ridiculous, I wasn't scared of getting married. Right? When I finished, Liam signed his name then passed it back. She went over the information, certified it, and then beamed as she said, "Congratulations and many happy blessings to you both."

It was sweet, and with the license in hand, we made our way to the Justice of the Peace. We moved like a swarm, and somewhere between the registrar's office and the Justice of the Peace, I just started giggling. It was—ridiculous.

We were a moving ceremony. The guys were all varying degrees of dressed up. Liam had on a suit, so did Kellan, and even Jasper had pulled out a really nice dress shirt. They were adorable. But the fact we were moving like a flock of birds was just—amazing.

Thanks to the call ahead, we were ushered right in. The Justice of the Peace, a man named Benson, greeted us with a smile and offered his hand to Liam to shake. "You brought plenty of witnesses with you," he said as he glanced around the room. We pretty much filled it up.

"We have a big family." The kind of family I'd always wanted, and I was so happy they were here.

"Well, you technically only need two to sign as witnesses," Benson told us. "So, which two will it be."

"Me," Lainey said, and I twisted to meet her smile. "Best friend privilege, I'm pulling rank."

Laughter rippled through the guys, then Bodhi raised his hand. "Can I get dibs on second witness? I'm good at it."

I hid a smile at Liam's pained look. "I think Milo would be the better witness," Liam said. "But thanks for the offer."

"Damn, fine, I'll just pretend I'm giving the bride away so I can play bodyguard if she needs it. You good with that, PPG?" Bodhi's smirk was adorable but so was Liam's attempt to not yell at him.

"I'd love that, Bodhi. Thank you."

He looked so pleased, but it was Lainey who rolled her eyes. "Such a pain in the ass."

"You know that about me," Bodhi said. "And you still like me."

As funny as it was, the distractions weren't working to ease the tension. Bless Bodhi for trying though. When we went over everything and confirmed the paperwork, Benson got us ready for the ceremony.

It was as straightforward as filling out the license had been. Except...

"Do you, Emersyn Sharpe, take this man, Liam O'Connell, to be your husband?" He didn't add any of the standard caveats. No richer or poorer. No sickness or health. No for better or worse. The simple truth was we didn't need those. We'd lived through all of them.

Shootings.

Car chases.

Fires.

Invasions.

A grave.

Lifting my chin, I smiled at Liam, but I also swept my gaze over the rest of the guys who were waiting with us. "I do," I said, and the words didn't waver and my hands weren't trembling.

Liam's grin grew when Benson said, "Do you Liam—"

"Hell yes, I do."

The Justice of the Peace chuckled. "Eager, son?"

"You have no idea," Liam told him, but he didn't take his gaze off me.

"Well, then as you are both certain this is your choice, and you are making it freely, and with full knowledge of the responsibilities of marriage, I now pronounce you husband and wife. You may kiss your bride."

The nervous flutters bursting inside of me just added to my laughter, and I was still giggling when Liam gave me a gentle kiss. Try as I might, I couldn't stop the amusement from bubbling up. He nipped my lower lip, but his smile was indulgent. "Mrs. O'Connell, you ready to get out of here?"

Oh, that dried up the laughter and replaced it with wonder. "I am absolutely ready, *Mr. O'Connell.*" It was both ridiculous, and sweet, and wonderful. The guys gave a spontaneous cheer. Lainey and Milo signed as witnesses, and the Justice of the Peace signed our copy and his. That was it. We were legally married.

The hustle to get out of the building took on a new strain, and it wasn't until we were back in Liam's car, with Jasper and Rome riding in the backseat with us, that I found out why.

"We've got watchers," Jasper said. "They took the bait, but we were there a fraction too long. Doc's guys are tagging them. We're sticking close."

My stomach clenched. "Then he knows I'm alive."

Good.

"If he didn't before," Jasper sounded almost apologetic. "He does now."

I didn't know how I felt about that, and they didn't discuss it as we drove. If anything, the ride back to the clubhouse was even more somber than the drive to the clerk's office. Dammit... "I hate this," I said. "We should be celebrating, and we're all thinking about Fuckbucket or King…"

"I'm not," Rome said. "I'm thinking about you naked and smiling."

The comment was just so him, I laughed. Glancing over my shoulder at him, I raised my eyebrows. "Naked and smiling?"

"Yes," Rome said. "Wedding nights should have you naked and smiling the whole night."

"Rome," Liam said. "This—"

"It's Starling's wedding night. Our wedding night. We're married, right?" The solemnity in his expression when he asked that settled something jagged and broken inside of me back into place. Gold filled those cracks, and the dark thoughts fled.

"Yes," I said, shifting my gaze to Jasper. "We're married. I like that…"

Jasper leaned forward to touch his finger to my nose gently. "We like that too. Now sit the way you should. Safety first."

The innocuous comment did the impossible, it splintered the tension. Where Rome had filled in the craters between the broken bits, making them stronger, Jasper swept away the debris to leave it shinier and happier.

Shiny happy people.

Happy.

I wouldn't let anyone take that away from us. Facing forward, I let out a little sigh then rested my hand on Liam's thigh. "Are we really having a wedding night tonight?"

"Maybe," he said. "Not that I'm not interested—but we have company and some of them would need to go. We don't want them all gone yet."

He had a point. Still…it was surreal. "We're married."

"Yep," he said in a sinful voice. "What do you want for a wedding present, Mrs. O'Connell?"

"I have the present I want." I had all of them. I didn't need anything else.

"Right, time to plan the perfect present," Jasper said.

"Read my mind, Jas."

"It's not really that deep," Jasper retorted. Liam just lifted his finger to flip him off, and they both laughed.

That was another gift.

All too soon we were back at the clubhouse. Security was tight here still, but the guys did sweeps of the interior, even after checking the security cameras. Once we were inside, Lainey gave me a hug and kissed my cheek.

"I've missed you," I confessed.

"Me too. We need to get rid of all the troublemakers so we can have some girl time."

"Deal."

I glanced over to where Milo eased down in a chair. He was still moving a little stiff, but his expression was foreboding as Mickey settled on the table in front of him. Their conversation was intense and focused. I didn't have to guess the subject. King had rattled everyone.

"You okay?" Lainey asked, and I blinked back at her.

"I am...I just—I wish I understood what King wanted, or why he showed up today..."

"He wants power," Adam answered from behind me, and I pivoted to face him. "Power and control. He'll leverage one to get the other, then use them both."

"What power or control does he get showing up there to see me?" Or had it been about me at all? He'd been taking little digs at Milo. Was I just a means to an end? A way to harm my brother?

"I can only tell you what I've seen about him over the years. He doesn't do anything without a reason. For nearly a decade, we didn't even have a face to put to the name. Now in a few short months, he's broken every protocol he put into place. He tried to have me assassinated. He wanted to recruit you. Now he wants a relationship with you—" Adam shook his head slowly. "Don't trust him."

"I don't," I admitted as Lainey hooked her arm through mine and held onto me. "I don't *know* him. The things I do know about him, I really don't like."

"Good," Adam said quietly, then he looked at Lainey. "Do you see why I wanted to keep you out of all of this?"

"Yes," she said. "And I still don't agree with it. You can't guard against what you don't know. If I let you make all the decisions, I'd be some feather head attending only the most elite of social functions and spending my days frittering about to find the perfect outfit."

Adam sighed and shook his head. I got it. I did, but I also understood Lainey. None of us wanted to be in cages or controlled. We had to be free to make choices. Me. Lainey. Milo. My guys. Even Adam. He'd been under King's thumb for far too long. Now?

Now, we had a shot at real freedom.

Freedom...

I looked at my Vandals.

They were my freedom.

"Hellspawn," Liam called. "You ready to do some bank paperwork?"

"Sexy," I retorted. "Sign me up."

He grinned, and Freddie laughed. "Boo-Boo, bank stuff? Really?"

"Sure," I told him as I hooked my pinky with his. "It'll be fun."

CHAPTER 37

EMERSYN

*B*ank paperwork was neither sexy nor all that fun. Liam's lawyers had drafted up a series of transfer orders and claim assumptions. The language was arcane in its own way, but the terms of the trusts were laid out.

"Do I want to know how they got the specifics for each one?" And just how many trusts were there? It seemed unreasonable.

"Alphabet helped," Mickey said.

"So did Moira," Milo commented and shock rippled through me. "After everything, she sat down and wrote out everything she remembered, including the names of every single trustee."

"Then she called them," Liam finished. "She asked for a lawyer—I sent her one of mine—and they did conference calls. She pulled all the information necessary, and I had the attorneys drafting the language. I wanted it ready, if we ever decided to pull the trigger."

It was so much. "This is millions."

"Closer to billions, Hellspawn." Liam tapped the top sheet. "Four separate trusts, each one multi-layered. That doesn't include the stock options attached or the companies themselves. He went to a lot of trouble to hide that money and tie it up in trusts where no one else could get to it. A nest egg…"

"And all we have to do is sign the paperwork and send the lawyers after it?" Was it really that easy?

Kellan moved to take the chair next to me as Milo eased down into the chair across from me. "Yes," Kel said. "And no. If we were going to physically get the cash, it would take a lot of time. What we're doing instead is draining the trusts into a series of numbered accounts outside of the country."

"It's the best way to secure it," Adam stated from where he'd come to join us. "It's a tax shelter for one, but that's only the basic part. What you want to do is make the money vanish."

"So we're adding my name to all the accounts," Liam stated, "and at the same time, we're changing your name. The marriage certificate is certified and copies will go out with every request. The lawyers will take care of filing everywhere necessary to update your last name. It takes around seventy-two hours to process, and once I'm on the account, we drain them."

"And take all of his money."

"Your money," Milo said firmly. "I don't care what you do with the money, stack it all up and burn it if you want to, but it's yours. They put it in trusts *for* you. Whether it was just another sick game or not. It's yours, and we're just leveling his playing field."

"Then we're going to level him." Freddie grinned. The whole plan was clever, and I wanted to make it hurt. Fuck-bucket loved his money because he loved his power. It took me a minute to master signing them as Emersyn O'Connell

—that would take some getting used to—but I had it down by the time I finished.

"Hey," Vaughn asked as he settled his hands on my shoulders. "What's wrong?"

I glanced up at him then down at the paperwork. "Not wrong precisely..." I'd grown up wealthy. The money had always just been there. I didn't think about it. We had security, cars, clothing, planes, trips overseas, education, all the dance classes I could ever want...the only thing I'd lacked for was real freedom from Fuckbucket's abuse.

"It's a lot," Liam said, and when I met his gaze, I read the understanding there. "You've never thought about it before." It wasn't a question.

I shook my head. Covering one of Vaughn's hands with my own, I squeezed his fingers. "I—I never had to think about money. It never occurred to me to think how much. I remember...I remember when I 'escaped,' I planned to get money to send to Mickey for the clinic. I could afford it from my own account, and I wanted to do something to help."

Surprise flickered over his face, and I gave him a small smile.

"I still want to help. I want to rebuild Kel's shop, and Vaughn's tattoo parlor, and everything you guys could want..." And the reality was, that might just be a drop in the bucket of all that money.

What the hell did someone do with all that money?

"We'll deal with that later," Kellan told me. "Is that everything that needed to be signed?"

"Yep," Liam said as he slid another page through a scanner. He'd been scanning them in and transmitting them to his lawyer as we signed. "I'll courier the originals over later, but this is enough to get them started."

Rubbing my cheek against Vaughn's hand, I blew out a shaky breath before I looked at Kellan. "Where is Fuckbucket going to be?" The hum of conversation throughout the sitting room died off at my question.

He pulled the slip of paper out and slid it over to me. It was what King had brought. Did we trust him? No. But if we had the info, maybe we could confirm it. "I don't know if we can trust it," Kellan told me. "And I don't know what game King is playing, it could be a trap. But even if it is a trap, we can use it."

"Exactly," Milo said as he moved over to the table. He was moving better. His wounds and burns were healing, but he was *still* healing. "I almost hope it is a trap, because I want to close in on that mother fucker and tear him apart."

Tension in the room climbed as I picked up the paper. Vaughn moved his hand to my nape and rested it there, stroking his thumb up and down along the corded muscle where it was tight.

I was worried about all of them, but they were equally worried about me. The group gathered around us, everyone waiting, even Bodhi and two of Mickey's guys who'd stuck it out for the rest of the day. I wasn't sure where Grace was, but they wanted to keep her at a distance from all of this.

I could hardly blame them.

Lainey slid into the seat next to me.

She bumped my shoulder gently while Vaughn kept massaging it. Right. Rip the Band-Aid off.

I unfolded the paper. It was on letterhead—King Industries—right, whatever. The handwriting was crisp, almost too neat, and disciplined. The address leapt out at me along with the arrival date. My stomach plummeted.

"He's going home," Lainey said, glancing up at me. "Could that be the trap?"

"Maybe. At least I know the place. Well, I know the fence around the property is now electrified." I curled my fingers into my palms. The scars there were fainter than the ones on my arms.

My tension must have communicated because Vaughn tightened his grip, a flex to remind me he was there. They were all here. I picked up the water someone had brought to the table and drained it before I lifted my chin.

"I know that place inside and out. If he wanted to set a trap there are more than a few places to do it... including the maze." There were secret passages too. Hidden rooms. Rooms locked behind other rooms. "His bedroom is also a panic room."

A dozen pairs of eyes locked on me.

"You up for drawing us a diagram, Sparrow?" Kellan's gaze held concern, and he wasn't alone. Adam's jaw had tightened. Milo's expression flattened. Their anger thrummed with my heartbeat.

"I can do anything. He said six days, so we have five to get ready... if we want to be there when he gets there, we should leave sooner rather than later."

"I'll get you paper, Boo-Boo," Freddie said.

"I'm getting you alcohol," Jasper commented. "Or do you want coffee?"

"Honestly?"

"Yes," they chorused, and it was sweet.

"I'd like both. Please."

As normal as everyone tried to make it, and as relaxed as they tried to be, I couldn't help the tremors. I was going home—to Fuckbucket's house. Was that why he was going there? To get me to come to him? Or something else?

A lot could happen in six days.

Six days. Why six days?

I didn't get that.

The next three hours were some of the longest in my life. I drew the layout for the house, what was on each floor.

What was on the property. Trying to remember the property lines was a little harder, but Adam actually knew them. When I gave him a bewildered look, he only shrugged.

"Know your enemies," he said in an almost gentle tone. "And there was every chance that Lainey was going to try and get to you. I needed to know how to get you both out."

Next to me, Lainey gave a little start. Adam barely flicked a look at her, but there was no mistaking the certainty in his voice. But maybe he should know something. "I would never have let her come there."

"I know," he said, regret tangible in those two words. "But in case you haven't noticed, Lainey doesn't listen very well."

Her snort was worth everything, and there was the barest of lip twitches from Adam.

"And she loves you," he continued. "Sometimes, she doesn't think about what it could cost her when she rushes out to do things."

That I knew, and I glanced at her to find her staring at Adam with the oddest expression. "I will never abandon my friends *or* my family."

"I know," he said, and that was it.

There wasn't much more to say after that. Kellan called a halt so they could go over what they had. Alphabet was already pulling property records and layouts. Anything he could get his hands on. When I told him there was a security system, he looked positively delirious.

In the kitchen, I rinsed out my mug, but I was swaying. Vaughn seemed to have become my shadow, and he came to rest against the counter. "Are you okay?" I asked him. It had been a long few days, and he was still grieving.

"I'm fine, Dove," he said, summoning a smile. "I'm just feeling protective, and you've got a lot on your plate at the moment."

"So do you."

"But I have you to look after me," he teased, and my heart did a little flop. Setting the cup aside, I shut off the water and turned to him. He wrapped me up into the best hug, and I sank into him. He smoothed a hand over my hair then down my back. "This is a lot for you."

"I'll be okay." It didn't sound certain. Then again, I wasn't all that certain myself. "It's hard because—I don't want you guys in that house."

A sound behind me was the first warning that Mickey was there, and then he rested a hand against my back. "That was the house where it started?" A simple question, especially if we didn't dig down into what it was that started.

"Yeah," I answered, turning so I could keep my cheek against Vaughn's chest, but the guys filling the room were just us. Milo...

"Sent Milo up with Lainey," Kellan told me. "Alphabet and his guys are getting to work. Bodhi is doing something."

"He wants to go poke a bear or something," Freddie said with a shrug. "I think he's restless. He said he'd be back when we were ready to move."

"We good with him going?" Liam asked, his expression guarded.

"I am," I said. "He's not going to betray us. He's had a lot of opportunities."

"What Boo-Boo said," Freddie agreed. "He just wants to help."

"Okay, we're getting you to bed," Kellan said firmly, and I raised my eyebrows. All seven of them were in here, did that mean... "You can sleep with whomever you want, but you need sleep, Sparrow."

"Yeah," Mickey agreed. "You're pale, and this has been a long day."

"It's supposed to be our wedding night..."

Liam grinned, but it was more indulgent than it was teasing. "Hellspawn, we've got all the nights ahead of us. The guys are right, you're tired. So are we. We've got a lot of planning to do and a lot of moves to make. I'm not opposed to sex, but I am definitely fine to wait for the celebrations for when you're really ready to celebrate."

Because I wasn't right now, and he was right. I wasn't. There was too much Fuckbucket in my head right now…

"Guys, I have a favor to ask."

"Name it," Jasper said.

"He has recordings…" I swallowed, locking gazes with Freddie. His eyes flattened. He'd been recorded—filmed for others—he understood. "He tried to torture Milo with them. I want them gone…completely and utterly gone. I don't want anyone to see them."

"We'll take care of it," Jasper said without hesitation.

"And no one will watch then," Mickey agreed. "But I do want a piece of him."

"Me too," they all echoed. So did I…whether I could actually do it or not? I wasn't sure. But I did want him dead.

I wanted to see him die.

They'd killed Reginald. He was history. I hadn't needed to see that he'd been erased.

Fuckbucket?

That I wanted to see.

I wanted to be the last thing he saw, so he would know he lost.

Then I wanted to forget him and everything about him. Closing my eyes, I burrowed into Vaughn, and he tightened his grip on me. "We have you, Dove. We have you."

CHAPTER 38

EMERSYN

Six days seemed far away, until we were forty-eight hours out. My trust accounts had been drained. Liam set up an account for my mother, at my request, so she would be free to do whatever she wanted. He promised to take care of it. Stock assets had been claimed, along with the voting shares for my mother that she signed over to me. It gave me a full forty percent of the companies, more than Fuckbucket's holdings.

There was a bizarre kind of irony that he'd given me his assets to hide them. I suppose he never thought I would go after them. To be honest, I probably wouldn't have. All I'd ever wanted was to escape. The idea of taking him down didn't occur to me because he was too powerful, held too much control, and he'd killed people.

Well, now so had I.

And I refused to be afraid of him.

Facing him in that graveyard, my fear had evaporated in

the wake of my hate. Hate for what he'd done to me. What he'd done to my mother. What he was doing to Milo.

"Boo-Boo?" Freddie slid onto the sofa next to me, and I glanced at him. I was up in our suite, Kellan had just gotten a call and said we might be moving, if it was the information we'd been waiting on.

"Hey…"

"You okay?"

They'd all been doing that, checking with me, asking, and I got it. Everyone was tense. Mickey wasn't sleeping. Even when I tried to get him to sleep with me, he would slip out as soon as I was asleep.

"My nightmares are not for you, Little Bit," was all he would say. "I won't risk you."

Liam spent more time on the phone and working with Adam and his lawyers. Ezra had been kind of quiet. Rome or Vaughn sat with me, or moved where I did. I was never alone unless I was in this suite. I loved them for it. I didn't have to be alone, but they needed to be where I was, because what had Liam said? Every time I left his sight something bad happened.

"I'm—worried." Though that seemed far too tame a word.

"This is going to work," Freddie said, moving to sit sideways so he could study me. "You believe that, right?"

The plan was solid. Alphabet had gotten the plans that had been filed for when the house had been built. I'd filled in all the missing pieces. The security detail he traveled with was the last part. Mickey's guys said they could handle it, but Kellan insisted we needed sign-off from the Network before we took them out.

They weren't planning to negotiate. In fact, there would be no negotiation.

At all.

"I want to believe it," I said, twisting the ring on my

finger. "But he's—so dangerous, and he has all these people working for him. The last time I saw him, he was torturing Milo."

"And then he put you in a coffin." Freddie placed his hand over mine, and I stopped fidgeting. "Boo-Boo, no one is letting him get anywhere near you. You're going because this is your fight too and you have a right to it, but no one will say a word if you don't want to do it."

If I didn't want to go... If I didn't want to face him...

"I can't stay behind. One—if I did, some of you would have to stay behind with me because splitting up is just a bad idea."

"You have a point." He stroked his thumb over the back of my hand, and it helped to settle some of my jangling nerves.

"Two—I owe him pain for everything he's done to us." Because he might have started out just hurting me, but so many others had been hurt along the way, including Liam's father and Ms. Stephanie. He'd tortured Milo. He tried to kill Freddie, Jasper, Vaughn, and Kellan... No doubt existed within me that he would kill all of them, given the chance. "I won't let that go. I have to see him die. I don't know if *I* can kill him." I wanted to say I could, but that was my shame and my fear. "I hurt him before. But I don't know if I can kill him."

"You don't have to," Freddie said. "Trust me, we're gonna be doing more than rock-paper-scissors to kill that asshole."

A laugh worked its way up through me, and I snorted. Then the laugh escaped, and I shook my head. "That should not be funny."

"It totally should be," Freddie argued. "It's funny as hell. You wanna place a bet on who's going to get to do it?"

I groaned, and he grinned then sobered. His eyes were so intense, I couldn't look away.

"Boo-Boo, I *know* you're scared," he said. "I know, cause *I'm* scared too."

At his confession, I turned one of my hands over, and he clasped it.

"I didn't see the coffin, and I am so very glad I didn't. I already hate that son of a bitch. But he's hurt you so many times, and I know this is going to hurt you—the videos, seeing that house—*him*. I know it will."

"But it might free me too." I was already free, right? So why did it feel like this?

Freddie nodded slowly. "Maybe. But the past is—it's a shackle that digs all the way down. Like it's tattooed on our bones. Sometimes, I think I've shaken it all off then it's just *there*, and I can't get out. That's when I want to get high or stoned or just—blur all the noise."

"Do you want to get high right now?" I didn't want him to fall into that pit again, but if he saw no other way, then he wasn't doing it alone. I would stay with him.

"Strangely," Freddie said, his expression a tad bewildered even as he fought to smile. "No. Cause if I do—then I can't go, and I can't help. I want to go, and I want to help. But I don't want to see you hurting, Boo-Boo. I can take a lot, but then I think about you in Pinetree and you being so out of it and disconnected. You barely even recognized me. You didn't recognize me at all. At least not at first."

I swallowed and tightened my grip on his hand as his knuckles went white. I didn't know which of us was grounding the other, but we were hanging on for dear life. As long as he wanted and needed me here, I would never let go.

"If I check out—you might end up like that again." He shook his head. "I'm not letting that happen to you."

"I won't let it happen to you either." I wasn't going to let it happen to any of them. "Freddie...have I ever told you that I love you?"

Surprise flickered in his eyes. "Boo-Boo, I'm—"

"Perfect, just the way you are. Perfect and flawed and you get me in a way no one else can. They understand, or they try to, and they are so good to me—but you *know*. I hate that you know, but at the same time..."

"...I'm also kind of grateful that you do too," Freddie finished. "Then I hate myself because I'm grateful."

"Don't hate yourself. I don't hate you for being grateful. I have a lot of reasons to be grateful for you, this is just one of them. I don't know where I'd be without you." That was the simple truth. He'd saved me. They'd all saved me.

"They would have gotten to you," Freddie promised. "I'm glad I was able to be there."

"And we got to meet Bodhi."

Freddie grinned then lifted my hand to kiss it. "This okay?"

"Yes. I told you, you can touch me anytime you want, however you want. Are you okay with me holding your hand?"

"I like it," he admitted. "It's nice." It was nice. "So—we're getting phoenix tattoos, right?"

I nodded. "Vaughn said we needed to wait until this was all done, cause they would be sore and need to heal."

"Agreed," Freddie said. "But—think you can help me pick something else out? The guys had an idea, but—I want to know if you like it."

"Anything," I agreed.

"You don't know what it is..."

"Well, is it a cock piercing?" Unease slid through me. Was that too much?

Freddie opened his mouth, then snapped it closed. Oh shit, maybe I shouldn't have—then he laughed, and relief whooshed through me as his eyes crinkled with his smile. His chuckle deepened, and he leaned forward, hesitating just a breath away from my lips. Lifting my free hand, I touched his cheek with two fingers and closed the distance.

It began as just a brush, then he formed his lips to mine as I opened my mouth. The sweep of his tongue sent shivers through me. It was the softest, most gentle kiss I'd ever received, and at the same time it left me panting for more. I didn't hold onto him, giving him all the control. Because he was letting me touch him, but I meant it when I said he could do anything he wanted with me.

I trusted Freddie. He needed that control, and I needed to give it to him.

When he bit down on my lower lip, a real shiver went through me, and he pulled back. "Too much?"

Licking my lips, I shook my head. "No, I promise—that was nice."

He grinned, his relief seemed to shudder over him. "You taste like coffee and sugar."

I laughed. "I just had coffee."

"I like it."

We were just staring at each other and his gaze dipped to my lips again, then he shook his head.

"You wanted to ask me something," I said gently, prompting him.

"I did," he said, then squeezed my hand before he let go to reach into his pocket. I folded my hands together again. That he could reach out and touch me and let me touch him sometimes was enough. He pulled out the paper and unfolded the sketch. It was a bird. "Rome and Vaughn were working on the phoenix idea, then Rome gave me this later."

When he handed it to me, I studied the image. It was a delicate looking bird. But I didn't know enough about them to identify it.

"It's a songbird," he said, almost sheepishly, and I glanced at him. Freddie could sing. He could sing beautifully. "But—

it's not a harmless one. A lot of songbirds are, you know, they just sing and look pretty."

Freddie was both pretty and could sing.

"But they call it a loggerhead shrike."

"Okay—what does a loggerhead shrike do?"

"Well," Freddie said, pursing his lips, then spreading his hands. I swore there was a flush to his cheeks too. "They are also called butcher birds or—" Now he looked almost shy. "A thorn bird."

"I don't get that. If it's a songbird—why do they also call it a butcher bird?"

Freddie ducked his chin, and the bit of color on his face deepened to a ruddier red. He was embarrassed. Now I had to know.

"Well, they aren't harmless, like I said…shrikes like to impale their prey after they catch it. I mean, I know it's insects and stuff. But they stab them with their beaks, impale them on barbed wire or thorns, and then come back to feast —when they want it."

"So—it's a beautiful songbird that enjoys stabbing their prey?" It was—*perfect*.

Freddie nodded slowly. "I've never really had one of the bird names. There have been a few suggested over the years, and I always said I didn't care but—"

Oh, Freddie.

"Shrike," I said, holding up the picture. "Rome and the guys want to give you Shrike as your bird name."

"Is that stupid?" And that was what he was afraid of. "I mean, Rome is a Hummingbird, and he doesn't care that it's not a predator like Raptor or Hawk. Liam's a Mockingbird. But it suits them and this…"

"Do you like it?"

He lifted his gaze to mine. "What?"

"Do you like it?"

Hesitation marked him, but when he nodded, his whole expression and posture seemed braced for me to reject it. "I kind of do, is that stupid?"

"No, not in the slightest, because I think it's perfect. You sing so beautifully—you really do. When you sing to me, I feel safe and cared for, but you are also so vicious with a knife. It's a thing of beauty. Startling and fast. People might think you're just a beautiful guy with a beautiful voice—and you are. But that's not all you are."

The marked hesitation and fear erased from his expression and his smile grew. "Shrike."

"Yes," I said firmly then tapped my thigh. "And we're going to add a shrike to the birds we put here."

His smile became a real grin. "I love you, Boo-Boo."

Elation feathered through me.

"And I want to take you on another date."

"Yes," I said with a firm nod. "Whenever. Wherever."

"You keep being so agreeable to everything and you're going to spoil me," he joked, but I smiled.

"Good." Because I wanted to spoil him. "I trust you, Freddie. I trust my shrike."

He let out a slow breath, then pressed a quick kiss to my lips. "Can we practice more touching—when we're done?"

The door opened to let Rome glance inside. "It's time."

We looked at him then at each other, and I grinned. "Yes," I told Freddie. "Like I said, whenever and wherever."

Rising, Freddie held out his hand, and when I would have given him the picture back, he shook his head, "Keep it."

I glanced at it then across the room to the stapler. After I let Freddie pull me to my feet, I crossed over and tucked the drawing under the stapler where it would be safe. Rome nodded to the image. "Shrike?"

Freddie grinned at him. "That's me."

Yes, it was.

"Good," Rome said. "Let's go."

The fear tried to flutter up, but the simple joy in Freddie's expression kept it at bay. Yes. Let's go and get this done. We had a life I wanted to get back to and a life to build together.

"Shotgun," I said as I skipped ahead and Freddie burst out laughing.

CHAPTER 39

EMERSYN

Getting underway meant cars to the airport, and then we were on a private plane. It was almost crowded with all of us. Lainey waded through the guys to claim the seat next to mine.

"Should I be surprised none of them are limping?" I nodded to where Milo sat with Kellan, Adam, and Liam. Ezra had followed Lainey back to where I was seated, but one scathing look from her sent him to take another seat.

"Did you really think I would let you go into this fight without me?" Lainey challenged.

"No, but I wouldn't mind if you were safe," I said, almost softly, and she sighed. She clasped my hand, and I rested my head against her shoulder. "Protecting you and our friendship is what got me through." I could confess that now. "A weekend escape here or there, phone calls, and messages—they were worth it for me."

"I know," she said, resting her cheek against my hair. "I will never not hate that I didn't know how bad it was."

"I didn't want you to know." I could admit that. "I didn't want anyone to know. It wasn't just that he killed the people I told." Saying that without choking was a step forward. "It always made me feel dirty and exposed and...I know you wouldn't have thought less of me."

"But it didn't mean you weren't afraid."

No, it didn't. "If he hurt *you*..."

"I know," she murmured again. "I really want to taser his balls until he shits himself."

That—was an image. Ezra twisted in his seat. "You don't touch his balls."

"You planning to hook him up?" Lainey challenged.

"Sure," Ezra said. "But you don't touch him. You can pull the trigger all you want."

She rolled her eyes, but I smiled at Ezra. "Thank you," I mouthed to him, and he nodded before he settled back in his seat. Planes were hardly quiet. While some of the guys might be aware of our conversation, they were leaving us alone.

"You think I can talk you out of going in there?" Lainey asked, and I blinked.

"Do you want to talk me out of it?"

Her sigh seemed to suggest she did. "I want to," she admitted. "I really feel like I should be doing everything I can to persuade you out of going. To holing up somewhere safe while we take care of everything."

Uh huh. I didn't say a word as she let out a longer sigh.

"But I'm not going to ask you for that," she said, finally. "This is your fight. It's been *your* fight longer than it has been anyone else's. I refuse to get in your way, even if all I want to do is make sure you're safe."

I smiled thoughtfully. The tears in my eyes didn't fall, but they did burn a little. "Same. And if I haven't said it yet...

thank you for coming. Thank you for always being there for me. This is not a fight you should have to—"

"Shut up," Lainey ordered. I lifted my head, and we glanced at each other. The twitch of her lips gave her away, then we were both giggling. Eyes half-closed, I settled my head back on her shoulder. I caught Milo flashing a look toward us and so did Adam. They wore similarly indulgent expressions, until they noticed me looking. Then they both went back to what they were doing, like they hadn't been watching us.

Uh huh.

I was wise to them.

I really wanted Milo to be happy. He deserved it. So did Lainey. I wanted it to work out for all of them, because Ezra and Adam could pretend all they wanted, but their blatant affection and possessiveness of Lainey could cause issues. Maybe they could all work something out—my guys had. Though it hadn't required me to navigate the messier parts. They'd all just done it.

Studying them where they were going over the plans, I couldn't help the smile pulling at my lips. Movement pulled my attention when Rome made his way to where Lainey and I were sitting. He carried a blanket with him, and he draped it over me and Lainey both. When I lifted the other side of it, he took the open seat next to me and let me tuck him in too.

With Lainey holding one hand and Rome holding the other, I did the impossible. I went to sleep. It didn't seem like I'd done more than blink when Rome brushed his knuckles against my cheek.

"We're here, Starling," he said, and the bounce of the plane registered, as well as the sound of the wheels. We'd landed. I stretched. Lainey was already sitting up and someone had buckled my seatbelt. She shot me a smile as she opened a bottle of water while Rome handed me one. "Drink. We're going straight from the planes and into cars on the tarmac. We're not going through the airport."

"Thank you," I told him, and he nodded. Only after I'd had a few swallows did he ease the blanket off and begin to fold it. Kellan walked back to where we were sitting.

"Nice nap?"

"It was." I wasn't the only one who hadn't been sleeping well. Liam was living on a diet of caffeine. Vaughn went through periods of restlessness. Jasper was almost pure agitation. Kellan, despite his calm, was on high alert just like Mickey. I didn't think anyone would be resting until this was done. "Did you guys get any?"

"We'll be fine, Sparrow. We're sleeping in shifts…"

"Cars are here," Liam called. "Arm up."

"Let's get you in your vest," Kellan said, holding out a hand. I unbuckled my seatbelt while Rome rescued the water bottle so he could recap it. Then Kellan tugged me up. Lainey was right behind me. We didn't pull up to a gate, but I didn't expect it. Not my first private plane flight.

A shiver chased up my spine. The last time I'd been on a private plane had been *with* Fuckbucket. Kel put his hand against my lower back, and Milo frowned. "I'm fine," I told him. I would keep saying it until we all believed it. But when I pressed a hand to Milo's chest, he pulled me to him for a quick hug.

"I know, but worrying about you is my job. Been doing it for nearly twenty years, not about to stop today."

"You have a point," I conceded, then pressed a kiss to his cheek. "You doing okay?"

His smirk was adorable. "I'm fine." Then he winked. "Get your vest."

"You guys are so bossy," I teased, and it helped to dislodge some of the unease jangling in my system. Kel tugged me away from Milo and held up the vest. Everyone not Milo or one of my guys wasn't on board anymore except for Lainey, so I pulled off my shirt and let Kel help me into the vest. He tightened the straps and flattened everything down before Rome held my shirt up, and then I was in it.

He smoothed the shirt down before Kel slid on my holster, and when we had that buckled, he added a jacket to cover it. Everyone else was armed too, but I hadn't been wearing my gun or vest when I got *on* the plane. A glance over at Lainey showed her sliding into a jacket too.

She met my gaze, and for a minute, we just stared at each other then we were both laughing. It was almost insane that this was my life, and at the same time—this was my life. I wouldn't trade it for anything else, not now.

Another check, then Kel said, "Down the stairs and right into the cars. We've got four of them. You ladies are in the two in the middle. Milo—are you riding with Lainey?"

"Yes," Milo said, then gave me a firm look. "Stick with the guys."

"We're splitting up?" All at once, my nerves were pulled taut.

"Different cars, but we're running together." Kellan wrapped his hand around my nape, and I closed my eyes as I leaned into the contact. Relief bled through all the cracks, and I would have fallen if not for him.

"Don't worry, Ivy," Milo said, and when I opened my eyes, I found rough sympathy in his expression. "We're joined at the hip until this is done."

That... helped.

A lot.

"Ready?" Rome asked as he moved to the door. He still had my water bottle, and I nodded.

I was right behind him and down the stairs. There were four SUVs. Mickey was at the one in the front with two of his guys. Liam was at the one at the back with another of

Mickey's guys, Jasper, and Vaughn. Freddie was standing next to one door, and Ezra was at the other with Bodhi.

Kellan and Rome rode with me and Freddie, while Lainey and Milo headed to the other SUV. Kellan was driving, and Freddie took shotgun while I settled in the back with Rome. As soon as we were all in the cars, we were moving.

The drive to the house from here wasn't more than ninety minutes, depending on the route we took. Fifteen minutes into the drive, Kellan's phone rang. He answered it with a button push and pressed the speaker.

"Traschel."

"Mr. Traschel, we've researched the issue you submitted. The team in question is made up of over a dozen men, roughly fifteen we believe, it was eighteen, but it appears that three of them have expired."

Expired. The three that Milo killed?

"They are no longer registered within the Network, as they declined to follow the new structure. I am sending you a text with their profiles and records. I've been asked to advise you that they were all dishonorably discharged, for various reasons, and should be considered quite dangerous."

"This is a lot more than I asked for," Kellan said slowly, and I frowned.

"I understand, but you have friends Mr. Traschel. Those friends have friends. You've also been a solid contact within the Network, and your transporters agreed to all the terms and conditions as set forth by the Network, which means you also reap benefits from the association—standby."

"Mr. Traschel." A woman joined the call. "We know who this team is working for, and as I informed you in Las Vegas, we were happy to deal with that problem. Can I assume you are going to deal with this one?"

Kellan didn't answer immediately, he drummed his fingers against the steering wheel a couple of times before he said, "You may assume that we have the matter in hand. We just wanted to verify that there would be no reprisals when we removed that team from the board."

"None from our end. If you wouldn't mind sending any verifications along when you're done, we'll update our files."

"Thank you," he said slowly. "We'd appreciate that."

"Of course, happy hunting."

There was a beat then the man was back. "Is there anything else I can do for you, Mr. Traschel?"

"That's all we needed," he said. "Thanks for the assist."

"Anytime—except let's not make this a habit." The man almost sounded like he was laughing. "We don't need any more blue-eyed foxes in the hen house." He was still laughing when the call ended, and I frowned.

"Did he just call you a blue-eyed fox?"

Freddie, who had been silent through the whole conversation, seemed to be struggling not to laugh.

"She did," Kellan said slowly.

"We met her in Vegas," Rome said. "She said I had nice eyes."

Freddie laughed even harder, and I bit the inside of my lip. "Well," I told him honestly. "You do have nice eyes." They were blue too.

Kellan finally chuckled. "You know, I'm just going to take this as good news. At least until I see what kind of problem these guys are going to be."

His phone chose that minute to begin buzzing. I didn't know who *she* was, but they all had great eyes. Freddie was practically chortling, then Rome said, "I like your eyes better, Starling. Beautiful bird. No foxes allowed."

Then we were all laughing, even Rome.

CHAPTER 40

FREDDIE

I hadn't seen where Boo-Boo grew up. We all knew it was an expensive house, how could it not be? They were a wealthy family. Too wealthy, considering the depravities she'd been put through. Still, staring at the tall house barely visible beyond the brick walls with their iron fixtures and verdant trees gave it another layer.

"Cameras," Kel said, nodding to where they were mounted. They weren't fixed, either. The fuckers rotated.

Boo-Boo leaned forward from the backseat. "They've updated it—at least since the last time I was here willingly."

I hated that last word, but I glanced at her. "What parts?"

"Well, the top up there is electrified, or it was when I came back before. That was how I burned my hands."

Kellan's hands flexed on the steering wheel, and his knuckles went white. "And the cameras?"

"I don't remember those, but I also didn't know he was

recording us," she answered in a tone far too even. Boo-Boo was holding it together, so we would do the same thing.

"So, it's possible they're new or upgraded." Daddy K's calm voice was exactly why he was the big boss.

"Yes," she said. "Normally there are security guards as well, but they used to be—subtle." She gave a little shiver as Rome shifted in the back seat, and I twisted to offer her a hand. A smile tipped the corners of her mouth as she gripped my hand lightly. "Last time, they were not so subtle. The guy in charge of them was scarier than the rest put together. Even the guy who cut me."

"He's dead," Rome said firmly.

"I know," she murmured, and her smile went from tragic to real for a miraculous moment. "The other one was really dangerous."

"So are we," Kellan said without missing a beat. Damn right we were.

"You see him, you point him out, Boo-Boo. I'd like to talk to him." Violently. With my knife. She squeezed my hand once.

"I promise, Shrike." The reminder made me grin. Probably made me look feral too. I was fine with that.

Kellan's phone vibrated, and he answered it on speaker. "Go."

"We've got eyes," Doc said. "Alphabet has almost taken over the security system."

"Almost?" Alphabet protested. "Bite me, Doc. I have it. Just need to rotate cause they have firewalls set up between interior and exterior."

"Like I said," Doc continued in a voice that promised all-business. "Almost. Jeff said he'd be back in six days, right?"

"Right," Kel answered. "What do you see?"

"They have a lot of movement for someone who isn't supposed to be there until tomorrow."

"Could be staff," Boo-Boo said. "He likes everything in a certain order. His expectations for perfection are pretty rigid. Staff doesn't last long if they don't adhere to his exact specifications and keep their mouths shut about everything else."

"We're looking, Little Bit," Doc said, his tone gentling for her. "Do you remember how many he has on staff?"

She gave a careless shrug. "At least a dozen in various capacities. More outside for the gardens. Interior staff—you had to meet different criteria. A housekeeper, a butler, three or four maids."

When she made a face, I raised my brows. From this angle, I could see Rome's hand on her thigh. Kel divided his attention between the rearview mirror where he could see her and the house itself.

"I don't know. I used to think the staff could help, but they never did so I started to pretend they weren't there. It was just—easier than looking at them. They knew, right?" Another shrug, but her hand trembled in mine. I hated this for her.

Hated *him* even more.

"No civilians," Kellan said, and Doc sighed.

"Yeah, that was my thought." A beep sounded as Doc spoke. and there was a click.

"We're looking at the rear approach," Liam said. "We've got a lot of activity back here. Doc, can you guys see this on the cameras?"

"Hang on," Alphabet said. "We can—now. Well, that's a lot of firepower. You think he welcomes all his guests this way?"

Since we couldn't see it, I didn't say anything.

"That's more than a dozen guys." Doc sounded grim. "Give us a couple. Liam, how many are you counting?"

"Maybe twenty—could be more since I think the cars all have drivers. They don't look like they are rolling out."

"Maybe coming in early," Jasper commented. "We need to get a better—what the fuck is he doing?"

Liam's sigh came in loud and clear. "Freddie—"

Oh crap. "It's Bodhi, isn't it?" He'd just shown up at the airport as promised, like he'd traveled there with us. I didn't know how he did it, but fuck, I admired it.

"Yeah," Liam said. "He's going for a walk." His tone was so bland and conversational, he might have been discussing a tour. Another beep joined the call.

"Let him."

"What?" Kel looked at me.

"Let him. Bodhi knows what he's doing. I had a nurse walk me down to his cell like she was going to toss me in there to let him kill me, and he just took her out. Then he took another walk." I glanced at Boo-Boo.

"He was out for a walk when he came into the doctor's office." Yeah, I'd gotten that too. The trembling in her hand steadied. "He was—so casual about it." A hint of wonder and amusement tangled in her voice.

"Bodhi's pretty cool," I agreed. I liked him, but I'd agree with anything to keep that expression on her face.

"He is…"

"A pain in the ass," Liam said, though I swore there was some amusement there. "Everyone hold position. You guys got eyes on him, Doc?"

"Yep," Alphabet answered for Doc. "Wish I had some popcorn too."

"Focus," Bones said, but there was grudging admiration in his voice. I kind of wished Doc had introduced us sooner. Then again, I wasn't a fan of strangers. So maybe not.

"Not sure these guys live up to the reputation," Alphabet mused. "They haven't noticed him yet."

"He moves like he belongs—and he just picked one of their guys off." Doc sounded surprised and impressed.

"Okay, I want video," I said as Boo-Boo's grip eased. A faint smile crossed Kellan's face, but he shook his head.

"He's in," Alphabet said. "Switching to interior, I've almost got the split in so I can see inside and out."

"Where did you find this guy?" Lunchbox asked.

"Pinetree," Boo-Boo answered. "Second best thing to come out of that place."

I quirked a look at her, and she grinned at me. "After you?" I teased. "I agree." To my delight, she stuck her tongue out at me. I caught Kel watching me, but he didn't scold. If anything, all he did was nod, and I waited. Shifting in the seat, I turned to watch the front gates. We were tucked just off to the side, using the trees to hide the car. The cameras kept doing their slow pan—wait.

"I'm in," Alphabet said as the camera nearest the car locked into place and just stopped. "And we have control of the system."

"Where's the crazy mother fucker?" Jasper asked.

"He's working his way through the building, and now he's heading upstairs. Wait—someone's talking to him. Too bad there isn't audio."

I appreciated the disgruntled note. I wanted to hear too.

A beep indicating someone else joined the call. "Do we go?"

Milo. Boo-Boo tensed all over again.

"Not yet," Kellan answered before anyone else did. "I want eyes on that son of a bitch. If he's in there, I want to know *before* we go in."

"Copy that," Alphabet commented. "Still skimming, not finding angles everywhere. If there is another internal system, it's not networked."

"Is that good or bad?" Boo-Boo asked.

"It's neither. Just means it can't be accessed externally. I'll have to go onsite if we're looking for files to delete... hold up, our guy has found something." There was almost an element of laughter in Alphabet's voice. "Or he's putting on a show. Phrase. Three words. First word. One syllable—"

"Is he playing charades?" I asked. "Do people even play that game anymore?"

Boo-Boo gave me a mystified look.

The silence seemed to drag on and on. It wasn't more than a minute, but before I could open my mouth, Doc said, "He's there."

"Repeat?" Kellan said even as he straightened in his seat.

"Bodhi just held up a note, it says 'he is here.'" Doc's voice was grim, but there was an edge of glee in his voice. It was weird. Vandal had always had that darkness in him, Doc didn't. Right now, I didn't think we were talking to Doc anymore.

Or maybe we were.

Boo-Boo let go of my hand, and I jerked my gaze to where she rubbed her hands against her thighs.

"We're going," Milo said. "Right?"

It was a demand as much as a request, but Kellan stared at the house. "Liam—"

"I'm here," Liam answered. "We have fourteen back here. They are offloading vehicles. They're armed. Heavily."

"Inside?" Kellan asked.

"Six—maybe seven from what I can see. Though it looks like our guy took out four already, and he's going after number five. If we leave him to it, I have a feeling he's going to do this without us."

"Staff?"

"Three I can see," Alphabet confirmed. "Not seeing the target. Wherever he is—there's no externally accessible camera on his location. Do we trust your guy?"

Kellan looked at me, and Liam said nothing.

"I trust him," Boo-Boo answered.

"Good enough," Kellan stated. "Everyone get ready. Doc, you and your team back Liam and Jasper. Wait until I hit the gate—Milo?"

"I'm right behind you," he said.

I wasn't the only one who twisted to see Milo's vehicle pull in behind us. Boo-Boo stiffened.

"You're with us. Stick close. Rome—you and Freddie stay with Sparrow." Then Kellan looked at her. "You good?"

The only sound inside the car was our breathing. She leaned forward. "I'm good. I want this." Then she looked at the house. "And I want to burn it to the ground."

"That's my girl," Liam said even as Jasper chuckled. "Hell, yes."

"Oh, I think we can do that," Vaughn added to the conversation.

"Focus," Kellan said. "No one moves alone. Do not leave *anyone* at your backs. Meet us inside. And if you find that prick—"

"We will," Doc—no, that was definitely Vandal speaking. "I might break his kneecaps just to make sure he has something to do until you get there."

"Thank you, Mickey," Boo-Boo said, and I nodded.

"Five minutes, then go," Kellan said before he slid out of the car. The call was over. Kel opened the back of the SUV. "Freddie, vest?"

"It's on," I promised. I hated the damn thing, but I had it on.

"Rome?"

"Yes."

"Good." When he returned, he had a shotgun, and he passed a Glock to me. "You don't have to use it, but I don't trust anything in there. So keep it with you."

"Copy that," I parroted Alphabet. Boo-Boo let out a laugh, and I winked at her. The shadows in her eyes roiled with all that chaos. "We got this, Boo-Boo." It was all the promise I could give her.

She blew out a breath, but the darkness in her eyes didn't retreat. "I'm ready. I can do this."

"Yes, you can," Kellan told her. "But if you need to get out —tell Rome and Freddie, then go. They'll cover you and go with you."

"Where are you going?"

"I made you a promise, Sparrow. I plan to keep it." He didn't look away from her. "Trust me?"

That really wasn't a question, not for Boo-Boo. "You know I do."

"Then stick with them. That's an order."

The corner of her mouth curved up. "I won't be bad, even if I wouldn't mind the spanking."

It was absurd, and at the same time, I loved it. A snort escaped me. "I'll be bad for you, Boo-Boo. Cause Daddy K definitely likes to spank your ass."

Rome chuckled. "So does Liam."

"Right," Kellan said before I could respond. "Put a pin in that. Seatbelts on. It's time."

Hell, yes. It was time. Kellan put the car into gear. The sound of the seatbelts clicking into place was almost a countdown.

One.

Two.

Three.

Four.

Go.

CHAPTER 41

JASPER

"*F*ive minutes, then go."

The words I'd been waiting for. Fuck, the words we'd all been waiting for. That crazy son of a bitch walked in there and got us the info we needed. He'd ridden with Milo, but then headed back here to join us after we were in position while Doc's guy got us access. Bodhi didn't seem to follow anyone's beat except his own.

"Four minutes," Liam said crisply as he checked his guns. He had three of them. He also had his fists. "Check my vest."

I checked his. Vaughn checked mine. Liam checked Vaughn's. Lunchbox just gave us a look. Yeah, we didn't have to check his vest, if he didn't want to.

"Three minutes. Earpieces in," Liam said. "Remember, stay off the line until we've finished securing the interior unless it's an emergency."

We knew this. But if he needed to say it, I was fine. I warmed up my batting arm. I'd brought the bat and the axe.

The axe was for the uncle. The bat was for everyone else. Vaughn cracked his knuckles, but the intensity in his eyes as he stared at the building was a little off.

"Hey," I said, nudging him as I climbed into the back. Liam was driving, and Lunchbox would handle shotgun. The man had a hand cannon. I wasn't going to argue with him. "You good?"

"Nope," Vaughn said in a quiet voice. "I'm getting there. This is gonna help. It's gonna be for Lauren. For Terry, Jahns, Rocky—everyone who died at the shop. Liam's dad. Ms. Stephanie…"

That hurt scored deep, but fuck, did I get that.

"And Dove." Vaughn glanced at me. "So no, I'm not good. I'll get there again. Dove needs me there."

"We need to do this." Fuck, did I understand that on so many levels. "For her and for us."

"Two minutes."

"Hey, Terminator," I said, and Liam spared me a look. "Lighten up. We get to kill people now." I grinned. Violence was a language I understood. It was both a sword and a shield. I'd been weaned on a diet of fists and abuse. Then I'd found a new home and a new family. Violence might have been the only love language I had at the time, but it had grown and evolved. Or so I liked to think.

"That's not what I'm worried about." His grin was all teeth and no smile. "We cannot let that fucker get away."

"We won't," I said in the exact same tone Vaughn did.

"Remind me when we have him," Liam said. "Until then…"

"Yeah." I got it. Violence had been a thread through all of our lives. For some of us, more than others. Our girl had suffered so much when we hadn't been aware of it. She'd learned to shield her heart and her mind so effectively. Lies with lies, to the world, to herself, and lies we'd embraced because it told the story we thought we wanted to see.

"One minute," Liam said as he started the car. When he held a hand out the window, he lifted his index finger. "You got the gates?" The question was to Lunchbox.

"I got the gates. Do me a favor boys—watch the fire zones and mind the friendlies."

"Yep," Liam said, then he dropped his finger. "Going."

The tension in me unwound. We were on our way to avenge our girl, our family, and ourselves. We would take the pound of flesh she was owed, then carve the rest of that son of a bitch up until nothing was left. This wasn't just vengeance. It was erasure.

Lunchbox was up and out of the passenger window. The boom of the shotgun was loud inside the car, but the satisfaction of watching the gate shiver as he blew the lock at the center and then the hinges, managing to slide back inside a split second before Liam crashed through them, was deeply satisfying.

The team we'd been watching pivoted at our approach. One guy already had a gun up, but a bullet slammed into him and knocked him on his ass. Dammit, I'd wanted to be first. When Liam cut the breaks and swung the SUV to a sliding horizontal stop. The tail hit another guy and sent him flying.

Goddamn. Everyone was getting their first shots in. Fine, I'd go for two for every one of theirs. I already had my door open, my bat a familiar weight in my hand. Guns were great. Fists were great. The bat though? I did one test swing as I adjusted my grip, then two-hand swung it for the nearest guy. The crack was so damn satisfying. Even better, catching another with a second swing. Ribs fractured. Jaws broke. There was definitely a meaty "thwok" of sound to the body blows I delivered.

A bullet slammed into the truck nearest me. It kicked off

debris. Turning, I half-ducked and spotted the gunman in time to see Doc take him down with two shots, both to the head. Yeah, he wasn't getting back up again. Vaughn slammed into another and lifted him bodily before he just slammed his whole frame right into the truck.

"Semi-automatics coming out," Liam warned, and I wasn't the only one crouching as our targets pulled out heavier artillery. The rapid-fire of bullets slamming into the trucks around us included cracking the glass of the SUV before it shattered completely.

More debris flew off the truck over my head. One of the guys came around the corner and ate two bullets from Liam's Glock. "Stay down," Doc ordered, then his guys were just there. They met heavy firepower with firepower of their own. They moved swiftly and efficiently, covering each other.

For some reason the song from Drowning Pool filtered into my head, and I laughed. It had been a while since we had this much fun or were around this much gunfire. The bullets flew, the sound left my ears humming. I'd been around this much gunfire. The smell of it in the air coupled with blood, sweat, and what had to be way too much green vegetation was an interesting combination.

"Clear," Liam said, and he was on his feet with me and Vaughn right behind him. The numbers were off. Doing a sweeping count of the bodies on the ground—we were dealing with more than a dozen men.

Touching my earpiece, I said, "Be aware. We've easily got twenty or more out here. There may be a lot more inside."

"Copy," Kellan said then the channel went silent. A guy rolled out from under one of the trucks, already raising his gun. I swung the bat and knocked the weapon from his hand. A half-step behind me, Vaughn lunged forward and picked the guy up. It was kind of funny to see this guy dangle from

Vaughn's large hands. He slammed him, head first, into the truck's side.

One.

Two.

And out.

He dropped the still form, and I paused only long enough to make sure there was no pulse before I continued on. Alphabet had slowed. He had a small device in his hands as he found a spot to lean, and then he was studying the screen.

"Yeah, we definitely have a few inside. It's a nice trap. They weren't expecting to be hit from two sides though."

"My heart bleeds," I commented as I eyed the man. He'd been limping. "You good?"

"Hell no," Alphabet said with a grin. "Where's the fun in that?"

I rolled my eyes.

"Don't worry about me, kid. I'm just making sure they aren't planning something special, keep going." Even as he spoke, he slid out a sidearm easily and fired back the way we'd come. I pivoted to see the guy who'd been pulling himself up go down again. "Like I said," Alphabet commented. "No surprises. I'm doing a sweep. Keep moving."

That left him heading back the way we'd come, and I nodded. Vaughn was a few yards ahead, shadowing Liam. Doc, Bones, and Lunchbox were trading fire with remnants near the house. Glass doors shattered, and there were tumbled over plants, broken pots, and a fountain that was now spilling out awkwardly onto the ground. The space was huge, including paths that led to a swimming pool in one direction and a maze in the other.

It took us time to root out more of the mercs. I got into more than one scrap when they tried to pull a Trojan horse maneuver. A half-dozen had been cooling their heels in the back of a truck. As luck would have it, Liam had every intention of being thorough. We'd been popping the trucks open.

One included what looked like a mini-apartment. Explained how Sharpe had been moving around. Sick mother fucker. Most had been empty though, or loaded only with boxes—supplies mostly, weapons, and money.

Vaughn and I had been taking turns when I cracked one of the cases and stared down at the cold hard cash. "Yeah, I don't even want to try and figure out how much that is." But it also made sense that they were transporting the money with them. I'd half-expected to find trafficking victims inside the trucks. The relief at not finding them didn't quite offset the growing anger at how much trouble this fucker had taken.

Then Liam popped that truck and took a bullet right into his vest. He'd have taken a second right in the head, but I hit him and took him down, even as Vaughn roared. The bullet that hit me between the shoulder blades *hurt*. The one that cut across my clavicle and thudded into the ground next to Liam just pissed me off. I rolled off him, and he lifted his gun and fired. One of the guys came tumbling down. Two more got lifted bodily by Vaughn. and he legit slammed their heads together then tossed them toward us.

Rolling away from Liam as he went the other way, we were on our feet. I brought the bat down on one of the guys trying to get up as Doc approached. He was firing into the truck, past Vaughn, who was beating the ever-loving hell out of the three guys who tried to tackle him.

One after another, those guys came flying out to hit the ground. Liam capped them, or I did. When he was done, Vaughn turned toward us. Blood speckled his fists and his face. He cut a look at me then at Liam and finally at Doc.

"We're clear," Doc told him, and Vaughn nodded, blowing out a breath before he turned back into the truck.

"Cameras."

"Alphabet," Doc called, and the other man limped toward us. Yeah, he was definitely limping. But since no one else said anything, I didn't. Vaughn returned to the edge and offered Alphabet a hand. He pulled him up into the truck one-handed then Doc passed a gun to Vaughn. "Watch his back."

After checking the gun, Vaughn nodded. "We got this."

"You two," Doc said with a look at me then at Liam, "with me."

As tempting as it would be to razz him, he sounded way too much like Vandal. The same guy who used to hand us our asses regularly when we got too fucking salty with him. That and I wanted in that house and after that asshole. We were several dead bodies closer too.

"Doors locked?" Liam asked as we scanned the area and trailed after Doc.

A low boom echoed over the yard, and I glanced up in time to see the big glass doors tremble then shatter inward before the doors themselves fell off the hinges that Bones and Lunchbox had just blown off.

"Not anymore," I commented, and Liam chuckled. My bat dripped with blood, and I still had the axe strapped to my back. I followed Doc and his guys into the house. The whole place smelled like money. Money and lemon polish. Someone let out a shout from ahead then a man crashed through the doors and onto the floor in front of us. "Party time…"

CHAPTER 42

ROME

I'd half-expected Kellan to crash the gates. It was the most direct way in, but we didn't need to. Nearly as soon as we reached them, the gates started to open on their own. Kellan's phone beeped with a message, but he barely spared it a look. Next to me, Starling's whole body seemed to vibrate with the tension. I wanted to offer comfort, but that wasn't what she needed right now.

What Starling needed was to finish this.

It was what all of us needed. Kellan accelerated up the long, tree-lined drive, and the silence in the car had texture. It had color too. A mixture of tans and greens, one bleeding into the other. Like the light outside. The sun had been playing hide and seek behind the clouds. It was gone entirely at the moment, with darker storm clouds rolling in.

When she reached a hand for mine, I threaded our fingers together. The dark didn't hold any fear for me. Not everyone was as comfortable. The house came into full view around the next bend. The huge manor had a kind of medieval quality. Stone walls, high windows, vaulted ceilings, all to better house darkness.

"It kind of reminds me of those fairy tale cottages," Freddie said. "On crack."

"More a dungeon than a cottage," Starling said. "Though he did like the castle theme—master of his domain, a king if you will." Then she snorted, the sound echoed in the car as Kellan swung around the circular drive.

"Rome…" Kellan warned even as he rolled the window down. I already had a gun up, and I shot the guard running down the stairs. He collapsed, dropping his weapon as he rolled down the remaining steps. Starling unbuckled my seatbelt for me, and I was out with her sliding out right behind me. She also had her gun out.

Milo pulled up behind us just as Kellan shot another man walking out the door. Another guard, dressed like the first one. This one though staggered backward into the interior, and Adam shot the one who tried to come around him, even as he caught Lainey's arm and tugged her back.

"Don't," was all he ordered. As soon as she stopped moving, he let her go. Probably wise. Milo didn't look friendly.

Starling put her free hand on my back. "I'm ready."

"Milo and I take point." Kellan was already striding forward. "Ezra and Adam, you have rear guard."

That put me in the middle with Starling and Lainey. I went a little wide so Starling could pull her in with me and Freddie.

"Fancy meeting you here," Lainey teased, though it didn't carry a lot of humor.

"It's so weird that you're seeing the house," Starling admitted.

"Yeah, my thoughts exactly. But we're not here for long."

Lainey sounded far calmer than Starling did, but her best friend's presence actually steadied Starling as we followed. Gunfire came from the back and inside.

At the door, I held up a hand. "Wait."

I eased up to the door frame and glanced inside. The hall was wide with a huge staircase that circled up to the second floor. Kellan and Milo had the foyer.

"Clear," Kel told me, and I nodded, moving in and beckoning the girls to follow. Freddie stuck close as we did a sweep.

"We need to split," Kellan said with a look toward Adam and Ezra. "We'll take upstairs. Milo, can you handle this floor with the guys?"

Starling paled, but she didn't hesitate. "Fuckbucket's office is on this floor, near the garden. The door is always locked."

Milo looked at her. "I'll take care of it, Ivy. You got this?"

She held his gaze, understanding flickered between them. The connection alive and well. I smiled. Brothers were good. Starling needed hers. I needed mine.

"I do. Take care of Lainey?" The friend in question snorted.

"If she'll let me…" Milo didn't roll his eyes or sigh. "And even if she won't."

That pulled a real laugh out Starling.

"Keep it up, Pretty Boy," Lainey said. "You boys better protect her."

"We will, Ball-Cracker," Freddie interrupted. "Keep Milo safe too, yeah?"

"Let's go," I said amidst the rolled eyes and snorts. Adam caught Starling's arm though before she took two steps.

"Be careful," he told her. "Take this." He pressed something into her hand.

"Panic button?"

"Yep," he said. "You find him or you need us. Press it. We'll come."

Surprise briefly registered then she closed her fingers around it. "Thank you."

He nodded once and ignored the rest of us before he turned to stalk across the foyer with Ezra right behind him.

"That man," Lainey muttered before she followed, Milo right with her. Starling resumed her path to the stairs.

"Same as before," Kellan said as he took point. Freddie moved next to Starling, and I followed, keeping my attention split between where they were and anyone coming behind us. The width of the halls was opulent. Paintings lined the walls. The windows at either end of the hall were huge, but the glass was frosted. It didn't allow much in the way of escape.

Our comms crackled to life. "Blowing the back door," Doc warned. Seconds later the sound of that explosion rippled through the building.

"Room by room," Kellan said. "Do you have a room here, Sparrow?"

"I did. End of the hall." She pointed. "On the other side of Fuckbucket's."

"Safe room in there?"

"Yes."

That told me where his room was. Freddie stiffened at the mention, but all Kellan did was nod. "Room by room. I want no one behind us."

The first two rooms were sparse. Guest rooms. No sheets on the bed. The walls bare, save for two covered paintings of landscapes. Kellan swept everything, including going into bathrooms and closets. Starling hesitated at the third door.

Kellan tested the door, but it was locked.

"Above the door," she said, and Kel reached up, found the key, and brought it down. He unlocked the door, and we shifted so he could go in first with Freddie right behind him, while I watched the hall. Starling was a little slower to go inside.

Only when she turned to watch the hall did I take a single step in to look.

It was a playroom.

There were dolls and dresses.

The photographs on the walls were all of Starling at different ages and in different dresses.

There was even one of her at a gala, and there was a leash on her neck.

"The room is clear," Kellan said in a steely voice. "Freddie, when we light the match—dump half the fuel in here."

Two more rooms—nothing.

Another room had blood stains on the wall and the chair. Starling gave a shudder as she glanced around it.

"He cut me there."

"The guard?" I verified, and she shifted her hand on her gun before she nodded.

"He's still dead, and he died hurting." A lot.

Liam had taken his time and I'd helped. A small smile flickered over her lips.

"Half the house is clear, and no one is up here…" Kellan's voice had grown chillier as we moved. He didn't like this place. He didn't like what it was doing to Starling. She kept her chin up, but there was a quaver in her voice. Her hands trembled. Her eyes—

I didn't like the darkness drowning in them.

"Still good to keep going, Boo-Boo?" Freddie asked. He'd started sweating in the doll room.

"We haven't gotten to his room yet." She said not looking at anything else in here. "If he's upstairs, he's probably there or in the safe room."

"Also in his bedroom?" Kellan confirmed. At her nod, he touched his earpiece. "Check in."

"Nothing down here except more guards. Found a room full of toys." Disgust curled through Liam's voice. "The yard is clear and the garage. No sign of the target"

"Found his office," Milo said. "Computers are locked, but Alphabet is on the way. Adam got the safe open. Notice I'm not asking how."

"I am," Lainey grumbled. "But later."

A smile flickered over Starling's face.

"Where is Bodhi?" she asked. "He said he was here, right?"

Freddie frowned and so did Kellan.

"No sign of him on the cameras, Dove," Vaughn said, and she closed her eyes as he spoke. "I'm scanning the interior now. We've got the security cameras locked. No cameras in the bedrooms that we've been able to find."

I scanned the room then moved toward a picture on the wall. Something was off about the eyes. Lifting the frame off, it revealed a camera behind it, where the eyes would be and an opaque lens.

There was also a red light on it.

"We're being watched."

Starling almost prowled over to the camera. She stared at it for a long moment then lifted her middle finger before she backed up a step and pointed her gun.

"Firing," Kellan warned a moment before she squeezed the trigger. The camera exploded in sparks. "That's one way to deal with it. There's another system here. And he's on it. We need to find it and him."

"We're working our way to you," Liam said.

"Still room by room?" Starling asked, but her voice gained in strength, and the tremble in her hands and shoulders vanished. Color flushed her face.

She was angry.

"Yes," Kellan said. "I know you want to find him. So do we, but nothing behind us."

She gave him one quick nod, but before we made it a couple of steps, an alarm went off and it was loud. The sound was repetitive and high pitched. It echoed through the hallway. Vaughn was saying something over the comms, but it was hard to hear him over the volume.

"Go," Kellan said. "Hit each room hard. Two by two." He cast a look at Starling then me, and I nodded. Keep her with me. "Freddie, you're with me." Even with him yelling, his voice didn't carry.

The sound hurt my ears. Starling kept watch when I went inside, but I never went far, not without waiting for her to step in. The alarm not only made it hard to hear anything else, it made it impossible to communicate.

I didn't want Starling too far from me, and she seemed to feel the same way. After an initial scan, I would nod to her, and she would follow me in, one hand on my back. When we came out, Kel and Freddie took their room while we watched the hall and covered them from here.

Every room was empty. It was like we'd come when no one was living here, and the rooms needed to be redressed for guests. Then, maybe we had. According to King, the uncle would be here the following day. Maybe he really had just arrived.

It didn't *feel* like a trap. But we'd come early because no one trusted King. When Kel left his room, we moved to the next, repeating the pattern until the only rooms left were the uncle's and her former bedroom.

I eyed that door. A part of me never wanted to open it. Starling hated this house, and these two rooms were the location of her pain.

While I didn't want her to have to go inside, she didn't

draw back. The alarm cut off abruptly, and it was so sudden, the silence seemed staggering.

"Why does that not feel like a good sign?" Freddie asked and Starling shook her head.

"I don't know what it is. I've never heard that alarm before."

"Do we have a lead on where that was coming from?" Kellan asked via the comm.

"No," Vaughn answered. "I can see you guys, but there's no angles inside the two rooms you're looking at. Alphabet is working on finding the power board and connections for the panic room, he thinks that's where the room cameras connect."

"Any sign of Bodhi?" Freddie asked.

"No."

"We're at the master suite," Kellan said. "We're going in."

"On our way to you," Liam said. "Downstairs is clear, as is the basement. We have a couple of staff members locked down. We'll deal with them in a bit." We were all ready to end this.

"Vaughn, watch our backs." Kellan said as he moved to the door, and this time, Starling was right behind him. Freddie and I moved to either side of the door. No one was stopping her from doing what she needed to do.

When Kellan tested the handle, it turned with a distinctive click.

CHAPTER 43

EMERSYN

*T*he now-silenced alarm still rang in my ears. The click from the door seemed abnormally loud. Like, why would the door—?

Kellan pivoted abruptly, all but picking me up as he rolled along the wall away from the sound. Freddie and Rome were on the far side of the door when a pair of blasts tore through the wood, striking the far wall and sending out a shower of powdered drywall. The shotgun fired again, further splintering the wood and exploding the paint off the wall. It even took down the Jackson Pollock, sending it crashing to the floor.

Another click. But nothing followed.

Then another.

"Stay," Kellan ordered me. "Please."

I nodded once as he shifted his weight. Rome was on the other side of the door, all of us flattened to the wall, then Kellan eased forward.

The clicks kept coming but no more shots.

Kel backed off a step and then planted his foot against the already-splintered door, kicking it in the rest of the way. The shotgun clicked again but it was empty. Rome was right behind Kellan, entering, with Freddie and me following him.

Freddie sliced the cord that was still clicking, as if it could keep pulling the trigger, while Rome gripped the gun and tore it out of the mount. As heart-pounding as the moment had been, I was almost grateful for the smell of the gunpowder or whatever it was. The acridness cut through the hints of his cologne and shampoo.

Everywhere I looked in the room, I could see *him*. Hear him.

Feel him.

A shudder worked its way through me and a warm hand settled at my back. I wasn't proud of the way I jumped or the fist I threw, but Liam caught my knuckles in his palm as his gaze held me steady. Understanding flared in his eyes and he shifted the grip on my hand until I could flatten my palm to his.

"Hey," I whispered.

"Hey," he answered, one corner of his mouth kicking up. Behind him, Mickey and Jasper both gave me steady looks. Blowing out a breath, I pivoted to face the room again. Almost instantly, I missed the contact with Liam—with any of them. 'Cause this room housed too many memories. Too many nightmares.

I'd lost a lot in this room.

Dragging my gaze away from the bed, I diverted it toward the closet. The heat at my back promised me I wasn't alone, and I didn't glance back for fear of losing my nerve. The smell of *him* in the closet was almost enough to make me gag. I missed a step and half-stumbled, but Freddie's hand was suddenly in mine.

He didn't say a word as I locked my grip on his palm. Closing my eyes, I forced shallower breaths and kept the breathing through my mouth. When I was a little steadier, I opened my eyes. The others were there, but they weren't following me into the closet—yet. Glancing at Freddie, I met his worried eyes and then nodded to him. I could do this.

"What are we looking for, Boo-Boo?" He took the verbal baton so gracefully I could have kissed him. This was not the time and this was very much not the place.

"Safe room," I said, proud that my voice didn't quaver in the slightest. "It's in here."

Liam slid into the closet with us. "Show me." That was definitely an order, but his eyes held the request. He didn't want me opening that door myself. Considering we'd just dealt with that bizarre shotgun trap, I didn't want any of us opening it.

"Behind the suits," I managed, despite my mouth drying up. The closet was meticulously organized—from the ties, to the cufflinks, to the dress shirts, suit coats, and pants. Organized by style, function, and color. Nothing left to chance. One maid had accidentally placed a shirt in the wrong place once.

Fuckbucket had given her a relentless dressing down until she was in tears. Then he fired her for sniveling. I'd had to watch the whole thing, and when he finished and she fled out of the room, literally running, he'd turned to me and said, "Never accept shoddy work or behavior, Princess. Let them get away with it once and you will never be able to trust them again."

The icy fingers of the past dug deep into my soul here, raking through muscle and bone to leave me bloody and raw. I hated this room. I hated this house.

I hated *him*.

"Back up for me," Liam beckoned and Freddie didn't

move until I did. If I'd objected or insisted, Freddie would have pushed it for me. But I didn't want to fight with them.

"Be careful," I asked and Liam brushed bloodied fingers against my cheek. I didn't care about the blood or the smell of gunpowder and sweat. If anything, I took a deeper breath to try to blot out the smell of this place. I'd rather drown in Liam's sweat than choke on Fuckbucket's cologne.

"Always, Hellspawn." The promise steadied me and Jasper gave my arms a squeeze as he eased around me. Freddie drew me back farther to the door, where Kellan and Mickey pushed into the closet to back Jasper and Liam. Rome stayed just outside, his gaze split between us and the door.

With one hand, Liam yanked the coats to the side, revealing the door and the keypad. It was on a timed lock. A camera blinked at us. Was he in there? We still hadn't seen Bodhi. Biting my lower lip, I shifted my hand from Freddie's so I could two-hand the gun. I kept it pointed at the floor. But I wanted to be ready.

"Code, Sparrow?" Kellan asked.

"My birthday," I said. Liam entered it but it rejected the numbers. I gave them the date of my adoption. No dice. Eyes closed, I swallowed bile, then gave them a different date entirely.

The red lights shifted to green.

Asshole used the day after my tenth birthday. Our "special" day.

The door slid open and Kellan and Mickey were the first two through, guns up. A sound drifted out...

A sound of me, crying.

"Motherfucker," Jasper swore, then glanced back at me. "You don't need to see this, Swan."

It was as much a request as it was a plea. The sound changed and the recognizable chaffing of skin on skin made me flinch. Honestly, the noise of Kellan emptying his gun was loud but far more welcome, and the sound cut out entirely.

"He's not in here, but he's got cameras everywhere." The grim words from Liam seemed a thousand miles away, or maybe that was how much my ears ached after the combination of gunfire and the alarm.

"If he's not in there," I said slowly, then glanced at Rome, who was watching the door to the room. "There's one room left."

Unless he added something else to the property. Bodhi said he was here. I pivoted on my heel and made my way to the door, with Rome and Freddie moving like my shadows.

"We heading to your room?" Freddie asked as he moved in lockstep with me. We paused at the doorway and I scanned the halls in both directions.

"I don't know where else he could be if he's not in his office, his room, or the safe room. Bodhi said he was here. So where is Bodhi?" Worry pierced me.

"Safe room is empty," Kellan said. "Make sure we wire it up. I don't want anything left in that room."

I was torn between collapsing and fighting. I didn't want anything else left in that room either.

"I'll take care of it," Lunchbox said over the comms. "Be up in a few. We're tracking down the last of these connections."

"You seeing any movement, Vaughn?" Liam asked, frustration in his voice. They were right behind us as I headed down the hall. But once I was at the door to my room, I just… froze.

My room.

For all that Reginald and Moira had been my parents, I'd practically lived with Fuckbucket after I went on tour. Instead of just coming here for weekends or holidays, I was here for every single break. Why go to their house?

They were never there.

This had been my home.

My home. My prison. My hell.

Awareness of the guys surrounding me filtered through the chaos of memories, as I choked in fear. I sucked in a deep breath. Then another one.

"Little Bit," Mickey said as he reached us. "Let us take the door first?"

They weren't telling me to let them do it; they were asking me. "I don't know where else he would be…"

"It's okay. We'll find him," Milo said over the comms and I'd half-forgotten he could hear me. "Let the guys take the door, Ivy."

It was a request. Adjusting the grip on my gun, I said, "A part of me doesn't want any of you to see that room—ever." I licked my lips. "I never wanted anyone to see this house. I didn't want anyone to know…"

They were quiet. But it was Vaughn who asked, "And now?"

"I just want this over. I want our life, and for this to just be the past." All at once, the lock that seemed to keep the chains in place, weighing me down, shattered and the chains slipped free. For all the sudden freedom I had, there should have been an actual crash of sound as my restraints gave way, and yet there was nothing.

Just understanding in the eyes of the men around me.

"Sounds good to me, Dove," Vaughn said. "Gentlemen, let's kick down all the doors? Yeah?"

"Copy that," Bones said. Words echoed by Lunchbox.

"I'm on my way to you," Milo said. "We're doing one more sweep."

After Fuckbucket's room, we took positions on each side of the door and Liam twisted the knob and shoved it open.

No obnoxious clicks.

No shots.

After a span of three seconds, Jasper and Liam went through the door together and then the guys followed, with me right behind them. The bedroom hadn't changed in my absence. It was still decorated in white lace and pink frills. There were dolls and stuffed animals on the bed, like it was waiting for me to come back.

Toys lined the shelves, most of them still shiny and new, not even dust to mark their disuse. The guys searched the whole room, bathroom, closet, and even went so far as to look under the bed.

It was... devoid of any real personality. The girl this room had been designed for was an act. I might have lived here but it really hadn't been my home. The ghosts of every night I'd spent in this place crowded around me, leaving icy trails everywhere they connected.

House.

Bedrooms.

Office.

Sitting rooms.

Entertaining rooms.

Basement.

Wine—

"A wine cellar." That memory shuffled out on zombie feet from the past. I'd only been down there a couple of times, but he'd wanted to test some wine and he wanted me with him when he did.

How had I forgotten it—?

Because the wine cellar was one of the places where he'd attempted penetration after the first time. It had hurt so much. He plied me with wine then bent me over...

I was going to throw up.

Pushing past those thoughts, I said, "There's a wine cellar. It's accessed through the butler's pantry in the kitchen.

Totally separate from the basement. I can't believe I forgot about it…"

"It's not on the plans," Alphabet protested.

"Built later," Adam suggested, and it was bracing to remember that it wasn't just us on this open line. "A lot of collectors do that, especially if they are after very particular bottles. You want it completely temperature controlled."

"Yeah, fuck his wine. We can dump that shit," Freddie said. "We need to find *him*."

"We will," Kellan said. "Finish the sweeps. Everyone keep your eyes open and we'll meet at the butler's pantry." Then he looked at me. "Does the wine cellar let out anywhere else?"

"I don't think so—but I don't know for sure. I hated going down there, and after the first couple of times…" I couldn't quite suppress the shudder. "I avoided it."

I hated the understanding kindling in their eyes, but it was Mickey who nodded. "Jas—bring the bat."

"Oh, yeah."

Eight minutes later, we were in the butler's pantry and it was Ezra who worked out where the door was. Why hide the door unless—?

The first bullet caught Ezra in the shoulder, then the arm, before Adam yanked him backward.

CHAPTER 44

EMERSYN

*M*ore bullets followed and Rome hooked an arm around my middle, dragging me backward, even as the guys emptied several rounds into the room. The sound echoed into my brain, leaving it humming. Freddie moved to cover me on the side as the guys kept firing. I cut a gaze to where Ezra hissed heavily as Adam put pressure on his injuries. Lainey was with them.

As abruptly as the gunfire started, it ended. The sudden quiet was downright unnerving. The ringing in my ears redoubled. I could see mouths moving but no sound penetrated. Mickey moved abruptly to where Ezra was sliding down the wall, and he replaced Adam to put pressure on the wounds.

When I attempted to step toward them, Rome and Freddie both pulled me back. Rome's lips moved and I shook my head. Words weren't quite—wait, he was saying *wait*. I nodded, turning a worried look to where Mickey hooked

Ezra up and over his shoulder before he was striding out, with Lunchbox following him. Lainey seemed torn between going and staying.

Adam wanted her to go, and when she turned those troubled eyes to me, I motioned her to go too. The moment Milo kissed her and then gave her a gentle nudge toward the door made the decision for her. Maybe it was the lack of sound, or how hard it was to hear, but there was no mistaking the dark look Adam gave Milo or the way Milo met his gaze. Liam cut between them and they both looked to the door of the wine cellar.

It was Liam, Jasper, and Kellan who went through with Bones. Milo and Adam were a step behind them. I wanted to go, but Rome held up a finger.

Wait.

Sound began to bleed back in, muffled as it was. Freddie sounded almost bleeped out. "What... fuck... that..."

I shook my head, then Rome caught my free hand. We both had guns in our other hands. Freddie still sported his knife and then we were heading into the wine cellar. The smell of gunpowder was nearly overwhelmed by the stink of wine and blood. It was—there were broken bottles and bodies everywhere. More than there had been anywhere else in the house.

And the cellar itself reeked of earthier scents and a breeze. Jasper appeared in front of us. He'd switched out his bloodied bat for the axe and his expression was fierce. His lips moved and I could track maybe one out of two words, but he repeated it twice and the words sank in.

"It leads out into a maze..."

"Goddammit," I swore. I knew it was out there. We'd discussed it briefly—one time. All at once, the dead bodies around me seemed to fade in importance. They were obstacles. Not the target. Not Fuckbucket. Now, Ezra had been hurt. He nearly got Kellan with the shotgun. Then all those videos in the safe room. "We have to get him."

"We will," Jasper said and it wasn't an empty promise or one made half-heartedly. "But I want *you* out of here. This is definitely a trap. He set this for all of us and he wants you…"

Rebellion surged in me. I released Rome's hand and planted it against Jasper's chest.

The corner of his mouth kicked up a little higher. "Yeah, I didn't think you'd go for it." He dipped his head and kissed me, fierce, hot, and demanding. "We're going to get him, Firebird. He's running like hell right now and he's afraid. I want him afraid. Then I want him in pain."

"Then he's going to be gone," Freddie finished and I nodded once.

I wanted all of that. But I wanted them safe… "Ezra?"

"I got him, Little Bit," Mickey said over the comms. "It's a lot of blood, but he's going to make it. We've got him locked down."

"I have an eye on him and on Lainey," Vaughn soothed. "I'm also searching on the cameras. This is all a setup, but they didn't anticipate how hard we'd come at them. We got this."

"I love all of you," I said, wanting to include them.

"Thanks," Ezra said. "I thin—ow."

Laughter bubbled out of me. Hysterical laughter maybe, but laughter. Jasper winked and Rome appeared to relax. We were still in the middle of this fight, but the mottled and frosted glass that had been separating me from everything else splintered, then cracked. Sound wasn't the only thing rushing back in to fill the crevices.

"I'm ready," I said, focusing on Jasper. Freddie and Rome had stuck with me through all of this. They all had, but we had our parts to play and I wanted this over.

"That's our girl," Jasper said before he dropped another kiss. "Do you know the maze?"

"Yes." As long as they hadn't changed it much in the last few years. I'd actually played inside it once upon a time. Played and pretended that there was a gate to another world inside that maze, where I could escape this life and find another one.

"Let's go…"

Jasper took point with the axe in his hand. There was a blazing strength to him at the moment. An energy that seemed to vibrate the air around him. It tickled against my skin, chasing away the chill and knocking out more of the cracked glass. I was so ready to be done with this.

I had *escaped* the life Fuckbucket wanted for me and I couldn't wait to keep building this one with my guys. The ring on my finger had been a comforting weight, one I was determined to never lose. Not the ring. Not the guys who gave it to me. Not the life we were going to have.

The wine cellar exited right into the maze. They weren't kidding. It wasn't just outside it or near an exit; it was in the maze. Milo, Kellan, and Liam waited for us with Adam. Their expressions were equal amounts of dark and sober.

"Huh," Freddie said as he did a slow turn. "I wasn't expecting some sci-fi shit on this trip."

A laugh escaped me. "It's a little more Jane Austen than science fiction."

"There was *Pride and Prejudice and Zombies*," Jasper suggested and I blinked at him even as Milo swung around to look at us.

"Yeah," I said slowly. "But maybe we skip the zombies."

Jasper held up his axe. "I got us."

And that just made me giggle all over again. I was still grinning when a sound rippled through the air.

"Princess…"

That fucking name. Liam's gaze snagged on mine and there was so much hate in his eyes. Yeah. Me too.

"I can't tell you how happy I am to see that you survived. I went back for you—"

See?

I twisted to look. The man had a thing for cameras. Jasper found it first and he slammed the axe right into the reflective dome that hid the camera. It was tucked right against the building. It sparked, then made a whining noise as the power severed.

"I'm really fucking sick of his games," Liam said even as he held a hand out to me. When I slid my palm to his, he tugged me to him gently and studied me with searching eyes. He must have found what he was searching for, because he dipped his head and pressed a kiss to my lips.

"Get your fucking hands off her…" Fuckbucket sounded positively unhinged. Not a sound I ever wanted to hear when someone was kissing me, but Liam's chuckle was all taunt and I opened my mouth to his at the first sweep of his tongue. "Get your hands—"

A gunshot sounded and I jerked against Liam, who pushed us up against the greenery like it would act as a shield.

"Who's firing?" Kellan asked but was met with only a chorus of *not its*.

"Bodhi?" I asked, hoping.

"Maybe," Milo said, before he gave me a once-over. We were all blood spattered in different ways.

"Let's go," Kellan said. "Which way, Sparrow?"

"Center or out?" I studied where we were. I'd been here a couple of times, but I wouldn't have known it had that secret entrance or exit into the house. The basement climbed up between the rocks. It looked like a little garden in the middle of the maze. The gardeners definitely kept it meticulous.

The guys glanced at each other, a wordless discussion. "Center," Kellan said. "This whole thing has been a trap to pull you in."

"So let's spring the trap." Milo nodded. To my surprise, Adam looked like he agreed and Jasper swung his axe.

"Right behind me, Hellspawn, one hand on my back. Rome?"

"I got her." Rome's hand settled against my back as I pressed mine against Liam's.

"Left," I said and I pitched my voice low. At this point, there was no reason to hide—a scream cut through the air.

Then another.

It was the third one, which carried a sobbing note, that made me flinch. I tried to focus on where we were going. Fuckbucket's disgusting baby talk as he tried to soothe me. And then another one where he had me begging.

Yeah, this was my own personal house of horrors. But I kept my mind on putting one foot in front of the other.

"You were so beautiful," Fuckbucket said. "Perfection. You know, I would forgive you if you asked to come back..."

We were almost to the center. The fact I could remember the path buoyed me until we came around the corner and found Bodhi. He was facedown, and a dark stain covered his back. Heart in my throat, I started forward when he turned his head. He didn't shake his head so much as point with one hand to the east.

"Fuck," Liam swore as two bullets hit his vest and he staggered back. It crashed him into me and I fought to keep him from falling all the way as Rome and I dragged him out of the line of fire. More bullets flew.

Kellan, Milo, and Adam just strode out there, guns out as they fired. Jasper moved to check Liam's vest as Liam fought to catch his breath. "Goddamn, kicks like a mule," Liam swore.

"Going for Bodhi," Freddie said and I would have followed, but Jasper was already with him. A moment later, they had Bodhi back and his shirt was soaked with blood. He gave me a faint grin and a thumbs-up.

"Hey, PPG. Almost had him."

"Are you okay?"

"I'll live." He touched a hand to his chest. "Hurts too goddamn much to be dying."

"Doc," Jasper said. "We got another wounded for you."

"Get me later," Bodhi said. "Go kill that prick."

"Are you sure you're going to be okay?" There was so much blood.

"I'll be fine." Bodhi grimaced. "Didn't see the big guy—my bad."

On impulse, I pressed a kiss to his cheek. "Let Bones take you to Mickey…" I glanced at the man. He'd stuck close to us. "Do you know how to get back?"

Bones nodded. "I'll catch up to you guys," he said before he picked up the protesting Bodhi and they were gone.

Then it was just us.

Liam wasn't steady on his feet, but we were up and following where Milo, Adam, and Kellan went. The gunfire tapered off. Three turns to catch up and I knew where we were going…

All the moisture left my mouth.

"The gazebo," I said. "It's this way." A special place for a special girl. I'd blocked that out because that was the last time the maze had been a place for me to play. "There's another way."

If we were going into a trap, I couldn't let the past keep trying to drown me. That was what he was doing. He wanted to tear me down.

No more.

"This way," I said as I doubled back. The guys didn't question it, just moved with me. Kellan and Milo insisted on taking lead, even if I was doing the guiding. The air seemed damp and cloying. There was honeysuckle near the gazebo. It always attracted the bees. The smell was sweet, but too heavy.

When we reached the gazebo, I spotted Fuckbucket before they did, but it wasn't Fuckbucket that arrested my attention.

It was Vaughn.

Bloodied.

Bruised.

Being held by two others and with a gun to his head.

CHAPTER 45

EMERSYN

*a*dam, Kellan, and Milo had their guns pointed. Jasper and Liam joined them. Fuckbucket had four men with him, beyond the two holding up Vaughn. The bruises on Vaughn's face made me angry.

"It looks like we're at an impasse, Princess," Fuckbucket declared. "I have one of them. They have you. Come back to me and they can have him."

"You really are a fucking whack-job," Freddie stated, knife balanced in his hand.

"What will it be, Princess?" He was completely ignoring Freddie and I focused on Vaughn. His head was down. Was he really okay? Were they just holding him upright to play a part? We'd just talked to him—where was Alphabet?

"She's not going anywhere with you," Milo said in a cold voice. "You are never touching her again."

"So this one doesn't mean as much to them?" Fuckbucket speculated. "That's a pity, Princess. My research told me he was the one most likely to have marred that beautiful skin of yours…"

"Why don't you just shut up?" I asked. I'd never thought of him as insane. But… "For real, you want to see me… then come out where I can see you." Because he was there but the men with him blocked my line of sight.

"Do you want to see me?" The hope sliding into his voice made my skin crawl. "I knew you missed me."

"I can't miss you if you come out…" I kept a hand flat against Kellan's back. Liam and Jasper framed on either side of me. They weren't letting him see me and I really didn't want to see him.

"Come over here, Princess," Fuckbucket said. "You need to just come to me. I don't trust those criminals you've been spending your time with. They've destroyed a lot of our home—have you seen the destruction? No respect. None. So, come here, Princess. Let's sort this out between us."

"He's completely delusional," Liam muttered.

"Maybe, but he has Vaughn." Vaughn. Wasn't. Fucking. Moving.

"You are not going out there, Ivy." Milo said through gritted teeth.

"Princess?"

I hated that name so much.

"Meet me halfway?" I called.

"What are you doing, Sparrow?" There was a distinctive edge to Kellan's voice.

"Not listening," Jasper responded.

"She has a plan," Rome said. "Leave her alone." I could have kissed him. But it was Freddie I looked at. Freddie and his knife.

He raised his brows then glanced at his blade before he looked at me. With care, he flipped it around and handed it to me, hilt out. I traded him my gun for the knife.

Kellan cut a look at me from the corner of his eye. "Sparrow…"

"I can do this. We need Vaughn." I needed him.

Swallowing back the bile the idea induced, I said, "Uncle Bradley?"

"I'm waiting," he said. "Come on, Princess. You know I wouldn't hurt you. Come here—let's talk."

Wouldn't hurt me? Right.

"If I come over there, you need to let their friend go." I had to distance myself. "Or they won't let me get there…"

"I knew they were forcing you to cooperate." Fuckbucket's voice grew stronger. "Let me see my niece—*now*."

"Hellspawn… if you get hurt, I'm going to beat your ass," Liam growled as he finally shifted to let me move forward. I was still wearing my bulletproof vest, but that wouldn't do anything if they shot me somewhere else.

"Promises, promises," I teased, keeping my voice down as I eased between him and Jasper. Vaughn still wasn't moving. I already wanted to kill Fuckbucket. I wanted to kill him for so many reasons, but I couldn't lose Vaughn.

I refused.

Why wouldn't he lift his head? Movement beyond them betrayed where Fuckbucket was. He looked… terrible. Dark shadows under his eyes. His normally well-coiffed hair was greasy and disheveled. He'd lost his jacket, and his sleeves were rolled up. Everything about him was off.

My stomach rolled at seeing him. It didn't matter that just a couple of weeks earlier, he'd gripped my face and bruised it, trying to order me to come back to him. Then he'd told them to bury me.

"Come on, Princess—keep coming." He held a hand out to me like I wanted him to touch me. I didn't dare look back at the guys as I started forward. I didn't head for my uncle, I headed for Vaughn. They were inside the gazebo. Two entrances.

The one in front of us and the one behind them. So I moved slowly. I needed some sign from Vaughn. Any sign. C'mon… My eyes burned as I edged closer to the steps. The men with Fuckbucket were not the friendliest looking. Thankfully, none of them appeared to be the scary guy from before.

"You heard her," Kellan said in a voice so devoid of emotion it sent a chill up my spine. "Give us Vaughn—*now.*"

"Or I'm shooting her," Jasper said; that was the rough voice that had once terrified me.

"Stay right there," Liam ordered. "Don't take another step until he's on his way to us…"

The men with Fuckbucket were split. Everyone had a gun pointed at everyone else and I was right in the middle of it. I held still, obeying the command to not take another step. This was a gamble.

I was gambling.

They were letting me gamble—more than that, they were *backing* me. This was already a risk, considering he'd been willing to let me die before. Would he really try to kill me again? I had no idea.

Vaughn's chest moved. It was hard to make out based on how they held him, but his chest rose and fell.

He was *alive.*

Relief had wings inside me.

"Uncle Bradley?" The nervous notes in my voice weren't hard to feign. They still had Vaughn and I was still right here…

"Let him go," Fuckbucket ordered as he hurried forward. Several things happened at once. Fuckbucket pushed through his guards and grabbed my arm. Disgust curled through me as he tugged me to him like he'd hug me. At the same time, the guys holding Vaughn shoved him toward the stairs; they were going to use him to block the guys from getting to me.

But when they shoved him, Vaughn snapped his head up and he yanked one of the guys forward and picked him all the way up off the ground, before he slammed his head into the roof of the gazebo. Shouts scattered the air and a gun went off, and then another. Fuckbucket dragged me to him and I gripped the knife in my pocket as he tried to retreat down the stairs.

"C'mon, Princess…" But he didn't get far.

Freddie and Rome were there.

The sound of a body falling and then rolling down the steps to hit the back of our legs had me stumble a half-step, but Fuckbucket shoved a gun into my ribs as he stared at the guys. Movement behind us had him jerking to see Milo and Kellan inside the gazebo. Liam came from another direction, and when we turned, Jasper was there.

"You're not going anywhere," Kellan said. "Let her go."

Fuckbucket jerked the gun up and pointed it right at Rome this time.

I twisted to see Vaughn move to the railing where he gripped it. He was still bleeding and battered, but he lifted his chin toward me.

"Head up," he said in a rough voice. "Wings out."

Agreed.

I slammed the knife right into Fuckbucket's leg. It was the closest thing I could hit at this angle and his attention was all over the place. He couldn't move very well as it was, and Freddie's knife slid in deep. I twisted it as he shrieked, but he was already collapsing and then Liam was there, and Jasper. One minute Fuckbucket was touching me, and the next he screamed as they each broke one of his arms.

The sound was like a violent score. Milo slammed his

foot down on Fuckbucket's bad knee—the one I'd broken—and the man let out another scream. I staggered right into Freddie. I had blood all over my hand and turned just as Kellan broke the other knee—the good one.

"Vaughn?" Kellan asked and he shook his head.

"I'm good. It's Dove's call."

"Agreed," Freddie said, squeezing my blood-coated hand. "It's Boo-Boo's call."

They looked at me.

Fuckbucket was screaming.

"Shh," I told him when he looked at me. "I know you like it."

His eyes widened. "Princess—" Was he really pleading with me?

"I hate that fucking name."

So much pain.

So much agony.

So much destruction. How many people had died because of his depravities?

"We're burning this place down, right?" I looked at Milo, then Adam who hadn't moved closer, but there was a savage satisfaction on his face, then Liam and Jasper. The hate in their eyes was a living thing and so was the genuine fury in Rome's and the rage in Freddie's.

Only Kellan's eyes seemed to be cool, but I didn't mistake his anger for anything other than what it was. "You want it gone, Sparrow?"

"Yes."

They looked down at Fuckbucket.

"And Mickey deserves his pound of flesh…"

"Blow his dick off," Mickey said over our comms. "I'm treating the wounded."

"I can do that," Kellan said as he checked the load on his

shotgun. One last glance at me and I turned away from Fuck-bucket. I squeezed Freddie's hand.

"Don't forget your knife… I didn't mean to let it go."

Freddie grinned. "You did fine, Boo-Boo."

I headed for Vaughn, but I stopped at Milo and Kellan. "If you guys need to make it hurt for him, I won't say no."

"Burning it all down, Ivy," Milo said. "Every damn piece."

I didn't look at Fuckbucket. Not again. He was the past.

"Thank you," I whispered, then gripped his bicep before I made my way up the steps to where Vaughn opened his arms. Leaning into him, I closed my eyes. Because Fuckbucket was actually pleading, throwing out insults, demands, and then flat-out begging before the shotgun blast seemed to drown out his words, and left him screaming.

They still weren't done.

I didn't leave though.

I wouldn't.

I wanted to know he was dead.

Vaughn held me, and my guys, my brother, and my friend erased Fuckbucket like he'd never existed.

For me, it was enough to end Bradley Sharpe once and for all.

CHAPTER 46

LIAM

"*H*e's completely delusional." Every goddamn time he called her "princess" it just raised my fury. She *hated* that name. The couple of times I'd referred to her as *princess* scored deeper marks in my mind. She should have hit me harder.

"Maybe," she whispered. "But he has Vaughn." The ache in her words left a bruise on my soul. A lot of this had gone right. And a lot wrong. Trading Hellspawn for Vaughn was a nonstarter in my opinion. But trading Vaughn's life for ours?

Yeah. Not happening.

"You are not going out there, Ivy," Milo said through gritted teeth. I felt for him. Fuck, did I feel for him. I wanted to send her out of here. One word to Rome and he *might* pick her up and go. Maybe.

But my mirror wouldn't shackle her any more than I would.

"Princess?"

Fuck you. I had to swallow the words. He had six guys with him. They were all armed to the teeth. Five had guns on us—the sixth had a gun to Vaughn's head.

"Meet me halfway?" Hellspawn called and my soul sank. Don't do this—I got it. I understood *what* she was doing. But going anywhere near the piece of shit was the last thing she wanted. Leaving Vaughn wasn't negotiable.

Fuck.

"What are you doing, Sparrow?" Kellan was not happy.

"Not listening," Jasper muttered.

"She has a plan," my mirror's absolute faith in her rang in every single word. Believe her. Protect her. Free her. I heard every single thing he didn't say. "Leave her alone." She needed this.

From me.

From him.

From us.

"Sparrow…"

"I can do this. We need Vaughn."

Goddammit, I needed *her.*

"Uncle Bradley?" Disgust, anger, and pain twisted up in those few syllables.

"I'm waiting," the shitstain called. "Come on, Princess. You know I wouldn't hurt you. Come here—let's talk."

Wouldn't *hurt* her? Yeah, delusional didn't cover it.

"If I come over there, you need to let their friend go." The distance in her voice could have cut, I supposed. Could have. The emotional divorce didn't remotely reflect the vibrant woman we loved. She was playing a role. *Trust her.* I could practically *feel* Rome's gaze drilling into me. "Or they won't let me get there…"

Or they won't—got it. She wanted us to play that part.

"I knew they were forcing you to cooperate." The son of a

bitch sounded so fucking pleased and arrogant. "Let me see my niece—*now*."

Play my part. I could do this for her, but she needed to understand one thing. "Hellspawn... if you get hurt, I'm going to beat your ass," I growled, shifting my stance so she could pass closer to me. I wanted her within arm's reach.

"Promises, promises," the low tease practically wrapped around my dick and gave it a stroke. Yeah, I'd spank her until her ass gleamed and then I'd fuck her until she couldn't see out of pleasure. That was happening.

It was a fucking date.

She moved forward on slow and steady steps. As much as I wanted to watch her, I didn't take my eyes off my target. Movement revealed the man who had been the architect of so much misery. He looked like the piece of shit he was. Someone had been pushed to the edge.

We'd taken his money. Isolated him from his wealthy friends. Pushed him into hiding. Forced him into a corner. He wasn't handling it well. Too. Fucking. Bad.

For a few scant months, we'd been doing to him what he'd done to her for her whole life. He deserved to suffer for so much longer.

Eternity wouldn't be enough.

"Come on, Princess—keep coming." He held a hand out to her, but she didn't go directly to him. Good girl. She slowed near the two steps leading up into the gazebo.

"You heard her," Kellan said in an icy voice. He shifted his target to point his gun at her. It was anathema to all of us. I trusted Kellan with her life. I trusted *us* with her life. Anyone else pointed a gun at her and I was going to take their goddamn heads off. "Give us Vaughn—*now*."

"Or I'm shooting her," Jasper declared in a rough voice. Yeah. I felt that brother.

"Stay right there," I ordered. She was too damn close as it was. "Don't take another step until he's on his way to us…"

I hated this play. It was a smart play. It catered to the sick fuck's ego, and he was clearly out on a damn limb already. Didn't mean I had to like it, and she was right between us and them.

"Uncle Bradley?" There was the barest hint of the little girl she'd been in her voice as she asked for him to cooperate. To help. To give up so that Vaughn could be released.

I. Hated. That. Sound. It just added another nail to the coffin I wanted to bury him in.

"Let him go," Sharpe ordered abruptly, pushing through his men and grabbing her. The moment he closed his fingers on her arm, I had to fight the instant urge to put a bullet in his head. The whole tableau seemed to slow down. The guards shoved Vaughn forward. He went from being limp and out of it to his head snapping upwards. Even as they pushed him into the field of fire to cut us off from Hellspawn.

I took a step, already moving as Vaughn yanked one of the guards on him forward and lifted him off the ground to slam him into the roof of the gazebo. The big guy was the gentlest of us in so many ways, but it was a mistake to ever think that made him *weak*. The guy behind him swung a gun in Vaughn's direction, but Jasper fired at the same time as Milo.

At this range, the bullets took the back of his head right off. I shot the next one, heading right for her. Vaughn was free; now we were backing her up. Guns went off all around me. I swore a bullet whistled past me, but it didn't hit any of us, so I didn't care. My chest ached from the shots my vest had already taken. When the last guard was down, it was us and Bradley Sharpe.

And he was still fucking *touching* her.

VAUGHN

Everything hurt. My sides. My chest. My arms. My soul. Being tased was an experience I could live without repeating. I'd killed two of them before they'd managed to take me down. Stupidity on my part. I'd gotten caught up staring at the cameras when Alphabet diverted to another access point. We needed to find where the feeds were for the safe room.

Frankly, neither of us thought that we'd found them all. In a straight on fight, five on one? I liked my odds. But they were heavily armed and they were taking me to that asshole. I wanted my shot. I wanted it for all of us. They didn't get me close enough though, and then the guys were there along with Dove.

When she moved to trade herself for me, I made myself wait. Wait for her to be closer. Wait for them to lose their focus, just once. If that gun moved from my head, all bets were off.

The moment it did, I slammed that guy so hard into the roof the crunch of his neck warned me he was dead, no matter how hard I hit him in the head. Guns fired from all around me. I half-expected to feel the hot punch of a bullet slamming into me, but it didn't. My brothers had my back and we would have hers.

"C'mon, Princess..."

Fuck. No.

I was moving, slow, and everything hurt. My legs. My arms. My head buzzed. But he did *not* get to walk off with her. She'd suffered enough because of him.

He didn't get to inflict one more piece of damage.

Ever.

Freddie and Rome blocked him as Milo shot the last guard between us and them. That body tumbled down the steps and nearly knocked them down. The bastard had a gun, and he didn't hesitate to pull her to him and shove that gun into her ribs. Milo and Kellan framed me, even as Jasper and Liam circled the gazebo.

He was not leaving with her.

It wasn't happening.

"You're not going anywhere," Kellan informed him. "Let her go."

I moved to the railing of the gazebo, gripping it to stay upright. The asshole pointed the gun at Rome, not that it seemed to faze him in the slightest. When Dove turned her head to look at me, I lifted my chin.

"Head up," I reminded her. "Wings out."

The spark in those brown eyes when she fastened them onto me was the balm my soul needed. She thrust herself into the lion's mouth to help me, but she wasn't toothless. No, my dove was a fighter, then she moved her hand and slammed a knife into the son of a bitch.

Slammed it into him and twisted it. I couldn't help the very bloodthirsty chuckle I released. That was our girl. He shrieked, his voice cracking at the agony.

The guys moved. Jasper and Liam hooked their arms to his and peeled him away from Dove, even as Jasper wrenched his left arm one way and Liam bent the right arm the other. Like some kind of twisted wishbone. The cracking of his bones was satisfying on a very primitive level. Just like his screams of agony.

The moment they dropped him on the ground, Milo stomped his foot down on the knee the guy favored. It made a meatier crunch and the agonizing screams climbed in volume and pitch.

Kellan was a step behind Milo and he delivered a similarly vicious stomp to the other knee. The man wasn't going anywhere. The death warrant he'd signed for himself was way past due.

"Vaughn?" Kellan invited me to the party, but I shook my head. The man needed to die for what he'd done to us. He definitely deserved to suffer for what he'd done to her. But I was satisfied that they would make sure justice was delivered.

It was enough for me.

Everything else? "I'm good. It's Dove's call."

"Agreed," Freddie said, his hand fast on hers. I was so proud of the little punk. He reached out to her more and more. Accepting contact, asking for it. "It's Boo-Boo's call."

I wasn't alone in my determination. Everyone looked at her and she glanced at the shrieking man on the ground.

"Shh," she said in the most dismissive, apathetic voice, ever. "I know you like it."

"Princess—" Maybe we should cut out his tongue.

"I hate that fucking name." Her whole life seemed to be summed up in that sentence. The pain she'd endured. The hell he put her through. The innocence he'd ripped away from her.

He'd killed so many. Hurt her so badly.

He deserved all the pain we could rain down on him.

"We're burning this place down, right?"

The moment she asked the question, I knew the answer. We all did. If she needed it gone, then fuck yes, we were burning it down.

Burn it all down.

JASPER

I'd forgotten how to breathe for a few seconds. The fight had been brutal to get here. Too much hurry up and wait. They'd left us bread crumbs, trying to pick us off on our way through with traps and ambushes. Then the tapes… between the audio and what video we'd seen—it turned my stomach.

If I didn't already hate him, that would have driven me to homicide in the moment.

My father had been abusive. Julius King, or Jeff Hardigan, or whatever his fucking name was, definitely qualified as a manipulative prick. This guy?

He was a monster. Pure and simple.

I thought I hated him before.

But the chance to rip his hand off her and break his fucking arm filled me with a very primitive satisfaction. I wanted to tear him apart. Chop him up into pieces, while he was alive. I twisted his wrist as I broke his arm, cracking it. Then snapped two of his fingers for good measure. I wanted to rip off every damn thing he'd ever touched her with.

"You want it gone, Sparrow?" Kellan knew the answer. We all knew the answer. But it had to be her choice. Life had robbed her of so many choices, starting with her deadbeat dad and ending with this fucker.

"Yes."

Shock rippled through Sharpe's eyes. Did he really think she'd defend him? Delusional didn't cover it.

"And Mickey deserves his pound of flesh…" The soft reminder carried so much sadness in it. Yes, Doc did deserve it. So did Liam. So did Vaughn. But this was her villain, the monster who'd not only lurked under her bed but in it.

"Blow his dick off," Doc said, his tone pragmatic and direct. "I'm treating the wounded."

That was our Vandal.

"I can do that," Kellan said as he checked the load on his shotgun. The asshole might bleed out fast after that shot gelded him. We wouldn't have as much time as I wanted to make him suffer. Suffer like we'd made Reginald Sharpe suffer.

Then again, Reggie Boy had adopted her and was supposed to be her father. He deserved that suffering. But my swan hadn't wanted to watch it. As much as she enjoyed the idea that we'd inflicted pain on Arlington, this guy? This guy had haunted her all of her life. She wanted freedom.

She didn't have to stay for this part, or watch.

She didn't have to do a damn thing she didn't want to do.

"Don't forget your knife… I didn't mean to let it go," she told Freddie who held fast to her hand.

Freddie grinned. "You did fine, Boo-Boo." She did more than fine. He released her as she moved away. She went around us, not taking a single step toward the soon-to-be-corpse on the ground.

When she reached her brother and Kellan, she said, "If you guys need to make it hurt for him, I won't say no."

"Burning it all down, Ivy," Milo said. "Every damn piece."

Yes, we were, and we waited as she continued to withdraw, but she didn't go far. She went straight to Vaughn and it helped ease a boulder off my heart to see her melt into him. The reality that one of us could have died on this trip hadn't been lost on me. She was worth it, but so were my brothers. I still wasn't willing to lose anyone.

"Please… I have money—"

Sharpe's pleading pulled my attention down to him. He had money?

"You're all criminals. You'd do the same thing. You can't tell me you can't be bought—" He said something else, but I tuned it out. Then Kellan lifted the shotgun and terror filled Sharpe's face.

His scream after Kellan fired was everything.

And he was still conscious.

I traded my gun for the axe. "Liam, grip his arm."

"Oh…" Liam said with a cold smile. "Yes."

CHAPTER 47

EMERSYN

*A*s quickly as Fuckbucket seemed to die, the guys had taken their time. I was pretty sure he bled to death. He definitely screamed until he passed out, but then they slapped him awake. I wasn't entirely sure why they *wanted* him awake, until they dragged him back inside, all the way up the stairs to his room. I followed with Vaughn. He kept one arm wrapped around me. I wanted him to go see Mickey, but he shook his head.

"When this is done, Dove. I promise." Then he pressed the gentlest of kisses to my forehead. It was so sweet and kind it made my eyes tear up. Freddie stuck with us as Rome moved ahead.

"Don't worry, Boo-Boo. If the big lug falls down, I'll help you catch him." Freddie shot Vaughn a sly look. "Wouldn't want him to squash you."

"Thanks," Vaughn said, his tone amused if dry.

"Just here to offer help, man," Freddie told him. "You know, don't be afraid to ask for it. We've got you."

Something passed between the two of them and Vaughn chuckled. It was a rough sound, but it held real humor. "Thanks, Freddie. I mean it."

"I got you," Freddie said with a nod. He caught me watching and he winked. "I got you too, Boo-Boo."

"I know you do," I said. "And I'm really glad you do." He looked pleased, only sobering when the guys emerged from the bedroom.

"Sparrow," Kellan said and I met his gaze. "Everything goes?"

"There's nothing here I want to keep except you guys— and our friends."

"Thanks," Milo said, the first real sign of a smile since our assault began. "Time for you and Vaughn to get outside, Ivy. Unless you want to light the match."

I considered it. "I already lit it—the day I tried to escape this place for the last time." The day I'd broken his knee and began to truly fuck up his world. It was the day I used what Liam had taught me to survive and to take back some control. It ended with me being shocked and blown off the fence. Then, eventually, Pinetree.

For all the pain, the fear, and the tears? Pinetree brought Freddie to me. I glanced at him now.

"I'm okay."

"Yeah, you are," he said, agreeing with me. "Let's get Vaughn out of here?"

I nodded, before I glanced at Kellan, Jasper, and Liam. "You got this?"

"Oh yeah, Hellspawn." Liam winked at me. "We got this. Rome?"

"Going with them." Rome moved around to Vaughn's other side. Every step I took away from that bedroom and what remained of Fuckbucket let me take deeper and deeper breaths. There were bodies all over the house, and the garden, and in the maze.

So many bodies.

I couldn't even call them a metaphor; it was another sad fact. With Rome bracing Vaughn on the other side and Freddie slipping around to move ahead of us, we made it down the stairs.

Mickey was coming in the front door as we got to the bottom step. He swept a look over me, his eyes assessing, and I summoned a smile for him. "I'm fine. Vaughn needs help."

"Just sore, Dove," Vaughn muttered. "Nothing too bad."

"Then it won't hurt you to let me give you a once-over and verify. That will make Little Bit feel better."

It absolutely would. Mickey took over from me and braced Vaughn to help get him outside. Freddie caught my hand and we headed out too. "We should move the cars," Freddie said.

"Already on it," Bones said as he pointed us to where a large van idled; although it was more ambulance inside than van.

Lainey looked up from where she was sitting with Ezra, her expression crumpled with relief as she rose and climbed out, before she collided with me. Freddie let go of my hand as I hugged her.

"I'm gonna check on Bodhi," Freddie told me.

I nodded as I hugged her. I didn't see Bodhi or Vaughn inside that van, but there were other vehicles pulling up, and other people. Lunchbox and Alphabet intercepted anyone coming in. I didn't know who they were or why they were here, but none of them looked at us so I contented myself with hugging Lainey.

When I would have loosened my grip, she tightened hers. "We're okay," I said. "We're okay."

"That house—the stuff he did…" Lainey's tears were wet against my neck and I squeezed her tighter.

"I made it," I whispered. "I made it because of you and because of them." When she squeezed even tighter, I huffed out what was left of my breath. "Breathing isn't optional," I reminded her and she let out a wet laugh as she pulled back. Somewhere there was the sound of an explosion. We pulled apart to stare at the house just in time to see the guys come out.

Jasper wore a grin, so did Liam. Even Kellan looked happy. Milo seemed more bemused, and Adam was unreadable.

Another boom sounded and then one of the upstairs windows exploded outward. I gaped at it until Liam blocked my view, tucked a finger under my chin, and closed my mouth with a light nudge. "Burning it down, Hellspawn."

Lainey squeezed my hand and then I let her go so I could wrap my arms around Liam. He picked me up with a huff and I pulled back a little. "You okay?"

"Little sore," he said, then hugged me tighter. "Just a little sore." The hug was everything, then he passed me to Jasper, then to Kellan. The ferocity in their hugs kept me grounded.

Eventually, we had to move. Mickey said Vaughn was a little bruised. He'd managed to crack at least one rib, but the electrical burns weren't bad. Bodhi had gotten stabbed at least twice, and he'd had to dig four bullets out of him. Most of them were flesh wounds, but they were still bullets. The biggest worry for him and Ezra both was shock, but they were getting transported to a private hospital.

"I'll take care of them," Adam said and Lainey seemed torn between going and staying. But Milo made the call for her when he offered to join them.

"Two are better than one for keeping watch," he'd said.

While Adam didn't look thrilled, he had merely nodded

before he pressed a kiss to my cheek. "Take care of yourself, Emersyn, and if you need anything, call."

"Thank you." Then Lainey was there with another hug before Milo wrapped me up into a tight embrace.

"Listen to the guys, Ivy," he teased. "But give them hell."

I laughed. "Be safe. Please."

"I'll call soon." When he flicked a look to Lainey and back, I nodded. I was safe. We needed to look after her now.

Then they were loading up and leaving. We weren't far behind them; the people who'd been showing up were dealing with the bodies. I didn't know who they were or where we found them, and I decided to not ask.

At least not today.

Mickey said goodbye and thank you to his friends. Then we were climbing into an SUV that wasn't damaged. It had three rows of seats and while it was a tight fit, all eight of us made it inside, though I was sitting in the very back, squashed between Rome and Freddie. Kellan drove and Vaughn was put in the front passenger. That put Jasper, Mickey and Liam in the middle row.

Thankfully, we were heading straight to the airport. They wanted me far away before the "cleaners" were done. They would not only erase any sign of our presence, but they would also verify that no one walked away. Fuckbucket was dead. He would be erased. In a few months, he might even die in a house fire.

Anything could happen.

There were more details, but I didn't care. Not anymore. We were going home. Vaughn was in pain. The guys were bruised in places. But it was done. He could never touch me again. We could tell Mary that the person responsible for Jonathon's death had paid for the crime. Mickey had avenged his sister.

Exhaustion weighed on me, I was half-asleep when we

pulled up to the airplane. We'd cleaned up some, but we were still filthy. I needed a shower and about ten years of sleep. Kellan picked me up when I stumbled; he didn't even slow down as he carried me right up the steps.

I wasn't the only one who was tired, but there was an intensity vibrating in the air around all of them. While I had to sit in my own seat for take-off, I curled up in Mickey's lap for part of the flight. I must have fallen asleep because I woke up curled up with Freddie, who grinned at me sleepily. It wasn't that far off dawn when we finally left the plane.

The drive back to the clubhouse included a stop at two fast-food places and one coffee shop. The giant caramel macchiato that Liam got for me was delicious. I didn't want food of any kind. Once we were home—and it was so much like coming home—I headed up for a shower while the guys sorted things out.

The nice thing was, by consensus, we all slept in the sitting room again. Vaughn got the longer section of the sofa. I curled up on the cushions on the floor next to him, where I could hold his hand. Freddie scooted in, to sleep next to me. The guys were still talking when I went to sleep.

No matter how hard I tried to keep my eyes open, I couldn't. My old life was over. For real this time. My new life? My life as a Vandal, with my Vandals? That was all just the beginning. I reveled in that feeling. I reveled in the soothing cadence of their voices as they talked, they laughed, they teased, and then Mickey shifted so I could lay my head in his lap and began stroking my hair, and I was out.

CHAPTER 48

FREDDIE

A WEEK LATER...

*B*oo-Boo sat in the chair facing me, hand in mine, as Vaughn worked on the first tattoo I'd ever let anyone put on me. Honestly, I wasn't sure what I expected. I knew it would hurt, but pain and I were old friends. Having Boo-Boo there helped, having her there *really* helped. Vaughn went over every step of the procedure with me and described exactly how it would go.

The trick, he told me, was to relax. Then he offered me a sympathetic smile. "Some people like the way the needle feels. They enjoy the scraping sensation as the ink is injected. Others hate it, but are willing to endure it because the art is worth it. This isn't a test. You don't have to love it; you don't have to hate it. And you don't have to finish it—we're not doing anything you're not comfortable with. My suggestion is to start small. We can draw a wing or a beak or, fuck it, a feather."

I turned those words over inside my head. No one judged me on this. I knew it. They didn't have to reassure me and at the same time, they did. Doc even reminded me that my bloodwork was in solid order. Despite all the crap I'd gone through, I didn't carry STDs or any other diseases.

But sitting here with no shirt while Vaughn waited to get started was the most exposed I'd been in a long time. Almost too exposed. Boo-Boo squeezed my fingers. "I can give you a blow job after," she offered. "Vaughn did that when he gave me my Vandals tat."

Surprise speared through me.

Her eyes were so calm. "Or you can eat me out—you know, I'm not going to complain."

Vaughn didn't say a word as a little bubble of hysterical laughter escaped. "Boo-Boo…"

"Wait," she said, squeezing my fingers once before letting me go. She stood up, whipped off her shirt, followed by her bra. Then she settled in the chair in front of me again and held out her hand. Her breasts were… really pretty. Even prettier was the Vandals tat nestled on her sternum and the abdominal tat that just—

"That's really gorgeous," I said, studying the way the hawk and the falcon circled her abdomen while my eyes trailed the words woven into the ribbons of their path.

"Thank you," she said. "What you do, I'll do. You get a feather, I'll get a feather. Vaughn said he'd do my thigh next or my back—I haven't decided which one to get first."

She was getting a phoenix on her back and the ring of birds on her thigh. Rome had been renewing the regular ink to keep it in place. I kind of liked it, and it was erotic as hell, considering he'd also added a shrike for me.

"Let's start with my Vandals tat," I said, the decision made before I could really process what I'd been thinking about. "I need it. I need that—and then the shrike. Then the phoenix."

Boo-Boo's grin grew.

"If I got you tatted on me, Boo-Boo, would that be okay?"

"Anything you want," she offered, and she meant it. Whatever I wanted. I still hadn't let her touch me. Not the way I wanted her to and each time I thought about it, the panic crept in and the nausea, and then I was sweating. But she let me touch her whenever I wanted and how I wanted. Her trust was so precious...

"Okay, that's the fourth tattoo and I don't get that until I let you touch me." It was a confession I hadn't shared with anyone beyond her. Vaughn didn't comment but I caught the rough sympathy in his eyes, along with pride. The first was something that made me want to duck my head, but the second stunned me.

"You got this," he said. "Whenever you're ready."

I blew out a breath. Then I glanced down at my bicep. There was a scar there. I knew every single one of them, even if I didn't always know where they came from. "Vandals tat," I said and did my best to relax my arm. "Right there, Boo-Boo?"

"Hmm?"

"Kiss it for me before he starts?" The request startled her but the swift pleasure in her eyes made me kick myself. I kept holding back from her and she didn't deserve that. One week ago, we managed to erase one of the worst people in existence. He wasn't the guy who abused me. But he had hurt her. He wasn't one of the men from the movies they made me do or the people they sold me off to.

But he was a monster. We freed Boo-Boo. Freed her and gotten her justice. I didn't think I'd ever be able to do the same, but Boo-Boo gave me wings. So maybe it was time I freed myself.

"Please?" I added and her smile was so beautiful it made my heart hurt. She leaned forward and my hand brushed her breasts, but she didn't withdraw as she pressed her lips right over that scar. Eyes closed, I just concentrated on the softness of her skin and the way her lips were feather-gentle as she kissed my arm.

When she lifted her head, I opened my eyes and stared at her.

"Thank you," I whispered and she smiled. When she sat back down, she stroked her thumb along the side of my hand and I savored that contact. "I'm ready, Vaughn."

"Okay, Shrike, let's do this..." The sound of the motor didn't distract me in the slightest from gazing into Boo-Boo's eyes. "Starting now," Vaughn said. "Remember: whenever you want me to stop, you say the word. You're in charge."

The first stroke of the needle was definitely a scrape, but I wanted this pain. I craved it. For once, I was going to match my brothers. My body. My choice.

My boo-boo.

KELLAN

TWO WEEKS LATER...

"Eyes still closed?" Sparrow asked and I chuckled.

"Yes," I told her, turning my face toward her. "They've been closed the whole drive. Is this a trust exercise?" The last couple of weeks had been tough. The nightmares started not even a full twenty-four hours after we were back. I'd expected them. Doc warned us too—Sparrow had been perfection and grace under pressure. She'd worked with us, trusted us, and followed our lead.

But killing the son of a bitch who hurt her was just shattering the last shackle of her past. The cage had been blown open, the past burned down, but she still needed to heal. We all did. Grieve. Heal. Then rebuild and go on with our lives. We were all doing it in our own ways. Today, she'd asked to take me out, then asked for my keys.

"I would have thought I'd proved how much I trusted you when you asked to drive my car," I teased her. Driving was a skill she was *enormously* proud of, and one she didn't use, because despite having dealt with Fuckbucket and Reginald and getting Moira secured, none of us were willing to let her out of our sight for very long.

Maybe in ten or fifteen years we could relax.

Maybe.

"You did," she said, her smile in her voice. "But I really want to surprise you."

"Whatever it is," I promised. "I'm sure I'll love it." I was with her; how could I not love it?

"I adore you," she said and I had to smile wider.

"That makes my day."

I'd been trying to keep track of where we were going since we left the clubhouse. But Sparrow was a deeply cautious driver. She didn't make sudden turns. She handled the car smoothly. The confidence in her as she accelerated or braked was something I wish I could enjoy watching, but I contented myself with letting her *surprise* me.

Still, nothing could have prepared me for when she pulled to a stop and turned the car off. "Stay there. I'm going to come around."

I put a hand on her arm to keep her from slipping out of the car. "Have you done a sweep?"

"Yes." All patience, no bite.

"And you're armed." That wasn't a question, but she covered my hand with hers and squeezed it gently.

"Yes, I am. Two seconds, I promise, and the blindfold is

coming off as soon as we're out of the car." But she didn't leave the car and I exhaled a long breath.

"Be careful," I asked her. "Okay?"

"I promise."

Then I forced myself to let her go so she could get on with her surprise. It was the longest two seconds of my life, between the sound of her closing the door and my door opening.

"I'm here," she said and her voice washed over me, soothing some of my jangled nerves. Then her hand was on mine and I eased out of the car. "You can take the blindfold off…"

She didn't have to tell me twice. I whipped it off and then stared at the shop. Well, the burnt-out remains of it. Liam and Jasper stood not a dozen feet away by the walls, and Rome appeared from the far side. I didn't laugh, but the idea they'd been right there settled me on a very deep and broken level.

"Well, if the guys are my surprise, I'll say thank you." I tried to keep it light but she laughed, then caught my hand in hers as she dragged me around the building. It was gutted from the fire. What was left standing was blackened and scorched.

The one remaining wall had a painting on it. Rome had added cars, including my own, to a road where they were racing. And, above, there were birds, along with a sparrow racing beside a kestrel.

"Sparrow," I began, then stopped when I saw the sign that had been added—Kestrel Automotive and Body Shop. "You bought it."

"We did," she said and I glanced down at her shining eyes. "Liam finished the last bit with the lawyers yesterday. It's in your name. But it's ours. Yours. Your shop to do whatever you want, and financed by Phoenix Vandal LLC."

Phoenix Vandal LLC. That was what she'd named the holding company to help manage her money. She didn't care about it, not really, but Liam had been bullying her to take it, own it, and do what she wanted with it.

"You bought Vaughn a shop—" I guessed.

"Nope," Jasper said. "Not yet. He's not ready. The fact Lauren finally got out of the hospital and is home is helping. But we're gonna give him a year to heal, then we'll build him a space wherever he wants it."

We.

"This isn't just me," Sparrow said as she grinned up at me. "We're an us. And you love this place. We can afford to make it whatever we want."

I turned, cupping her face, and she was already pushing up on her toes to meet my kiss. Her smile softened as our lips connected and her sigh was everything. Raising my head, I grinned down at her. "Thank you, Sparrow."

There was a sound of bottle caps coming off and I glanced over to find Jasper holding out a beer to me. "Drink up. Just because we own it doesn't mean we're done yet."

I laughed, and when she drifted over to Liam and wrapped herself around him, I sighed. I lifted my bottle to them. "To our girl and our future."

"Hell yes, I'll drink to that." Jasper clinked our bottles together, then Rome and Liam added theirs. Sparrow wasn't drinking and she grinned as she held up the keys.

"I'm still driving."

That made me laugh and it dislodged another boulder of the past. We may never forget it all, but we weren't going to let any of it control us.

Not anymore.

CHAPTER 49

DOC

A MONTH LATER...

"Y ou don't have to sell it if you're not ready," Little Bit said from where she sat on the counter in Steph's house. It had taken me forever to even be willing to come here. I half-expected to find the weeds choking out her garden, or the power to be shut off. But, no, it was all in pristine shape. Then Little Bit told me what the guys had been doing.

"I know," I said. "But this is never going to be my life." I motioned to the house, the yard out back, and the suburb. "White picket fence, wife, 2.4 kids."

"2.4?" She made a face. "How do you have a .4?"

I chuckled. "I have no idea, and to be fair, I don't want that anyway."

"Well, you have me," she said. "I might not be the wife you wanted—"

I crossed the room and pressed a finger to her lips. "Hush," I ordered. "I mean it. One bad word about you, and we will have a moment, Little Bit."

She bit my finger, impudent as always, then grinned. "You should never threaten me with a good time."

Laughter swelled up inside me. "What am I going to do with you?"

"Whatever you want, I hope." Then she wrapped her legs around my hips and dragged me closer. She was dressed in leggings and an oversized t-shirt. With her hair pulled back into a ponytail, she looked every inch the soon-to-be twenty-year-old she was. Fuck me, not even of legal age to buy alcohol.

Cupping her face in my hands, I met her gaze and sighed. "You're beautiful," I said. "You should be told that, and often. But that beauty, it's not just in this admittedly gorgeous and flexible body, but it's your mind, Little Bit. Your mind and this heart—how you kept that heart intact after everything you went through… everything you're still going through."

She took my breath away. Physically, she was a twenty-year-old. Emotionally and mentally? No, there was no measuring that. She was the girl for me. The girl with the survivor's heart and the incomparable soul.

When she wrapped her arms around my neck and used her legs on my hips to leverage herself a little higher, I met the sweetness in her kiss with the hunger in my own. I fucking loved this woman, loved every single stubborn inch of her. The stroke of her tongue to mine sent a bolt of lust right to my dick.

Sliding my hands under her ass, I picked her up, and she let out a little hiss. I paused, breaking the kiss to eye her. "Problem?"

"Um, just a little sore today," she told me with the cheekiest grin.

"Your ass is sore?" One corner of my mouth pulled up in spite of myself.

"Mhmm. Pretty much."

"Need a doctor?"

Her smile grew. "Maybe—think he could fix me up?"

"Never know until we take a look." I settled her onto her feet and then turned her to put her hands on the counter. "Let me do all the work, okay?"

"Okay." With care, I peeled down her leggings. The permanent ink of the tattoo on her thigh was as hot now as it had been the day after Vaughn finished it. It completely circled her thigh, and I loved it. Erotic and emotional.

Her ass was definitely redder than normal and there were hints of light bruises in the shape of handprints. With care, I kissed each one, careful of the welts. "Liam?"

"Kellan," she said on a sigh when I traced one welt with my tongue. "He wanted to do something new."

The dampness on the inside of her thighs said it was something she enjoyed. "Did he now?" I massaged her ass, until I was kneeling behind her, and pressed my lips up to her cunt. "Lean forward, Little Bit." Her swift obedience sent languid heat spiraling through me. "Such a good girl for me."

I traced her labia with my tongue and lapped up the sweet slickness. She clenched even as she tried to relax her thighs.

"You definitely need a doctor," I informed her as I rose and nudged her feet a little farther apart. She was flat across the counter, her ass on display and her smile relaxed and pleased. A cat with her cream.

"Can you help me out?"

"Oh yeah," I said as I opened my jeans and lined myself up. "I have what you need right here..." Thrusting into her was like sinking into home and her delighted sigh was everything I wanted. I wasn't gentle, or easy. My hands on her hips kept her in place. The hot heat of her cunt soaking my cock was everything I could wish for, but the sweet, rapturous sounds she made just added the cherry to the top.

I wasn't going to last long, but I teased an orgasm out of her before I came. I leaned against her back and trailed kisses along her throat.

"I think I should see the doctor daily," she panted and I chuckled.

"For you, Little Bit," I said, giving her a gentle push that had her inner muscles twitching and fluttering around me. "The doctor is always in."

Her giggle was perfect and I lay there, just soaking up her nearness. We'd get back to the packing later. Right now, it was enough to have her, and one of the bruised areas on my heart shrank just a little bit—because of my Little Bit.

VAUGHN

TWO MONTHS LATER...

Having Dove flat on her stomach with her shirt off while I worked on her phoenix was just the soothing I needed. Freddie's tattoo—his Vandals mark—had been the first I'd managed to do since the shop burned down. Then Dove had me do the ones on her thigh. Freddie was back for his shrike, not even a week after the first one.

'Course, I thought it helped that Dove would come and sit with him. Between her playful, raunchy jokes, and going topless just to give him something else to concentrate on, it was one of my favorite things. Freddie had two tattoos and he wanted me to finish Dove's phoenix before I did his.

Fair enough.

"You going to sleep on me?" I asked as I added color to one of the wings. We'd been working on this for the last month, on and off. A week on, a week off. I wanted it to heal fully but she never complained about discomfort.

"Hmm, no, I was thinking about the tour we've been discussing."

Ah. "How many cities?"

"Twelve," she answered with a sigh. "I thought, keep it small, but do slightly larger venues. Spread it out. Four shows a week, twelve weeks, then back home."

Three months.

"Freddie already said he wanted to go with me, and I know Jasper and Kellan can't go the whole time, but they promised to come to at least one of the shows. Rome will be there. Would you like to come too?"

The invitation surprised me. I paused in my drawing to consider *why* it surprised me.

"Vaughn?"

"Sorry, Dove," I murmured, pressing a kiss to her shoulder. "I just had to think about that for a minute. I would love to go with you—I can work rigging, be the guy who takes care of all of that and makes sure they set you up right."

Her smile settled something in me. "Thank you. That would make everyone feel better. I didn't want to pull you away, though, if you had other plans."

I went back to filling in the tattoo, taking care to blot up the blood as I moved. "I don't really have other plans at the moment." The only reason I even had equipment for tattoos was because Liam picked it up and brought it here. Ostensibly, it had been for Freddie, but I got that it was also for me.

"Okay, then I would absolutely want you to go. 'Cause that means I won't have to miss you."

Chuckling, I said, "You'd think you'd be sick of us sometimes."

"Hmm, maybe. But you guys are all working really hard to not hover. You support what I want to do, and the only places none of you budge is security. I can live with that."

"You weren't this serene two days ago," I teased.

"That's because Jasper and Liam were playing a game of pool to see who I slept with that night." She sniffed. "They didn't ask me. They just decided they were playing for those stakes."

"They're always going to do that and you know that." The wing was really looking good. "But that wasn't what bothered you…"

"Adding mind-reading to your list of talents, Vaughn?" The tease in her voice erased any kind of sting or criticism.

"No," I said slowly. "But I know when something is bothering you, Dove. The last couple of weeks, you've been distracted and a little cranky."

"That's a polite way of saying I've been a bitch."

Pausing, I settled a hand on her ass and gave it a light swat. She jumped and glanced back at me, her mouth forming a little "O."

"Don't ever call yourself a bitch," I informed her. "I would never and you shouldn't either." I'd cheerfully break the face of anyone who called her that.

"Okay," she said. "And I have been cranky, but mostly because the guys said I needed to wait and I don't want to wait."

"Don't want to wait for what?" I studied her and checked the ink load on the pen before going back to work.

"Don't want to wait to talk to you about opening another studio."

A jolt went through me at that admission, and I was glad that I didn't have the needles on her skin. "They don't want you to talk to me about that?" To be honest, after what happened, I wasn't sure I was ready to ever hang my shingle again.

"They want to give you time to heal, but something Liam and Rome did for me reminded me that sometimes you have to push, or the fear and the pain won't let you heal." The genuine note of caution in her voice had me turning off the machine and rolling the chair around so I could meet her gaze.

"What did they do?"

"They took me up in the silks. I hadn't... done that after Pinetree. After what happened to my arms. I was dancing and working out, but—" She extended one of her arms. The scars were still there. They would always be there, but they would also fade. "I wasn't sure I'd have the strength. I definitely didn't have the confidence. They took me out and helped me dance in them, and it reminded me of how much I loved it."

"I'm glad they did that for you." I owed them a personal thanks for that, because she found such peace when she was flying. Then reality flickered through me. "That's why you and Freddie... the tattoos."

"Partially," she admitted. "To be fair, Freddie really did want his tattoos and I really want this phoenix. But you make such beautiful art, Vaughn, and you love what you do. If you genuinely don't want to do this anymore, I get it—but if you're afraid of opening a new place because of what happened, then I want to help you like they helped me."

"You're worried about me." That was—when was the last time someone really worried about me? I wasn't usually that guy.

"I love you," she said, lifting her shoulders before she grimaced a little. "I'm always going to worry about you. I want you to be happy."

"I am happy, Dove," I promised her. "And maybe I do need

to think about setting up shop somewhere. Maybe after your tour, 'cause I want to go on that with you. I want to be there."

Her smile grew. "Can I help you look at places? To pick one out?"

Maybe her enthusiasm was contagious. "You can do anything you want, but let's finish this phoenix. And, Dove?"

"Hmm?" The smile in her eyes was all the embrace I needed.

"Thank you," I whispered before I dropped a kiss on her lips. "Thank you for being you."

For being our phoenix. Yeah, maybe it was time and she was right. I was letting fear win. No more.

After the tour, we'd get right to work on that.

CHAPTER 50

ROME

THREE MONTHS LATER...

I studied the different bouquets the shop had on display. We were meeting Mary O'Connell for dinner. Liam invited her for the birthday dinner we never had. I didn't much care about the birthday, but I thought flowers would be good.

Starling studied the flowers, then me. "Do you know what kind you want to get her?"

"Something pretty," I decided. "But not something that smells too strong."

"Hmm..." Starling traced her fingers over the blooms. "What about this one? It has daisies and snapdragons. It's simple and it's elegant. I also think she'd like this shade of blue."

It was pretty but not what I wanted. "No, I don't like

those." After another few minutes, I said, "Maybe not flowers." None of them seemed pretty enough.

The thing was Mary O'Connell needed demonstrations of affection. Flowers would demonstrate that. Tonight was important. It was important for Liam, for his mother and for Starling. I wanted the flowers to be special. I didn't find the right ones until we turned to go. There was a bunch of flowers in a glazed, pink, glass vase near the window. So many different kinds of flowers and greens, including roses and spray roses.

When I picked it up, Starling let out a little sound. "Oh, those are pretty."

They were various shades of pink; the differing types of blooms gave it texture. They almost looked like a painting. The greenery they'd added to the arrangement reminded me of paint brushes.

"I like this one," I said and Starling grinned.

"Then let's get her that one." Ten minutes later, bouquet in hand, we walked the five blocks to the restaurant Liam had chosen. My other half was already there with his mother when we arrived. Starling's face was flushed and her smile happy as she accepted Mary's hug.

When she released Starling and faced me, I offered her the flowers. Mary's expressions shifted as she stared at them, two fingers pressed to her lips, then at me.

"For you," I said, in case it wasn't clear. I had brought them with Starling.

"You did not have to get me flowers, Rome," she said, her smile growing and her eyes wet. I made her cry?

Happy tears or sad tears?

"I wanted to."

I understood the surprise. I didn't do things for Mary that often. I didn't think about it. But since Jonathon died, and

Liam had been so torn up and worried about her, I worried about her too.

My mirror needed her. So I would need her and look after her too.

When she started forward and then hesitated, I took the last two steps and gave her the hug she seemed to want. Her little startle vanished quickly as she held me tighter. I didn't like these as much unless it was Starling, but what had Vaughn said? Sometimes moms just needed hugs and we needed to let them hug.

When she broke the embrace, she wiped at her eyes and beamed up at me. "I love my flowers and thank you, my sweet boy."

"You're welcome." I meant that part.

"Okay, everyone sit. We're going to have a proper birthday dinner and we're going to celebrate." Liam and I sat across from each other on the four-top table so we're both sitting next to Mary and we were both sitting next to Starling. Mary's happiness lit the room and I was glad I got her the flowers.

Liam grinned at me. The flowers made him happy too. That was good. I didn't even mind how long dinner took or that she insisted on having the staff sing us "Happy Birthday." Starling and Mary were both happy.

This really wasn't so bad.

LIAM

FOUR MONTHS LATER...

The sound of the door unlocking alerted me to her arrival. I'd all but moved back into the clubhouse, but I kept my apartment. It was nice for getaways, and nights like tonight—

a date. When Hellspawn let herself in, I grinned at her. She looked amazing. Her dress was one of the ones she let me pick out at the shop. Every month, I was allowed to get her one thing. Last month, she permitted two.

Her grin was open and free. The funny thing was she could afford anything she wanted, but the clothes become a game. This dress—I loved this dress. It had a wrap-around feature but the skirt flared and moved. While the top was solid black, the skirt was a whole rainbow of colors that just popped.

"You look amazing," I said as I finished lighting the candle. She laughed and did a twirl.

"Imagine my surprise, Mr. O'Connell, when I came back to my room after rehearsal today to find this dress and this note." She held up the card I'd left her.

"Were you really surprised, Mrs. O'Connell?" I teased as I moved over to greet her.

She glanced at the card. "Your presence has been requested at my apartment, seven promptly, with this dress on and nothing else under it. Obedience will get you all the orgasms. But go ahead and try me, Hellspawn."

"Sounds like what I'd write," I said as I settled my hands on her hips.

The silk of the dress was so soft and there was nothing on under it. Her nipples beaded against the front of the material, but the dark color kept it from being see-through.

"Also, I love an obedient woman," I whispered a moment before I claimed her lips. She sighed into the kiss and then bit me. The sharp sting of her teeth had me laughing as I lifted my head. "That's my hellspawn."

She grinned, then wrapped her arms around my neck. "You like it."

"Oh no, like is far too tame a word for what I feel for you," I informed her as I nuzzled another kiss. "But you are right. I do enjoy every sharp bite and claw mark you give me." Her stomach rumbled and I laughed. "Let's feed you so I can get to my treat."

"I see…" She was laughing as I led her over to the table. "…the reason for me to go commando."

"No, it's just because you got mad the last time I ripped up the lace panties. The rest is just a perk." I lifted the silver lid to reveal the lasagna. "I hope you brought your appetite. I know you've been training but I kept your carb intake in mind."

Her smile grew as she stared up at me. "I am starving."

Words I wanted to hear. Especially since we still had to battle the old voices that said she had to stay so painfully thin. But in the last few months, she'd begun to fill out again. Her muscle tone was excellent as she trained for the show she wanted to kick off the following year. I loved the swell in her hips and her breasts. The healthy glow to her.

Most of all, I loved the fire in her eyes.

"You okay?" she asked as she broke a breadstick in half. She loved garlic sticks and she didn't allow for cheat days often, so I was probably banking three of them with this one meal, but our girl *loved* pasta. Then again, who didn't love forbidden fruit?

"I'm fine. No worrying about me," I said and she wrinkled her nose.

"I can worry about you if I want." There was the bite again.

"Fine, fine—I just wanted to take a moment, and I was going to save it until after the meal. But since you insist, let's do it now."

"I'm not insisting." There it was again, the fire sparking in her eyes. I loved riling her up. I loved it even more when she pushed back.

"But you are and that's fine. I'd rather you were the impatient one." With that, I stood and moved around the table. She tracked me and when I went to one knee, she lowered her fork slowly. "Emersyn O'Connell," I said, savoring the syllables of her name. "A few months ago, we all surprised you with a very personal—but also business—proposal. You said yes to becoming my wife to get access to your accounts."

When she went to open her mouth, I held up a finger and she closed it again. I reached into my pocket and pulled out a ring. "Today, I'm asking you to marry me for just me. To be my wife. You're going to be with the others, and you can be their wife or girlfriend or whatever label you want to put on it, Hellspawn, but my world is so much brighter with you in it."

Mom had brought me the box when she came up for our makeup birthday. I'd told her then what I intended and she'd been over the moon.

"I want you to be my wife in every way that matters. I want you to know that I love *you* and that I want *you* and that I will support you in everything you do, and I want your support for the same. I need you in my life. I want you in it. You were the way home for me—that's what I used to think. But you're the family I want and you're not just the way home. You are my home."

I'd been working on the words for days, and instead of any of my carefully planned speeches, I just went for it, and then she was in my arms and kissing me. I half-forgot about the ring when I had an armful of this soft, beautiful woman.

"Is that a yes?" I teased and she laughed as she pushed me back, tumbling me onto the floor. "Oh, that's my girl... tell me yes and then come sit on my face. I've been starving for you all day."

It made my whole week that she lifted her skirt and did exactly as I asked. Face to face with that gorgeous pink pussy, I licked my lips.

"Liam?"

"Hellspawn?"

"My answer is always going to be yes."

That's my girl.

JASPER

EIGHT MONTHS LATER...

"You ready for this?" The SUVs were loaded with the gear. The advance team had already begun the set up at their first venue. Emersyn *Sharpe* was returning to the performance circuit. While I didn't like her using the Sharpe name, she pointed out that it was only for the stage and she would be introduced as Emersyn.

"I'm nervous," she admitted and I frowned.

"What do you have to be nervous about, Swan?"

"Everything," she said with a little shrug. "I haven't done a show in almost three years, Jasper. That's a long time. When we first announced it, I wasn't even sure we'd be able to get a good venue."

"But you did, and you sold out in less than three days." Dazed didn't begin to describe her expression. "You're going to be amazing," I told her. "Kel and I will be there for opening night. We already have the tickets. Milo and Lainey are coming too. Probably bring Adam and Ezra."

Goddamn if that wasn't a story, but her laughter was what I craved for her. Not the shadows or the pain or the fear.

"You're not alone. Freddie, Vaughn, and Rome are on the road with you. Liam said he was coming to each city, right?" Rich bastard said he had "work" to do. Yeah, work like see our girl. Not that I could blame him. "Doc will be there as well. He's just finishing up the safe house. And don't worry, we'll look after him too."

Doc had turned Ms. Stephanie's place into a safe house for the abused. Men. Women. Kids. Didn't matter. If they needed a safe space, he'd set it up. We had a half-dozen houses in the city ready to go. More soon, at the rate Doc was going. It was a project that Swan and Freddie both loved. Me too.

Ms. Stephanie would be really fucking proud.

"Three months is gonna feel like forever."

"It is," I agreed as I looped an arm around her. "But you're going to be fantastic. We'll talk every day. I want to hear about every single show. Maybe we'll try some phone sex. I've heard good things…"

The last of the melancholy vanished from her eyes. "I love you."

"I love you too. I have, for longer than I've known it was possible to love like this." Raising a hand, I cupped her cheek. "You are going to be amazing. You're going to fly, Swan, and you're going to dominate and I can't wait to see you up there."

"If I call," she asked, a playful look in her eyes. "Will you kidnap me again?"

That sent laughter shaking through me. "Damn straight. You just lift a pinkie and I'll come for you."

When she surged up to hug me, I held her tight. "I'm going to miss you," she complained.

"Make it up to me when you're back," I whispered.

"It's a date."

Then I walked her over to where Vaughn was putting the last of their bags into the car. "Take care of our girl."

"You know it." He gripped my hand. "When I get back, gonna look at some places downtown."

"Sounds good to me."

Kel came to join me as they pulled out. Freddie waved, Swan blew us kisses, and all too soon, they were out of sight. I lit a cigarette and took a long drag.

"It's going to be a really long three months," I told Kel and he nodded.

"But she's coming home. To us. We're going to be here," he reminded me. "In the meantime, I gotta get down to the shop. You good here?" There were rats showing up and I turned to see where they were getting to work unloading one of the trucks.

"Yep," I said as I blew out a stream of smoke. "I'm damn good." With that, I clapped him on the shoulder and headed across the warehouse. "Don't stack the pallets that high..." Damn kids. Time to teach them how it was done.

EPILOGUE

EMERSYN

ONE YEAR AND A FEW MONTHS LATER...

"Ms. Em! Ms. Em!" Amy raced over to me, bouncing in her brand-new tutu. They'd come in today and it was costume fitting for the recital. She half-slid to a halt before she went into first position. "How do I look?"

A smile spread my lips wide as I applauded her. "You look amazing." The rest of the class was hurrying in, each of them sporting their brand-new bright-blue tutus and ballet flats. I swore my heart was so full for each and every one of them as they posed, showed off, and wore their biggest smiles—they all lived at one of the group homes four blocks over.

When I opened the dance school, they'd been the first place I approached. Every single one of them attended with the Stephanie James scholarships I offered. I didn't need the school to be profitable in terms of cash, but watching these girls was everything I didn't know I needed in life.

I'd do another tour and for those three months, I'd bring in rotating teachers to give my kids exposure to different styles and experiences. Everything else, we would play by ear. By the time we wrapped for the day, I was happily exhausted. I locked up the studio and glanced across the street to Vaughn's new tattoo parlor. We opened it at the same time I opened the school. He was by appointment only right now. And Lauren accepted the job we'd offered her to manage the place.

In time, we'd hire more artists. Vaughn had actually taken on an apprentice. One of the rats who turned out to have some talent. So, Vaughn decided to nurture it. I checked my watch as I walked out to my car. I had time to stop for food if the guys wanted to order in. I fired off a message, but the response I got back was immediate.

They had it covered. Fine by me. It had been a long day. Long, but good. I glanced at the painting on the wall. The kids playing in the yard—it was the guys long before I ever knew them. This was the perfect spot for my school, Vaughn's tattoo parlor, and in the not too far distant future, there was a whole row of shops opening. We'd bought all the abandoned buildings and begun to rehab them. Turned out, having all that money let me do something about the neighborhood, and I loved it.

Starting the car, I let out a satisfied hum. The Phoenix Dance Company was an extension of my rebirth. If I had my way, we'd rebirth the whole neighborhood and fill it with opportunity, and more. It helped that the gangs who tried to slide in didn't last long.

Vandals didn't allow anyone in their territory. Period.

It worked for me.

Backing out of my slot, I headed for home. There were a

couple of rats finishing up a truck when I pulled into the warehouse. They lifted hands to wave at me. It was funny... I actually knew them all on sight now. That was Pedro and Ronnie. They were good kids. They'd aged out of one of the group homes and we'd given them jobs while they worked on community college.

"Evening, Ms. Emersyn," Ronnie called and I grinned. He was all of two years younger than me? Three? But none of them called me anything but Ms. Emersyn, and I was okay with that. The guys didn't allow them to be more familiar. It made them happy, but it was still weird.

It was kind of funny that no one was outside to greet me. Usually one of them did, but they'd also been working on relaxing some of the hypervigilance. But only some.

"Boo-Boo!" Freddie called as I came in the door and then he was there. "Happy Birthday!"

Birthday—

Shock rippled through me as Freddie picked me up and swung me around for a hug. The next moment, his lips crashed into mine. The kiss stole my breath, all demand and heat. His tongue tangled with mine and I just let my bag fall while I wrapped my arms around him.

Kisses with Freddie were a treasure.

The kiss was dizzying as he deepened it and I forgot about everything except the feel of him. Laughter eddied in the air around us and then, finally, there was a whistle.

Heat suffused me as he lifted his head. The gorgeous length of blond curl fell into his eyes and his lips were wet and a tad pink.

"Hi," I managed, more than a little breathless. This was not quite the welcome home I'd been expecting, but I was definitely *not* opposed. Freddie's grin grew.

"As I was saying," he touched a finger to my nose. "Happy twenty-first birthday, Boo-Boo."

Was it really—? I glanced around at all the guys. There were balloons, cake, and even a sign. Laughter spilled out of me. "I forgot it was my birthday…"

Kellan's smile was indulgent. "That's why we remember these things." When he held out a hand, I was floating on air to go to him. Thus began my merry-go-round of kisses that had my heart racing and me practically panting by the time I ended up in Mickey's lap.

They had dinner—huge steaks and baked potatoes, wine for me and beer for them. Though I didn't mind beer. The cake was for afterward. The best part, all of us were together. We'd spent the last year doing *so much* that I loved having all of us here.

"Tonight," Kellan said as the cake was being served out and I looked across the table at him. "We decided that the birthday girl doesn't have to choose."

"Choose what?"

"Choose where you're sleeping," Liam said.

"Who you're sleeping with," Jasper added.

"Or how many orgasms you're going to get," Vaughn served up.

"Everyone wants to have sex with you tonight, Starling," Rome said. "Together, apart, but all of us, with you. If you want to have us. But no one wants to miss out."

But I looked at Freddie and he grinned. "I may not be up for the full-sex part with everyone around yet," he said. We were getting closer and I was happy to wait ten years if he needed that. Sometimes, when he really needed it, he would rub off against my back, and I was fine with that. But Freddie could sleep with me now and I could touch him more and more. These were all wins. "But I can totally cheer you on."

My cunt clenched at the offer and I looked over at Mickey, who raised his beer. "Little Bit, you can handle us—"

Oh, I could do that. I licked my lips and my heart did a

high-five against my ribs. I was still hot from Freddie's welcome home kiss. The combination of having them all here? That was just a heady experience. Now, they wanted to fuck me together? All of them?

I was going to be so sore tomorrow.

"Hellspawn?" Liam said, leaning forward with concern in his eyes. "You good?"

I nodded slowly. "I just have one question."

"Name it," Kellan told me.

"Do we have to finish the cake first?"

The breathless question escaped me even as heat unfurled in my system. Sharing was something they were good with, but all of them? Together? With me? This was new.

New and enticing.

No lie.

Soft laughter rippled through the room and Freddie slid over to eye my cake then me. "You want the salty to go with the sweet?" His smile filled his eyes and I tilted my head back.

"I want anything you want to share."

"Yeah?" He raised his eyebrows, the cheerful light in his eyes reflected his playful smile. "Talking dirty to you is my love language."

Laughter exploded out of me as I dipped my fork into the cake and held the bite up to him. "You know, I knew that about you."

The laughter around us was like a group hug and Freddie's grin just grew. He opened his mouth and let me feed him the bite of cake. His happy sigh soothed some of those broken and jumbled bits inside of me that were always there. I didn't feel them all the time, nor did they keep from doing the things I wanted to pursue—but they also never went away. Little things could trigger the memories.

A piece of music.

A scent.

A turn of phrase.

Those memories had teeth. For me and for Freddie. We were hardly unique, the nightmares came for all of us. At the same time, we worked hard to meet those challenges and support each other.

"I think I know what I want to do," he said after he washed down the bite with a drink of coffee. The record scratch of the subject change silenced everyone. The declaration buoyed me at the same time.

"Yeah?" We'd been talking sex but Freddie had spent the last year either traveling with me, helping out Mickey with his safe houses or Jasper with the trucking business, sometimes going to the shop with Kellan and even wandering with Rome. If he wanted to talk about him, I was all in. The guys waited, their interest as piqued as mine.

"Yeah," he said, the corner of his mouth quirking upward. He ran a hand over his face then glanced around the room at everyone. "Sorry, we were celebrating."

"You making a decision is worthy of celebration," Kellan told him, his voice as firm as it was kind. We were in this together. All of us. "Now don't keep our girl hanging. What have you decided?"

"Or do you need a minute alone?" Mickey offered. "If you just want to talk to Little Bit."

For a minute, I thought Freddie would take them up on that, but he shook his head. "No, I want to share with all of you guys—been thinking about this for a while and you know I've been a floater. I like helping out, but I've never really been driven to do much for myself."

I nodded. That was one area where I still worried about him.

"Not sure I really need a calling. I'm not a dancer. Yes, I know I sing, Boo-Boo, but that's for you and sometimes for them." His smile was quicksilver, a flash and then gone again. "But last week—you told me about one of the boys in the dance class and how he didn't like to be touched."

Some of the joy in the room dimmed. "You were going to talk to him."

"I did," Freddie said. "You were right. He's like us."

That broke my heart.

"He's going to be okay, I talked to Doc about him." He motioned to Mickey who raised his beer in salute. "We're already getting him help. I got him to talk to me because I got where he was coming from. I liked helping him. It might take a while...but I want to go to school."

I straightened.

"Going to put what I know to work—I want to help abuse victims. I want to help the way Ms. Stephanie helped me... not sure I'll be good at it." A smile flickered over his face. "It could take a lot of time away from here at first, you know, I wasn't always that great at school. Not even sure they'd take me and school costs..."

"I got you little brother," Liam said without missing a beat.

"We all have you," I promised.

"Yeah?" There was a shy hopefulness to him that just twisted my heart. Taking the risk, I set the cake aside and bounced up to throw my arms around him. Freddie caught me and squeezed me close.

"Absolutely," I told him as I hugged him. "Anything you need." Then I dropped my voice a little lower. "I know you can help anyone you put your mind to—you helped me."

He'd helped me name my abuser and the abuse out loud. Secrets, lies, and deception all fed that beast, tightening the choke chain of control. If I hadn't been able to tell Freddie in Pinetree, maybe I wouldn't still be here.

"I love you, Boo-Boo," Freddie whispered.

"I love you too." I closed my eyes as I savored the closeness. When he spread his fingers against my back and rubbed a slow circle, I relaxed into him and he gave a slow shudder.

The motion had me loosening my hold, but Freddie shook his head against my neck and tightening his grip. "No," he whispered. "This is good. Real good."

Then as if to prove his point, he eased back and held up a steady hand. My heart fisted as I grinned up at him. The happiness in him, the determination? That was one of the best birthday presents ever.

"You want to keep hogging her all to yourself there, Freddie? Or are you good for us to get this celebration back on the road? We don't mind, we can wait." The droll, absolutely dry note from Jasper was exactly what we needed.

It alleviated the wild vulnerability of the moment giving Freddie a graceful exit from all the attention. I loved how they loved each other so much. How they loved each other and how they protected each other.

When Freddie dipped his head to give me a light kiss, I took a chance and nipped his lower lip. Surprise flickered in his eyes and he grinned. "Boo-Boo has teeth."

"Yes, she does," Vaughn said almost on a sigh and I wasn't the only one laughing.

Dancing backwards, I clapped my hands as I did a little spin. "How do we do this?"

To be perfectly fair, I expected guidance or maybe even a suggestion. Rome just swooping me up and over his shoulder sent another wave of laughter through me as he made his way to the stairs.

Currently, only the eight of us were here. So it wasn't like we had to be quiet. Frankly, we didn't have to go upstairs either, but Rome's long legs made ate up the space between the downstairs and our suite.

Once we made it to the suite though, he set me on my

feet. Turning me to face the door, he covered my eyes with his hands. "This is okay?"

"Yes," I promised him. I leaned back against him, trusting he would keep me upright.

"Eyes closed, Starling," Rome said not removing his hands from my eyes. With one hand still over my eyes, he opened the door. The scents of lemon cleaner, touches of roses, and coffee tickled my nostrils.

Someone had been busy today. I felt more than heard the guys make their way into the room with us as Rome ushered me forward. The lack of snickering and teasing laughter didn't mean they weren't having fun.

It tended to mean they were more interested in my reaction to their surprise than picking on each other. If I hadn't already been humming with excitement, this would have stoked my curiosity and my happiness.

Rome's hushed, "Ready?" wasn't directed at me. Not that it prevented me from saying, "Yes please!"

A gentle pinch. Those were Vaughn's hands. "Behave, Dove," he chastised gently. "Or we'll keep you blindfolded for the first half."

First half? "Is that a promise or a threat?" I loved when they would play with me. I loved it even more when they dared me to play with them.

"Both," Liam whispered before he pressed a kiss to my cheek. "Let her see, Rome."

"Surprise," they all said in unison as Rome's hand fell away from covering my eyes and I blinked them open.

Of all the things I could have anticipated my surprise being, this—this one floored me. Never in a million years would I have imagined.

"Rome," I whispered as I crossed to the wall behind the sofa. His latest work took up most of the wall. "When…"

"Today," he said. "I started right after you left."

I still couldn't fully wrap my mind around how he did this in so little time. My days were usually six to seven hours, nine if I warmed up in the school studio rather than dance here.

The entire wall behind the sofa was now—me. But not only me. It was silk dancing with all of their birds around me. In some ways it was as if they were flying with me, but it was more than that.

It was them flying to keep me safe, watching over me, and elevating me all at the same time. I was about ready to burst into tears. Pressing my fingers to my lips, I stared at it. Because the more I looked the more I saw.

"It needs more," Rome said. "But I wanted it ready for your birthday."

Twisting around, I hugged him. His strength wrapped around me as he lifted me. Then he was kissing me. The sweep of his tongue teasing mine lit me up.

He alternated between deep, wet kisses and fluttering teases with his tongue. The warmth of a body caging up against my back had me sighing as Vaughn settled his hands on my hips.

"Ease back," he said and I wasn't sure whether he meant me or Rome and then I was leaning on Vaughn as Rome retreated a step.

His lips were wet and hinted toward pink as he gazed at me. Gentle hands framed my waist before Vaughn tugged my shirt upward. Then Kellan slid into place in front of me.

The intensity in his eyes grounded me even as my heart and soul soared. The liquid heat unfurling within me reminded me of the phoenix Vaughn painted on my back.

"Eyes on me, Sparrow."

I could in no way ignore that command even if I wanted. Kellan wrapped his hand around my throat. It steadied the race of my pulse which beat like a bird. What tension from the day remained slipped away.

Here, I was home and I was safe. We were stronger together. Three years—three years since they first took me. Not that long after my eighteenth birthday and I had no idea *any* of this was possible.

The dream I didn't dare have.

"Sparrow." The crack of command brought me back to the moment.

"Sorry," I whispered. "I was lost thinking about how happy I am."

His eyes softened. "And how happy are you?"

Sighing, I leaned all of my weight into Vaughn, aware of him and of Kel. Aware of all of them, really. Their gazes were a caress all their own. "So happy. I never even knew I could dream of this. Just—just teaching at the school and having that would have seemed immeasurable once upon a time."

"Good," he murmured, stroking his thumb over my pulse point. "You know there's nothing we won't do for you, right?"

"I had gotten that impression," I teased, a little even as I melted. Not even a question in my mind. "You know I feel the same way, right?" Anything they wanted.

"I had gotten that impression," he parroted back at me with a smile. "Then tonight—it's all about you."

"Yeah?" I drifted under the contact.

"Oh yeah," Kellan said then Vaughn shifted, steadying me on my feet before he pulled a blindfold over my eyes.

Surprise speared through me. The low chuckle from my left was all Jasper, but Kellan never let go of my throat as Vaughn tightened the blindfold.

"Is that all right?" Vaughn pressed his lips to my ear. The whisper of his breath combined with the sweetness of his croon sent an entirely different kind of shiver through my system.

"Yes," I answered. I was sinking fast. Could you die from pleasure? Drown from it? They were barely touching me and I was already coming undone.

Then as if summoned by the thought, the hands on my hips moved to hook into my leggings and like my shirt earlier, they were peeled off. Someone was at my feet and before I could even decide to balance, Vaughn lifted me.

I moved my hands to his, and he chuckled before sucking my earlobe against his teeth. "Relax, Dove. I won't let you fall…"

I didn't really get a chance to respond to that before my bra vanished, then there were lips wrapped around my right nipple. The combination of light teeth scraping followed by the lave of a tongue sent heat spiraling through me.

After a long, teasing lick along the shell of my ear, Vaughn set me down. The cool air in the room was a balm on my heated flesh. The mouth teasing my nipple went away, and Kellan spun me until I leaned back against him.

The firm grip of his hand around my throat seemed to alternately excite and relax me in equal measures. When he tilted my head back and began to devour my mouth, I let go.

They wanted to neutralize my senses, take away all distractions like getting to enjoy looking at them while they stroked, teased, licked, nipped, and kissed.

There was a sound of fist slapping skin in rhythm. It registered when Liam muttered, "Asshole," that they'd been doing rock paper scissors.

Asshole had to be—Jasper's low chuckle skated over my belly and I smiled into Kellan's kiss.

One hand on my thigh, Jasper lifted it and then his mouth was on my cunt. The hot, tongue penetrating erotic kiss to my pussy turned me inside out. There was no gentle coaxing or teasing, he alternated between the thrust of his tongue against my channel to the circular teases against my clit before he sucked on it like I was his favorite treat.

The first orgasm hit and I was bucking against his mouth but Kellan barely let me up for air as Jasper drove me mad and then Mickey's mouth fused to mine as fingers trailed against my anus.

I knew their touch, I knew them all and when it was Kellan lining up to take my ass, I was still vibrating from the first round of orgasms. Thanks to Jasper. Mickey let up on my mouth as they shifted me around.

They hadn't been kidding. I didn't have to worry about holding myself up. The burn of where Kellan stretched me, left me aching for more. Not for long, because there was a cock filling my cunt as Kellan rocked against my ass. Then there was another mouth on mine.

Liam.

Rome.

The gentle tweak of one of my nipples followed by another fiercer one. The pinch and the pull were just enough pain to edge the pleasure that unfurled and bloomed throughout me.

A shout escaped Kellan as he came. The hot warmth of his release was there to comfort me when he eased away and then I was laid over the sofa and a cock teased against my lips.

Rome traced his fingers against my face as I opened to take him. Mickey's orgasm came too soon and I wanted to be greedy for more. I wanted to feel him come again, but he no sooner left me than Vaughn thrust in to drive me mad.

So they went in turns. Rome came and I swallowed every drop, nearly choking as Vaughn teased another orgasm out of me. I was a shaking, sweaty mess when Jasper turned me over and thrust into me from behind.

There was another kiss, this time from Mickey as he teased my lips apart and then we were moving again and when Liam pushed into my cunt with Jasper still buried to the hilt, I lost the thread of all of it.

It was too much and not enough. I needed more. My mind seemed to kaleidoscope. The hours bled into each other, awash in so many colors of pleasure. I rode Vaughn, Mickey filled my ass as did Liam and then Jasper was there again with Kellan.

Rome drifted in and out, more than once he eased me down through the tremors before he pushed into me and another orgasm rattled out. They were drowning me.

I craved them and this so much.

The next time I roused there was a damp cloth being worked over my skin. Another eased between my thighs and I jerked a little. Too much, not enough and then the sweetest kiss teased my lips.

"Freddie," I exhaled as he kissed me. He kept two fingers pressed against my cheek as he teased my lips apart. When I fluttered my eyes open, I drank in the sight of him. Freddie deepened the kiss, pressing past my defenses as he teased my tongue.

Then when I began to duel with his tongue, he took my hand. When he pulled my hand to his chest, I nearly gasped at the bare skin and the scar present beneath my fingertips.

Only the fact I was so loose-limbed and floating from multiple orgasms put my reaction in check. Freddie was letting me touch him. I didn't mind if he couldn't bear it, if he needed to control the contact and he could get off rubbing against me.

Whatever he needed whenever he needed it. But being able to touch him?

Tears burned in my eyes when he used my hand to stroke down his chest to his cock and the velvety skin against my palm was electric. Freddie lifted his head, teasing his tongue against the seam of my lips.

I studied his eyes and his expression. Neither was tight nor withdrawn. The light in his eyes pulled me in and all at once, it registered—there were no other sounds. Just us.

"Freddie?" I let him move my hand against his cock as he wrapped my fingers around him.

"I know," he whispered, then pressed another kiss to my lips. "I asked the guys if I could do this part alone…"

This part. Let me touch him.

"I never want you to think I don't want you," Freddie said as he began to rock his hips against my hand. "I do, Boo-Boo. I want you so much. Sometimes—i don't think I'm good enough."

When I opened my mouth to protest, he kissed me again. He thrust his tongue in clear imitation of how he rocked his hips against my hand.

Pulling back, he smiled and then took my free hand to press against his chest. "See—no panic."

Tears burned in my eyes as he kept rocking, the velvety heat of his cock was just so much and I gave into the temptation to give him the barest of squeezes as he moved.

His pupils dilated and he let out an explosive breath. "Wow…"

"Wow good?" I asked, finally remembering how to talk. "Wow bad?"

The kiss he gave me was so fierce and demanding, I forgot where we were or even what I'd asked. Then cupping my face, Freddie grinned.

"Wow good…I want to fuck you for real, Boo-Boo…I want you to fuck me. I want…I want to feel your mouth and your hands…I want all of it and I don't know how long I'll last."

"Then we do it all."

He laughed, the sound was so damn freeing it lifted one of the last boulders still weighing down my soul. "I like your confidence in me, Boo-Boo. Might not recover that fast."

"Freddie, we have forever."

All at once he paused. A look of wonder filled his expression and I wished I could capture it. Capture it and hold onto it forever. Hold onto him the same way.

"What do you want to do first?" I offered instead and he bit his lip.

"Birthday girl's choice..." he whispered, stroking his thumb against my lower lip.

"Freddie," I said, letting go of his cock and giving him a little—where were we? Oh, my room. Cool. I gave him a nudge back onto the bed. "I'm going to blow your mind..."

When I dipped my head to teased the head of his cock with one teasing lick, he grinned wildly. "You did that the day we met Boo-Boo."

I swallowed his cock and savored his expression. Definitely a happy birthday to me.

* * *

The... beginning of a beautiful life together...

AFTERWORD

And that's—the end. At least for this chapter of their beginning. So I guess, in a way, it is the beginning of the rest of their lives. It seems like it happened so soon and then I remember that the first book came out in March of 2021 and now it's May of 2023. 9 books. Just at a million words. 2 years, 2 months. So much blood, sweat, and tears.

Yes, I say blood because as some of you may recall, I herniated a disc in my back a month before the first book came out and I had to have surgery later that year. I'm still recovering from that surgery in some ways.

But our scars, as Doc and Em say, are proof that we survived. So I'll embrace those scars and the memories of diving into the darkness of Emersyn's past and the tragedies that not only brought the guys into the group home, but also bonded them together.

There were a lot of things that I knew going into this story. I knew that Emersyn's brother was Raptor and that he would not be present when the guys "kidnapped" her. I knew he was in prison and I knew it was for a crime he didn't commit.

Milo has a whole history and story we have not fully explored yet, but that was not always meant for Vandals.

All of this said, I have a bit of a confession, not every character who survived was supposed to survive—at least not originally. While I would never confirm in the beginning how many were in Em's harem, it was supposed to be six.

Then Doc happened. Doc walked on the page and he was definitely there to stay. So now I had seven, and I didn't want seven, at least not initially. I thought it would be so hard to have seven. Not going to lie, seven was hard.

There were ideas for the twins that I thought would happen and then the twins did what they did and said nope, this is us. Then there was Freddie who was so difficult and damaged in the beginning. A tragedy really and I thought that if Doc was in then maybe Freddie was out.

Before you come at me with the knives and the pitch-forks, there was a very active campaign from those in the know to keep him. To be honest, I knew if we lost Freddie it would hurt—but this is a dark story. Dark stories have consequences and stakes.

Originally, Freddie was going to die at the end of the fourth book saving Em. That was what I saw way back in the beginning of the first book.

But the more we got to know Freddie, the harder that reality was to embrace. So, I ultimately added a book to the series and for those of you have wondered—that book was Dirty Devil. While her time in Pinetree was somewhat inevitable, how it developed and the very pivotal role Freddie played—that was all Freddie.

One hundred percent Freddie.

He was perfect just the way he was. His damage and Em's damage mirrored each other in a way that gave them a profound insight to each other. It helped that they were close in age and that their experiences were somewhat similar.

Something that came full circle in this book with her offering him raunchy jokes and sexy come-ons to make things easier for him when he needed it.

I have waited nine books to tell this story. I can say with absolute certainty that I love how this story ended. I love that the characters told us what would happen and even when we pitched them a curve ball, they made the calls.

We met so many other characters along the way from Lainey to Adam to Ezra to Bodhi to Bones, Lunchbox, Voodoo, and Alphabet. We had a few cameo appearances including Vienna and Cash. We got to talk to Fletcher on the phone. There were even a couple of Untouchable cameos if you caught them.

This whole world is filling in with shadows and color and depth. So many more stories to tell. I legit cannot wait to get to them all.

Thank you again for coming on this journey with me.

Head up. Wings out.

xoxo

Heather

Reader group:
facebook.com/groups/heatherspack
Spoiler group:
facebook.com/groups/teammadatheather

VANDALS GLOSSARY

HAWK

Hawks are often revered for their keen eyesight. While there are numerous types of hawks, the red-tailed variety is the most common in the United States and they flourish in deserts, forests, and cities. They are also known to mate for life. Jasper earned the nickname for how often he saw what others did not, even if he doesn't always understand *what* he is seeing.

KESTREL

They are colorful birds, the smallest of the types of falcons, but they are a fierce predator. Kellan earned the name because of his fine suits and cars that he earned on his own. His quiet manner tended to be dismissed and most didn't see him coming.

HUMMINGBIRD

Hummingbirds are fast and they are colorful. You can't always see them, but you can hear them. While they tend to be nectivores, they are also very good at hawking insects and other prey when the mood strikes them. The guys gave Rome the name because they could never pin him down and he moved to his own beat.

FALCON

Like hawks, falcons are known for their keen eye for detail, and their swiftness. While Vaughn's size might have lent itself to a name like Condor or a larger bird, it was his artistic talent and specificity in what he drew that earned him the name.

MOCKINGBIRD

Known for their mimicry, mockingbirds are not really considered birds of prey. Yet, they are territorial and will defend that territory against others. When Liam was adopted, he never truly left the Vandals, but he fit in both worlds. That ability got him the name Mockingbird. Not that he uses it much cause Jasper stuck him with it and Jasper's a dick.

RAPTOR

The first of the Vandals to get a bird nickname, Milo took the name Raptor for his ferocity in defending his brothers and his baby sister. Raptors in general are known for their ability to swoop down on their prey before they even know the predator is there—and Milo was always ten steps ahead.

VANDAL "DOC"

When Mickey J first got the name Vandal, it wasn't for a bird. It was because he proved vicious in street fights. His nickname was a street name than it was a predator. Eventually, he shed that name for Doc after his stint in the military, but he was the first Vandal and Milo named their gang after him.

SHRIKE

Loggerhead shrikes are songbirds with a raptor's habits. They impale their prey. Freddie never thought he cared about having a bird name until Rome suggested this one and since he prefers his knife to other weapons and he can sing, it's a name he's embraced.

PHOENIX

A firebird. When they die, they are reborn in their own flames, remade, stronger and more perfect than they already were. Mythological or not, phoenix are revered and admired because they are the ultimate survivor.

EMERSYN'S NICKNAMES

DOVE

Doves are often considered spiritual creatures with spiritual meanings. They represent love, purity, faith, and peace. Vaughn gave Emersyn the name Dove not only because of her grace as a dancer, but also the peace she gave him.

SPARROW

Sparrows are small, social birds that can thrive in the most inhospitable of environments, like the bottom of a coal mine. American kestrels are also referred to as sparrow hawks. Kellan gave her the name because of the darkness she has survived in and thrived despite the life she has endured.

STARLING

Starlings are vocal mimics, and aggressive. They have a unique alarm to alert when danger is near. They are known for bonding with caretakers and seeking them out for companionship when they develop trust. Rome saw the struggle as well as the fierceness in her and he wanted to show her he would always take care of her.

SWAN

Beautiful, elegant and graceful. They can fly, and swim with incredible speed and agility. Jasper sees the absolute beauty in Emersyn, along with her intelligence. Her ferocious temper when standing up to him and others suggested just how perfect she was to him.

LITTLE BIT

Clearly, not a bird. When compared to the Vandals, Emersyn truly was a tiny thing and why Mickey calls her his little bit. His little bit of happiness and joy. Even when he screwed up, he saw her as the little bit he wanted and needed in his life.

BOO-BOO

Freddie dubbed Em Boo-Boo from their first meeting because of all the bruises she sported. The vulnerability in her mirrored one inside of himself, and while he often used ribald comments as a defense, she enjoyed them and it helped build the first connection between them.

HELLSPAWN

She was no one's princess and the fact she punched Liam more than once, was all the proof he needed that she was definitely a hellspawn.

IVY

Milo will forever think of her as Ivy, her birth name and his baby sister. Ivy is a twisting vine and it bound all of them together and eventually bound the brotherhood he found to her.

ABOUT HEATHER LONG

I *love* books. Not just a little bit, but a lot. Books were my best friends when I was growing up. Books didn't care if I was new to a town or to a class. They were always there, my trustiest of companions. Until they turned on me and said I had to write them.

I can tell you that my own personal happily ever after included writing books. I've always said that an HEA is a work in progress. It's true in my marriage, my friendships, and in my career. I am constantly nurturing my muse as we dive into new tales, new tropes, new characters and more.

After seventeen years in Texas, we relocated to the Pacific Northwest in search of seasons, new experiences, and new geography. I can't wait to discover what life (and my muse) have in store for me.

Maybe writing was always my destiny and romance my fate. After all, my grandmother wasn't a fan of picture books and used to read me her Harlequin Romance novels.

Follow Heather & Sign up for her newsletter:
www.heatherlong.net
TikTok

ALSO BY HEATHER LONG

A Marine Affair

Marine Ever After

Marine in the Wind

Marine with Benefits

A Marine of Plenty

A Candle for a Marine

Marine under the Mistletoe

Have Yourself a Marine Christmas

Lest Old Marines Be Forgot

Her Marine Bodyguard

Smoke & Marines

Blue Ivy Prep

Problem Child

Mad Boys

Party Crashers

Bravo Team Wolf

When Danger Bites

Bitten Under Fire

Cardinal Sins

Kill Song

First Chorus

High Note

Last Word

Chance Monroe

Earth Witches Aren't Easy

Plan Witch from Out of Town

Bad Witch Rising

Her Elite Assets

Featuring:
Pure Copper
Target: Tungsten
Asset: Arsenic

Fevered Hearts

Marshal of Hel Dorado
Brave are the Lonely
Micah & Mrs. Miller
A Fistful of Dreams
Raising Kane
Wanted: Fevered or Alive
Wild and Fevered
The Quick & The Fevered
A Man Called Wyatt

Going Royal

Some Like It Royal
Some Like It Scandalous
Some Like It Deadly
Some Like it Secret
Some Like it Easy
Her Marine Prince
Blocked

Untouchable

Rules and Roses

Changes and Chocolates

Keys and Kisses

Whispers and Wishes

Hangovers and Holidays

Brazen and Breathless

Trials and Tiaras

Graduation and Gifts

Defiance and Dedication

Songs and Sweethearts

Legacy and Lovers

Farewells and Forever

Wolves of Willow Bend

Wolf at Law

Wolf Bite

Caged Wolf

Wolf Claim

Wolf Next Door

Rogue Wolf

Bayou Wolf

Untamed Wolf

Wolf with Benefits

River Wolf

Single Wicked Wolf

Desert Wolf

Snow Wolf